THE CAJUN SNIPER

To Tony Little,

I hope that you
enjoy the story.

Wayne W. Talley
1/12/05

THE CAJUN SNIPER

WAYNE TALLEY

iUniverse, Inc.
New York Lincoln Shanghai

The Cajun Sniper

iUniverse, Inc.

For information address:
iUniverse, Inc.
2021 Pine Lake Road, Suite 100
Lincoln, NE 68512
www.iuniverse.com

ISBN: 0-595-31446-5

Printed in the United States of America

The book is a fictional novel for reading entertainment only. The characters used in the story are fictitious and do not represent anyone. Any representation of a person that is living or dead is purely coincidental. The story is that of a vigilante, which makes for a good story, but a terrible defense in a court of law. Be warned. The high quality manufactured products that I recommend are listed below.

The book is dedicated to my wife, Janet. Her love and understanding made this book possible.

A note to the reader:

If you are a reader that enjoys technical information, see the glossary and the Lagniappe section in the rear of the book prior to reading the story. Figures in the back of the book include a state map, a local map, and my rifle's data card. You may download the figures for free from www.cajunsniper.com. The password is Pichou.

CHAPTER 1

▼

*Elevator doors open a*t the end of a Biloxi, Mississippi hotel hallway. Large wooden double doors, with the muffled sounds of hip/hop music coming from the other side of them, are at the other end of the forty-foot long hallway. Four red doors are on each side of the hallway, and murals of Vikings battling are on the walls. Scott Meyeaux, a forty-year-old ex-college linebacker, steps out on the red and black-checkered carpet. He's wearing a gray sports coat, open collared shirt, and black slacks. Scott checks his watch and runs his fingers through his neatly combed short brown hair that is parted down the middle. As the handsome two hundred and forty-pound package of muscle walks towards the double doors, a look of determination replaces his smile. He reaches behind his back and pulls out a high capacity pistol with a threaded barrel. His pace slows as he slightly pulls back the slide and verifies that there's a live round in the chamber. He puts on a fake smile and puts the pistol back in its holster. He stops at the double doors and waves his keycard in front of the scanner. As the door lock pops, he pushes open the left door.

Cautiously, he walks into a large hotel suite where there is a small private party well in progress. Two large diameter concrete columns that divide the room in half are located in front of him. He thinks to himself that they can provide excellent cover if he needs it. He looks to his right and sees three couples on the wooden dance floor in subdued light with a strobe light flashing on them. Scanning left and looking over the beige carpet, he sees the catered food table against the opposite wall. In the middle left half of the room is a brown leather couch with a matching lounge chair, a glass coffee table, and a big screen TV located against the wall between the two bedroom doors. Near the wall to his left is a bar where his best friend Billy is standing with a drink in one hand and waving at him with his other. As usual, Billy is already toasted. An uneasy feeling comes over him as he notices the left bedroom door is closed. He walks behind the two level bar, puts his pistol on the counter, and fixes himself a drink.

Billy is the same age as Scott, and almost the same muscular physique. He's wearing an open long sleeve white shirt and blue dress slacks. Billy leans over the bar, looks at the pistol, and looks at Scott. "Put it away Scott. Everyone is having a good time, and everything will calm down if you let it."

"Who's behind the door?"

"It's just Kim. She had to freshen up. Do you know that she use to be a Vegas showgirl?"

"Yeah, you remind me at least three times a week. Have you ever heard of variety?"

"Scott, she's the one and only for me."

"Two years ago, you were standing in that very spot saying the same thing about your present wife."

Billy looks back at the pistol. "Tony and Mike got you a present to smooth things over. Let's not blow it."

Scott looks out on the dance floor and sizes himself up against Mike and Tony. They're ten years younger than him and look like twin professional wrestlers with tan skin and long tight curly black hair. He laughs to himself at their matching pastel blue shirts and black leather pants. They have only been with the organization for two weeks and are already trying to muscle into Scott's position. "Billy, I don't want anything from those two."

Billy turns around and faces the dance floor. "Trust me, you're going to want this one."

Scott looks at his boss Joe on the dance floor. Joe's the casually dressed fifty-year-old with a long, thin face and thin brown hair that is badly receding. He has a cigarette in his hand, and the old man is doing a poor job of imitating the movements of Mike and Tony. Scott is Joe's right hand man, but Joe's sudden bonding with Mike and Tony has him worried.

"Billy, when did Joe loose his gray hair?"

"This morning. Mike and Tony took him to a spa. From what I heard, he got the works."

Scott makes a face. "What happened to his brown three piece suit that he always wears?"

"Mike and Tony also took him shopping."

Scott shakes his head in disgust. "Is there anything else that I should know?"

"Yep. They took him for a workout and got him using steroids."

"Just great. The man that is supposed to be making rational decisions is going to make all aggressive ones. This is not good. Where's my date?"

"She's running a little late."

"One more reason for me to be concerned."

"Scott, would you relax? Look, they are not going to do anything with the girls here. You're starting to make me nervous. If they come over to get a drink and see the pistol, who knows what's going to happen? Come on Scott, put it up."

Scott pulls open a drawer, puts the pistol in it, and leaves the drawer open.

They continue to look out on the dance floor. "Scott, just look at the three babes in the micro dresses. If that don't lower your stress level, you better start taking some medication." They both laugh. "That's more like it."

"Billy, is that dancing or flexing for body building competition?"

"Scott, you're just jealous, but you got to laugh at Joe. Would you look at the size of those two? Talk about steroid overdose."

"They're not any bigger than us."

"Are you kidding? Look at them. They are the same height as us, but they got us by fifty pounds."

Scott takes a sip if his drink. "I still can take them."

"Yeah, you more than proved that last night. Putting that pistol in Tony's face wasn't such a good idea."

"Billy, after I saw what Tony did to that woman last night; I should have pulled the trigger."

"Relax friend. It's over with. We have plenty of time to talk to Joe. Your girl should be here shortly, and you'll forget about the whole thing. Trust me."

"Look at them. They look alike. They even dress alike."

"There is one major difference."

"Do you mean that Tony has a beard, and Mike has a three day stubble?"

"Nope. One is a whole lot weirder than the other."

"Billy, what do you mean?"

"You see that leather pouch around Tony's neck. He calls it his Ju-Ju bag. It's supposed to have a mixture of crushed up human bones, bat bones, and magic dust."

"Thanks Billy, I'm going to have some fun with this one."

"Don't mention it."

Scott laughs.

The bedroom door opens and Scott puts his hand on the pistol. Kim steps out of the bedroom. She's a tall blonde in her upper twenties with milk white skin.

She has beautiful blue eyes with pinpoint pupils and is wearing nothing but glitter, spike heels, and jewelry. She walks by the bar. "Hi, Scott. How's it going?"

Scott smiles and shakes his head from side to side. "Just fine. You know, some people think that you might be an exhibitionist."

She laughs. "What do you mean might be?" She steps back and stands in a beauty pageant pose. She looks directly at Scott and has a smile from ear to ear. "Are you going to say something or what?"

"Nice earrings." Scott and Billy laugh.

"Scott!" She shakes her head. "You're too much of a gentleman."

She grabs Billy's hand and pulls him towards the dance floor. "Come on Billy, I want to dance."

"Gotta go, Scott. The girl loves to dance. What can I say?" Billy and Kim walk out on the dance floor, and Scott sits on a barstool facing the dance floor. He is taking a sip of his drink when both of the double entrance doors fully open. A sixty-year-old high roller wearing a powder blue leisure suit and a loud flower shirt parades in with a woman on each arm. He has silver hair combed straight back and pulled into a ponytail. His face is tanned and has multiple age spots. He is in decent shape, and he doesn't wear glasses, which is uncommon for a man of his age. The men on the dance floor see him, stop dancing, and begin to walk towards him as Scott discreetly closes the draw with the pistol in it.

The old man throws up his hands and in a cheerful voice, "Satinito says, let the party continue."

Mike and Tony howl, continue dancing, and pull off their shirts showing the results of years of weight lifting and steroid abuse. Satinito walks towards Scott, and Joe soon joins him. Satinito stops at the bar. He looks at each of his girls. "Go find something to do. I've got business to attend to." He watches the girls go wiggling off and sit on the couch. Like keen waitresses, they watch Satinito's every movement. He turns around and sees Joe behind him. "Joe, glad you're here to listen to this. Scott, Joe told me what happened last night. I don't want it to ever to happen again. Is that understood?"

"I understand Mr. Satinito, but we need to draw the line…"

Satinito holds up his hand towards Scott and interrupts him. In a stern tone, "You're paid to do what Joe tells you to do—nothing more, nothing less. You've been working for me for fifteen years. You know how our operation works. Joe does what I tell him to do, and you do what Joe tells you to do."

"But the kid…"

Joe makes an evil face at Scott and interrupts him. "There was no kid, Mr. Satinito."

Satinito continues, "What's done is done. Let's forget about it and move on. Now that we have all of the business out of the way, let's live to my motto." He points to large gothic print on the wall above the double doors. "'Live today because there is no tomorrow.' Let's party. Scott, where's your girl?"

"She hasn't shown up yet."

"Don't worry. Mike picked you a good one, or at least I hope so. If she's half as good as the money that I paid for her, you're in for a real treat. Let me know what you think of her. Maybe, I can negotiate a cheaper long term rate." Satinito laughs and motions to his two girls. They get up and run over to him like two puppies. They parade out on the dance floor and begin dancing.

As Scott watches Joe put out a cigarette in an ashtray on the bar and lights another one, he fixes Joe a drink. He can see the dark rings under Joe's eyes from trying to keep up with Tony and Mike.

Joe is talking with the cigarette in his mouth. "Scott, I need to know if I can count on you?"

"Sure boss."

"Good, because if I need something done, I need to know that you'll do it. Even though you might think that I'm insane for letting things get out of hand, there are sound reasons behind it. You've been at this for fifteen years. Me, I've been at it for twenty-five. The number of people that we had to kill in the last two years is more than we killed in the ten years before that. The people today have no sense of responsibility, and they have no value on human life. They are not even worried about their own lives. The lives of their girlfriends, wives and kids; they do worry about. I'm hoping the scenes that we leave behind are gory enough to deter anyone else from even thinking about stealing from us. We might even be able to stop the killing all together."

"Is that why you hired the two goons?"

"Scott, not long ago; you were a goon yourself."

"Tony just enjoys it too much."

"That's why Tony's so good at what he does. It's just a new way of handling a new generation. I tell you what, give it two months. If we don't see any results in two months, we'll go back to the old way."

"Two months, starting with last night?"

"Deal, now get out from behind the bar and onto the dance floor." Scott walks from behind the bar, and Joe puts his arm on Scott's shoulder as he walks with him to the dance floor. "Scott, forget about last night, put a smile on your face, and dance with my girl until yours shows up. One other thing, if you ever do that to me in front of Satinito again; I'll take that big pistol of mine and put six holes in you."

"Sorry, Joe, I slipped."

"I know, but don't let it happen again. Now, get out there and show Satinito that you enjoy the hell out of your job."

As they are walking to the dance floor, there's a light knock on the door. Scott opens the door to see the most beautiful woman that he has ever seen. She is a tall, twenty-year-old, redhead wearing a short green sequence, spandex dress.

In a cute voice, "I'm lookin fer Scott."

All of Scott's defenses are let down. In his deep voice, "You found me."

"I'm Laura Lee." She giggles, smiles, and turns around in front of him. "You like?"

"Oh yeah, Scott likes."

He escorts her in, walks her to the bar, and fixes her a drink. They make conversation at the bar. She takes a pack of sugar and puts it in her drink and stirs her drink with her finger. "In Alabama, we like everything sweet." The idle conversation continues as they finish their drinks.

Laura Lee gets up off the barstool and grabs Scott by the hand. "Come on Scott, let's show them how to dance." They walk to the dance floor and join the other five couples. They continue to dance through three more songs. While Tony changes the CD, Mike walks to the bar and brings back five bottles of liquor. Tony turns the stereo up and the music continues. Everyone holds their bottle up, make a toast, and begin to power drink out of the bottles. Scott is letting his guard down, but he's not stupid. He knows better than to get drunk and make it easy for a team to take him out. Scott takes the girl by the hand, leads her down the hallway into one of the rooms, and closes the door behind him.

When he returns, Satinito and his women are gone; and the party is in full gear. Mike, Tony, and Joe are still on the dance floor with their dates. Mike is down to cowboy boots and his leopard skin briefs. Tony is barefooted and is down to his white cotton briefs and the leather pouch. Joe lost his shirt and shoes but kept his cigarettes. All the women are down to their jewelry. Billy looks like a zombie sitting on the couch with Kim sitting on his lap. Scott walks to the couch, and Kim pulls her legs up to make room for him. He sits down, and she puts her feet on his legs.

Billy with slurred speech, "Scott, where's the redhead?"

"She'll be back in a minute."

A couple of minutes later, Laura Lee walks in, fixes a drink for Scott, and brings it over to him. She looks around and notices that the other women are naked. She hands Scott the drink and starts to pull her dress off, but Scott stops her. Billy raises his eyebrows, smiles, and begins to speak.

Kim puts her finger over Billy's lips. "Scott is just being a gentleman."

Laura Lee smiles at Scott and imitates Kim by stepping out of her shoes and sitting on Scott's lap. She feels comfortable, and in a girlish way she pulls her knees up against Scott. She wraps her arms around his neck, and snuggles her head to his chest.

Mike walks up behind Scott and puts his hands on his shoulders. Scott looks up at Mike. "Thanks for the girl."

"She was Billy's idea. He gave me the description of the girl that you always talk about. She was hard to find, but I think that I found her."

Scott looks at Billy. "Thanks Billy. You're the best friend that a man can have."

Billy just holds his glass up to Scott and says nothing.

Mike squeezes his shoulders. "We might have gotten off on the wrong foot big guy. We just want to be part of the team. You seemed a little uneasy about us last night. What do you think of Laura Lee?"

"Mike, she's a goddess. Your finding skills will contribute greatly to this organization."

Mike laughs. "Do you mean fine art skills?" Everyone laughs.

Joe staggers over to the bar and grabs a liquor bottle that is one-third full. The three women walk over to the other side of the coffee table, kneel down, and start drawing six perfect lines of coke. Tony is wasted beyond belief and is running around the suite saying things in some weird language. He trips over a chair and lands near the end of the coffee table. He gets on his knees, unties the leather string that holds the leather pouch on his neck, sprinkles some brown dust from the pouch on the table, and carefully ties the pouch back around his neck. He makes a line, grabs a straw, and snorts it. He throws his head back and screams in pain. Everyone laughs at him as his hair stands straight out like he put his finger in an electrical socket. He roughly pushes the girls aside, snorts their lines, and licks up any traces that are still left on the table. Tony's really freaking, and everyone is still laughing at him. He gets up screaming and runs around the suite like a wild man drinking everyone's drink. He grabs the bottle out of Joe's hand and guzzles it. He runs up to Mike's girl, picks her up, and throws her over his shoulder. When he turns around, his date is standing in front of him. He stands there staring at her for a few seconds with a confused face. He puts the girl down next to his date and studies them. He pushes Mike's date aside, throws his date on his shoulders, grunts, and slaps her butt. He screams as he runs down the hall. As she's bouncing on his shoulder, she laughs and waves back to the crowd. He goes into a room, and closes the door behind him.

Everyone is still laughing, and Joe's still trying to figure out what happened to the contents of his bottle. Scott looks at Billy. "I'm not going to try to top that one, and I don't care to see anyone else try. See you in the morning." He puts his arms under Laura Lee, picks her up, carries her down the hall, and into a room.

CHAPTER 2

▼

The next morning in a little south-central town in Louisiana called Houma, an elderly man wearing a white tee shirt and blue jeans watches a white Cadillac Escalade pull into the paved driveway of his white wooden house. An attractive five-four, forty-year-old woman with shoulder length, straight jet-black hair gets out of the SUV and walks to the front door. She's elegantly wearing a pair of pants and a flowing blouse. In her left hand, she's carrying a bible with a rosary hanging from it. Before she can knock, he opens the door and greets her.

"Good morning Malynda, I'm so glad to see you."

"Good morning Mr. Robichaux."

They walk into the simple house, and she sits at the kitchen table while he fixes her a cup of coffee.

"Mr. Robichaux, I received a beautiful card from your daughter yesterday."

"Your stopping by means so much to all of us." He puts the coffee in front of her.

Malynda smiles. "Thank you. How's Mrs. Robichaux doing?"

"She mostly sleeps, which I think is a good thing." He sits down across from her.

She reaches across the table and holds his hand. In a soft and gentile voice, "And how are you doing?"

The smile leaves his face. "I have my moments. It just causes me so much pain to see her like this. I just want to know why it's taking so long?"

"It's all part of cancer. I can't tell you why, but I know that she needs you to be strong for her."

His eyes water, "I know Malynda. I'm trying, but it's tough."

They finish their cups of coffee. "Mr. Robichaux, are you ready?"

She gets up holding his hand, and they walk into the bedroom together. In the bedroom, there's an elderly woman in a hospital bed with an oxygen tube under her nose and an IV drip in the back of her hand. Her mouth is open, and she remains motionless with her eyes closed. On the dresser, there's a statue of the Blessed Mother and a rosary. He picks up the rosary, and Malynda walks him to the left side of the bed. He kneels down and grabs his wife's hand. Malynda walks to the other side of the bed, kneels, and grabs her other hand. They make the sign of the cross and Malynda with a warm and caring voice begins saying the rosary. Tears begin to fill his eyes. He looks up at Malynda and sees sunlight beaming through the curtains making Malynda glow. Forty-five minutes later, they finish and make the sign of the cross. She kisses the woman's hand, stands up, and kisses her on the forehead. The elderly woman does not move. The man also gets up, turns the radio on to big band music, and they softly walk out the room.

He hugs Malynda as soon as they get into the kitchen. "I know you are tired of hearing this for the past two years, but thanks for coming by. I almost forgot to ask—how's your daughter and your husband?"

"Celeste is doing fine. She's with my next-door neighbor—Debbie. Scott is coming home today. That's why I really can't stay. I have three more people to see in the hospital, and I want to make sure everything is perfect for Scott when he gets home. You should stop by and see us. I'm making a big pot of red beans."

"Thanks for the invitation, but I think I better stay with my wife as much as I can."

She hugs him again. "I'll bring you a bowl tomorrow. In the meantime, keep your head up and look on the bright side. She's been through the worst part of it. It shouldn't be long before she'll be in a better place."

"I know you're right."

He walks her out the door and waves as she pulls out of his driveway.

CHAPTER 3

▼

In the early afternoon, Scott and Billy are wearing casual attire traveling eighty-seven miles per hour on a south central Louisiana highway in complete silence. By the look on their faces, the silence is more than the boredom of the endless two-lane highway with eight-foot walls of green sugar cane on each side. The ear piercing noise of the radar detector redlining breaks Scott's concentration. His foot hits the brakes of his Lexus LS-430, and they cruise through the speed trap twenty miles an hour over the speed limit. Billy turns in the seat, looks through the rear window, and studies the cop car.

"Scott, that was a State Trooper with instant-on radar; I think he nailed you."

Scott looks up in his rearview mirror until the trooper's car disappears into the distance and laughs. "Billy, just call me Mr. Lucky today, because he's still on the side of the road."

"Man, what an icebreaker. The tension in the car was beginning to get to me. Does Mike know how to pick them, or what? I wish I knew how Mike found that redhead. How was she? Was she a true redhead?"

Scott makes a face. "She was Ok."

"Ok. Just, Ok. Scott, Mike got you your fantasy girl. What more could you ask for? The girl was hot! Now, Mr. Ass Connoisseur, wasn't that the best looking derriere that you ever saw or even dreamed about?"

"Ok, you're right. Enough!"

"Face it Scott. She was the hottest thing you ever slept with."

"Billy, we're talking about a messed up twenty-year-old little girl with a kid."

"Well, that explains the hips?"

"Maybe that's a good thing."

"Don't tell me she was terrible in bed."

"Billy, you're hopeless. She was great. No, she was better than great. Now, will you just shut-up!"

"What's wrong with you? You have to appreciate girls that make their living by pleasuring men. Do you realize how many hours in the gym she must…"

"Billy, you just don't get it. We string these women out on dope, and they just become a toy to us. As soon as they get too strung out to do us any good, we throw them out on the street. I want out! I'm tired of ruining other people's lives."

"Are you going through a mid-life crisis or what?"

"No, it's Mike and Tony; they're freaking nuts! Did you see their eyes? They actually enjoyed beating that woman to death the other night. That's the last time I ever want to see something like that. Look, I have a family to think about. It's time I find another job!"

"Think about what you are saying. You know there is no way you can leave the company. Mike and Tony, they just get a little carried away sometimes. Talk to Joe, maybe he can calm them down."

"Joe is the one that orchestrated the scene. He gave me a line of crap last night, but he's enjoying it too. The couple was what—thirty or thirty-five? The girl was maybe fifteen or sixteen at most. What pleasure could Tony get out of beating a sixteen-year-old girl to death after she watched her mother last a little over two hours?"

"Scott, putting a bullet in her head didn't help her any."

"It saved her from the hour or so that it would have taken Tony to beat her to death. What did that girl do? She had two doped out parents. I'm telling you Tony and Mike are bad news. They're getting higher on brutality than they are on their drugs. How could someone do that?"

"Ok, I admit that Tony went a little too far. What's done is done. Once word gets out, we probably won't have to do this again for a long time."

"Billy, I don't want to do it again—ever." Billy makes a face. "Don't act as if it didn't affect you!"

"You do realize that they stole about a hundred "K"."

"Do you understand that we are responsible for that?"

"Scott, how do you figure that?"

"Remember ten years ago, we would give them only small amounts on their first time. We knew full well that they were going to screw up. We would go in and bust their heads, and they would straighten out. We would then have a good distributor."

"Scott, don't give me that crap. You've killed more than a few guys that got out of line."

"Yeah. I killed a few, but it was a rare event. Most of the time, we just busted them up to say that we mean business. Now, every week we are killing a few. When I did it, it was quick and painless. I just put a bullet in their head. What we are doing now is pointless. We torture them for hours and then put a bullet in their head. We should be putting a bullet in their head in the first place. What is the point of making a messy scene for the cops to find? What's with Tony licking the blood off the girl's face? The man belongs in an insane asylum!"

"I don't know about an insane asylum, but I thought you were going to put him in his grave when you shot the girl with his face right next to hers. The way he jumped up, I thought you hit him too. Tony is extremely superstitious and practices Voodoo. He calls it the fountain of youth. He believes that by consuming the blood of his enemies, he gains their strength and the years that he robbed them of."

"You don't find that a little psychotic?"

"Everyone has their quirks. Tony is only thirty and is already fixated on living forever. Mike is fixated on women, but he uses so many steroids that his nuts have to be the size of peas. Joe is fixated on Satinito's position. I'm fixated on trying to keep up with my twenty-two-year-old wife. You, you're fixated on living your double lifestyle. You have the opportunity to marry some of the most beautiful women in the world, but you stay with your forty-year-old wife. When are you going to wake up and trade her in?"

"Trade in Malynda?" Scott laughs, "Not a chance."

"Come on, Scott, the holy rolely can't be as good as what you had last night."

"Malynda is not only as good, but she's better."

"There's no way that Saint Malynda can compete with that redhead. You're just getting settled in your old age."

"Old age, hell. I can still tangle with the best of them."

"Scott, get real. There is no way you can go hand to hand with Mike or Tony without getting a few bones broken."

"They'll know that they were in a scrap. Besides, I'm not going to have to worry about it. I'm out."

"Scott, let's face reality. You can't be ready to retire. Where are you going to find another job? What are you going to put on your resume for the past fifteen years? I was high paid muscle for a drug organization, and I killed people for a living? Look at the lifestyle you are giving up. Do you realize that, within the last two days, we broke all of the Ten Commandments and laughed about it? Saint

Malynda is all right for a visit every now and then, but you're still living in the fast lane. Don't give me that crap about Malynda being better. Since you married her, you haven't been faithful. There's a reason that we have been in the business for fifteen years—we are good at what we do. The reason that we are good at what we do is plain and simple—we enjoy it."

"You mean, did enjoy it."

"I hear you, but face the facts—they won't let you quit. If you do, you're committing suicide. You would stand a better chance at living if you killed Joe and then took his place. You better make it look like an accident though. Hell, I'll even help you if you want. Think about it, you're top dog and me at your side. We could run the operation like it should be run."

As he pulls into Billy's driveway, "Nope, I'm just quitting. I took out a little insurance policy this morning. With it, they'll have to let me go."

"I hope it's a life insurance policy with me as the beneficiary. Just don't make any rash decisions. You should give it another week. What's one week? This last trip was rough on all of us. You will probably want to get back on the road after a couple of days of doing Malynda's honey-do's."

Scott shakes his head as he pulls out of Billy's driveway and continues home.

CHAPTER 4

▼

In late afternoon, the August record high temperatures are scorching Houma. Malynda is lounging in a dream like state in the shade of her back porch of her powder blue Arcadian style home. She is barefooted and is wearing red denim shorts and a white sleeveless blouse. She's watching her six-year-old daughter, who's the spitting image of her; playing in the cool running water of a garden hose. Using her thumb and forefinger, she's rubbing a small gold crucifix that is hanging from a thin gold necklace. She smiles as she looks down at her large golden retriever that is having a dream of his younger days. Tranquility overcomes her as she over looks the emerald green St. Augustine grass that is shaded by the moss covered limbs of the majestic oak trees that extend over the bayou in her back yard. The roar of a passing eighteen-wheeler on the highway in front of her house snaps her out of it. She looks at her watch—4:00. With a slight lisp, "Celeste, Daddy is going to be home soon. Turn off the water and help Momma roll up the hose."

As she walks into her professionally decorated home, she smells the aroma of the spices applied to the red-beans that are on the stove cooking since morning. With a gentle shove, "Go make yourself presentable and make sure your room is clean." She puts on the rice and cornbread, and lets it cook while she heads to her bedroom to freshen up. Sitting in front of the vanity mirror, she applies ever so lightly a base to cover some of her freckles. She then brushes her hair. Carefully looking over herself one more time, she finds a single imperfection—a single eyebrow hair that needs plucking. She removes it, tucks in her sleeveless, nearly shear, white blouse with small red polka dots into her short shorts. Standing back from the mirror and admiring herself, "Do I still say fun, sassy, and good looking?" She pauses as she playfully turns left and right a few times in front of the mirror. A devilish grin comes over her face, "You bet I do!" She prances into the kitchen, stirs the rice and beans, checks the corn bread, and makes one more pass through the house to make sure that everything is in order. While in the weight room, she can't resist planting her foot into Franky's external obliques. The loud thump of her tennis shoe hitting the rubber kickboxing dummy echoes throughout the house.

She hears the Lexus pull into the driveway, and she runs into the kitchen. She looks out the window and watches the black Lexus pull into the detached garage alongside of the Escalade. She congratulates herself on marrying well. She accepts the heavy price tag of having her husband away so much for the high society lifestyle that she's grown accustom to living. She reminds herself that Scott's trustworthy. She overlooks his one case of infidelity that occurred early in their marriage as a test that made their fifteen-year marriage stronger. She's glad that he got it out of his system early, and he now knows what makes a good wife and mother. She's confident that single event is the reason why she has not been replaced by a younger trophy wife like so many of her sorority sisters have been. She knows that Scott is happy with her, and she is with him. As she watches her handsome husband walk to the back door, "Yes, Scott's definitely a keeper." The back door opens, and Scott walks in after being away for four days and three nights. Her daughter comes running and screaming "Daddy! Daddy! Daddy!" Scott picks Celeste up, gives her a welcome kiss, reaches into a bag, and pulls out a new teddy bear. "I want you to take real good care of this one and don't let Rex get it." Celeste's eyes light up, a big smile comes across her face, and she promises. Malynda watches her gentle six-four, ex-LSU linebacker and daughter for a few seconds. Scott puts Celeste down, and she playfully runs up to him "Hubby!, Hubby!, Hubby!" He catches her at the waist and effortlessly lifts her one hundred and ten-pound frame over his head. He slowly lowers her down where she wraps her arms around his neck and gives him a welcome kiss. In her girlish voice, "Did you miss me?"

"Malynda, I've been thinking about you the whole trip." He carries her into the kitchen. "Is that red-beans I smell?"

"You've been gone for three nights, and all you can think about is food?"

"Not only food, but your food and my favorite dish. Have you been working out because you're feeling pretty toned to me."

"Franky and I have been getting along at least half an hour every day."

As he carries her to the kitchen table, "I can tell."

Scott and Celeste sit down, and she serves the food. They say grace and begin to eat.

"Did you and Billy make the big sale this time?"

"I think we did. We'll know soon enough. Honey, this traveling is really beginning to take its toll on me. I think that I am going to find something local."

"You're a good salesman, and there are plenty of oil and gas supply companies right here in Houma. With your success, they would be crazy to turn you down. You wouldn't have to travel as much, and I'll see more of you."

"It probably won't pay as much."

"Scott, you paid your dues. We're debt free—no house note, car note, no nothing. Almost all of your commissions go straight into the savings anyway. It will be a nice change to have you around the house."

Celeste finishes dinner first. She excitedly interrupts the conversation, grabs her father by the hand, and tugs him away from the table. Scott is only half finished, but there is no stopping motor mouth Celeste. "Daddy, I colored pictures. I decorated my room. I cleaned my room three times. I got a new fish. I learned to read another book. Let's have a tea party. Come on daddy—hurry up."

Malynda looks at Celeste and then Scott, "Go on, just save some time for me." Scott and Celeste leave the kitchen while she starts on the dishes.

CHAPTER 5

▼

*1700, **the gentle breeze*** blows the eighteen-inch tall grass of a green pasture in southern Oklahoma. A clump of grass slowly begins to move. A forty-year-old man's face begins to appear through the camouflage—it's a sniper in a ghillie suit. His natural vegetation that is woven in his ghillie suit blends in perfectly with his surroundings. He remains motionless and looks forward. Another clump of grass in front of him moves back towards him. It's his twenty-six-year-old spotter that is easing back to his position.

The sniper whispers to his spotter, "Randy, what do you think?"

"Jacques, it is going to be an easy shot, because we are going to be within a hundred and twenty-five yards. Getting there is going to be the problem. Our primary target is in a foxhole two hundred yards on the other side of those bushes. There are eight alert sentries on elevated positions looking for us. The bad news is, to get to a clear shot and concealment, we have to cross seventy-five yards of some pretty short grass."

"So, let's get some fresh vegetation in our ghillies and get a move on. I want to get the shot off before dusk so they can't see my muzzle flash." He and Randy backtrack, locate similar grass, and weave it into each other's ghillies and drag bag. They ease back to the bush line and start their long seventy-five yard journey. Being the sniper, Jacques takes the lead. The breeze blows causing the grass around him to move, and he slides forward an inch or two. He waits for the next breeze to move the grass, and he moves another inch or two. Forty-five minutes later, he slides behind an eighteen-inch mesquite bush and slowly pulls out his rifle from his drag bag. Randy covers the seven yard lag during the time he's extracting his rifle. They lay side by side, and he waits as Randy scans the potential targets. Using a pair of binoculars, Randy studies the face of each of the men in front of him. He whispers, "There he is—second from the left." Jacques brings his rifle over and focuses his Leupold Tactical 6 x 20 scope. He checks his windage and elevation. "I got you now. Let's get this over with." He eases the bolt back and pushes it forward putting a round in the chamber of his custom 300 Winchester Magnum. "Ready."

He waits for Randy to make sure that the sentries are looking in different directions, "Ready."

"Safety off. Sniper up."

A couple of seconds pass then "Send it."

Jacques applies two pounds of force to the trigger, and the rifle rockets perfectly back into his shoulder as the sentries nearly jump out of their skin. He and Randy freeze as the sentries scan the area with their binoculars.

"Jacques, they're looking behind us."

"I know, just sit tight. I'm going to pop our secondary target. He's out there. Find him for me."

"Jacques, you're pushing our luck. We're too close for a second shot. We need to start escaping and evading."

"Find the second target and keep reminding yourself that you are invisible."

"I hope you know what you are doing."

CHAPTER 6

▼

Scott is two hours into a tea party with Celeste when Malynda interrupts them,—"Bath time." Picking up Celeste, Malynda heads off to the bathroom. Scott gets up and heads into the living room. He's sitting upright in his recliner with the TV off, his hand over his mouth, in deep thought. "Scott, why don't you go take your shower?" He does not respond. "Scott, wake up!" He shakes his head and looks at her. "What's wrong, you look like you are a million miles away."

"Just thinking about the trip."

"Relax, about the trip. You did all that you could do. It's all anyone could ask of you."

Before they tuck in Celeste, they say their prayers as a family, and then proceed into their bedroom. He climbs into the bed as Malynda goes into the vanity room. He stacks the pillows behind him and sits up. He begins to think about how much is at stake. He has a loving wife and a beautiful daughter. In his line of work, how much is he putting them at risk? He hears the vanity door start to open. He tries to put all of the crazy thoughts out of his mind and concentrate on the treat that Malynda normally prepares for him. He knows that she loves to manipulate men's minds, because it is so easy for her. This talent coupled with her strong sexual desires sent her to the confessional numerous occasions while they were dating. Now that it is done within the sanctity of marriage, she has become bolder and more creative in her techniques. The woman that he had last night was good. She did what she had to do to get what she wanted. His wife, on the other hand, has everything she wants. She does it out of pure enjoyment and self-satisfaction. It's a game to her—a game she's truly perfected. Getting the response she wants is a given. Now, she challenges herself on how quickly she can get that response. Knowing Malynda, she probably has a diary full of her techniques, formulas and stuff.

Malynda opens the door and steps out. He sees her standing there in the doorway with her hands on her hips, feet in the typical model pose, a red boa threaded behind her back, and a halo created by the vanity light. His eyes almost pop out when he becomes fixated on her tight, strapless, red, waist cincher. Scott's head is swimming in a blur. He nods his head, "What......What would the nuns...think of their little catholic school girl now?"

"They would think she's all grown up. Would you agree?" With his mouth open, he continues to nod his head. "For a ladies man, you aren't very articulate right now. Since men are visual creatures and I am your wife, I guess it would be all right to ogle for a while; but I want you to pay careful attention to the fine details of what I am wearing. There is going to be a test." He tries to regain his composure and takes in the whole picture. He sees her slim figure with the waist cincher exaggerating her already small waistline, adding flesh to her hips, and giving cleavage to her rather small bust line. As she slowly turns around for him, his eyes focus on her toned buttocks covered in red lace panties that are about an inch below the cincher. She continues to turn around. He stares through the thigh high stockings at her firm legs that are enhanced by her strapless two-inch heels. "I'm going to give you one more turn." She continues to turn around, and Scott thinks to himself that she's better than what men only dream about. As she sashays towards the bed, keeping her left hand on her hip and swinging the boa with her right, "I want you to keep silent and perfectly still." She steps out of her shoes, climbs on the bed, and sits on his thighs. She brings her face within an inch of his. He smells her lightly applied perfume, and he stares at her seductive, big, dark, brown eyes. As she slowly pulls back, he is overtaken by the by the infinite details of her face; then hair; then neck and bare shoulders. He notices her small gold hoop earrings. A red ribbon tied into a bow around her neck that he did not even notice before jumps out at him. She's sitting upright, and he is totally paralyzed by her beauty. All of his tensions stresses, anxieties, and conflicts are replaced with inner peace and calmness. She leans over and kisses him to break the mystical trance he is in. "Close your eyes." He reluctantly does. "I told you that there was going to be a test, and here it is. I want you to visualize me in my red outfit, and answer my questions. If you answer them correctly, you will be well rewarded." Scott thinks to himself that she's smiling now, because she's getting use out of her Child Psychology degree. Malynda begins, "I want you to picture everything about me—the jewelry I'm wearing, my body, my hair, and my attitudes. I'm going to start asking you questions. You need to answer them as quickly as you can."

"Did my shoes have straps?"

"No"

"What was the first thing you saw?"

"The waist cincher"

"What was my neck bow made of?"

"Red ribbon"

"How was my stockings attached?"

"With little straps." His thoughts are turning from the image to lust.

"Describe how my panties fit."

"They're low in the front and the sides go over your hip bones."

"Scott, I've been working out really hard. HOW DID THEY FIT?" The image of her tightly wrapped in lace pushes him over the edge. He reaches up to grab her, but she fights back and holds his hands at his sides. "We're not finished. How did they fit?"

"Very nicely"

"Correct"

In her serious voice, "Ok, you missed one. If you miss one more, you lose. This is going to be a speed drill. Answer as fast as you can."

"What color are my shoes?"

"Red"

"What color are my stockings?"

"Red"

"My panties?"

"Red"

"Waist cincher?"

"Red"

"Neck bow?"

"Red"

"Hair?"

"Red"

"Wrong, you lose. I'll guess I'll have to give you the consolation prize—*me!*" She wraps her hands around the back of his neck, and they laugh and wrestle for a while. The wrestling calms down, and they begin passionately kissing one another. Within minutes the outfit is on the floor, and they are under the covers making love. They fall asleep naked in each other's arms.

Malynda wakes to the silence of the house. She strains to hear and hears nothing. The familiar sounds of the frogs in the bayou and the crickets in the lawn are silenced. She looks around the dimly moonlit room. She turns to see her husband, who is sound asleep. Rex is lying on the floor next to her side of the bed. His head is up looking at the bedroom door, and he's softly growling. She looks at the digital clock, which reads 2:00 a.m. A board on the front porch creaks, and Rex starts barking. Before she can react, she hears the noise of the front door being busted in. Scott jumps up to the sitting position and reaches for the pistol in the nightstand. Rex bursts in a full run towards the front door barking the whole way. She hears the dog's barks turn into one yelp and then silence. Before Scott can get the pistol out, four armed intruders are in the bedroom doorway heading towards the bed.

The two bigger guys grab Scott and roughly throw him face first against the wall. He is hit by a kidney punch, which drops him to the floor. They manhandle him back to a standing position with his back against the wall and the muzzle of the silenced MP-5 touching his left cheekbone. The two smaller guys go after Malynda. She surprises them by shoving the heel of her hand into the base of one of their noses and kicks the other in the nuts. Scott yells, "Run! Malynda! Run!" She manages to make it out of the bedroom, and runs towards Celeste's room. From out of nowhere a metal object hits her across her face, and she drops to the floor. A hand grabs her by her hair and drags her back into the bedroom

Scott hears her scream in pain, and then he sees his wife in the kneeling position being violently dragged by her hair back into the dark bedroom. The man that drags Malynda back into the bedroom turns on the bedroom lights. When the lights come on, Scott sees four men wearing black body armor and one in slacks and a tan short sleeve shirt. The picture in front of him is what he feared the most. The two men that are holding Scott against the wall are Mike and Tony. Mike is holding the MP-5 on him, and Tony is pressing him against the wall. Joe's holding a stainless steel revolver in one hand. His other hand has a handful of Malynda's hair jerking her to and fro. On the other side of the bed is his best friend Billy holding his crotch, and a five-ten, one hundred and ninety-pound, twenty-one-year-old kid with short curly brown hair and a bloody nose. He looks at Malynda and sees blood coming from a deep cut under her right eye. Scott remains silent knowing that anything he says will be used against him. He is going to have to wait for his opportunity.

Joe picks up Malynda by the hair and throws her like a rag on the bed. "Tony, take care of her." As Mike laughs, Tony quickly moves to the opposite side of the bed and grabs Malynda by the wrist. Still full of fight, Malynda quickly stands and extends putting the perfect distance between her and the giant. With all of her quickness and strength, she lands her foot solidly into Tony's spare ribs. Even though it's ideally placed, it has no effect. In response, Tony pulls her in closer and backhands her across her face so hard that she flies over the corner of the bed, crashes head first into the headboard, and is soon spitting out blood and pieces of a tooth. Partially unconscious, she stays where she is with her torso on the bed and her legs hanging over the side. Scott screams, "Stop, I'll give you anything you want. Just Stop! What do you want? Anything! Just Stop!"

Everyone looks at Joe. Joe stops and lights a cigarette. "Ok, let's stop for a moment and determine if this is all necessary. I want the roll of film. Where is it?"

"In the trunk of my car."

"Keys?"

"On the dresser."

"Cliff."

Scott watches the new guy pick up the keys and leave the room.

Malynda begins to move and moan. Tony steps behind her and using his left hand on the small of her back puts his weight on her. She tries to kick him in the nuts and hits him in his thigh. Tony slaps her in the back of the head with his free hand, "Move again bitch, and I'll kill you."

Joe waves his pistol in the air. "While we're waiting for Cliff, let's see if we can entertain ourselves." Tony and Mike begin to laugh. "Scott, tell me. Does your wife know that you kill people for a living? Does she know that you have seen this same stage set so many other times—from a different prospective of course?" Malynda with a confused expression struggles to look up at Scott. "That's right sweetheart, until just a little while ago Scott worked with us." He begins to struggle, and Tony has to assist Mike to keep him against the wall, while Billy holds her down on the bed. Tony lands a punch into his stomach and slams his head back into the wall. Joe continues, "Scott, don't make me kill you just yet. Think about it. If I kill you now, you'll die not knowing the un-pleasantries your lovely wife is going to go through."

"Does Satinito know about this?"

"Are you kidding? It was his decision."

"Not, Malynda. He would never…"

"You're right, he's got a thing for your wife. She and your daughter wasn't supposed to be around. He actually thought that by having you out of the picture, he could make the move on her. He wanted me to use his nephew to snipe you, but you know how I like to take care of business myself. It's only way that I'm sure the job gets done right."

"You bastard, let her go. She doesn't know anything. She thinks that I'm a salesman. I'm giving you what you want. Let her go."

"Now, she knows that you're a murderer. You kill people for a living. Tell me, does she know about the twenty-year-old redhead that screwed your brains out last night?"

Scott screams out, "This is not necessary. I'm giving you what you want."

Malynda looks at Scott, and he just looks at the floor. "You see Tony and Mike physically beat people. Me, I'm way smarter than that. I cause much more damage than any physical beating can ever do. Satinito taught me the basics, and I now elevate it with the drama in front of you. Now answer, how was that young redhead last night? What about last week? Was she a blonde or brunette? What about the week before, and the week before that? Did your husband tell you that he has a thing for young redheads that are half your age?" Malynda's face turns red with anger. "That's right honey, you married a Don Juan. Were you thinking about your wife tonight, or were you thinking about that cute thing you had last night?" Cliff comes back with a 35mm camera with a telephoto lens. Joe re-winds the film, opens the camera, pulls out the film, and puts it in his pocket. "Tell me, what were you planning on doing with these pictures?"

"I was going to use them as a bargaining chip. I want out. Without something to hang over your heads, I knew that you would kill me."

Joe stays at the foot of the bed pacing back and forth. "Well, you no longer have something to hang over our heads. Do you? You're one unlucky bastard. Ironically, we were taking pictures of the same thing you were for the same purpose—blackmail. Who does Mike see through his telephoto lens? You, that's who. Talk about bad luck. Who were you planning on giving the pictures to— the cops? You're a bonehead because of pictures like this, we own the cops. How do you think that we're able to operate without interruptions? You lose. Let the games begin." Tony lets go of him and moves back to the other side of the bed, picks Malynda up by her hair, slams her face into the night stand, picks her up again and throws her back into the bed.

"No wait! What about Satinito?"

"What about him? I think that Satinito is just getting a little stupid in his old age."

"You bastard, just kill us and get it over with. Billy, just kill us and get it over with! You're my friend. Please, Billy."

Billy looks at Joe and begins to speak. Joe quickly interrupts him. "Billy is not in charge here. I am. I want to introduce you to your replacement—Cliff. Cliff, do you think you could replace this cry baby?"

"Yeah, boss."

"Do you really think that you could replace him? Let's see if his wife thinks that you can replace him?" Malynda looks at Joe. Her face is blue and swollen. Cliff also is looking at Joe with a puzzled look. Scott starts screaming again, "Billy, just shoot us. Do you hear me?" Tony moves back to Scott, holds his mouth shut, and forces him to watch.

"Do I have to explain everything? That is a nice piece of ass with your name on it. If you're replacing him, it's your piece of ass." Scott can see that Malynda is out of fight, and she's accepting that the worst is going to happen to her. As Cliff unzips his pants, Scott hears Malynda beginning to pray. Scott can't make out what she is saying, but she is repeating it over and over. As he watches, all the strength from his muscular body is drained. As soon as, Cliff clears out of the way, Tony picks up Malynda by the hair and begins unmercifully beating her to death while Scott is powerless to do anything. Her lifeless body falls to the floor one more time.

Billy sees that Malynda is obviously dead, and he steps in front of Tony before Tony has the chance to pick her up again. Billy looks closely at her and sees that her open eyes are in a fixated state. He looks at Joe, "It's done, enough." Joe nods at Mike, and Mike squeezes a single round off into Scott's head. Celeste runs into the room screaming. Like a rabid dog, Tony runs across the room; and picks Celeste up with his bloody hands. With a crazy look in his eyes. "Boss, let me do her to. It will be like bonus points."

Joe runs up to Tony and rips the kid out of his arms. "Not the kid." Joe carries her off and locks her in a hall closet. Everyone is standing in the living room. Joe looks at Billy. "Just to make sure, I want you to go back and put one in her head. Hurry it up, it's almost light outside."

"Ok, boss."

Billy walks back into the room and looks at his college teammate with blood still draining out of the bullet hole. He walks over to Malynda, who he knew almost as long as he knew Scott. He points the silenced pistol right above the tip of her ear. As he looks at the emptiness of her eyes, he remembers being best man in their wedding and begins to tear up. He can't do it. He points the pistol above her head and shoots through the wooden floor.

CHAPTER 7

▼

0230 Wednesday, the windows in a Witcha Falls motel room are vibrating from Randy's snoring. There's shooting equipment scattered throughout the room, and the room smells like powder solvent. Jacques is sleeping in the other bed, and his eyes suddenly open. He slowly scans the darkness of the motel room and sees nothing. He looks over at his shooting partner sleeping in the other bed. He remains motionless in the bed as every hair on his body stands up. His antenna goes to full alert. He thinks to himself. "Something woke me. Now, what was it?" He strains to hear movement and hears nothing but the occasional vehicle on the interstate outside of the motel. His nostrils flare as he tries to smell anything out of place with empty results. He sees that his partner senses his tension, and he watches him roll over to face him. He sees him sliding his hand under his pillow where he knows there is a Colt 1911. Randy makes a face with tension at him to silently ask him, "What is going on?" He shrugs his shoulders. Randy whispers, "Is it serious?"

"Yeah." The two men in white tee shirts and boxers using the movements of cops search the room and come up empty handed. Randy is six-one and is the type that hits the weight room three to five days a week. Jacques is forty years old, five-ten, has a little bit of a gut, a little balding on top, and is in the shape of a guy that hits the weight room only once or twice a week.

Randy looks across the room towards him. "Jacques, what's going on?"

"I don't know. Something woke me out of a dead sleep."

"What about the truck?"

Jacques looks out the window. "No, the truck is fine."

"Relax friend, it must have been the wind blowing at the door. You should have had some of that group tightner with me before we hit the sack. People laugh when they see me having a few beers, but I get a good night's sleep. Everyone else is wired about the shots they missed, the shots they're going to miss, or dealing with the aches and pains that will not let them sleep. Not me, I sleep like a baby. Come on friend, we have a big day ahead of us. We need to get some sleep."

As they climb back in their respective beds, "Yeah. You're probably right." Jacques tries to go back to sleep but fails. He gets up, takes a leak, and climbs back into to the bed while scratching his ass. He tosses and turns for the next two hours and finally falls back to sleep.

0500, the alarm clock goes off, and Jacques turns it off. Randy quickly jumps out of bed, "Come on old man, today is the last day of this sniper match. Last night, we were in the lead by over fifty points, and the only two events left are your favorites—unknown distance and 1000 yard. What's the matter, you still look rattled?"

Jacques slowly drags out of the bed, "Have you ever had one of those feelings that you know something is wrong, but you just can't put your finger on it?"

As they get dressed and make their equipment ready, "Jacques, you're probably just worried about today. On the last day, you always do. I'm charged and ready for whatever today brings me. When you fired that shot yesterday, three of them lost their hats. Even with the walker within ten yards of us and they knew the shot was coming, the second shot made them jump almost as much as the first. Do you realize that we were within one hundred and twenty-five yards with a walker within ten yards of us, eight of the world's best snipers with binoculars looking for us for three minutes in ten inch tall grass; and they still could not find us after two shots. We kicked their ass!"

Jacques looks at Randy packing all sorts of electronic equipment in his pack. "Randy, does your department supply you with all that electronic equipment?"

"Are you kidding? If you are on the force and you want something good, you have to buy it yourself."

"Do you really need all of that?"

"Nope, I just like to have it."

"You ought to think about loosing it and making your pack lighter."

"No way, I like my toys."

The realization of what Randy said earlier sinks in. "Wait a minute, we were in the lead by a hundred points at lunch time. What happened?"

"I checked the board while you were doing your night fire. We lost a few points with the moving target event and the KIMS (Keep in Memory) game."

"We?"

"Ok, I lost a few points with the moving targets, but we both lost in KIMS. Even if we don't win, we will make enough money in the money shoot to make up the difference between first and second place."

"I wouldn't be so sure of that. A lot of people back out of it when I sign up."

They load the truck and drive to the 1000 yard range.

Randy sees that Jacques is driving slower than normal. "Jacques, come on get with it. What's up?"

"I don't know. I still have that weird feeling that I had this morning—like something's wrong."

"Old man, you're just second guessing yourself or worried about the wind. Just get in your zone."

"It's not the shooting. It's something else—something I can't explain."

"Well, snap out of it. We're here. Time to put your game face on. Hoo-ah!"

"You still have too much Ranger in you."

They exit the truck and carry their gear to the 1000 yard firing line.

Jacques rolls out his shooting mat along side of the other competitors, sets up his rifle, and positions his spotting scope in front of his left shoulder. He looks up at Randy, who is looking down range with his binoculars. "Randy! Get your ass in gear!" Jacques lies down behind his rifle. Randy takes a sitting position by Jacques' right shin and sets up his spotting scope overlooking Jacques' right shoulder and rifle. Jacques records the temperature and humidity in his shooting log book. He studies the wind. "Do you see what the wind is doing 700 yards?"

"Yeah, it looks like it decreased from ten miles per hour to about five miles per hour."

"You are looking down at the grass straight in front of the target. There is a little valley right there. Look at each hilltop. Remember, at 700 yards your bullet is going to be eight and a half feet above line of sight."

"Man, it's blowing. It must be about twenty miles per hour."

"More like seventeen. Look at 300 yards. The wind is blowing in the opposite direction. So, at 300 yards we have a left to right at about five miles per hour. At 600, the wind is blowing from five o'clock at seventeen miles per hour. At 1000, the wind is blowing from three o'clock at fifteen miles per hour. Low humidity, so the mirage is going to be minimal. The adjustment for a thousand yards with a fifteen mile per hour cross wind is 10 MOA [minutes of angle (100 inches)]. The adjustment for three hundred yards with a five mile per hour wind is 1 MOA. Ten minus one is 9 MOA. What do you think?"

"When it comes to a thousand yards, you're the man. I'm not going to question you."

The range official tells the shooters to stand away from their rifles and everyone complies. "Good morning shooters this the third and last day. The sniper match is nearly over. We have two events remaining. This is the thousand yard event. You will have five minutes to shoot ten rounds at the target. The target looks like this." He holds one up. "It is a paper silhouette target of a bad guy, with the ten ring the size and shape of a beer can. The five ring is twice the size of the ten ring. Any hit on the silhouette is worth two points. The target spacing is only four feet. If you shoot someone else's target, the points will go to your competitor. If there's more than ten holes in your target, you will get the higher score hits. As always, there will be no sighters—every shot counts. Snipers will be on the line first. Time begins now."

All the snipers dive on their rifles and their spotters position themselves on the spotting scopes. Jacques checks the wind as he obtains his natural point of aim. He squeezes his hand sock, quarters the target, and begins to communicate with his spotter. "Wind?"

"Same."

Jacques waits for the wind to blow hardest. "Ready."

"Ready."

"UP!"

"Send it."

Jacques exhales, waits for the pulse of his heartbeat to quarter the target, and squeezes the trigger. The rifle rockets straight back into his shoulder pocket. Instinctively, he draws back the bolt, picks up another round, drops it on the feed ramp, and shoves the bolt forward. Randy watches the vapor trail of the bullet land one quarter left on the target.

"Favor right."

They follow their communication routine, and Jacques sends another round down range. Randy sees the vapor trail end at the center of mass. "Center of mass."

They work as a team to get as many rounds down range before the wind changes direction. They finish in plenty of time.

"Shooters! Cease-fire! Cease-fire! Unload and remove your bolts. Back off of your weapons."

The scores are radioed in, and Jacques scored a ninety-five out of a possible one hundred.

"What were you so worried about? You picked up the fifty points that we lost yesterday."

"Your turn, and remember follow through."

"Snipers remove your equipment from the firing line. Spotters set up on the firing line. You will have a two minute set up time."

They go through the same routine with the spotters. Randy scored a thirty-one.

"Shooters you have ten minutes to relocate to the unknown distance range." Everyone loads in their vehicles and travel a mile down the red dirt road to the unknown distance range. "Shooters, there will be a cash shoot. Entry is one hundred dollars." Jacques takes fifty out of his wallet, and Randy gives him the other fifty. Only one other shooter comes forward, and the rest of the shooters laugh at the new comer. "Come on shooters, you all can't be afraid of Jacques?"

"That gun of his should be banned from sniper competition. He's pushing a two hundred grain bullet over three thousand feet per second. His windage is only half of our .308's, and his drop is less than half. No way, not this time."

Jacques interjects, "I'm only pushing twenty-nine fifty. I tell you what. I'll only take head shots if it makes you feel better."

Ten of the other competitors come forward with their money.

"Jacques, what are you doing? We've got a fifteen mile per hour wind; you know that the targets are going to be spaced over a hundred and twenty degree arc; and fifty bucks of that is mine. Not to mention that we can lose the whole match with this nonsense."

Jacques has a confident smile on his face. "What's the matter youngster, are you beginning to lose faith in this old man?"

"Shooters pay attention. Spotters will not be allowed to assist the money shooters. Where there will be no unfair advantage, money shooters will be called to the firing line one at a time. Money shooters are to remain here until your name is called. Jacques, you shoot last. The rest of you may approach the firing line to observe. For this event, you will be shooting ten eleven inch wide by twenty inch tall steel silhouette targets. Jacques, you will be shooting at a six inch wide by eight inch high head. Only shots that knock over the target will count. You will have a fifteen minute time block to locate and engage all ten targets. A first shot hit is ten points. If you miss, you will have five seconds to make a second shot hit that is worth five points. Jacques, you will have five seconds after the target resets." Jacques watches the match director lead the crowd through the mesquite trees to the firing line.

Jacques walks off and sits by himself.

As soon as Randy clears the mesquite trees, he gets bombarded with the questions from the other competitors.

"What drives Jacques to shoot so good? I mean before his wife died, he was just a little better than most of us. Now, we can't even touch him."

"It's his way of letting out hate."

"If he has that much hate, why don't he just shoot the bastard that killed his wife and kid."

"Shoot, tell me who did it; and I'll shoot the bastard. We might then stand a chance of winning one of these things."

"This is getting old. Instead of mailing my money to the match directors, I think that I should just mail it to Jacques."

Randy interjects, "I shouldn't be telling you this, but he don't hate the guy that caused the accident. He hates God himself. He's obsessed with showing God that he has the power to take away life just like the Almighty does."

"Do you think he's stable?"

"I've been shooting with him for a couple of years, and he seems all right to me."

Back along the road, Jacques opens his data book and makes a table of ten rows for the targets and ten columns for the shooters. He hears the first shot go off, and he counts real fast—one, two, three, four, five, six, seven, eight, nine, ten, eleven.

He hears a second shot go off and counts again—one, two, three, four, five, six, seven, eight, nine, ten, eleven, twelve, thirteen, fourteen, fifteen. *Plang!* He puts 800 yards in shooter one target one. There's fifty seconds of silence before the next shot goes off—one, two, three, four, five, six, seven. *Plang!* He puts 350 yards in for shooter one target three. After the first five shooters finish, he maps out the target's approximate distances. As he figured, there is a close target and then a far target. He keeps watching the wind and making notes as the other six shooters completed their course of fire. High score is nine hits. Many shooters have problems with targets number 3, 6, and 8, and no one hit number 10. The high score is ninety. Jacques figures that the targets are only partially visible. There's a delay after the eleventh shooter finishes. Finally, he's called to the firing line.

He walks through the mesquite trees to the firing line, which is on a gradual downhill slope. The crest of the hill in front of him is twenty-five hundred yards away. The vegetation is a mixture of grass and mesquite trees of various sizes. There is a barbwire fence in front of him. He knows the properties are divided into half mile tracts, and he is about eighty yards inside the fence line.

Before he gets his backpack off, "Fifteen minutes begins now! We repainted the targets to verify your head shots."

Jacques drops his backpack, pulls out his Leupold 12x40 spotting scope with the Gen2 reticle in it, sets it up, gets his rifle in place, and pulls out twelve bullets. He starts scanning about a hundred yards inside the barbwire. He finds the first target close to the fence line. It's camouflaged painted and is placed behind a bush so that it is only half-visible. He mils it at 780 yards with a 15 mph wind from nine o'clock. He dials in his dope and communicates with the scorekeeper in the same manner as his spotter. He squeezes the trigger and the rifle rockets perfectly back into his shoulder. Confident in his shot, he moves his rifle to the second target before the hit is confirmed. The scorer yells, "Hit" Using the scope's reticle, Jacques mils the second target at 375 yards with almost full value cross wind. He dials in the dope and fires again. "Hit." He looks at his watch, and he says to himself, "Two targets down within a minute. Time looks good." He continues with his spotting scope to locate target number three. Mils it at 625 yards. Dials in his dope and fires. "Hit" He continues to locate and engage targets without missing. By this time, the one hundred plus degree temperature starts affecting his judgment. As the salt of his sweat fills his eye, he finds target number ten. It's painted solid white and is out in the open. He mils it at 1200 yards. "Can't be." He mils it again—1200 yards. He looks at his charts. He dials in his thirty-four minutes of elevation and holds one and one quarter mils high. He gets his natural point of aim, his pulse down, exhales, and starts to apply pressure to the trigger. He stops and pulls his finger out of the trigger guard. "Wind! I have a fifteen mph tail wind. I need another one point five MOA, which is about half a mil. Aim high one point seven five mils. Wait. Double for the scope. Three point five mils."

"Thirty seconds left."

"Ready…"

"About time…"

"Up…"

"Send it…"

Jacques holds three point five mils at center of mass and squeezes the trigger. The rifle rockets back perfectly again. After follow through, he quickly sets back up on the target and tries to read the trace. The rifle gets back into position just as the target falls.

"Jacques, get ready for a repeat. I think you missed the head."

Someone calls out "There is a coyote right behind target number three. Jacques loads two shells as the target resets itself. The target pops up. Using his spotting scope, he sees a silver dollar size circle of paint missing four inches below his aim point. "You have five seconds to repeat the shot."

Jacques holds the three point five mils on top of the target's head, communicates with the scorekeeper, and fires again. This time instead of trying to see the trace, he concentrates more on follow through. Nearly two seconds later, the crowd begins cheering, and the sound of the impact is then heard. Jacques trains his rifle on the coyote as the target is resetting. The coyote freezes, looks towards the 1200-yard target, and begins to run towards target number one.

"Hit. Jacques Boudreaux wins the money shoot with a score of ninety-five. Good shooting Jacques."

One of the competitors screams, "Get him Jacques." Jacques has the dope, the wind, and the lead; but he can't do it.

"Randy, what's wrong with Jacques? How come he don't shoot?"

"He won't."

"I thought you said…"

"I did. He wants to think it himself, but he was brought up under the philosophy that you only kill for two reasons—food or survival. You see he considers all life to be sacred—nothing is wasted. Even though he eats nutria, he doesn't eat coyote."

Jacques ejects the shell and stands up away from his rifle as the crowd comes to congratulate him. The scorekeeper watches the coyote run until it is out of range. The score keeper gets out of his chair, walks over to Jacques, and hands him the twelve hundred dollars. "Ok shooters, we all know who won the top gun position. We have three teams in the contingency for first place. Let's finish up the event with the other shooters. Snipers on your rifles and prepare to engage target number one. They do and finish out the match. Randy scores enough points to maintain the team's first place standing.

After the awards ceremony, Randy and Jacques pack their gear in their vehicles. "Jacques, why don't you come spend some time with me? My wife is a good cook, and we can get some shooting in."

"I'm sort of getting use to the single life again."

"Liar."

"Well, maybe in a couple of months."

"Liar."

"I still need some time."

"Jacques, it's been over a year and a half. You can't keep going on living your life like you are. It's unhealthy. Come on, take a week off spend some time with the wife and me. You'll have a good time."

"Sorry, I just can't do that right now."

"Ok, but remember the offer is always open. If you need anything, just give me a call."

"I appreciate that." They get in their vehicles and drive off in separate directions.

CHAPTER 8

▼

On a Houma highway, a pleasantly plump brunette in her mid-twenties is driving home from the grocery store in the pouring down rain. She is sitting on a pillow to help her see over the steering wheel. Her shoulder length hair and stripped blue and white blouse are soaking wet. She has a concerned facial expression because she's having a difficult time seeing the road in the heavy downpour.

As she passes her next door neighbor's house, she thinks that she sees the front door open. She continues home, parks her vehicle in her driveway, and then sloshes through the wet lawn to investigate. As she comes up the stairs, she sees Rex's body lying in a pool of blood. She starts frantically calling for Malynda. She sees the chair propped against the closet door. She slowly removes it, and picks up a crying Celeste. Carrying Celeste on her hip, she continues through the house. She walks into the bedroom and immediately sees Scott's naked body sitting in a puddle of blood and sees the blood on the opposite wall and bed. "Mon Dieu!" With her hand over her mouth, she slowly walks over to the side of the bed to see Malynda lying on the floor. She starts hysterically screaming and runs out of the house and back to her own. She picks up the phone and calls her husband's cell phone.

In a black and white patrol car, a sharp looking deputy in his mid-twenties with sandy blonde hair and a mustache is patrolling a Houma neighborhood.

His cell phone rings, and he answers it. A woman is screaming, crying, and incoherently speaking a mixture of boogulie French and English.

"Debbie, honey, calm down. Are you all right?" Debbie continues in her hysterical state. "Are you at home?" He deciphers a definite "Yes."

"Are you in any danger?" and he deciphers a definite "No." He immediately turns on the siren of his patrol car and speeds homeward. He continues screaming over the sound of the siren, "I'm on my way home. Calm down and pull yourself together. I need you to slow down and tell me what is wrong. I need to know if you are all right?"

She screams, "Steve, it isn't me;" and she becomes incoherent again.

"Who is it? Is anyone hurt?"

"It's Malynda and Scott, They're...They're dead. Scott and Malynda are dead!"

"Calm down. Where are you right now?"

"I'm at home."

"What about Celeste?"

"There's blood all over the place—over the entire house! It's a mess! There's so much blood! Hurry Steve!"

"What about Celeste? I need to know if Celeste is hurt? Is she all right?"

"Celeste is fine! Malynda is full of blood, Scott is full of blood, the dog is full of blood! There is so much blood! Steve, please hurry!"

"I need to call this in. Stay on the phone with me—Ok. Do you understand? Don't hang-up."

"Ok."

"Dispatch, this is Unit 24. I need to report a multiple 30 at 1624 Main Street. Presently, in route."

"Unit 24, roger. Wait, that's your house."

"No, next door."

"Malynda Meyeaux?"

"Roger"

"Unit 13, in route." "Unit 26, in route." "Unit 18 in route" "Unit 6, in route." "Unit 3, in route." "Unit 11, in route." "Unit 1, in route." "Unit 8, in route."

"This is Unit 1, I want everyone to stay out of the house. I want you to secure a perimeter. Unit 24, when you arrive on the scene, call me on your cell phone."

"Unit 24, Roger. I need someone to look over my wife."

Unit 13 is the first on the scene. He pulls his patrol car into the hundred foot long driveway at a high rate of speed. He speeds across the front lawn, jams on his brakes and slides parallel to the front door, "Unit 13 on the scene. I'm parked in front of the house." He jumps out of his patrol car with a sawed off shotgun and points it across the hood of the car towards the open front door.

Steve comes off the highway, onto Malynda's lawn, and accelerates to the rear of the house. He jams on the brakes, and the car slides into a defensive position. "Unit 24 in position at the rear of the house." Steve also jumps out of his patrol car and secures the rear of the house with a shotgun.

Unit 11 pulls off the highway speeds down Steve's driveway. "Steve; I'll look after Debbie. Take care of business."

The rest of the units arrive within seconds and strategically place their vehicles around the house.

The sheriff is the last to pull into the driveway. "Unit 24 and Unit 18, enter and clear the house from the rear and flush them out through the front. Unit 8 set up some crime scene tape to keep the crowd back. This woman touched a lot of people. It won't be long before word gets out."

Using nothing but hand signals and the leapfrog method, Steve and his fellow officer clears the house room by room. When they are sure that the house is clear, Steve calls on the radio, "All clear."

The detectives arrive, and Steve walks them into the house. He watches one of them walk over to Scott and by inspection declares him dead. The detective then walks over to Malynda, puts two fingers on her neck, and declares her dead. The detectives then begin to look for signs—hair, footprints in the blood, fabric fibers, and anything out of the ordinary. They make their tape-lines of the victims' bodies and take countless pictures.

Debbie watches from under her carport with Celeste on her hip. The Deputy tries to comfort her and brings her a folding chair. By the time the ambulance arrives, a crowd of at least a hundred is standing in the rain against the yellow crime scene tape. She hears the town's church bells begin to ring sadness through the town as a pregnant woman seeks shelter next to her. Debbie gives her the chair that she's sitting in.

"Thank you, you know this is a sad day for this town. Even the storekeepers are closing shop and most of the flags in town are already being reduced to half-mast. Why would someone do such a thing?"

Debbie puts her hand on the woman's shoulder. "If any one of those deputies find out who, I'm afraid he won't live long enough to say why." They watch the ambulance back up towards the front of the house. The paramedics wheel out the gurney in the pouring rain and disappear inside of the house. When they reappear, the ten deputies form an alleyway, remove their hats as the gurney with the sheet-covered body is loaded into the ambulance. As paramedics retrieve the backboard, the deputies put their cover back on to try to keep as dry as they can. As they load out Scott, again the deputies remove their hats. Once the victims are loaded into the ambulance, it's police escorted to the hospital; and the crowd of people follow.

A young female intern at the hospital acts as a sentry for the arrival of the ambulance. "It's here!" Half of the emergency room staff in a semi-organized method rushes out the sliding doors to meet the ambulance. As the young intern wheels a gurney to the ambulance, other staff members unload the ambulance's gurney with Malynda and swiftly take her inside. The orderlies remove the backboard and load it on the intern's gurney. Once inside, she and the others push the gurney into a room. The doctor pulls back the cold and wet sheet off of Scott, sees the bullet hole in the head, and declares him dead. He then walks over to Malynda's gurney. He pulls back the sheet, looks at the extent of her head wounds, shakes his head, and realizes that he is wasting his time. He feels for the carotid pulse. When he touches her, he feels that her body is at room temperature and does not feel a pulse. He puts his stethoscope on her chest and hears nothing. He then pronounces her dead. The doctor barks to two orderlies to bring the bodies to the coroner's office. The young intern feels robbed of her opportunity to try to assist and walks out of the hospital to get some air. She wipes away a tear that is running down her face, and the crowd that is impatiently waiting to hear of any news immediately bombards her with hundreds of questions. She turns to rush back into the hospital; however, the crowd surrounds her. Without raising her head, she softly says, "They're both dead."

The two orderlies push open the double doors to the morgue. Loud symphony music fills the morgue. There are two shinny stainless steel tables in the center of the concrete floor. On one side of the tables is the stainless steel vault. On the other side, there is a counter with lab equipment on it. They look at the end opposite of the entrance doors and there is an old man in a shirt and tie with a green lab coat on. He's reclined back in his swivel chair with his feet on the desk. His eyes are closed, and he is making motions as if he is a composer.

One orderly calls out, "Colonel Green!" There is no response. He calls out louder, "Colonel Green!" Still, no response. He screams, "Colonel Green!"

The elderly colonel green turns off the CD player, looks over his half reading glasses, and sees the two orderlies with the gurneys standing in the morgue.

They're a little choked up. "Colonel Green, this is Mrs. Malynda and her husband. Where do you want to us to put them?"

"Did you say Mrs. Malynda? Malynda who?"

"You didn't hear? Mrs. Malynda Meyeaux and her husband were found murdered this morning."

His glasses fall to his desk and the blood drains from his face as he fights to stand up. He uses the desk to support his weight. "Did you say Malynda Meyeaux?"

"It's a terrible thing Colonel. The whole town is practically shut down. At last check there were over three hundred people praying in the parking lot. The Churches are full. No one understands, and everyone wants answers. Where do you want me to put them?"

The coroner is unable to answer.

"Colonel, are you ok? Do you want me to call someone?"

"No, No. I'll be ok." He walks over to the blood stained sheets and pulls them back. "Oh! My God, how could someone do this? He looks at Scott and tells the orderlies to put Scott in one of the vaults and to put Malynda on table one. He returns to his office and puts on his gloves and mask. He loads the tape recorder and returns.

The reality and full impact of her death hits him when he sees her naked body laying lifeless on the cold seven foot long stainless steel table with her hair matted in dry blood and the absence of muscle strength to keep her body symmetrical. He puts his glove-covered hand on her shoulder and looks at her repulsive face. The old veteran doctor of Korea and Vietnam, the one who stared at death countless times and unmentionable medical horrors of war begins to tear up. "Who would do something like this to you? What terrible horrors have you gone through?" The lights blink as a loud clap of thunder vibrates the glass windows. "You would think that God and the Angels would be rejoicing to have you in their mist; however, this horrible thunderstorm says otherwise. I just hope you can hear the people praying, and the Church bells ringing. They say how much your works were appreciated. You touched the community as a whole by selfless-ness, caring for the terminally sick and their survivors. I can still picture you tak-ing care of my Claire, how you would visit nearly every day. Your visit meant so much to her. Your caring charm, grace and persistence pulled me through. I thank you so much, ever so much; and I am sure others are saying the same. You sure were a special one. I vividly remember how skillfully and gracefully you delivered the Eulogy. You had a way of turning the words that were spoken thou-sands years ago into emotions, into life, to be applied to life, and to become life itself. You had a God given special peace about you that you couldn't help but to share with others." The knot that was developing in his craw starts to close off. He struggles to get out a few more words. "Malynda, I am going to ask you to make one more contribution to your community. I need you to give me the evi-dence we need to capture the evil that did this to you." He drops to one knee and breaks into tears. "God, please give me the strength to get through this." Wiping the tears from his face and regaining his composure, he uses the table to help him to his feet. He reaches up and turns on the overhead microphone and opens the file. He clears his throat and begins: "Case Number 200300054, Malynda Meyeaux, forty-year-old female." He looks at the digital weight, "Weight: forty-nine kilograms." He stretched the tape measure, "Height: one hundred, sixty-three centimeters. By initial observation, Malynda's cause of death was due to multiple head injuries." He wipes a tear off the side of his face and grabs the camera and begins to take pictures. He puts the camera down and ever so gently rolls her over. He continues taking pictures as he describes to the recorder his actions. He then rolls her back over on her back. He positions her to remove fluid samples from her. He inserts the fluid into vials and catalogs the samples. Feeling uncomfortable by having violated the very woman that served him Holy Communion, he quickly repositions her in a more presentable position. He grabs for the fingernail scraper from the assortment of surgical tools. "I hope you put up fight and have something for me." He starts with the right thumb, scrapes and collects the powdery substance in a vile. He scrapes her right index finger and her hand pulls back. "Relax, I didn't mean to hurt you. With more than twenty years as a coroner, the nervous system reflexes still gives me the chills." He continues on the middle finger. As he scraps the middle finger, the reflex jerk is more obvious. "What?" He does it again, and she jerks back again. He drops her hand and the scraper bounces off the concrete floor. He runs over to the phone, quickly punches an extension, and starts screaming into the phone. "Get someone down to the coroner's office. MALYNDA MEYEAUX IS ALIVE. DID YOU HEAR ME—YOU IDIOTS? SHE'S ALIVE."

CHAPTER 9

▼

0900 Thursday, at the FBI New Orleans' Field Office, an attractive blonde with unkempt short hair nearly fills the height of an open doorway. The thirty-two-year-old woman is wearing a navy blue jacket with a matching skirt, a light blue blouse, and a pair of black heels. The sleeves of the jacket are too short, and the length of the skirt is barely acceptable office attire. The muscle definition in her thighs and calves clearly shows that she is not only attractive, but also physically fit. The nameplate on the wall to her right is of Frank Harris, District Head, FBI Narcotics Enforcement Section. The immaculate dressed and groomed short man sitting behind his desk is in his early sixties. The oversized wooden desk is empty except for two folders that are perfectly placed side by side in the upper left corner. He's ignoring the woman and is concentrating on something in the open desk drawer. The spacious office has a wooden bookcase that occupies the entire wall to her left. The wall to her right is covered with diplomas, awards, and pictures of Mr. Harris with presidents and foreign leaders. The entire wall behind his desk is a window overlooking Lake Pontchartrain.

She knows that the old bastard is just ignoring her. She begins to stare out of his window. A little over a minute passes. Without looking up he turns in his high-back swivel chair and closes the blinds. He turns back around and finally looks up. "You're five minutes late Special Agent Susan Rodred. Well, don't stand in the doorway. Come in and sit down while I finish organizing my paperclips."

She walks in and sits with her legs crossed in a chair across from his desk. Even with a special platform that his desk and chair are on to elevate his head above his guest, she sits at eye level with him, which he totally despises. He takes exactly five minutes to finish organizing his paperclips as she patiently waits.

"Your business suit looks good on you—all trim and proper for a change. You're almost fitting for the FBI. You know that you are not in the military. You can let your hair grow out a little more. Speaking of hair, you could use a new coloring job because your roots are showing. Don't make a face and roll those grey eyes. We are after all the FBI, and we have an image to uphold."

She bites her lip and cheerfully answers, "Yes Sir, I'll schedule an appointment as soon as possible."

"There is something I've been meaning to ask you for over a year. With your height and figure, how come you ended up a FBI sniper instead of a model?"

"On the South Dakota farm where I was brought up, I shot prairie dogs all the time. Etiquette school was not a high priority growing up in a farming community."

"It's never too late to start. Is everything in place for your surveillance on the Satinito's group tonight?"

"Yes, sir; but Scott Meyeaux was killed last night."

"So, one less criminal on the street. Any idea who did it?"

"I would bet that it was Satinito's bunch."

"So, they finally turned to cannibalism."

"His wife was attacked also."

"So, two less criminals on the street."

"Sir, she survived."

"What do you mean she survived?"

"They thought she was dead. She was even pronounced dead at the hospital, but she survived. I would like to put a security detail on her."

"It's a local problem. Let the locals handle it."

"You know that the locals can't protect her from Satinito's bunch. She will be dead by the end of the week."

"And your point is?"

"We should give her protection."

"Like I said it's not a federal case. Satinito is a federal case. Let the locals handle Mrs. Meyeaux." She rolls her eyes. He continues, "You obviously don't understand that Mrs. Meyeaux's life is not worth blowing our cover in this case. I only have two years to make my twenty, and I want to go out as a winner."

"You're not planning on dragging this case out for the next two years are you?"

"You need to become a team player Sue. I know how much ass kissing you have done to get as far as you have. You're a team leader—a field team leader at that. Not many women in the Bureau can say that. If you file a report on me, it wouldn't matter. I can coast my last two years. They'll slap me on my hand and might even give me early retirement. You, on the other hand, can loose everything you worked so hard for. You could be blackballed and never get another leader assignment your whole career. I know you wouldn't want that. Besides, cooperate with me, and I'll even recommend you for my position." She makes a face. "Sue, I don't make the rules. I just play by them. You should learn to do the same."

"At least let us get some information on Satinito in the Casino's."

"You can collect all the information you want as long as you stay within the borders of St. Tammany Parish. We have local law enforcement support, and we are sure that they are not on Satinito's payroll. Any investigation outside of St. Tammany could jeopardize the case. I will not jeopardize this case. Is that clear?"

"Crystal, Sir."

"Good."

"But, Satinito never goes in St. Tammany Parish. We have over a year's worth of drug trafficking evidence on Satinito's right hand man, Joe and Joe's bodyguard—Mike. If we are not allowed to get evidence against Satinito, how are we to build a case against him?"

"I'll let you know in about another year. Do you have anything else you want to talk about?"

(Silence)

"Good, keep me informed of your progress on the case."

"Yes, Sir." And she walks out of his office and under her breath, "What a prick!" She turns a corner and opens her cell phone and dials a number.

At a crowded, loud craps table in a Biloxi casino, Satinito is ready to throw the dice. He gets a twenty-five-year-old woman that is standing next to him to blow on the dice, and he throws them.

He rolls a two and a six. "Point is eight."

Everyone places their bets. As he puts out his bet, his cell phone starts ringing. He answers it.

"Franky, how's the FBI treating you? Hold on."

"Roller's coming out. Eight is the point." He gets the girl to blow on the dice again, and he throws them while he has the phone to his ear.

"Come on baby!" The crowd roars as he rolls double fours. "Yeah, baby!"

"Satinito, stop what you are doing. I need to talk to you right now. Do you hear me?"

"Franky, hold on a second and let me pick up the ten grand I just won." Saninito picks up his ten grand and then continutes, "So tell me, how're they hanging?"

"They're pretty swollen! Your idiots didn't do to good of a job last night."

"What do you mean? Everything went just fine."

"Malynda Meyeaux is still alive?"

"Hold on. Let me get somewhere I can talk to you." He walks through the casino and walks through a door and into an office. "So, I told Joe not to involve Malynda or the kid."

"Well, they did. She's in ICU this morning."

"Relax Franky. As soon as, she gets out of ICU and…"

"Relax! Satinito your guys really screwed up this time. I want you to kill her. I want it done sooner than later. I want to know what she knows. I want to know if my name was mentioned. Your guys are too much into the gory scenes. They want to make an example. This is an example of what happens when you screw around and don't do things the simple way. I thought you said that you were going to use a sniper?"

"Calm down. If Joe didn't want to use my nephew, I'm sure that he had a good reason. As far as Meyeaux's wife, I'll make sure the job is finished. Just wait until she gets out of ICU. There's just too many people around. Trust me. She won't leave the hospital alive. In the meantime, I'll give you the ten grand I just won. Come on over and enjoy yourself."

"I don't want to enjoy myself. I want that bitch dead, and I want her dead now. There's no telling how much she knows, or what she's willing to do to seek revenge."

"Franky, you need to learn to relax. Just give me a little time, and I'll take care of everything. I tell you what. Come over and I'll give you the ten grand and this beautiful and lucky woman. That should calm you down until I fix this little mess."

"You can keep your money and your women. This is serious."

Satinito laughs. "You know me and my blood pressure. This woman could give me a heart attack. You don't want that to happen. Come on over and enjoy yourself for a change."

"Get serious. Do you realize this whole thing could come apart if she lives? I'm not ready to do a twenty year sentence to cover for you."

"Don't worry. I'll handle this. I'll call you when I know more." They both hang-up.

In a cubical in a FBI Building in Washington, D.C., a tall and lanky thirty-year-old man with brown brillo hair is sitting back in his chair waiting on two computers to finish running their programs. He's wearing brown dress slacks and a cream long sleeve shirt with the sleeves rolled up. He stares at the running program logic through his thick seventies style glasses shaking his head. One of the computers starts throwing strange characters on the screen and locks up. He throws his hands in the air and then his palms crash onto his forehead. His phone rings, and he answers it while he watches his other program crash.

"Agent Merrit."

"Danny, this is Sue. Don't make any plans for this weekend. After I give my Friday status report tomorrow, I'm headed to get a drink, and I'm on the first plane to D.C. Harris hit an all time high today."

"What has Napoleon Junior done this time?"

"We'll talk about it when I get there."

"Come on Sue, you know I'm seeing someone."

"Does she have a ring on her finger?"

"Not yet. What kind of question is that?"

"Who is she?"

"You know who she is."

"Is she better looking than me?"

"You know she's not."

"Does she have a rack like mine?"

"You know she doesn't."

"Is she better in bed than me?"

"Sue, what kind of question is that!"

"I'm just trying to size up my competition."

"She's not your competition, and no she's not."

"She can cook, can't she?"

"Best red gravy I've ever eaten."

"So, she can cook. Is that the only reason that you are picking her over me?"

"Did you forget about a little thing called lack of commitment?"

"Oh, yeah. I sort of."

"Oh, yeah is right. We've been sleeping together for how many years, and you're still afraid of commitment."

"It's not that I'm afraid of it. I just have so much that I still want to do. Look, just let me be the other woman. I'm fine with that. Please Danny. I need to talk to someone."

There's silence on the other end.

"Danny, I'm not asking you to marry me. I just need some company. I need someone to talk to who understands me. We don't even have to go out. We can just get a hotel room and stay in all weekend."

"Sue, are you that desperate?"

"Oh yeah, I'm real desperate. Please. Come on, I'll do anything."

"Ok…Don't fly into D.C. Fly into Knoxville. I'll get a cabin in the mountains. Maybe a weekend in the mountains will calm you down. Let me know what flight you catch, and I'll try to meet you."

Joe and Mike are watching television in Joe's living room of his 1960's, sixteen hundred square foot, Gulfport, Mississippi house with white vinyl tile floor, tile counter tops, white walls and ceilings. The phone that is mounted on the wall with a short cord rings. Joe answers it with a cigarette in his hand and the TV blaring.

"Joe, this is Satinito. I have a problem with you. How many years have you worked for me?" He motions for Mike, who is sitting on the couch, to turn down the volume.

"Twenty-five. Why, do I get a twenty-five year anniversary party?"

"How about a twenty-five year funeral party? How many times did you screw up in twenty-five years?"

"None."

"Well, you screwed up last night. In this business, do you realize how many times you are allowed to screw up before there is a bullet in your head? I thought I told you to leave Malynda and the kid out of it."

"Mr. Satinito, it was personal. I wanted to see that the job was done right. We treated him just like any other traitor. It was painless Mr. Satinito—one bullet in the head. She didn't even know what hit her. Now Scott, we roughed him up pretty good."

"Oh, you did a good job on Scott; but Malynda lived through it."

"Can't be the same person. Malynda is at room temperature in the morgue."

"She's alive."

"Impossible, we put a bullet in her head."

"Then, she's alive in the hospital with a bullet in her head."

"I don't understand."

"Joe, since you showed me years of loyal service; I'm going to give you one chance to fix your wrongs. Don't screw it up. Do I make myself clear?"

"Thank you Mr. Satinito. I'll take care of it right away."

"Don't rush into this, she's a smart girl. Take care of her at the first opportunity, and make sure it looks like an accident. Get someone at that hospital, and make sure we know where she's at all times. They'll try to transfer her to put her in safekeeping. If they do, find out where."

Joe covers the microphone of the phone and looks across the room. "Mike, Meyeaux's wife is still alive. Get over to the Houma hospital and make sure she doesn't leave. I'll call you later." Mike gets up and runs out the door.

"Mr. Satinito, I'll take care of this."

"You better."

"Don't worry, I will."

"We have another problem. You excited Harris again."

"Do you want me to take care of him also?"

"Are you kidding me? As long as he has a federal investigation ongoing, local law enforcement has to stay clear. We are untouchable until he retires. Besides, he's a materialistic fool. A little money and a few whores every now and then is all it takes to keep him happy. Where are we going to find another dummy like him?"

"All right, I'll get the girl; but you know we are going to have to take care of Harris sooner or later."

"For now, it's later. Make sure you get the girl." They both hang up.

Sitting on top of a hill in a Mississippi pasture, a mean looking bald man with bushy eyebrows and a clean mustache is looking through the scope of his bolt-action rifle. He is viewing a silhouette target at 600 yards. He's wearing woodland BDU's and combat boots. He uses his toe to push himself a little forward and squeezes the trigger. The rifle rocks back, the explosion is heard, then the sound of the bullet hitting a metal plate is heard. He ejects the brass, comes off his rifle, and records the data in his logbook. He picks up another round when his cell phone rings. He answers it, and it's Frank Harris.

"Sergeant, we had an accident last night. Satinito's guys didn't do a thorough job. They killed Scott Meyeaux, but Malynda Meyeaux survived. She's in St. Ann's hospital. If she appears outside of that hospital, take her head off. In fact, if you get a clear shot through her window, take it."

"Why don't you let her get into protective custody in a remote area or let us do her in the hospital? It will be much easier to cover up. Hell, we could even blame it on the food."

"Satinito's men will get her in the hospital. I don't want her to make it into protective custody. She's a real liability that needs to be taken care of as soon as possible. Do I make myself clear?"

"Crystal, Sir. I'll get on it right away. If she steps one foot outside the hospital, she's dead."

Joe dials Tony's number, "Tony, I want to have a meeting in two hours at the Sea Shell Motel. You know the dump on the coast right past Pass Christian. Call Cliff and Billy and make sure they show up. Mike already knows about it. Oh, tell Billy to show up in two and a half hours. I have a surprise for him."

"What's up Boss?"

"I'll tell you when you get here?"

Two and half hours later, Billy walks into the door of a simple motel room. Tony grabs him and throws him against the wall and starts strangling him with both hands. Joe walks up to him. "Why? Just tell me why—Billy? Why didn't you kill her like I told you to?"

He struggles to speak, "Boss, she was already dead. I mean really messed up. What was the point of putting a bullet in her?"

"The point was to make sure she was dead."

"Ok, I screwed up. I didn't put a bullet in her head—Big deal! She's still dead."

"It's a big deal because she's still alive you idiot."

"What do you mean? There's no way."

"She's in St. Ann's in ICU."

"She ain't going to live, she can't. Tony worked her over really good. Even if she lives, I don't think that she's going to say anything to anybody."

"Billy, you should have put a bullet in her head—just like we did her husband."

"Boss, I never saw anybody so messed up before. I'm surprised that she lived through it. Did you see all the blood? Tony backhanded her one time, and I thought her head was going to come off."

"Billy, you have seen Tony's work before. Was this time any different?"

"Boss, this was a woman. When Tony was finished, you could barely tell what she was. By the time men are that messed up, they are begging for the bullet. All she kept screaming for was the kid."

"So she had a kid."

"Boss, what about the kid?"

"What about the kid? Maybe we should have let Cliff have his way with her too—the horny bastard."

Everyone in the room starts laughing, except Billy.

Tony interrupts, "Boss, why didn't you let me do the kid like I wanted to? You wanted to make a statement. That would have made a statement."

"It would have been ok with me, but I was told to leave the kid alone. What are we doing talking about the kid? Billy we need to be talking about what we are going to do with you." Joe pulls out his revolver, cocks the hammer, and points it in Billy's face. "Satinito might have a hit planned for me already, because you can't follow simple directions. A bullet in the head might not be so bad after all. Do you realize what is going to happen to me if he finds out what we did to Malynda?"

"Wait, we don't know if she's even going to live. At least, let's see if she's still going to die. I didn't betray you like Scott. Please, give me a chance. Think about it. You would have to train two new guys. If she dies everything will be cool."

"She still might talk to the police, or worst yet to Satinito."

"She's not talking to anyone. She's smarter than you think. Please Joe, think about it."

Tony tightens his grip on him, "Do him Boss. He deserves it."

Joe pulls the pistol away from him, "It's against my better judgement, but you live for now. If she lives, you die. If Satinito finds out, I'll make sure that I kill you before he kills me. Tony tie him up. You have a baby sitting job."

Cliff rips out the lamp's wire and hands it to Tony, and Tony ties Billy's hands behind his back.

"Wait, what are you doing this for. I'm not going anywhere. You don't need to do this."

"You do this or you die. The choice is yours."

As Joe walks out the door, "Tony, I have some business to take care of. You watch Billy. Come on Cliff, you can drive."

"Wait, don't leave me here with Tony. He's crazy."

"I'm sure that Tony will take real good care of you while we are gone."

CHAPTER 10

▼

Saturday morning in the bed of a Houma hospital ICU room, Malynda lies unconscious. She is clearly visible through the glass walls from anywhere within the ICU unit. Her swollen face is black and purple, and her scalp is completely covered with a head dressing. The motor sound of the IV pump and the beeping of the heart monitor can be heard throughout the quiet room. A woman wearing green scrubs is sleeping in a chair next to Malynda's bed, and she's holding Malynda's hand. She's in her early fifties, but her slightly puffy face does not have a single wrinkle. Her jet-black hair is short and styled and accents her beautiful brown complexion. She's still wearing a pair of half-reading glasses that she forgot to take off the night before.

Malynda's eyes begin to open, but everything is a blur. Sounds are clear, and she tries to focus on each strange sound and identify what it is. The fuzzy images become clearer to her. The IV bottle is dripping; the sound of the heart monitor is beeping. She jumps up, "*Celeste! Where is Celeste?*"

The woman in the scrubs jumps up. "Calm down, Celeste is all right. She's here with Debbie. Relax."

Several medical staff members rush in and push the social worker to the side. They start scratching Malynda's skin with objects, someone injects something into her IV, someone is shining a flashlight in her eyes, another person is rotating her head, and everyone is asking her questions at the same time. She feels light-headed again and fights the pain medication. "I want to see my daught..."

That afternoon, she wakes up again. Afraid that the same thing will happen to her again, she remains motionless. She looks at the woman in the scrubs. "Don't let them do that again. I want to see my daughter."

"Ok, honey. Just let me stay in here long enough to hold off the doctors."

This time, only one doctor and one nurse come into the room. The doctor has her chart folded in his arms, and he walks towards her. He stands close to the bed. "Well, Mrs. Meyeaux, you gave us quite a scare."

She demands, "Where's my daughter?"

"Calm down Mrs. Meyeaux. We sent someone to get her. She should be here in just a few seconds."

"Where's my husband?"

"He is not doing good. He is down at the other end of the hall. We have another surgery planned for him tomorrow morning."

"I want to see him."

"I'm sorry I can't do that. We need to work on getting you better. Perhaps, we can wheel him by after surgery tomorrow. Is that ok?"

She fears the worst, begins to cry, and nods her head, "Yes." She sees a crowd gather outside the glass walls of her ICU room. Debbie fights through the crowd with Celeste on her hip and makes her way into the room. "Momma! Momma! Are you going to be all right?" Malynda crying rubs her hand on Celeste's face, "Yes, baby. I'm going to be all right." The doctor and nurse back away from the bed and give Malynda some space.

"Why are you crying? Are you hurting?"

"No baby, I'm happy you're here."

Debbie sits Celeste next to her mother's side. The doctor watches Malynda and Celeste for about fifteen minutes then interrupts. "Mrs. Meyeaux, I really need to cut this visit short. You are still very weak, and I don't want you to get excited."

Debbie in her heavy Cajun accent, "Don't you worry about Celeste, Malynda. I'll take good care of her. How are you feeling?"

"Debbie, I need you to be careful."

"Don't worry, Steve's full time assignment is to protect Celeste. You take your time on getting better. Imagine how much I'm getting done around da house by having him home all day." They laugh and look through the glass at Steve. He just raises his hands with a confused look. Debbie grabs Celeste and starts out of the room. "Malynda, you take care of yourself. Dey say Celeste and I can visit two times a day 'til you get a regular room. I'll see ya tomorrow."

The Doctor has the nurse escort Debbie and Celeste outside the room. "Mrs. Meyeaux, for the next two days I'm going to keep you heavily sedated. Your body will heal better that way. Your body has been abused, but it will heal with time. We have a little oral surgery to do on you, but other than that you have no broken bones. The trauma to your head concerns us the most. You have a major concussion, and your brain is still swollen. Just a precaution, we will be doing daily CAT scans. We are looking for blood clots that may form in your brain. Don't look so worried; we haven't found any. We want to keep a close eye on you for the next few days. I'm restricting visitors to just Debbie and your daughter and only twice a day for fifteen minute stays. With your permission, we would like to do the oral surgery tomorrow." She nods her head, "Yes."

"Also, the police want to have a few words with you."

"No. I don't want to see the police. Keep them away from me! Do you hear me? You keep them away from me."

"It is important for you to talk to them as soon as possible. They have special people that can question you and bring many things out of your memory that you probably didn't realize you saw."

"I said *No*! No police. I don't want to talk to them. I don't want them near me or my daughter."

"Ok, maybe tomorrow. Before I give you your pain medicine, I want you to hear a little something. It is going to take a few minutes so just wait." He picks up the phone and dials an extension. "Ok, tell them that she's still in critical condition, but we expect her to make a full recovery."

She watches the doctor as if he is expecting something from her. A few seconds pass, then she hears a crowd rejoicing and applauding. She looks at the doctor with a puzzled look.

"It is your devoted fan club. They have been in the parking lot in the rain for twenty-four hours a day. There are over two hundred people down there." She then hears the town's church bells begin to ring, and a smile comes over her face.

The doctor motions to the woman in the green scrubs. "Mrs. Meyeaux, this is Violet Johnson. She's the social worker that has been assigned to you. She has been here from the beginning. Well, don't try to do too much to soon. It will be a long recovery process. I'm going to give you some pain medication, and I'm going to leave you and Mrs. Johnson alone for a while." The nurse injects Malynda's medication in the IV tube, and they leave.

"You can call me Violet."

"Is my husband dead?"

"He is in bad shape. It's day by day. For now, let's concentrate on getting you better."

"I have something for you. It is the only thing that you came in with." Violet puts the crucifix necklace back on her neck. "Honey, Lord must have decided that your job on earth was not finished yet, or he could have just got tired of going against the wishes of your fan club."

"I'm scared. What is going to happen when they come back?"

"Excuse me for a moment." Violet steps out the doorway with attitude. "Do you all have something you should be doing?" The crowd moves on and she walks back to Malynda. She sits at the foot of her bed. "Sorry about that. You don't have anything to be scared about. There are two policemen stationed at the elevators, one at the stairs, the one right outside your room, and one making rounds on this floor. Debbie's husband has been assigned to Celeste and there is another patrol car watching Debbie's house. No way—no how darling. You're protected."

She begins crying again. "You didn't mention Scott's protection. Scott's dead; isn't he?"

"You were going to figure it out sooner or later. Scott was killed instantly. There was nothing that anyone could have done to save him."

A mixture of anger and sorrow overtakes her. "Why did you lie to me?"

"We wanted to break it to you slowly. It's standard procedure."

Her sorrow overcomes the anger. She turns away from Violet and pulls her covers up and begins to cry. "I want to go to sleep."

"I'll be here when you want to talk."

"I don't want to talk. Go away."

CHAPTER 11

▼

2100, Joe returns to the motel room to find Billy standing in a galvanized wash tub naked with his hands tied above his head, duct tape across his mouth, and totally hairless. His body is one big bruise with hundreds of small cuts. His hands are bright purple. There are several black candles burning on the dresser and weird music coming from a CD player. Tony with nothing on except a natural leather loincloth is sitting on the floor heating the metal blade of a spear with a propane torch. Tony turns to look at Joe, and Tony's face is completely painted in black and white.

Joe rushes over to Billy and rips the tape off his mouth. "Tony, what's going on?"

"Boss, he's crazy. He is planning on quenching his spear with my body. Please, cut me down."

"Tony put the spear down! How did you get all cut up?"

"He shaved me with a straight edge razor. Took my hair and made a voodoo doll and started shoving pins in it. When it did nothing, he began shoving pins in me instead of the doll. He keeps telling me over and over that he is going to rob me of my powers before he kills me. He's crazy. You got to cut me down. Don't leave me with him again." Joe puts the tape back over Billy's mouth.

"I was just trying to scare him boss."

Joe turns back to Billy, "Malynda is going to live that means you die. Sorry, Billy."

Cliff walks behind him and shoves a needle in Billy's neck and pushes out the contents of the syringe. Within seconds Billy can no longer stand up. His knees give way, and he is left hanging by his hands. Cliff pulls out a pocket knife and cuts his hands free.

Tony picks up his spear. "Boss, I want to do him. I have a special surprise for him."

"Ok, Tony, but do it up I-59 and make sure nobody finds the body. Cliff back the car up to the door and go with him to make sure the job is done right." Cliff makes a strange face. "Tony's all right. Aren't you?"

"Yeah Cliff, you don't have to worry about me."

Cliff backs the car up, and Tony manhandles Billy into the trunk of the car.

Tony carries his spear and the propane bottle and walks over to the driver's side of the car. "Move over kid, I'm driving."

They drive about an hour, and Tony swerves to miss a black cat that is crossing the interstate. He goes onto the median and looses control. The car spins completely around, and Tony jumps out. "Did I cross its path? Did I cross its path!"

"Hey, you hit it. It's dead. Let's go."

Putting his hands on his face. "Which wheel did I hit it with?"

"Left front. Let's go."

"Good, I didn't cross its path."

"How do you know? It might have walked out to the median and then back."

"Don't mess with me man. Did I cross its path?"

"No, you killed it before you crossed its path."

"Good, because it's bad luck. You do know that. Don't you?"

"Come on Tony, Let's get out of here before someone sees you."

Tony jumps back in their car, and they continue North on I-59.

CHAPTER 12

▼

Sunday morning, Violet wearing her green scrubs is walking down the hallway of ICU. She gets to Malynda's room and walks in.

"Malynda, what you doing there?"

She responds in a real snotty tone. "I'm writing a letter to my daughter. Can I please have some privacy?" "Please!"

"Honey, I know the last few days have been bad; but you should be moving to a normal room pretty soon. We need to see about you talking to the police."

"I told you that I'm scared. I still have my daughter to think about."

"You don't need to flare that little nasty attitude with me. I'm here to help you. Maybe, you will feel different in a normal room where every passer by can't see what you are doing every minute of the day."

"What about the police protection? Are they going to still be here?"

"Don't worry dear, the police will be here to protect you."

"For how long?"

"As long as need be."

Malynda tears off a piece of paper. When Violet is not looking, she hides it under the covers. A short time later Debbie walks in with Celeste, while Steve stays outside and talks to the security detail. Malynda sits up and hugs Celeste.

"Momma, your hair is growing back. I like you better with hair. Look your bo-bo's are going away too. Don't worry when you get home, I'll take good care of you." Everyone laughs. Before they know it, the fifteen-minute visit is up. Malynda hugs Celeste again and whispers in her ear, "Momma is going to slip a secret note in you underwear. You give it to Mrs. Debbie. Don't let Mr. Steve see it. Do you understand?"

"Yes, ma'am."

"Remember, it is a secret. Don't let anyone else see it." She pushes Celeste back and hands her the note that she wrote her. "Here, I wrote you a letter." Debbie grabs Celeste, "I'll see you tomorrow," and she walks out the door.

As soon as Debbie is out the door, Malynda can see the security detail grab the letter and read it. Malynda protests.

"Malynda, calm down. I don't..."

"It's private, they don't have a right to read that."

Violet sits on the bed. "Honey, let me finish. I don't think that they saw the note that you shoved under Celeste's dress. I use to be a second grade teacher, and I have eyes in the back of my head. I'm sure that you had your reasons, and I'm sure that your note is going to get out."

Malynda starts crying, "I'm scared. I'm really scared."

Violet reaches out to her, and they hug. "It is going to be ok. You just keep praying, and it is going to be ok."

Later that day in Debbie's house, "Steve, come see, Celeste handed me dis earlier today. I wasn't supposed to show you, but you should see it."

"Debbie,

Go into my house in my memory box on the top shelf of my bedroom closet. There is a small purple piece of paper with Jacques Boudreaux's phone number. It's his parent's number. Get his number and tell him that I need his help immediately, and he needs to be careful. He'll know what to do. Don't show this to anyone—not even Steve. The police are involved.

Love,

Malynda

"Well Debbie, that explains why she's not talking to the police, but who is this Jacques Boudreaux?"

"I don't know, but I'm sure dat we're going to find out. Do you think dat the police are involved?"

"I hate to admit it, but it's a possibility. Wait, that house is still a crime scene. I don't want you messing around where you shouldn't be messing."

Steve grabs his mic, "Unit 24, we are going to get some clothes for the girl."
"Roger that."

Debbie and Steve walk over to the house. Debbie goes to get some clothes for Celeste, and Steve goes into the bedroom and hunts for the phone number. Steve goes into the closet, and there is only one box in the closet. He opens it, roots through it, and finds the phone number. He neatly replaces all the papers and puts the box back on the shelf.

"I got it. Let's get out of here."

Later that night, "Any luck."

"No, I got in touch with his parents. Dey seem like good people, but I just get his answering machine."

"Did you leave a message?"

"No, I not sure dat I want a stranger having our phone number."

"Leave a message without a phone number."

2200, Jacques is strapped into his rifle standing in the hallway of his house wearing nothing but his boxers and a white tee shirt. He's dry firing from the kneeling position at a target that is illuminated on his back yard fence. "Number 30, 29 to go." *Click*. He drops the rifle off his shoulder, works the bolt, puts the rifle back into his shoulder pocket, and tries to controls his wobble. The phone begins to ring. He concentrates on the sight picture, and he squeezes the trigger. Click. "Number 29, 28 to go. When are they going to realize that I'm not going to answer that phone?" He works the bolt and re-shoulders the rifle.

The answering machine picks up. A woman with a heavy Cajun accent begins to leave a message. "I'm calling for Jacques Boudreaux. It's about Malynda Meyeaux. No, I mean Malynda Thibidoux. Are you there?" Jacques runs to the phone with the rifle still strapped to his bicep. "Hello!"

"Sorry to call you so late. Are you Jacques Boudreaux?"

"Yes, you said something about Malynda Thibidoux. How's she doing?"

"I'm afraid, not good."

"What do you mean?"

"She was brutally attacked and almost killed. Her husband was killed."

"Where is she?"

"She's still in ICU. She say dat she needs your help immediately and dat you to be careful. She say dat you would know what dat meant."

"I'm on my way. What hospital?"

"St. Ann's"

"What city? What state?"

"Good God, when was da last time you seen her."

"My sophomore year at LSU."

"She's in Houma. The hospital is on Main Street."

"The one by the IntraCoastal?"

"Dat's the one, but you have to see her social worker before you can see her."

"What's her name and phone number?"

"Violet Johnson, her phone number is 985-555-1212."

"Ok, if you see Malynda tell her I'm on my way. Who else knows I'm coming?"

"Just me and my husband."

"Good, keep it that way."

He hangs the phone up, puts his rifle down, and starts packing. "I wonder what my old college buddy Judge is doing now a days. It's been a couple of months since I spoke to him."

Jacques picks up the phone and dials a number.

In a dark living room of a small Houma home, a heavy set man is alone sitting in an oversized recliner watching a DVD on his big screen television. The phone rings, and he picks it up.

"Hello."

"Judge, how you're doing? I hope I didn't wake you."

"Oh, just fine. You didn't wake me. You know me; I'm a night owl. How've you been? I hope you called to go fishing. We loaded the boat up the other day with white trout in Terrebonne Bay."

"Not fishing this time."

"Sorry, about that."

"Do you still work in social services in Houma?"

"Yep, going on ten years."

"Do you know a Violet Johnson?"

"Yep, she use to work with me for a while. She then moved to treating battered women. Why?"

"An old friend of mine that is in the hospital called me up and wanted to see me. I understand I have to go through Violet to see her. I was wondering if you could grease the skids for me."

"You mean Malynda Meyeaux is a friend of yours."

"A long time ago. Do you know her?"

"Everyone in Houma knows her."

"Do you know what happened to her?"

"Some people broke into the house in the middle of the night. They shot her husband and the dog. They nearly killed her too. A neighbor found her the next afternoon almost dead."

"How about greasing those skids?"

"Jacques, she's a tough cookie. She plays strictly by the rules. You know after a woman has been battered, they won't allow men visitors. I'll give it a try, but I can't promise anything. In fact, I'll give her a call as soon as we get off the line."

"Wait, it's 11:30."

"It's ok, she's a workaholic. Anything else?"

"I could use a place to crash for the next couple of nights."

"Sure thing, but you have to let me buy dinner this time. How's Dave's sound?"

"Great, if I have time. I have a feeling that there's going to be some serious business ahead of me."

"Nowhere is it written that you can't take care of serious business on a full stomach of good food."

"Ok, see you tomorrow." They both hang up.

Jacques immediately heads for his walk-in closet and shoves his sniper rifle in his drag bag. He opens the gun safe, pulls out his AR-10T, and shoves it into a drag bag. He grabs his AR-10's web gear that is hanging on a heavyduty wooden coat hanger, loads all clips, and verifies that it's packed with the bare essentials for a three-day mission. He then repeats the process for his sniper rifle's web gear. He reorganizes and checks the niceties in his ruck sack. He realizes that in a crisis situation that the ruck sack is disposable; therefore, all its contents are also disposable—expensive but disposable. He grabs an athletic bag and throws some clothes in it, sets his alarm for 0200, and tries to get in a little nap prior to getting on the road.

Violet is talking to the nurses at the nurse's station when her cell phone rings. She looks at the number, recognizes Judge's number, and answers it. "Hey boo, what are you doing?"

"Watching a movie. How are you doing?"

"I'm fine sugar, but why are you calling me at this hour?"

"A friend of mine named Jacques Boudreaux called me just a little while ago, and he would like to see Malynda. He said that she asked to see him."

"The note."

"What?"

"Nothing, I'm the only one that is allowed to see that girl. I'm having a tough time holding off the police."

"He said it's important. When this guy says something is important, it means life or death."

"Wait, I'm right outside her room. Let me ask her about this matter."

She wakes Malynda. "Malynda, do you know a Jacques Boudreaux? I have someone on the phone that said you wanted to see him. Is that right?"

"I need to see Jacques. He is the only one that I want to trust right now."

"Ok, Judge. I'll meet this Mr. Boudreaux, and I'll make a decision after I meet him. You need to make sure that he understands that. Now, what type of person he is?"

"He's a really calm person, level headed, high morals, extremely resourceful, and a great problem solver. We went to school together at LSU. He graduated in engineering."

"So he is a extremely bright individual with morals."

"Wait I didn't say he was extremely bright, he's just bright. What makes him special is that he is persistent. I've seen him in action before; the man never gives up until whatever he sets out to do is done. He doesn't know how to quit."

"I'm still not sure."

"The other thing you should know is that he is extremely protective of his family and friends. He was raised in the swamp with old time values. Something like this happening, I'm not sure what he is capable of."

"What is that suppose to mean?"

"Well, do you still have that direct line to God?"

"Yeah, my faith has never been stronger. Why?"

"You might want to start praying for the people that did that to Malynda. May the Lord have mercy on their souls because when Jacques finds them—and he will find them—he won't show any mercy."

"I like him already, but you know the rules honey. Men visitors are not allowed. I tell you what, give him my cell number and have him call me at eight a.m."

With that, she folds up her phone. She turns to Malynda. "Looks like you've got a boyfriend coming by tomorrow to pay you a visit. Don't get your hopes up. If I don't approve of him, I won't let him in."

CHAPTER 13

▼

0200 Monday, Jacques wakes up to the sound of the alarm clock. He quickly showers, shaves, gets dressed, loads the truck, and drives in an almost dream state thinking about Malynda.

He only knew her for about a year and a half. It seemed that she moved into the neighborhood the summer of his freshman year and moved out the day after Thanksgiving their sophomore year.

During that time period, he was "The Man." He just received his driver's license was the full back for the football team and a track star. The summer of his sophomore year, he was five-ten and 180 lbs. with a washboard stomach. He thinks to himself, those were the days. He was lean and mean. He thought that he was indestructible until he found out his heart was his Achilles heel.

He lived in a blue collared neighborhood. His family's social economic status was the lowest part of middle class. They had enough money to make ends meet, but not much beyond that. Like his parents, Jacques always made the best of what he had. Instead of buying new, everything was fixed over and over.

During that period, he had some very fond memories of an attractive girl with black hair and deep brown eyes. They were neighbors the first summer, then friends, then a close relationship developed. The relationship started the beginning of the last summer and ended the day she moved. It wasn't a boyfriend-girlfriend relationship—just a relationship of friends. At the time, they were both going steady with someone else. She was more than a girlfriend to him. She was a true friend. They spent a lot of time together, mostly talking about life and their good and bad experiences. He remembered how she could take his very complicated relationship problems and make them so simple. He could also remember the times they laughed and the times they hurt. She made him realize that being held can express so much more emotion of how a person feels than countless meaningless words could ever do.

The most beautiful part of their relationship was the simplicity. For some reason, he was going steady with a parish beauty queen. She was going out with a wealthy parish beauty king. He thought to himself, "It only took me eight years and four serious relationships to realize that having a trophy means more than having someone that is beautiful on the outside. To be with the beauty kings and queens were to impress others and not yourself. A true trophy is one that is beautiful on the inside. They are warm and caring people that make life worth living."

He remembers that she was very competitive and not willing to accept defeat. She even ran track in high school. He remembers racing her in dashes between street light poles. Unless she was really mouthing off and aggravating him, he would almost always let her win. He did this for two reasons. The first reason was that he knew he could easily beat her and her feelings would get hurt. The second was that she always wore sleeveless, one-piece terry cloth jump suits. Since she was thin and a little on the tall side, the jump suits fit very short on the bottom. When they would race, the shorts use to ride up her derriere; and the view was always worth loosing a race for. She knew what she was doing, and they always laughed about it after the race.

The last kiss good-bye was another memory. The kiss occurred the day after Thanksgiving. That Friday, he went hunting in the morning, came back, cleaned ducks, cleaned his gear, showered, and fixed a sandwich for lunch. What made that Friday so unforgettable was he fixed himself a turkey, oyster dressing, and cranberry sauce sandwich on toast for lunch—a tradition for him the day after Thanksgiving. He was just about to sit down when she knocked on the door. He answered it with a smile on his face. She returned a little one back. He could see her eyes begin to water. She told him that they were leaving in less than an hour and hugged him. He didn't know what came over him. With her head buried in his shoulder, she began to cry. His face turned towards hers and hers to his. They embraced in a life long memory kiss. While getting on her toes, she wrapped her arms around his neck. He wrapped his arms around her back. For a split second, he realized what was going on, and he tried to pull back. She also realized what was going on and pulled his head towards her. She was so warm, so soft, and so willing. The kiss seemed to last an eternity. As their mouths separated, he realized how special she really was. They gave each other one last hug, and she ran back to her house where the moving truck was waiting. There were no phone calls or letters back and forth. The good-bye kiss was it.

Three years later at LSU, he was sitting on a bench in front of Hatcher Domoritory. He saw a fairly attractive girl walking from the Quad towards him. She looked like one of those million dollar sorority types. She had a cream white silk shirt, cream white silk pants, and sort of resembled Malynda. She had the same color hair, same hair length, same body build, and the same face. As she got closer, he started to get his hopes up and started wishing. Sure enough, she screamed "Jacques!"

"Malynda?"

He ran towards her, and they hugged. Malynda was all smiles, as he always remembered her, and she had a radiant glow about her. They went back to the bench, sat down, and tried to catch up on old times. He was so glad that he was given a second chance with this girl. She then dropped the bomb on him. She showed him a rather large diamond solitaire on her finger and excitedly announced, "I'm engaged to be married." His face dropped with disappointment. He then realized how selfish he was being. He could see how happy she was and became happy for her.

"So should I go have a talk with this suitor?"

"No, he's really nice. I'm really in love with him. Besides, he's pretty big. He's Scott Meyeaux." Jacques looks at her with a puzzled face. "You know the starting line backer for the football team."

"Oh, yeah."

"Are you still dating that beauty queen?"

"No after four years, she broke-up with me the day before final exams. I'm now dating her arch enemy."

She talked about life in Houma, and he talked about life in Meraux. They both talked about school, and their relationships.

"Are you still shooting those metal animals? What do you call it?"

"Silhouettes. No, I just shoot for beer money these days."

"Jacques, it was really nice to see you, but I've got another class in five minutes. It is in the chemistry building all the way across campus. I'm going to be late again."

"My next class is right across the street in the math building. Look me up when you get some time. Well, I wish you the very best. It was really good to see you."

"You too."

They parted their separate ways, and they never heard from each other again.

Jacques keeps driving east on I-10, and he begins talking to himself. "Those fond memories are great, but I need to start thinking about myself. Why is a woman that is in the hospital calling me after not seeing me in eighteen years? My motto, always prepare for the worst and hope for the best. You know the worst has never happened to me. Maybe the worst never happened to me because I always prepared for something much worst than actually takes place. What if things are not as they seem? What does she need from me? What if this is a trap? Could it have anything to do with Colombia? Why would she set a trap for me? Why does she say to be careful? Apparently, she wasn't supposed to be alive. She probably knows that she's now a target. Why not go to the cops? She's smarter than that—they could be involved. I don't know the answers to a lot of questions, but I do know how to be careful. Also, as soon as she comes out of intensive care, she's an easy target. I need to get her out of that hospital. I need a plan."

He's approaching Houma, and he picks up his cell phone and dials a number. After the phone rings a few times, a woman's voice answers. "Hello, this is Mrs. Johnson."

"Mrs. Johnson, this is Jacques Boudreaux. How are you doing this morning?"

"I'm doing ok. Mrs. Malynda is in much better spirits since I told her you were coming. Where are you?"

"I'm on US 90 and just passing Hwy. 311. Hwy. 24 exit should be just ahead."

"Well, do you want to come in my office at the hospital for a chat?"

"Actually, I don't want to be seen around the hospital or Malynda. If she's in some sort of trouble, I can't help her if the trouble decides to want me too. Is there a nearby café that we can get a cup of coffee and maybe some breakfast?"

"There's a little café right here in town. I forget what it's called, but you can't miss it. As you drive into town on Hwy. 24, Houma will start looking like the New Orleans' French Quarter. On the left hand side you will see this corner café. There's a parking lot just past it."

He drives through this unique little town, whose streets are defined by waterways. Two hundred feet on his left, is Bayou Terrebonne. There are mostly acre lots with single dwellings between the road and the bayou. To his right are mostly businesses—majority of which are oil and gas related. He finds the little café and parks his truck in the lot just past it. As he walks in through the glass doors of the café, he thinks that he just went through a time portal that takes him back fifty years. The café is a hole in the wall joint. There's a bar with a grill behind it. Along the unpainted brick wall are booths. Between the booths and the bar is less than six feet. The food must be good here because all the booths are taken, and there are only three barstools available. Jacques stands at the door for a while trying to identify Mrs. Johnson. A woman waves at him. She's sitting by herself in a booth midway down the wall. She's in her late forties to early fifties with green scrubs on and a pair of half glasses with a chain that goes behind her neck. She looks like she can handle herself.

"Mrs. Violet Johnson?"

"Yes, you must be Mr. Boudreaux."

"Call me Jacques."

"Well Jacques, call me Violet."

"Did you order yet?"

"I'm fine with my coffee. You go ahead."

Jacques flags the waitress and orders hot cakes and a tall glass of orange juice.

"Well Mrs. Johnson, what's the score?"

"What do you want with that girl? Are you one of the guys responsible for this? I bet it has to do with drugs or something. Do you do drugs? Why does she think that you are going to protect her?"

"Calm down Mrs. Johnson. I haven't seen Malynda since my sophomore year at LSU—eighteen years ago. She must be real desperate to call me. What did she say happened?"

"She won't talk to me. She hasn't the whole time she's been in the hospital. She's scared, very scared. Her daughter and Debbie are the only two that she'll talk to. Your name sure has a positive effect on her."

"She realizes that she isn't supposed to be alive. They are just waiting for an opportunity. As soon as that opportunity presents itself, they'll finish the job."

Violet gives Jacques a folder. He immediately goes to the police pictures of the house.

"That's their dog. The next one is of her husband."

"It was a head shot." He looks closer at the picture "Face shot and the bullet exited out the back of the head".

"That's her blood scattered all over that side of the room."

"You can see that they used a battling ram because of this square indentation of the door and how the hinges were ripped out of the frame. Where are the pictures of Malynda?"

"I took them out. I didn't want you to see her without her make-up. Jacques, you realize that this poor girl was raped then almost beaten to death. I spoke to Judge, and he said that you would take matters in your own hands. I don't agree with that, but it is none of my business. Malynda is my business. This woman needs some loving hands to look over her."

"Mrs. Johnson, I understand. If I don't get her out of that hospital, the only hands she's going to need are praying hands. The house was a professional hit.

They will be back, and you and anyone else around will be killed to cover their tracks."

"I wasn't sure that I was going to let you visit her, and you are already taking her out of the hospital. Now hold on there."

"Slow down. How hard do you think it would be for a professional to kill a hospital patient?"

"Why doesn't she go to the police, instead of calling someone that she hasn't even seen in eighteen years?"

"Probably, because she thinks the police are involved."

"Jacques if the police are involved, what makes you think you can protect her? What can you say to me that will convince me that you won't let any harm come to her?"

"Mrs. Johnson, I can't offer any guarantees. If they want her dead, eventually she'll be killed. The only thing that I can guarantee is that if they want to kill her, they will have to get through me. I don't want to tell you the details, but I do have a well thought-out plan to protect her. It should work at least for a little while. By then, I'll think of a more permanent fix."

"You mean you just have a temporary fix?"

"After looking at the pictures, I'm thinking it is going to be hard keeping her alive for the next ten days."

"You're at least an honest man, and you do have character."

"Is she still in ICU?"

"Yes, they are planning on moving her tomorrow morning."

"Why don't you come by the hospital this afternoon, and we can talk to Malynda about this."

"I would rather not. I'm sure that they are watching the hospital twenty-four hours a day. Give me a call about four o'clock this afternoon."

"What if Malynda doesn't want to go along with this?"

"Tell Malynda that I am planning on taking her out of the hospital tomorrow night, and ask her if she's willing to go with me. If she says, "No"; you can tell me at 4:00. If she says, "Yes," I'll need talk to her doctor. Who is watching her now?"

"There is a police officer watching her."

"Who is watching him?"

"He is the police. Nobody needs to watch him."

Jacques makes a face at her. "Mrs. Johnson, please get a hospital security guard that you trust to help watch her."

"I see your point. I need to get to work. I'll call you at 4:00."

Violet gets up and leaves. Jacques throws a ten-dollar bill on the table and walks out right behind her.

CHAPTER 14

▼

0805: At the FBI Field Office, Sue Rodred is wearing the same blue business suit. She tries to sneak into her eight foot by eight foot cubical without Frank Harris seeing her. Just as she turns into her cubical, he picks up his head and looks at his watch. He calls out to her. "Sue, I'm glad you can finally make it in. May I have a few words with you?"

She drops her laptop in her cubical and proceeds towards his office.

"Close the door."

"I rather leave it open."

"Suit yourself. Where were you?"

"I took off for the weekend."

"I'm surprised that you can take an unplanned vacation with the latest developments."

She lies, "I sent you a memo about a month ago, and I tried to remind you on Friday. Do you want me to hunt up a copy of it?"

"If you sent me a memo, I'll find it. Sorry that I missed your status report on Friday. The golf course was calling me. Thursday night, did they continue their activities as usual?"

"Yes sir, but"

"No 'but', we still have a case. How much money do you think was involved?"

"Probably a little over two million, but Mike wasn't there. There was a young guy in his place."

"Maybe, Mike had the flu."

"Billy and Tony also dropped off the screen."

"How do you know this? Did you disobey my orders?"

"No sir."

"Well, they all might have gone on a vacation."

Under her breath, "Or they could be waiting at the hospital like a bunch of vultures."

"What's that?"

"Nothing Sir."

"Since you seem to know everything about the planet today. How is Mrs. Meyeaux doing?"

"No change, she's still in ICU."

"Do they expect her to live?"

"They're not sure."

"Thanks for the update." He motions her to go away. "You can leave now." As she starts to get up, "Good job on your hair and your suit, but you could expand your wardrobe. I'm sure that you can afford more than one suit. A push up bra might also help. One more thing—what is that nasty red spot on your neck?"

"A spider bite that I got on my stakeout Thursday night."

"Use a bit more make-up to cover it up." She hurries out of his office before she gets more abuse. As soon as she clears the door, "That little prick, I mean no good little prick."

CHAPTER 15

▼

Jacques drives from the café to the hospital. He wants ever so badly to visit Malynda, but he knows that isn't a good idea. He starts taking mental notes as he makes a single pass around the hospital then drives on a high-rise bridge over the Intracoastal Waterway. He sees a wooded piece of property below and across from the hospital and finds a way to get there. He parks his truck along side the road, dons his ghillie suit, and grabs his spotting scope, data book, and a can of Coke. He walks through the wooded property to the edge of the intracostal waterway. He eases up on a small dirt hill to see everything, draws a map, and makes notes. "The hospital is located on the southwest corner of the intersection of Bayou Terrebonne and the Intracoastal Waterway. It's a six-story structure that looks like it's built to withstand the worst of hurricanes. It's mostly concrete with small windows. It's only accessible by land from the north, south, and west side. The east side faces the Intracoastal Waterway, which is located a hundred and fifty yards to the east of the hospital. The south side of the hospital is set up for receiving deliveries with only one roll-up door. The north side is the building front. The main entrance is located two thirds westward on the front building face and the emergency entrance is located a third eastward. In front of the north face is a large parking lot. Beyond the parking lot, there is a picnic area under the Hwy. 24 overpass. The area east of the east wall is a well-maintained and well-shaded grassy area. The only access to the receiving door is a service road that passes on the west side and wraps around the backside. By setting up surveillance in the northwest corner of the parking lot, a person can observe every vehicle that drives to or from the hospital. I'm interested in the one hundred fifty yard area between the hospital and the Intracoastal Waterway. There are no lights in this area, and the lights from the hospital's parking lot will throw a good shadow on that area. The grass is cut, and there are many trees. If someone is set up in the northwest corner of the parking lot, they can't see the east side of the building. That's my escape route." He opens his can of Coke to slow himself down. He sits there and thinks a while. "Where is the surveillance team in the parking lot? I'm looking for someone sitting in their car with the windows rolled down and reading the newspaper or a magazine." He moves to a different position to look at the parking lot from a different angle. Still, he finds no one. He moves to a third position and scans the parking lot again. "There you are. Ok, where are your friends?" He backs away from his spotting scope and looks around. Something catches his eyes west of the hospital. He keeps gazing in that area, and there it is again. A glimmer in a third story window two hundred yards away from the hospital. "Whoa!" He covers his Coke can. "I wonder if he saw me." He slowly goes flat and eases backwards. He resets his spotting scope. "You bastards." He sees a sniper set up on a platform inside the window." He looks towards the north across Hwy. 24. He sees an abandoned six story building three hundred yards away. On the sixth floor, all the windows are in place, except for one. Jacques tries to see inside the window but can't. He ranges the sniper locations using his mil dots and puts them on his map. He spends the next four hours looking for other sniper positions and finds only one other possible. He eases back to his truck, drives to a boat launch with a pay phone, and calls Mrs. Johnson. "Mrs. Johnson, I know that I was supposed to call you at 4:00; but, can I meet with you today perhaps for dinner? I would like to meet Malynda's doctor also."

"I'm in with Malynda's doctor now. He said dinner would be fine say five o'clock"

"I need the number of the woman watching Malynda's daughter. Do you think that I can trust her husband?"

"I suppose so. Malynda is. Here is her phone number."

Jacques calls Debbie, "Debbie this is Jacques. I saw you going to the hospital today."

"What makes you sure it was me?"

"Malynda's daughter—no question about it. She looks just like her mother. Is the cop your husband?"

"Yeah, how did you know?"

"Just by your reactions towards one another."

"Ask him to meet me at the boat launch on Bayou Terrebonne about two miles past the hospital. I have something to show him."

"He can't do that. He has been assigned to watch Celeste."

"Can I talk to him?"

"This is Deputy Steve Herbert. Can I help you?"

"This is Jacques Boudreaux. I was told that I could trust you. Would you throw away your badge to save a woman's life?"

"Without hesitation."

"Good, I need you to meet me at the boat launch on Bayou Terrebonne about two miles past the hospital. I have something I need to show you."

"I'm bringing Debbie back to the hospital in about an hour. Can it wait until then?"

"No problem. See you then."

Jacques calls Randy. "Randy, I need you to assemble a team for a little extraction training exercise."

"Cool, where and when?"

"St. Ann's Hospital in Houma, Louisiana—tomorrow night. Get some people that can swim."

"Tomorrow night is a little soon. Can you give me any more time?"

"Nope, are you in or not?"

"A water extraction, I wouldn't miss it. Are we are going to need some inflatables?"

"No, there're plenty of boats down here already. There is a friend of mine named Judge. Here is his phone number. Just tell him that you need a place for your team to stay. I'll call you on your cell tomorrow 1200."

Jacques waits a few minutes and a patrol car pulls up. Jacques approaches the patrol car, "Steve?"

"Yeah, you got something you want to show me?"

"Let's take my truck. It will be less obvious." They climb in and drive back to the wooded area.

"Here put these BDU's on, I don't want us to be spotted."

They ease within forty yards of the edge of the wood line. Jacques sets up the spotting scope. "Here look at the black trans-am in the corner of the parking lot."

"So, it's a guy reading a newspaper."

"Is he one of your guys?"

"No, why?"

"That guy has been there all day. He walks up to the pay phone every hour and calls someone."

"The parking lot is full of people since Malynda was attacked. There is an ongoing 24/7 vigil. If you like we'll have him arrested for loitering, but he's not posing a threat."

"You see that six story building. Sixth floor, third window from the left."

Jacques helps him with the spotting scope. "All I see is a broken window."

"Look at all the other windows, they are all intact."

"That proves nothing. If you like, I could have someone search the building."

"Look on the other side of the hospital. That blue three story structure, third floor, far window."

"Whoa! There is a muzzle of a rifle."

"He's the stupid one. He can't keep still, and he is too close to the edge of the window. The one in the six-story window is the smart one. We can't see him, but he's there."

As he reaches for his mic, "Thanks, we will end this quickly."

"No! Don't tell anyone. If you arrest these guys, they'll just put in better people that will be more careful. We need to let them think that they are comfortable where they are. If we cause them to move, we will need to come up with another plan. Remember, I asked you if you were willing to risk your career to save a woman's life. What was your answer?"

"Of course I would."

"Are you still sure?"

"What kind of question is that?"

"I need to get Malynda out of the Hospital, and I need your help."

"What if I don't go along with you?"

"I'll get her out the military way."

"The what?"

Jacques' warm friendly face turns to ice. "Get my team, go in the front door, move fast, and kill everyone who stands between me and our objective. It's not a pretty procedure, but it is highly effective."

"Ok, you made your point. How do you plan on getting her out without being seen?"

He opens his data book. "This east wall is the only way. We make sure that her room is on the east wall, take her out of the window, cross that grassy area to a boat, and boat her off to the boat launch where you met me. If we do it right, they won't know anything until the shift change. If we time it right, we could have a four-hour head start. By that time, she will be safely stashed."

"What do you need me to do?"

"Two things. Since you have access to the hospital, I need you to get on the roof; secure two lines; and drop them over the side of the building for repelling. The other thing I need you to do is convince her doctor and that social worker that this is a necessary thing. I have supper plans for five o'clock at the seafood house. I would appreciate you attendance."

"Ok partner, let's get out of here before we are seen."

Jacques walks into the seafood shack. The place has wooden floors, wooden picnic tables and benches, and loud festive Cajun music blaring from the juke-box. Violet meets Jacques at the door.

"Jacques, I've got a room in the back. It is a little more quiet back there."

Violet leads Jacques to a glassed off room. "This is Malynda's doctor. Doctor Landry, this is Jacques Boudreaux. The one that Malynda has been asking for."

The doctor extends his hand out. "How you doing Mr. Boudreaux?"

"Well, Doc I'm going to have to go on a diet when I get back home. I've only been here a day and I think I put on ten pounds." All three laugh.

"Are we expecting anyone else?"

"Steve and Debbie should be showing up. In the meantime, can you fill me in on her status?"

Violet flags a waitress. "I know you two are not talking business without ordering an appetizer. Come here honey, I'd like to get a large order of frog legs and two orders of crab patties. And bring a picture of beer."

Jacques looks up at the waitress, "I'll have ice tea."

"Malynda has made a remarkable recovery. We plan on moving her to a private room tomorrow. Her blood pressure is good and there's no fever. We are just keeping her hospitalized to monitor her and for medication purposes. She should be able to go home within a week."

Steve and Debbie show up. "Debbie, this is Jacques Boudreaux. He was the man I went to meet, while you were visiting Malynda." Debbie grabs Steve by the arm says in French "He's an outsider. I don't like him," and sits quietly at the opposite end of the table.

Jacques responds in French, "Old Jacques has come to take care of Malynda. Who is this beautiful little girl?"

In a harsh tone, "Celeste."

"Well, Jacques has come to take care of Malynda and Celeste." Jacques looks at the confused faces around the table and begins to speak English again. "I can understand your concern, but believe me I am here to protect Malynda—not to do her any harm."

Violet puts both her hands on Jacques' shoulders, "Honey, wait until everyone has ordered before you start. In fact, you might want to wait until everyone has finished eating."

In a heavy Cajun accent Debbie asks, "Where you from—Plaquemines?"

"Ah, you noticed my dialect. Close to Plaquemines. Meraux, it's a small town east of New Orleans."

"You know Malynda long?"

"We use to be neighbors in Meraux."

"She has many friends right here in Houma. Why she calls you?"

"I guess she thinks that I have a special talent to get the job done."

"Well, do you?"

Her husband whispers into her ear, "Debbie, he is not the type of person that you ask those types of questions to."

"Answer my question—do you?"

"I can keep her alive for a little while longer than the police can do here, but not forever. Eventually, they will find her and me. It's just a matter of time."

"Then, what good are you?"

"Once I have Malynda in a safe place, I'll look at taking care of the problem in a permanent way."

The waitress comes back, and they order and eat.

Jacques starts, "Well, I guess it's time to tell you why I have gathered you here. Malynda is in great danger in the hospital. I don't know to what extent the people that want her dead are willing to go through, but they are still waiting to kill her. There are two snipers—one on each side of the hospital. There is also a sentry in the parking lot. I plan on removing her from the hospital tomorrow night."

The table erupted in objections.

Violet stands up with her hands reached outward, "Whoa people! Honey, you need to work on being a little more subtle. Let's look at everyone's objection, including my own, one at a time. After all, this is Malynda's idea. Ok. Doctor Landry, you first." Violet starts pacing around the table.

"Medically speaking, she needs to be in a hospital. How do we know that there are snipers hunting Mrs. Meyeaux?"

Steve interjects, "It's true. Jacques showed them to me this afternoon."

Doctor Landry replies, "Well, arrest them. It is your job."

"I can't arrest them because they will just be replaced by ones that will be less obvious."

"What about her medical needs?"

Jacques interjects, "You told me earlier. You just have her in the hospital for medication and observation. I can provide that for her."

Doctor Landry still refuses to go along. "I think that the hospital can provide her better protection than you can. We have guards all over the hospital."

Steve interjects, "Doc, Jacques is right as soon as she's in a private room anyone can get to her. I agree with Jacques that she has to be secretly removed from the hospital, but to a police safe house."

Debbie chimes in, "Steve, Malynda's note you saw. How safe can she be?"

The doctor stands up, "Wait, are you telling me the police are involved?"

Steve shakes his head, "We're not sure, but they could be."

The table is silenced.

"And I was telling Jacques to be all subtle and stuff. I take the silence to mean we agree that she has to be removed from the hospital. Now, let Jacques explain his plan."

"Doctor, can we get her in a private room on the east wall? Say the sixth floor."

"No, that is all offices."

"What about the fifth floor?"

"We would have to move a patient, but we can do that."

Steve interjects, "Wait Jacques, if we are going to take her out the east side why not put her on the ground floor?"

"Steve, if we put her on the ground floor; they'll realize it's a potential escape route. No one will guess the fifth floor window is an escape route."

Doctor Landry stands up. "Wait a minute, I said I agreed to let you take her out of the hospital. I didn't agree to this. The woman is just coming out of intensive care. Are you crazy?"

Violet rolls her eyes, "There you go being all subtle again. Jacques, you really need to work on that."

Steve stands up and starts walking around, "I was there. It should work. The department trains us to perform rescues like this. Go ahead Jacques finish."

"The plan is to load Malynda in a litter, feed her out the window, lower her to the ground, boat her to the boat launch, load her in a vehicle, and drive off."

Violet walks to the window, "Jacques, please tell me you're not planning on taking her off in that beat up pick-up truck."

"No, first thing tomorrow I'm going to rent a mini-van with the seats removed."

"Celeste, what about her? Da poor girl is going to want to be with her Mère."

"We'll have you meet us at the boat launch with Celeste."

"Honey, I can put all her medication in pill form, but what about her IV?"

"Doc, all we are talking about is starting an IV drip?"

"Yes."

"I can do that."

"Jacques, you're going to need a IV stand. I'll make sure we load it in the litter when we put Malynda in."

The table is silenced again and Violet asks, "Is everyone satisfied that this is what we need to do?" Everyone nods his or her head. "Are there any more objections?"

Skeptical Debbie makes a face, "Jacques, we don't know you. Jacques what certain...proof...AH! guarantee you keep her alive?"

"None. She just stands a better chance with me than in the hospital. If they want her dead bad enough, nothing is going to stop them. Right now, I just want to keep her alive for a couple of weeks until I figure something out."

"Honest. Jacques, you a good man. We pray for you."

Violet continues, "Jacques now that everyone agrees, when will this happen?"

"Doctor Landry, I need you to have her drugged for 2:00 a.m. I need her to be silent so do a good job. I also need all her medication in a ziplock bag with legible instructions. Violet, I need you to stay with her the whole time she's in the room. At 0030 Steve, I need you, Debbie and Celeste to sneak out of the back of your house and wait for me to pick you up by boat. We'll boat to the boat launch and then to the hospital. Once there, I need you to go into the hospital and stretch two ropes over the east side of the building. I need you to repel down, and I'll climb up. Is there anywhere closer than Baton Rouge where I can get some mountain climbing equipment?"

"I already have everything you need in the trunk of my car. I can give it to you tonight."

"The only other thing I need is complete secrecy."

Jacques pays for the bill, and they leave the restaurant. Outside, Steve gives him the climbing harness and ascenders.

At Judge's house, Jacques calls Randy. "Randy, how's the team coming."

"All present and accounted for, Sir. We're driving in now. I already have the satellite images, and what is a Fais Do Do?"

"It's a party. You must have spoken to Judge."

"He seems like a really nice guy."

"Almost all of the people down here are. What is your ETA?"

"We are looking at 1400."

"Good, I already have a plan in place. I'm using a local deputy to help."

"Jacques, how do you know that you can trust him?"

"I don't. I figure no matter which side he is on he will want to get her out of the hospital. He won't be expecting you. I'll go over his little surprise when you get here."

CHAPTER 16

▼

0030 Tuesday, Steve, Debbie, and Celeste sneak out diagonally from their house to the Bayou in the darkness of their backyard. They use the house to hide them from the security detail parked in front. Steve motions to Jacques, who is paddling down the bayou in Judge's sixteen-foot flatboat. When Jacques gets near, they get in as quietly as possible. Steve and Jacques continue to paddle until they think that they are in the clear, start the outboard motor, and get on top. While Jacques is working the tiller of the outboard motor, he pulls out a small bottle of Skin-So-Soft from his cargo pocket and hands it to Debbie to keep the gnats off. Debbie laughs, reaches into her purse, and pulls out her economy sized bottle to show Jacques that she's already prepared. They travel through the marsh to keep from passing in front of the hospital. As they approach the back down ramp, Jacques takes the motor out of gear and idles in the middle of the bayou for awhile. He scans the remote boat launch. It's completely dark, except for one mercury vapor light located at the end of the back down ramp. Since the light is between him and the land, it hinders his sight instead of helping it. Jacques hears two clicks in his ear piece. He puts the boat in gear and idles to the dock. Steve helps Debbie out and hands her Celeste. "We should be back within two hours."

Debbie turns back to look at Steve. "Steve, you be careful. You hear. And you two bring back Malynda safe and sound." As they cast off, she waves and makes the sign of the cross.

Jacques and Steve motor through the swamp again to the Intracoastal Canal. They continue down the Intracoastal, and Jacques kills the motor six hundred yards from the hospital. Steve grabs his athletic bag, wishes Jacques good luck, and starts jogging towards the hospital.

0120 Jacques is completely blacked up with the climbing harness on. He re-checks the litter for the climbing rope and black sheets inside of it. He lies flat in the boat, and begins to silently paddle the six hundred yards to the hospital. He hugs the shoreline near the hospital and hides within the shadow of the timber bulkhead. He reaches the hospital, ties off the boat, eases the black litter over the bulkhead onto the grassy area, and slithers over it himself. Having confidence in his woodland BDU's that have been dyed black will not give away his position, he uses the low stalk while staying in the shadows of the trees to make his way to the hospital wall. The litter is clipped off to his belt loop, and he drags it behind him like his drag bag. Once he reaches the wall, he picks his head up and sees the two ropes. He unhooks the litter and clips one end of the rope that is in the litter to his belt loop and the other to the litter. He pulls out the ascenders from his pocket, and starts ascending up the left rope. Starting is a little hard for Jacques; but once he gets off the ground, he's able to use his legs to do most of the work. As he reaches the fifth floor window, he locks into position; reaches over; and tugs on the right rope. He looks up and watches Steve ease over the edge. With the movements of a jumping spider, Jacques inverts himself. He uses his legs to keep him away from the wall so that his body is thirty degrees away from the wall. He silently pulls up the litter. The doctor opens the window just as Steve repels to it. Steve climbs in as Jacques continues hoisting the litter. Jacques hears two clicks in his ear piece, and a smile comes over his face. He grabs the litter and hands it to Steve while he rights himself. Then they ease the litter into the room. While the doctor and Steve load Malynda into it and cover her with the black sheet, Jacques connects the pulley to an ascender that is located a couple of feet above his head. He threads the line twice through a carabiner that is located on his waist belt and then through the pulley. The doctor and Steve begin to ease the litter out the window feet first. Steve hands Jacques the safety rope, and Jacques clips it off to his carabiner. Jacques reaches over Malynda's head and grabs the top of the litter with his right hand. Steve and Doctor Landry continue to ease it out until it clears the window. As soon it clears the window, the weight pulls Jacques' arm straight. The safety rope is too long, and Jacques doesn't have the strength with one hand to pick it up and clip it off. He rolls his eyes at Steve, who quickly clips off and gives the necessary assistance to tie off the litter. Steve holds the weight of the litter as Jacques prepares to lower her. Once Jacques' carabiner is loaded with the weight of the litter, Jacques motions to Steve to repel and catch her when she reaches the ground. He watches Steve expertly descend as he hears the rope rip through the belay. Jacques holds tight and waits to hear the sound of Steve hitting the ground. Within a second of Steve hitting the ground, Jacques sees three black images engulfing him. He begins to lower Malynda as one of Randy's team members starts ascending on Steve's rope, and the rest of the team takes a defensive position on one knee. As the litter approaches the ground, three of the guys grab it and gently lower it to the ground. Once the litter is secured, Jacques repels down pushing off the wall only one time during his decent. Once on the ground, he drops to one knee to evaluate their situation. Not including him and Steve, there are six men on the ground, one climbing up the side of the building, and Randy is not with them. They are in a human wedge formation with rifles up on their shoulders, safeties off, and constantly scanning their kill zones. Jacques sees the two point men have AR-10 carbines with twenty round magazines, night vision, and silencers. One team member has an M-60, and the others have AR-10's with night vision. He grabs the closest man with night vision, points to his scope, and runs his thumb across his throat. The man mouths, "They're off." He looks at Steve hog tied on the ground, pulls out his knife, and cuts the nylon cuffs off his arms and legs. He motions to Steve to be silent and pulls the duct tape off his mouth. Steve starts to protest. As his lips begin to move and before the first sound comes out, six pairs of eyes are on him. They wait for the man to repel and gather the ropes. Jacques and Steve grab the litter. They hear one click in their ear piece and everyone freezes. They wait a few seconds and hear two clicks. With rifles up and moving in a low wedge, they run across the open area, load onto two sixteen-foot flatboats, and paddle along the bulkhead away from the hospital. In the front boat, the M60 man lays on the bow, and the other four shooters paddle. The second boat holds Malynda, Jacques, Steve, and two shooters. They have a gun on the bow, while Jacques and the other team member paddle. Steve sits low on the floorboards of the boat. Once they are beyond six hundred yards, one man from each team starts the motor; and they speed away down the bayou.

Jacques looks at the disarmed deputy, who is obviously upset with Jacques. "Steve, it's standard procedure. It's not pretty, and it doesn't do any good for your ego. Look at the situation from their point of view. They don't know you; therefore, they don't trust you. You need to keep things in perspective with the end result. No one man is bigger than the mission. My mission was to get the girl out. Each individual here tonight had the same mission. No matter what happened, the last man standing would get the girl out." Jacques taps the shooter on the bow, "Give me his pistol." He does. Jacques empties it and hands it to Steve. "Steve, if it would make you feel any better, your reputation won't be hurt because no one breathes a word of the techniques of these missions." Jacques goes back to the bow, "Where's Randy?"

"He's in a hide. We'll pick him up when we drive back."

"I thought there were ten of you."

"Yeah, we had to leave one with that crazy Cajun bitch that we almost had to shoot. She just didn't want to cooperate."

"I hope you didn't rough her up too badly."

"Naw, she took the hint when Jimmy put his pistol on her forehead."

"That's good."

"Hey, I can't guarantee that she's still alive. She gave us way more trouble than we expected."

Jacques ear piece comes alive, "Team leader this is Red 1, I think you need to let me take one of these out. It is a target of opportunity."

"Negative, escape and evade."

"This guy is serious. He's got some expensive hardware and by the looks of things knows what he's doing. If I don't engage now, you will be seeing him again."

"Red 1, escape and evade."

"WilCo. Red 1 out."

"Team Leader out."

Instead of turning to follow the planned route, the boats keep going straight. Steve tugs on Jacques' sleeve, "Where are we going? You missed the cut."

"Change of plan."

Ten minutes later, they pull into another remote boat launch. Jacques watches with pride as all the shooters of the first boat exit and take defensive positions behind anything available.

In his ear piece, "The babysitter is ok." And the van door opens. The team on land sets up a four-point perimeter around the nearly empty shell parking lot with the M60 being closest to the back down ramp, which is the escape route.

Jacques' boat pulls up to the back down and docks.

Debbie jumps out the van and starts her non-stop French jabbering. Steve runs over to her and tries to calm her down.

Jacques and another team member load Malynda into the mini-van. Jacques starts the van and turns on the A/C. Jacques signals to the corpsman. "Doc, get her IV started and get her vitals. Use the pay phone to call her doctor." Jacques walks over to Steve and Debbie. "Celeste, are you ready to be with your Momma?"

Debbie starts off, "You know, you should have told us about this. I want dat one arrested. He pointed a gun right at my head. He kidnapped me."

"Debbie, I appreciate what you and Steve did. I'll take good care of them."

Debbie handed Celeste over to Jacques, "Celeste, tu vas avec Monsieur Jacques et ta Mère."

Jacques sees the corpsman getting out the van. The corpsman raises his hand to show everything is ok and heads to the pay phone. Jacques looks at Steve. "Jimmy has another little surprise for you two to make it look real." Debbie and Steve look at each other with a puzzled look, and Debbie starts to protest. Jacques just ignores the protesting and says, "Thanks again." Jacques waves at the team, loads Celeste in the van, and drives off into the darkness.

After the three hours of an uneventful drive, Jacques drives across a draw-bridge; takes a hard right; and drives down a highway with a bayou on the right side of the road and houses sitting on twelve to sixteen foot piles on his left. He drives for a mile and a half and pulls into an oyster shell driveway of a twenty foot by twenty foot house sitting on top of twelve foot piles with a screened in porch on the front of it. Jacques stops the van and gets out with his grease paint still on. The next door neighbor's porch light comes on; and an elderly couple appears on their porch.

A man's voice comes from next door. "Jacques, dat you?"

"Weh, Monsieur Melerine."

The elderly couple comes down the stairs of their pile-supported house. The short, bald man that is wearing overalls and white shrimp boots grabs Jacques by the hand and pats him on his back. "Bonjour, mon amie."

A white haired overweight woman wearing shorts and a white cotton blouse wraps her arms around him, gives him a tight hug, and kisses him on the cheek. "Bonjour, Jacques. Comment ça va?"

"I've been good. Let's get inside before the mosquitoes tear us up."

Mrs. Melerine opens the passenger door and carries the sleeping Celeste up the stairs while Jacques and Mr. Melerine carry the litter. They walk into Jacques' simple fishing camp. One half is the kitchen and living room, the other half is two bedrooms. The half bath sits right behind the kitchen. Jacques and Mr. Melerine no sooner get Malynda out of the litter and on the bed of the front bed-room, and Mrs. Melerine runs them out and closes the door behind them. A few minutes later she re-appears. "What the hell happened to dat poor girl?"

"I'm not sure Mrs. Melerine. I plan on finding out as soon as I can talk to her."

"Jacques, dat girl, she's been through a lot. A lot more than you told me over the phone. Tonight, I stay here. She may need me."

"Mrs. Melerine, you can have the back room. I'll sleep on the couch."

"I'll hear no such nonsense, Jacques." She waves her hands at her husband. "Melerine, you go home and get some sleep."

"Ok, Jean." Mr. Melerine waves to everyone "Bon nuit. We'll have beacoup time to talk in the morning."

Mrs. Melerine grabs an afghan and snuggles next to Celeste on the couch. Jacques heads to the back bedroom and closes the door.

CHAPTER 17

▼

0500 In Jacques' fishing camp, Mrs. Melerine knocks twice on Jacques' door and walks in with a broom in her hand. "Bonjour Jacques, time to get up. Sleeping past sunrise is a sin. I'm sure dat you have some t'ings to do. It's time you start doing dem."

"How's Malynda?"

"She's still sleeping. I know you are going to be passing through town so I made you a grocery list. I also called Père Andrew, and he's going to be stopping by."

"As long as he's gone by the time I get back, that's fine."

She smacks Jacques on the thigh with the broom handle. "Jacques, that's blasphemy. I will have no blasphemy. You hear." She hits him with the broom handle again. "You will treat Père Andrew with respect."

"Ok, ok. Let me get moving." He walks out of his room into the kitchen/living area. It shines of cleanliness. He notices three blessed candles burning on the kitchen counter. He sees a wooden crucifix that he threw away years ago hanging between the doorways of the bedrooms again. "Where's Celeste?"

"I put her in bed with sa mère."

He takes a shower and re-appears in kakki shorts and a green tee shirt. "Mrs. Melerine, why do you have three candles burning?"

"Mais, one is for that girl. The other is for her daughter. The third, well, it's for you." He makes a face. As she waves the broom stick at him. "You don't make a face. You should be glad dat I care enough about you to light dat dere candle."

"I thought I threw that Crucifix away."

"I saved you from dat sin 'cause I knew you didn't mean it. What you planning on doing today?"

"I need to go back to Houston to get my boat and some other stuff."

She rushes him out the door and on the porch, "Now, you be careful and here's da grocery list."

"Wait, what about breakfast?"

"Dat's your penance for sleeping too late. The kitchen is closes at sunrise. Now, get." She pops him with the broom handle one more time as he walks out the screen door of the porch.

He walks down the stairs of the fishing camp rubbing his leg. Across the highway, Mr. Melerine is in his Lafitte skiff and is casting off. He sees Jacques get his last pop, begins to laugh out loud, and screams to him. "You should know not to smart-mouth Jean." As Mr. Melerine continues to laugh, Jacques just raises his hands, shakes his head, and continues down the stairs.

Mrs. Melerine calls out to Jacques. "Jacques, I'll be cooking some good couvoun for supper. What time do you think you'll be back?"

"Probably about midnight or a little after."

"Well, I'll leave some in the refrigerator for when you get home."

"Mrs. Melerine, I really appreciate what you are doing. Are you going to spend the night?"

"Mais, weh."

"Go ahead and sleep in that back bedroom. I'll sleep on the couch tonight. I'll see you about midnight." Jacques gets in the mini-van and drives off. He returns the mini-van and continues to Houston in his truck.

0700 in the patrol car outside of Steve's house, the policemen are reading books about the recent changes to the state and local laws. "Unit 24, this is Unit 1. Do me a favor and check on Steve and Debbie."

"10–4. What's up?"

"Mrs. Meyeaux is missing."

The two officers cautiously walk up to the front door and ring the door bell. There's no answer. They knock on the door and call out for Steve. With their adrenaline rushing and pistols drawn, one of the officers kicks in the door; and they rush the house. They get to the bedroom and find Steve and Debbie tied up and duct tape over their mouths. They pull the duct tape off of Debbie and Steve. Debbie immediately starts her French.

"Steve what happened?"

Steve tries to console his wife. "They got the girl about three hours ago. It was six of them. They were quick and silent. It was like they knew the inside of my house. They knew exactly where to go. Malynda is going to kill me."

"Unit 1 this is Unit 24. The girl is missing too."

"Is Steve and Debbie ok?"

"Steve and Debbie are fine. Must have been the same guys. They must have come in from the back of the house."

"Do you realize this could cost me my job? Here we go again. This time we are going to need some help."

"What do you want us to do?"

"There is nothing you can do. Three hours—they can be anywhere by now. I'm calling the FBI."

0800 At FBI New Orleans Field Office, Frank Harris is in his office. His cell phone rings. Frank looks at the incoming number of his sergeant and answers his phone, "This better be important."

"I think that you can sleep a little better Sir. From the looks of things, I would say one of Satinito's men finished the job. The local cops sealed off the hospital at seven this morning."

"Thank God."

Sue storms by Frank's office, turns and heads towards her cubical.

"Sue! Get in here." She stops in mid-stride, about faces, and walks into his office as he is hanging up the phone. "How is Mrs. Meyeaux doing this morning?"

With a lot of attitude, "I don't know. She's probably dead by now."

Frank can hardly keep from smiling. "What happened?"

She notices the false concerned face. "She was kidnapped. Probably Satinito's bunch. You should have let me put a security detail on her."

"Sorry to hear about that. This time, you were right. Next time, we'll offer the assistance needed. That will be all."

Sue throws her hands up and continues to her cubical.

A few minutes later, Frank exits the building and goes for a drive along Lakeshore Blvd. He calls Satinito.

Satinito is lounging at poolside in a hotel robe when he answers the phone. "Frank, how is our little problem?"

"How'd you do it?"

"Do what?"

"Get the girl out of the hospital?"

"I didn't do anything."

"Don't kid me. How did you do it?"

"No kidding, I don't know what your talking about. Mike called me this morning and said that the hospital was closed off. I figured she died or......"

Frank starts screaming into the phone, "You idiot, she didn't die. She disappeared."

"You're the stinking FBI, you should know what's going on. Look, stay calm Franky. You have a serious problem of going overboard. I'm on top of it. Mike said that she didn't leave. If he said she didn't leave, she didn't leave. The hospital only has a front exit and a rear exit. Mike is on the front and my nephew is on the back. There was no way she could have gotten out of that hospital. A lot of times before they try to move someone into safekeeping, they create a distraction. This is just the distraction. I was expecting it. As soon as Mike called, I put extra men in place. While all the commotion is going on, they'll try to sneak her out. It's not going to be long now, trust me."

"You're right—a distraction. Just make sure you get her when they move her. Keep me informed of the situation."

Satinito laughs. "Satinito's always right. You remember that Franky." They hang up.

Harris calls his sergeant. "Sergeant, this is Harris. She's not dead. The way I figure it. It is a distraction to sneak her out of the hospital. If you get any shot, take it. I don't care if you have to shoot through someone to hit her. I want her dead. Am I clear?"

"No problem, Sir."

"That is not the response that I wanted to hear."

"Crystal, Sir."

"Much better. Keep me informed of the situation." Frank hangs up the phone.

Jacques backs his truck into the driveway of his large two story Houston house that sits on a matchbox size lot. He rushes out the truck; pulls his blue nineteen foot, tri-hull, center console boat out of his detached garage; and connects the trailer to the truck. He rushes inside and immediately heads for the gun safe. "As tired as I am, I'll take everything and determine what I need when I get back to Hopedale. At least that way, I won't forget anything." He loads shotguns, pistols, and all his ammo cans into this truck. His next trip is to the cedar robe where he stores all his nylon gear and camouflage. He then loads the truck with arm fulls of clothing. He locks up the house, checks his trailer lights, and is back on the road within an hour.

Malynda is lying on her back with Celeste's arm across her stomach. Celeste stirs and wakes her mother. Celeste squeezes her. Malynda's eyes open, and she remains motionless. She begins to panic. A million thoughts run through her head, "Where am I? Who got me here? Am I a prisoner?" She looks down at Celeste, who is looking up at her with a big six-year-old smile. She looks around the ten foot by ten foot room. She sees the faded yellow paint, the holes in the threadbare green curtains, the garage sale dresser with a mirror, and the noisy air condition window unit. There are no decorations—just plainly painted walls. She hears a television outside her room, and she smells the spices of the red gravy of the couvoin. As she sighs, a sense of calmness spreads throughout her whole body because she realizes that there are bayou people right outside her door. Malynda can tell that Celeste senses her calmness too. In a calm soft voice, "Where are we, baby?" Celeste just shrugs her shoulders to indicate that she doesn't know. "Did Mr. Jacques bring us here?" She nods her head up and down, "Uh huh." She can't wait to see Jacques. She fights the medication. Using the IV stand for support, she wobbles to the bedroom door. She gets there and realizes that she's still in her hospital gown. She turns and sees herself in the mirror and becomes depressed. She begins to head back into the bed and begins to cry, "I'm a monster. I'm so ugly."

"Momma, you're not a monster. You're real pretty. Momma, I love you."

As she stands there rubbing Celeste's hair, "That's because you are so beautiful yourself that you can only see pretty things." She realizes that her daughter sees beyond her appearance. "Maybe, Jacques will too. Well, here's for first impressions." She slowly cracks open the door, and peeks out. The cayenne pepper aroma rushes through the crack and hits Malynda square in the face like a sludge hammer. Her eyes begin to water, and her nose begins to run. Celeste grabs her nose. Malynda sees a white haired woman wearing shorts and an apron standing in front of the stove. She then sees the three candles burning on the kitchen counter. Malynda's now positive that she's in good hands and continues to open the door.

Mrs. Melerine turns around and rushes towards Malynda, "Oh Lord child. I'm not sure you should be up. You need to get back in dat bed." Malynda makes a face that is universally understood by all women that she had to use the rest room.

"Ok, I help you; but it's back to bed after. Weh?"

Excitedly she asks, "Where's Jacques? Is he here?"

"Jacques, he be back tonight. He say he had to get some stuff from Houston."

Mrs. Melerine helps her back in the bed and pulls the covers up to her neck. "My name is Jean. You need anything—you stay here. I'll get it for you."

"Tell me about Jacques. I haven't seen him in years. What's he like? Is he married? Does he have any children? What does he do? I don't know anything about him."

"You calm down. Jacques is Jacques. Always was, always will be. He never change. You see. Maybe tomorrow, he tell you all these t'ings himself." The smile leaves Malynda's face. "You not worry about nothing. Jacques, he's educated. He see past your appearance. You see." A little smile comes back. "Jacques, he a real good boy. He'll take good care of you. You get your rest. Come on little perch. I teach you to play a card game named—Booray. Then you teach your Mère. Malynda, I'll bring you something to eat the next time you wake up."

Malynda gives Celeste a little shove. "Go ahead with Mrs. Jean and play cards."

After they leave the room, Malynda's troubled. "Why didn't she ask me anything about what happened? Or why did I get Jacques involved? I'm sure she cares."

A few hours later, Mrs. Melerine walks in with a bed tray with a bowl of soup. "Celeste, she says you like vegetable. It's my favorite too." Malynda sits up in the bed, and Mrs. Melerine sets the cheap metal tray over her legs. Mrs. Melerine sits on the end of the bed.

"Thank you, Jean."

"Malynda, in time those marks will heal real nice. You just need some good living and some loving care."

"Aren't you curious about what happened?"

"A little, but it's a sin to go prying in others business. I figure when you ready, you'll tell me."

Malynda smiles, "Now, tell me about Jacques."

"No such thing. He tell you about hisself when he get back."

"Are you upset that I got Jacques involved?"

"No, child. I'm happy you brought our Jacques back to us. Whatever, you two are involved with; Jacques will straighten things out right fast. You'll see."

"You have to tell me something about Jacques."

"I tell you this. Jacques, he's a good boy. I treat him like my own son. He still has plenty of respect for God, nature, and his elders. He's raised properly. Lately, he's been through beaucoup tough times, but he'll find his way back. I probably say too much already. You go ahead and eat. If you hold it down, I'll take that nasty IV out of your arm. The Lord given us a mouth. That is the way we should get our nourishment. When given the choice, we should always do it the Lord's way. Père Andrew, he'll be coming by shortly. If you want, I can talk about him because he won't mind none."

CHAPTER 18

▼

Joe is standing behind the crowd in the hospital's parking lot. He's upset as Cliff walks up to him. "What took you so long? Did you take care of Billy?"

"Billy has adventured to the next world from the bottom of a four foot deep hole."

Joe takes a drag from his cigarette. "Don't give me that. Tell me you put a bullet in his head."

"I put a bullet in his head while he was at the bottom of a four foot hole."

"Good, you are going to be all right kid. Where's Tony?"

Cliff can hardly hold back the laughter. "Oh yeah, it's two o'clock."

Joe throws his hands up in the air. "What's that supposed to mean? It's freaking two o'clock."

Cliff starts laughing, "Tony thinks he is going to die at two o'clock." Joe looks at him with a strange look. "I'm not kidding, he's sitting in the car with that big .44 magnum. He's so scared that he looks like he's ready to pee in his pants. He's been that way ever since we saw that old colored woman in the woods."

"What are you talking about? Are you high or what?"

Cliff continues to laugh, "No sir, I'm straight."

"Ok, what happened? It was supposed to be simple. You drive up I-59, kill Billy, and bury him."

"Tony's one weird person. Tony's driving, and we're heading up I-59. A black cat crosses the interstate in front of the car."

"Oh, no! How many miles did you have to go around not to cross its path."

"None, he hit it."

Joe, slaps his forehead and starts laughing. "Tony hit a black cat!"

"He tried to miss it, and we spun out of control on the median. Tony gets out of the car wearing his Indian cloth, war paint, and his spear in his hand. He starts screaming about if he hit it before we crossed its path. I'm doing everything possible to get him back in the car and get moving before a cop shows up. I mean, we still have Billy in the trunk."

Joe starts to snicker. "Tony takes a little time to get use to."

Cliff is still laughing. "I finally convinced him that he hit the cat before it crossed our path. The rest of the way up there he's preaching to me how much bad luck we are going to have because of that stupid cat. We pull off on one of those logging roads and go deep into the woods. Tony opens the trunk and throws Billy on the ground. He takes his propane torch and heats his spear until it glows, tells me to cut Billy loose, and tells Billy that he has a ten second head start. The naked man starts running down a hill and stops when he runs into some briars. Tony draws back, throws, and thump. The spear sinks into Billy's chest, and Billy falls. Tony pulls out the spear and holds it like he is about ready to make love to it. He walks off into the woods without telling me anything. I dig a hole, roll Billy into it, put a bullet in him, and cover him up. I must have waited for two hours at the car, and Tony finally shows up."

"Cliff, it's funny, but not that funny."

Cliff is still laughing. "Wait, the strange stuff hasn't happened yet. He's driving back down I-59 and takes another detour into the woods. He drives up to this two hundred-year-old, ready to fall apart, slave shack in the middle of the woods—no roads, no nothing. A skinny, hundred year old colored woman wearing something like in those old plantation movies is waiting on the porch for us. She has an empty mason jar in her hand that she hands to Tony. Check this out. She said that she was expecting us. It's like midnight, and this woman is waiting on us in complete darkness on her porch. She said that in order for her to give us what we wanted, we had to catch a black widow and a violin spider. She points to the woodpile. We get a flashlight out of the car and head for the woodpile. Finally, we find this big black widow and get her in the stupid jar without her biting us. Man, those spiders are quick. Before we could get the lid on, it got out to the outside of the jar twice. Then we go under the house for the brown recluse. There are thousands of brown spiders on the underside of the wooden floor, and I can see the candlelight through the cracks. Do you know how hard it is to determine a brown recluse from another brown spider in the middle of the night? We finally find one. Now, we have to open the jar, put the brown recluse in there with the black widow before the black widow gets out. To make matters worst, we didn't have any room to work and nowhere to escape. We're lying on our backs, and Tony's chest is touching the floor joists. We get the spider in the jar and go inside. The whole house is just one room without indoor plumbing or electricity. Along one wall is a wood burning stove, the opposite wall had a fire place, the other wall had mason jars full of I don't know what, and a cot with a mattress made of moss on the other. This old woman with her bandana is sitting on her knees in the center of a large circle made with candles. Tony hands her the jar. She inspects it and places it in front of her. We sit across from her and watch the black widow kill the brown recluse. She says something in some weird language, pulls out this red handkerchief, and throws out freaking chicken bones on the floor. She leans forward and covers the bones with her body and then sits back up. She carefully studies the bones, and her eyes almost pop out of her head. Tony doesn't like the look on this woman's face and starts questioning her. Without saying a word, she picks up the bones, wraps them up, and throws them out again. Again her face is in shock. She then tells Tony that he is going to die a horrible death. Tony turns white and begs her to do it again. She does and says that the bones don't lie. So, now Tony's scared out of his mind. He asks her when, and she studies the bones some more. She said that the bones say two. Now, Tony is totally freaking out. He wants to know two what—minutes, hours, days, years. This bright woman tells him that the bones only say two. It could be anything associated with the number two. I look at my watch, and it is two a.m."

Joe and Cliff are laughing so hard that tears are coming out of their eyes. "Wait, it gets better. Tony asks what does he need to do? She tells him that he must sacrifice two chickens and pour a magic potion that she gave him on the sacrificed chickens. Check this out. He has to do this at Marie Laveaux's gravesite before daylight. She says that if the voodoo queen is satisfied, she will show mercy on him."

Joe's laughing so hard he can barely speak. "Where did you get the chickens from at two in the morning?"

"Are you kidding? The woman's yard is full of them. The problem is that it couldn't be just any two chickens. We have to catch one white for some sort of purity mumbo jumbo and the other black for some type of evil mumbo jumbo. Every other place in the world, chickens sleep at night—not this place. As soon as we walk outside, they all begin running around. Tony's a big guy, but imagine him wearing his Indian get up trying to catch a chicken in the middle of the night. We catch the chickens, throw them in the trunk, and drive like a bat out of hell to New Orleans. We break into this spooky cemetery; and check this out, he knows exactly where to go. He kills the chickens, puts the magic potion on them, and then puts three X's with the blood of the black chicken on the tomb of Marie

Laveaux. He makes three more X's on top of the other X's with the blood of the white chicken. We sneak out, drive back to his place, and get some sleep. The next thing I know he's waking me because you called."

They're still laughing full heartily. "Cliff, We are going to have some fun with this one."

"It might even last a whole two months."

Joe stops laughing. "Look, they are starting to remove the tape off the hospital doors. Mike is at the rear entrance, and I'm in the front. I want you to get in that hospital and find out about the girl."

"No problem boss." He jogs to the front door of the hospital.

Frank Harris is teeing off the third tee, and his cell phone rings causing him to slice. He looks at the incoming number, and it is his sergeant calling. He answers, "What do you have for me?"

"I've got two vehicles with government plates, with eight guys in fancy suits. The way everyone is getting out their way, I'm guessing an FBI ERT (Evidence Response Team)."

"They either must be classifying this as a kidnapping, or they are going to try to move her in protective custody. Can you get me the plate numbers?"

"No, they are turned away from me."

"How concealed are you?"

"Real good, why?"

"If you take a shot, will you be compromised?"

"Negative on one shot. Probably so on two shots."

"Good. If you see her, take the shot."

"I'm on my way down. I'll have a box of papers in my trunk. When I park at the hospital, have one of your men remove it and place it in the Meyeaux's house. I'll arrange cover at the house to do this."

"WilCo and out."

Frank Harris dials Sue's phone. She's sitting in her cubical at the Field Office, and she answers.

"Sue, this is your Boss. Do you still want to help Mrs. Meyeaux?"

"Yes Sir, but I think you are a little too late."

"I'm on my way back to the office now. Meet me out front. We're going to the hospital."

An hour and a half later, Sue and Frank arrive at the Houma hospital. They walk by the crowd and are escorted to Malynda's hospital room. The eight FBI ERT men are alone in the room. Franks looks at the one most senior. In a superior voice, "What do you have?"

"We think that it was an inside job. The only way out is through the door or the window. The window is riveted shut. She had to be carried out the door."

Frank watches Sue walk over to the window, and she looks at the one rivet in the bottom left corner of the window. She turns the window handle and pushes on the window. It's secured. She uses the heel of her hand and hits the window near the rivet. The window doesn't budge. She hits it again harder. The conversation in the room stops. She hits it one more time even harder. The window opens. Sue throws a smile at the ERT guys. "They cut the rivet and super glued the rivet head in place. After they got her out, they super glued the window shut."

Frank thinks to himself, "Good looking and brains too. I'm glad I brought her." He pulls the senior guy to the side. "I have a case being built against this woman, and your interference could jeopardize two years worth of work. I want you to go back to the office and forget you ever heard about this woman."

"Mr. Harris, we were given this case. I don't think you have the authority to pull us off."

Frank uses his cell phone and dials a number. He talks into the phone for a couple of minutes. He then hands the phone to the senior agent. "It's your boss. Tell him that you think you should remain on the case."

The young agent listens to the phone and hands the phone back to Harris. "This is wrong, and you know it." He walks to the center of the room, "Come on guys we're yanked off. We need to immediately report back to the office." The eight men protest as they walk out.

Harris walks over to Sue. "What do you think?"

"I overheard what happened. I don't have enough experience to work kidnapping."

"Come on Sue, you are a bright individual. Think of this as a challenge."

"I'm just one person. If I bring my team in, we'll blow our cover with the Satinito case."

"Well, we'll have to put our differences aside and work this one together. You said that you wanted to help this woman."

"Ok, on one condition."

"What might that be?"

"You let me gather information on Satinito in Mississippi."

"Ok, you have it. After you find Mrs. Meyeaux, you can start collecting information on Satinito in Mississippi, but not a second before. Am I clear?"

"Crystal, Sir."

"Realize that this case is added to your work load, Satinito is still your primary case."

Frank can see that Sue is excited, and she actually thinks that she has a case that she's allowed to solve. The way the blood is rushing through her body with the challenge of working two cases at the same time is obvious to him. He thinks to himself, "What a fool."

Frank looks at Sue, "It's been a long time since I've actually worked on a case. How do you propose we attack this one?"

"We need to get some of those ERT guys back in here."

"I can fix that." He picks up his cell phone. "This is Harris, maybe I was a little harsh on you. Did you make it out of the building yet? No. Good. I would like the assistance of four of your men to help Ms. Rodred solve this case. I would appreciate your immediate return." He hangs up the phone and looks at Sue. "That was easy enough. Now, what?"

"The ERT's will sweep the room." She looks outside the open window. "They fed her out the window, lowered her five floors, carried her across that grassy area, and put her into a boat. We need to get a list of the people that were around her and start questioning them. We need to find out what the sheriff knows." Four agents return. "And we need to search the inside of her house."

"You keep two of these guys and tell them what you need them to do. I'll take two of them and search her house. Say we rendezvous about eight o'clock?"

"I prefer you use the word reconvene."

"Very well, reconvene at eight o'clock."

Frank Harris leaves, and Sue puts the two ERT's to work.

1830: Sue Rodred is standing at the edge of the wooden bulkhead looking into the muddy water that is two feet below the top of the bulkhead. One of the agents calls out to her. "Mrs. Rodred, I found where they drug the litter over the bulkhead." She rushes over where the agent is standing. "See right here. There are fresh cuts in the wood. I hate to say it, but this is probably where our trail is going to end. There are just too many boats in Houma to get a search warrant for all of them."

"They had to come out the water somewhere. Find out where."

"Again, there are over twenty boat launches and most of the boats never leave the water. They stay docked in the bayous on private piers. Have you started questioning people yet?"

"No, I want to get in as much daylight as possible out here. We'll question the list of people tonight."

"I don't think anything is missing. We figured out step-by-step how they got her out of the room, and it leads to a dead end. I think it is time you start questioning some people."

"We're not finished out here. You figured how she got out, but you didn't figure out why?" She looks back at the hospital then all around. "Why not go straight out to the bayou? How come they went on this angle to get to the bayou?" She stands at the water entry point and looks around. As the young agent follows, she walks ten yards along the bulkhead and looks around again. "They were using the building to conceal them." She scans the part of the parking lot that is visible, then beyond under the overpass, and then beyond it. "That's it." She looks straight at the broken window where Harris' sergeant is hiding. "I want you…"

A deputy grabs her by the arm and interrupts her. "Ms. Rodred, you and these other guys, need to come see this in a hurry." She's rushed back into the hospital where everyone is silently staring at the television sets that are blaring. The screen has a table draped in a dark blue cloth with large bright yellow FBI insignia on it. On the cloth are papers, weapons, and bottles of chemicals on it.

"Again, we are reporting from Houma, Louisiana where the FBI has unraveled a potential terrorist plot to blow up the Louisiana Super Dome. On this table are the plans and chemicals that a Scott & Malynda Meyeaux were planning on using for the attack. Ironically, Scott Meyeaux was killed a week ago. His wife is at large, is armed, and considered extremely dangerous." A picture of Malynda comes on the screen. "There is a two-hundred and fifty thousand dollar reward for the assistance in the capturing of this woman. If you know or think that you have seen this woman, you are asked to call the FBI directly at the number on your screen. The FBI is not releasing anymore information at this time, but we will keep you informed of the latest developments."

Sue storms out of the hospital and dials Harris' cell phone. "Mr. Harris, what are you doing? This is not the 1960's. That evidence you found was used for our training exercise last year. What are you trying to accomplish?"

"I figured that we are going to need the help of the people to find her. The best way to get the support of the people is to offer a reward. Most of the top ten most wanted only have a fifty thousand dollar reward—except terrorist. Now a days, the easiest way to get large rewards approved is to associate it with terrorism. Brilliant, isn't it?"

"Mr. Harris, you don't understand the people's mentality down here. We are the outsiders, and she's an insider. They are extremely secretive people. They'll protect her from us. Now, whoever has her, is going to be more cautious then ever."

"She'll be spotted sooner or later. She has to get money and buy food."

"You just don't get it. You're not in New York or Chicago. The people down here work as a community. If one member of the community needs help, the whole community is there to help. Do you realize that there are people down here that don't even speak English? As far as money and buying food, the people only work because they want to. Once in the swamp, these people can comfortably survive without any outside help. This aggressive move is going to backfire on you."

"What do you want me to do to fix it?"

"You can't change what you already done. Please, just leave. Get in you car, and drive back to New Orleans."

"Ok, but I want you to keep me informed. If anything comes up, I want you to call me before you do anything. Am I clear on that?"

"Crystal Sir."

"That's my girl." And they both hang up.

Sue with her entourage of agents walk back into the hospital. As they are walking down the hall Sue says, "Let's make one last pass of the room. I also want the names and phone numbers of every person that was on duty in this hospital last night." They exit the elevators on the fifth floor, and she sees Cliff at the end of the hall coming out of a broom closet. She slows her pace. He knocks on a hospital door, opens it, sticks his head in, and closes the door. He does it one more time before he notices the agents. Once he sees the agents, he walks directly towards them. Sue puts her hand in her purse and grips her S&W 649. She eyes him real hard as he makes her give way and walks right through the middle of the agents. She looks at one of the agents that is wearing a pair of binoculars. "Let me have your binoculars." She walks into a room where she can see the parking lot and searches for the members of Satinito's bunch. She sees Joe standing by his car. He's smoking a cigarette with one foot on the bumper. She goes into a room located at the rear of the hospital and finds Mike leaning against his car down the street of the rear entrance. She thinks to herself, "This is interesting."

2400: Sue Rodred is sitting at the desk of her Houma motel room. She has just finished questioning the last person on her list. She has four suspects that she knows are lying—Malynda's doctor, her social worker, the deputy and his wife. She tries to put this case together as she undresses and jumps into the shower. She begins thinking to herself. "Satinito's bunch is still looking for her which means that they don't have her. The police don't have her. The doctor and social worker being involved might mean that they snuck her out, which means that she left on her free will. So it's not a kidnapping, but why has Harris all of a sudden taken an interest in the case. Maybe he figures that he might lose the Satinito case if it turns into a kidnapping. Why did he plant the evidence? He's part of the narcotics enforcement. He claimed that it was a terrorist plot. Does he know that he could loose the case to the terrorist task force?" She turns off the water, dries herself, wraps herself in a towel, puts the blue business suit in the hotel's dry cleaning bag, and hangs it outside her room. She pulls back the covers and jumps in the bed. "At least I can sleep better knowing that a bunch of bayou people have her instead of Satinito's bunch. What am I going to do? If she's hidden from Satinito's bunch, she's safe. If I find her, she's in the limelight and becomes a target again. If Satinito finds her, she's dead. Do I really want to find her?" She tries to go to sleep, but she tosses and turns with the conflict raging in her mind.

CHAPTER 19

▼

Wednesday morning in Hopedale, Jacques wakes up in time to eat breakfast; and he unloads his truck. When he finishes, he asks Mrs. Melerine, "How's Malynda doing?"

"She's a strong girl. In time, she'll be fine."

Jacques starts walking towards her bedroom, and Mrs. Melerine stops him. "You better let her get her sleep."

He realizes that she's probably right and heads out the back door. He sees a cargo ship a half mile north in the Ship Channel (Mississippi River Gulf Outlet). He looks at the saltwater marsh grass between his camp and the tree line of the Ship Channel. He walks back through the house to the front porch to find Mrs. Melerine sitting on the steps watching the sunrise above the marsh.

"Jacques you come sit down and enjoy the sunrise wit me." Jacques sits one step below her. "Jacques, it's a sin for her to be running around dat camp in a hospital gown. Today, I take Celeste, and we go to town to pick up some clothes for Malynda. You come wit us."

Jacques hands her a hundred dollar bill. "Mrs. Melerine, I wish I could; but I have some things that need to be done around the house."

Mrs. Melerine looks at the hundred-dollar bill. "Jacques, it takes more money than dat."

He pulls out another hundred and hands it to her.

"Jacques, I got to do da groceries too since you forgot."

He hands her another hundred and says, "That's it."

"Dat's good, I can get every t'ing she needs." They sit in silence and take in the beauty of the sun coming up over the marsh. A flatbed truck delivering drill pipe passes on the highway that is a hundred feet in front of them. Jacques looks ten feet beyond the highway and there is the one hundred and fifty foot wide Bayou Loutre with the tree covered spoil levee on the other side of her. He hears some noise across the street, and it's Mr. Melerine trying to manhandle the mamoo's onto the Miss Jean. Jacques calls out to him, runs across the street, and helps him put the heavy frames into their hinge pins. During the installation, Mr. Melerine and Jacques have an idle conversation.

"Enough with the chit chat, what's going on with that girl? I saw all the hardware you pulled out of your truck. It looks like you brought your whole wardrobe."

"She's just an old high school friend that needs some help that is all I know. Things are happening so fast. As soon as I get some time, I'm going to talk to her."

"Jacques, I know you are old enough to make your own decisions; but Jean and I worry about you. Jean told me how bad she looked, and we don't want you coming home the same way or worst. The people who did that are bad news. You need to find out what is going on, and you need to do it soon. Jean also saw your rifle. You better think it through. You know that they will be judged on judgement day."

"I plan on talking to her today. I figure if I want to save her life, I might have to take one or two. It is not something I am proud of; but in this case, it probably has to be done."

A priest pulls his old beat up pick-up truck that is belching white smoke in the Melerine's driveway. The truck used to be gold with a white top. Now, it's a bucket of rust. Over twenty-five percent of the bed is rusted through. The cab is mostly covered with surface rust except for the large hole in the driver's door. The Friar Tuck looking priest in black pants, black short sleeve shirt, a white collar, and white shrimp boots walks across the street to where Jacques and Mr. Melerine are standing.

"Like I said, you're a grown man. You need to make your own decisions."

The old burley priest extends his right hand towards Jacques. "Bonjour, Jacques. Comment ça va?"

Jacques shakes his hand. "I've been good, how about yourself?" Jacques can't help but notice how the priest's callused hands cuts into his own.

"You're hands are like da skin of a baby. What type of work do you do over dere in Houston?"

"I'm still an engineer."

"Mais, not today. Today, you come with us and be a shrimper. Old Père Andrew, he knows just da spot."

"Père, I have some work to do on the house."

"Da house, it can wait till we get back. Come on and be a shrimper, and I'll help you booby trap da house after we offloads da beaucoup champagnes dat we're going to catch. Weh."

Jacques thinks about it for a minute. Père Andrew's help would be handy and being away from Mrs. Melerine might allow me to get some sleep. "Weh, today I'm going to be a shrimper." All three laugh as they board the Miss Jean, wave to Mrs. Melerine, and motor down Bayou Loutre. On the ride out, Jacques is still amazed about the design of the Lafitte skiff. Twenty-five foot long and twelve foot beam, a nearly flat bottom, and an air-cooled, inboard, Chevy 350 motor makes it perfect for getting around in the shallow bays of the South Louisiana marshes. The fantail, kangaroo boom with winches, and awning makes it perfect for daytime trawling. The mamoos finishes off the masterpiece for nighttime shrimping. He still hasn't figured out why all the Lafitte skiffs are painted blue on top and below the water line and white on the sides.

They reach Bayou Pitre, and Mr. Melerine tells Jacques to lower the fifty-eight foot trawl. Mr. Melerine slows the boat to a near idle. Jacques ties the tail of the trawl and throws the tail overboard. The passing water sucks the net off the fantail. As the trawl boards clear the boat, Jacques works the winch brakes to add tension to the cables to make the boards dig and open the net. He reaches the three painted marks on the cables that indicate one hundred fifty feet of cable out and locks the winches. Mr. Melerine looks at his watch and keeps the boat in the channel of the bayou. Once Jacques thinks that everything is in place, he lays on the bow and takes a nap.

Thirty minutes later, Jacques wakes to the engine speed increase as Mr. Melerine packs the net's contents into the pocket. Jacques walks back to the winches and brings in the net. When the boards clear the water, Mr. Melerine turns the wheel as Jacques passes the lazy line on the sheave and two wraps on cat head. He brings in the tail, and it is so heavy that he needs to put another wrap on the cat head to lift the pocket out of the water. Père Andrew brags on himself. "Jacques, you take note how lucky Père Andrew is. When's da last time you saw a pocket full like dat?" Jacques unties the tail, and it fills the pick box. The excited Père Andrew walks back to the pick box. "I bet dere's four champagnes in dat pick box. See Jacques dis is da good life." Jacques re-ties the tail and lowers the net back into the water. Jacques and Père Andrew each grab a rake and start separating the fish, crabs, and shrimp. "Jacques, you need to move more faster than you are if you want dis box empty by da next time we pick up da net." Jacques just makes a face. "Jacques, so tell Old Père, why you come to Hopedale with dat girl?"

"I needed someplace safe for her."

"Funny, whenever you need someplace safe, you run down here. Why's dat?"

"Père, Hopedale is a great place for what I'm doing. Strategically, it is sitting near the end of a dead-end highway. There's the drawbridge just prior to getting to Hopedale. If you are in a car, the bridge is the only way in or out. Bayou Loutre is ten feet on the south side of the highway, and the houses are just across the street. My boat is sitting right across from the camp. It's fueled up and ready to go. Then, there's the swamp. I grew up down here and know the swamp like the back of my hand. If I have to make an escape, I can get to Venice, Grand Isle, Biloxi, New Orleans, Chalmette, or Slidell through the swamp much quicker than any road can take me. The second reason is because of the people. I know almost everyone down here. Even the people down here I don't know, I can trust my life with. I haven't seen many of these people for years, but in a time of need I know I can count on them. It's the unwritten law. The third reason is that I just feel safe around the swamp. I mean that I can comfortably live in the swamp almost indefinitely. It's rich with fish, crabs, shrimp, rabbits, deer, and ducks. The swamp can provide all of my needs."

"Jacques, if you like Hopedale for all of dose t'ings. Why do you only come back when you in trouble? Why you not stay and make a life down here?"

"It's complicated Père. There is a little thing called money. There is no money down here. You would never understand."

"Perhaps one day, you explain it to Old Père. Come on, let's get that net in again."

They empty another full pocket into the pick box.

"Jacques, dat Malynda, she's a cute girl—nice too."

Jacques' curiosity reaches a high. "You talked to Malynda?"

"Weh, we talked about many a t'ings. She's mainly interested in you."

A boyish smile comes across Jacques face. "What did she want to know?"

"I tell you what, if you promise to take her to Mass on Sunday; I'll tell you." Jacques makes a face. "Jacques, I know you have issues wit God. You and He aren't right yet, but I know dis. God, He has a good plan for each of us. Sometimes we like his plan. Sometimes we don't. Many a time, God, He put a turning point in your life. Somet'ing to give your life more meaning, more purpose. Maybe dis Malynda is one of those turning points. You just remember dat he has a reason for everything that happens in our lives. Maybe, he's telling you something. Maybe you ought to listen."

"Père Andrew, I respect you plenty; but please stop the preaching."

"Ok, Jacques. Enough with da preaching. Old Père, all he suggests; if she wants to go to mass, you should take her."

"I'm trying to hide her. Bringing her to a public place is not such a good way to keep her hidden."

"Relax Jacques, you're among friends. If you like, I'll keep a low profile about it. Bring her to Church."

"Ok Père, you win. I'll take her to Mass on Sunday. Now, tell me what she wanted to know?" Their conversation continued until mid-day. By two o'clock the shrimp box is full, and they're heading back.

CHAPTER 20

▼

Joe's team of bullies is sitting on the couch in Joe's living room of his Gulfport house. The sliding glass door opens, and Joe has a cigarette in his mouth, a plate full of BBQ steaks in one hand, and a beer in the other. They're brainstorming about how they are going to find this woman, and how they are going to explain it to Satinito. The phone rings. Joe hurries to put the plate down and answer the wall-mounted phone with a twelve inch cord. It's Satinito on the other end.

"Joe, you let the girl escape. You were my go to guy because I could count on you to get the job done. That's two strikes against you. Let's hope there is not a third."

"Mr. Satinito, does Harris know about the film?"

"No, he's just worried that Meyeaux's murder can be linked to him. You do have Meyeaux's film, don't you?"

"Yeah, it's in my pocket." He reaches in his pocket and pulls out two rolls of undeveloped film. "I'm going to send Tony to get both the rolls developed right now, Mr. Satinito?"

"Joe, just relax about the girl. She has nowhere to go. She's afraid of the cops, and she's more afraid of you. Sooner or later she's going to call me. She doesn't have a choice."

Joe rolls his eyes and thinks to himself, "Is this guy living a fantasy or what?" He answers, "Yes, Mr. Satinito, I'm sure she's going to. It's just a matter of time."

"Joe, I want you to continue your little operation. Also, we're going to have to plan a little surprise for Harris. Don't do anything yet. Just get a plan together. We might need him to get to Malynda if she makes it into protective custody."

"Ok, Mr. Satinito, I'll get on it right away. Is there anything else?"

"Just don't let me down again." Joe hangs up the phone.

Mike asks Joe, "Well, what did he say?"

"We're alive as long as Harris is. He's talking about making a plan for us to take Harris out. Tony, get these two rolls of film developed."

"No way, man. Two rolls of film at two o'clock. No way."

"You can't still believe that crap you heard from that Voodoo woman?"

"You don't understand. She knows things that ordinary people will never know. No way, send Cliff."

"Cliff, take the film and wait for it to be processed."

As Cliff walks by Tony, he slaps Tony's knee and laughs. "You big sissy. Maybe we need to put a dress on you."

Tony in one quick move jumps up, grabs Cliff by the throat with one hand, and lifts his feet off the ground. "Don't mess with me kid, or I'll crush you like a bug."

Cliff uses both his hands on Tony's wrist to keep his weight off his throat. "I'm just kidding. Let me down."

Joe screams, "Tony, put him down."

Tony brings Cliff's face within inches of his, "Do it again, and I'll kill you." He then throws Cliff over the coffee table and onto the floor in front of the TV. The choking Cliff grabs the film and walks out the door. They watch TV and wait for Cliff to return.

Cliff returns in an hour and a half. "Boss, you're not going to like this. One of the rolls of film is blank."

Joe jumps up and looks at the blank negatives. "Oh NO! Oh NO! Oh NO! Where's the other roll?" Cliff hands it to him, and he pulls them out. "Tony, are these the ones you took?" Tony grabs them and flips through them. He gets to just about the end of the stack and there is a picture of Scott with his camera.

"Yep, these are the ones I took." A scary look comes over Tony's face. "The number two is going to plague us. You'll see. This is just the beginning. In the end, it's going to kill all of us."

Joe looks around, "Shut up about the number two. You better lay off whatever that crazy woman is giving you to smoke and get with the program. Meyeaux switched the film. We need to find the other roll. Satinito is going to have a fit. That lying bastard Meyeaux, he probably thought that I would have pulled out the film from the camera without rewinding it."

Joe picks up the phone and dials Satinito's number. "Mr. Satinito, we don't have the film. Meyeaux must have switched it."

"Joe relax. It's got to be in the house. I'll just have Harris get it for us."

"But, he'll find out what's on the film."

"Are you kidding? I'm going to tell him what's on the film to make him more aggressive in finding it. He's going to find out sooner or later anyway. It's better that he finds the film than someone else finding it. It's just inconvenient timing. I was planning on using it after he stopped taking the women and the cash. Look at the bright side; the FBI has the house off limits to everyone. He can send in a team, and they can spend days tearing the house apart without anyone questioning them. Relax, Joe. This is not that big of a deal. Let me call Harris. Just continue business as usual."

Harris is sitting on a park bench in the shade of an oak tree on Lakeshore Drive. He's staring out over Lake Pontchartrain as his sergeant pulls into the parking space along side his car. The muscular, bald, forty plus year old sergeant wearing a black suit with mirror sunglasses on looks like a typical G-man that uses intimidation to get his way. His face has a neatly trimmed mustache and is expressionless. He still has a hint of grease paint in the lobes of his ears."

"Mr. Harris, whatever possessed you to put Rodred on the case?"

"Excuse me, I thought that I'm the one making the decisions around here."

"I'm sorry Sir, but she's just too smart. She can solve this case and put us in jail."

"What makes you say that?"

"When I was in my hide, it took her just a few seconds to find me. I saw those cold gray eyes looking right at me. I'm telling you, you need to take her off."

"Don't worry about Sue. I still have her on a short leash. Besides, I'm looking at retiring in about a month anyway. What do you say? Let's make one big cash in and call it quits."

"Why don't we do it this week and get it over with?"

"Satinito is shaken up pretty good. He's going to be real cautious for a couple of weeks. Let's give him about a month."

"What about Rodred?"

"Let her continue her worthless surveillance on Satinito and let her find the girl. If she finds Mrs. Meyeaux, you can kill her."

"Kill which one?"

"Both if you want." They both laugh. "You see, I'm not as dumb as I pretend to be. For years I've benefited from the sweat of others. I mean no offense. Sue is my brains, and you are my brawn. It's a pity that you hate her so. That's where I come in. I'm a liaison. I get the best out of both of you. You might want to reconsider working with Sue. When I'm gone, she will be going places. You really should meet her. I could introduce you to her, and who knows you might even become lovers."

"Fat chance on that. I already know enough about her to stay clear of her."

"Funny, you know everything about her, and you haven't even met her."

"I'll just keep my distance. Besides, she's still just trying to save the world. She doesn't fit in my plan for early retirement."

"True, but she's young and doesn't really know how the world works. She'll figure it out someday and make what we're doing look like child's play."

"So what do you want me to do?"

"Simple, leave Satinito and his bunch alone. Let Sue find the girl, and kill her. We'll figure out what to do with Satinito later."

Frank's phone rings. He looks at the incoming number. It's Satinito. His sergeant gets up, leaves, and waves good-bye as Harris answers the phone.

"What is it Satinito?"

"We might have a little problem. I don't know how to put this, but we took out a little insurance policy on you to make sure that we have your loyalty. Tony took some pictures of you with me a couple of weeks ago. Meyeaux did too. That's the reason that we killed him. The problem is that Meyeaux's film is still missing. We think it's in his house. I would like for you to use your team and get it." The sergeant starts his car, and Frank waves at him to come back.

"Satinito, nobody blackmails Frank Harris! Do you hear me? Nobody, I mean nobody! I want the film and the negatives! Do you hear me?"

"Relax Franky, get the film, and we can talk about it. Right now, my roll is in safe hands. The other roll is not. Call me back when you find it. Look at it this way. If you find the film, you have pictures of me and I of you. Neither one can use it without incriminating themselves. Get the film, Franky. Come on over here, and we'll have some drinks and laughs."

"This isn't over. Good-bye." He slams the phone shut. His sergeant comes back. "Get your team in Meyeaux's house. There's a roll of film that we need to get. I need you to tear that house apart and find the roll of film. I want it brought back to me in its canister undeveloped. Do I make myself clear?"

"Crystal Sir." He gets into his vehicle and speeds away. Frank storms to his car and drives off.

At Jacques' camp, Père Andrew and Jacques work on the camp while Mr. Melerine takes the Miss Jean to the shrimp sheds. Jacques and Père walk around the camp and inspect all the windows.

"Jacques, dat chicken wire looks fine to me. The porch screen is covered in da chicken wire too. No teargas or grenade gets through dat. You brought da home made clay mortars for your cans?"

"I figured I could use what I had before. I just need to replace the powder." Jacques goes into the wooden twenty by twenty T-11 shed and pulls out eight homemade clay mortars. He empties the old powder, fills with new powder, verifies the battery is not hooked up, and puts the caps on them. He grabs four cans, and Père grabs the other four. Jacques walks to the back left piling and pulls a plastic box off of a metal can made of half inch steel in the shape of a square loud speaker. He verifies that the alignment is facing the base of the stairway. He puts the clay mortar facing outward, connects the wires to the igniter that is in the cap, and puts the plastic cover back on. He repeats the process with the right rear and the two corners of the porch. He helps Père get the last one in place on the front side of the camp.

"Jacques, you got yourself a mighty good scatter gun, but tell me—how you know the ball bearings, dey go forward, and you not just blow out the pile and make the whole camp fall? You got some formulas for dat type of stuff."

"Père, I look at it, and say by inspection that it is going to work."

"By inspection, ha. You're guessing."

"It's simple. You have equal and opposite force. I figure that it is going to take less force to push the bearings than it will take to shear the pile. Besides what's the worst thing that could happen. I loose four piles; I still have plenty left. Quit worrying, and let's get the flash bangs in place before it gets dark."

"You mean, you got some more."

"Nope, extras from last time."

Jacques has six wooden boxes with trap doors—one on the underside of each side of the house and one in the ceiling of each porch. Père holds the ladder while Jacques climbs up with the 175 dB flash bang in his hand. "Père, you might not want to stand down there." He moves way back. Jacques pulls the pin of the flashbang, opens the trap door to find a large paper wasp nest in the closure. He slowly and carefully pushes the flash bang against a spring with the handle wedged in the box without disturbing the wasps, slowly closes the trap door while holding the flashbang in with his thumb, and slides down the ladder. He repeats the process for the other five wooden boxes.

Jacques looks at Père Andrew. "Well, all we have to do now is hook up the battery."

"Before you hook up da battery, you might want to move Melerine's truck. One of those cans is pointing right at it."

Jacques moves the truck, makes sure both the bedroom switch and the kitchen switch are in the off position, and begins to hook up the battery.

"Jacques don't you think you should test it before you hook it up. You know those storms blow beaucoup saltwater through here. Dem wires could be corroded."

"Where your faith? Just make sure no one is out front."

"It's all clear out here."

Jacques closes his eyes, says a silent prayer, and connects the battery. After the battery is connected, Père Andrew makes the sign of the cross. "Jacques, there's more dan you in dis house. You need a safety on dem switches." Jacques holds up a roll of gray duct tape that he covers the light switches with. Père looks out the front window and sees the Miss Jean pulling up to the dock. They walk out, stretch the net, sit around in the boat, and talk about how good of a day they had. They see Mrs. Melerine carrying a big pot and a loaf of French bread over to Jacques camp.

"Père and Jacques, you both know Jean. We better hurry, or we'll miss supper. It looks like seafood gumbo tonight, and we don't want to miss that." As they walk in, they see Celeste putting the silverware on the table. After washing up, they sit down to eat. Mrs. Melerine is coming out of the front bedroom just shaking her head. Jacques looks at her with a concerned look.

"Jacques, you are going to have to give her some time." She serves the plates and places them on the table. After grace, they begin to eat and carry on conversation.

After a couple of hours, Père hits Mr. Melerine on the arm. "Come on Melerine, let's carry this conversation outside." They get up and leave out the front door. Jacques starts on the dishes while Mrs. Melerine bathes Celeste. After giving Celeste a bath, Jacques is confronted by Mrs. Melerine. He expects to get a lecture about going shrimping instead of going to the grocery. He thinks to himself. "At least she doesn't have a broom in her hand."

"Jacques, it's good you went wit Père today. Maybe he teach you something. Today, Celeste and I pick out plenty of nice t'ings for Malynda and her, but clothes can only do so much. Jacques, I going to leave you two alone tonight. You just remember that she's been through a lot, and I know how you are. You always want to solve all your problems right away. This time, don't push so hard. She needs time and lots of prayer."

Jacques entertains Celeste with a few new toys until she falls asleep on the couch. As soon as she falls asleep, Jacques jumps into the shower, puts on a clean pair of dress slacks and a polo shirt, and just a little of his after-shave. He prepares as if he is going to meet a blind date. He wants his first impression to be flawless. He looks in the mirror and makes a face. "This is not me." He takes off the fancy clothes and puts on a pair of shorts and a colored tee shirt. He looks at himself in the mirror again. "It's not much, but at least it's honest." Jacques picks up Celeste, walks to Malynda's bedroom, softly knocks on the door, and walks in. He lays Celeste down next to Malynda and asks Malynda to come out into the living room so they can talk. Malynda's reluctant to, but Jacques convinces her that it's necessary. Once they are sitting on the couch in the living room, Jacques begins his planned speech that he has been working on for the past two days; but he forgets everything when their eyes meet. He knows exactly what he is going to say, but the words don't come out. He sees her for the first time. Her disfigurement surprises him; and his emotions are glad, sad, happy and angry all mixed up at the same time. Her presence still has the same effect on him as it did in High School. Jacques can see that she's ashamed about her marred body and nearly shaven head.

She starts the conversation with a laugh. "Does my nightgown look that bad?"

Jacques looks at the hot pink, silk, tie-died nightgown. "It's a little on the bright side. You're a little wilder than I remembered you."

She points a finger at Jacques and laughs. "It's Celeste's choice. Somehow she convinced Jean that this is what I wear all the time."

They both laugh. "Malynda, I'm just happy that you're here. I don't care what you wear."

"I'm happy to see you too. How many years has it been—about eighteen? I tried to write to you; but every time I started, I just didn't know what to say. Jacques, I'm sorry about bringing you into this, but I didn't know where else to turn."

"I'm glad you remembered me. Don't feel so bad about not writing. I could have written you too." They continue with all the catching up of the years that they were apart. All of a sudden, the smile leaves Jacques' face.

"Malynda, I have to ask you some difficult questions. I need to know the truth. I'm not here to judge you. I am here to protect you, but I need to know the truth. My first question is 'Is this drug related?'"

"No, definitely not me. Well, maybe. I'm not really sure."

"Are you on drugs or have you done drugs?"

"No. I tried a little coke at a party once in college, but that's it. I never touched it again."

"How about your husband?"

"He used to smoke every now and then. He said he quit, but every now and then I would find a joint."

"Did you or your husband deal drugs?"

"Jacques, why are you asking me all these questions about drugs? Don't you understand that my husband is dead, and someone tried to kill me?"

"Malynda, I saw the police pictures. It was a mob hit. The only reason that the mob kills everyone like that is to make a statement—an example, so that others never would consider doing the same thing. What I am trying to find out is what you or your husband did to cause this."

Malynda starts to cry. "I'm just a housewife, and I thought my husband sold oil industry supplies. What do you mean? You're saying that I caused it to happen."

"Do you know, who did it?"

She looks down at the floor. "No."

"Malynda, I see it in your face. You know, now tell me."

"You're just going to get yourself killed."

"If you don't tell me, you're just going to get both of us killed. You see, we only have so much time before they find you. When they do; you, me, and Celeste are all dead. Do you understand that?"

"We are down here, and they'll never find us."

"They will find us. It is just a matter of time. How we use that time is all up to you."

"Ok, Scott, my husband, he was working with some gang members. Believe me, I didn't know until that night. The whole time I thought he was a salesman. They could have been into drugs. I'm not sure."

"Why did they do this to you?"

"They did it out of meanness. They were beating me, but they were killing Scott. He tried to help me. He really did, but there was nothing he could do."

"Why were they doing this to him?"

"He took some pictures that he wasn't supposed to."

"Where's the film?"

"They got it."

"Ok, they got what they want. That could be good. Were they wearing masks?"

"No, they weren't."

"Did you see them?"

She nods her head. "Yes."

"Could you identify them if you saw them again?"

She nods her head again. "Yes"

"Did you know any of them?"

"Yeah, my husband's best friend—Billy Chauvin."

"That is all I need to know. Let's change the topic and talk about all the times that we missed out on."

"Wait, you didn't ask what happened."

"I saw the police photos. I know what happened."

Jacques looks at the fear that's in Malynda's face. "Relax, Jacques is going to take real good care of you." As he gives her a big hug, Malynda tries to smile. Jacques thinks to himself that he is also going to take real good care of them.

"Malynda, one other thing about living down here, you must never use the phone, Internet, or go into town. You must remain hidden for the time being. You can travel around here and go outside, but you can't cross the bridge. If someone recognizes you, or they trace a phone call; the game is over with."

Malynda's pushes away from him and her attitude flares, "I'm not stupid. I didn't talk to the police. I didn't talk to anyone. I know what they can do."

As Jacques reaches out to hug her again, "Ok, ok. Let's get some sleep. We can talk again in the morning." Jacques walks Malynda into her room, tucks her in, gives her a kiss on her cheek, and says, "Good night."

CHAPTER 21

▼

Thursday 0530, Jacques is in his fishing camp, and he calls Randy. "Randy, this is Jacques."

In an energetic tone, "Hey, you crazy coon-ass. Glad you called. How's the girl doing?"

"She's doing fine. I appreciate the help the other night, but I need another favor."

"Man, is it going to be as exciting as the last favor you asked of me? We're still talking about it."

Jacques laughs. "I'm afraid not. Can you access police records without anyone knowing you did it?"

"Sure, I do it all the time."

"Good, I need you to access a William Chauvin that lives in Houma."

"No problem, I'll do it later today. I need to talk to you about that sniper you wouldn't let me take out."

"He was hidden behind who knows what. Probability of you hitting him was slim."

"Ah, but you didn't know what I had. I had a new toy—a barrett .50 BMG with an EM scope. At three hundred yards that 700 grain bullet would have found it's mark."

"You can't hit what you can't see."

"Did you hear me? I had an EM scope. It allows me to see through concrete walls. Well, not all concrete walls; but I could see the guy's piddle pack."

"How did you afford that?"

"I didn't. I convinced the manufacturer to loan it to me for a month for our department to test it out. It's a great toy, but no one can afford it. I returned it and told them that the fifty-pound battery pack is to heavy. Hey, give me a call a little later. I'll tell you what I've come up with." They both hang up.

0810: Sue passes by Harris' office ten minutes late, and he says nothing. Before she heads into her cubical, she glances down the corridor at him. He's in a trance. His cell phone is in the center of his desk, and he's just staring at it. She shrugs her shoulders, steps into her cubical, sets up her laptop, and gets lost in her paperwork. Thirty minutes later, she feels a presence and looks up. It's Harris holding an extra cup of coffee.

In a kind tone, "I thought you could use a cup of coffee."

She doesn't know what to do. After working for this man for over a year, he's so out of character. She plays along. "Thank you, Sir."

"How's my girl doing?"

"Just fine." She thinks to herself. "That's two sentences, can we try for three?"

"How is the Meyeaux case going?"

She points to her laptop. "It's a waiting game."

"What's it doing?"

"You see I think Mrs. Meyeaux escaped from the hospital with the help of some of her friends."

He points to her guest chair, "You mind?"

She thinks to herself, "Wait a minute something is definitely wrong. This absolute control freak is asking me if he can sit in my cubical. I've got something he wants dearly. Now, what is it?" She continues the little game. "Sure, go ahead."

"If you think these people are involved, why not pick them up and grill them until you get the information you want. That's the way we use to do it. Just keep pounding on them until they slip or just give in."

"The problem is that these people might have helped her escape, but they don't know where she is."

"What do you mean" The laptop comes alive, and she holds her finger up to Mr. Harris to be quiet.

It's Violet Johnson's voice, "Hey honey, any word yet?"

Deputy Steve's voice, "Not a thing."

"Darling in this case, no news is good news."

"Debbie's getting worried."

"Just tell her we did the best thing we could do and to keep praying for her."

"Ok, talk to you later."

"You too boo."

The computer records the conversation, the numbers, the date, the time, and the length and automatically stores it.

Harris looks surprised, "What was that?"

"That is the way we solve cases in the twenty-first century. I got a federal district judge to give me a court order to tap the phones of my four suspects. Whenever one of them makes a phone call, the computer recognizes the callers and records the conversation. It's called multi-tasking. I can sit here and do all my work, while I ease drop on my suspects."

"And you can do that from anywhere?"

"As long as I can tie in through the Internet to the FBI mainframe." She smiles. "Computers are great. Aren't they? You see eventually whoever has Mrs. Meyeaux is going to call one of these suspects. As soon as he does, we have him."

"What happens if he calls us from a pay phone?"

"We go there, dust for finger prints, and question people. As long as, they think that we are no longer pursuing them, they will become more relaxed. The more relaxed, the more of a chance of them making a mistake."

"Don't you think that this could take some time?"

"Fortunately in this case, time is a luxury, because I don't think that she's in any danger."

"What makes you so sure?"

"Face the facts, her doctor, social worker, and her two next door neighbors, who were watching her daughter, are involved. I think that this case is much more complicated than we first thought." Harris looks at her with a confused look. Sue continues, "I don't want to say anything until I have more proof. Just give me some time, and you'll be able to chalk another one up."

"Sue, when I agreed to give you this case. You agreed to keep me informed."

"Mrs. Meyeaux is way over her head. Someone else besides Satinito is hunting her. I saw a hide at the hospital." She notices the blank look on Harris' face. "A hide is a place where a sniper hides."

"Satinito has a sniper. It was probably him."

"No, it wasn't him. Satinito's sniper is a complete moron. This guy is real professional."

"If you think this guy is a professional, why did you find him?"

"Because I would have picked the same spot to set up."

Harris' cell phone rings, and he answers it with a smile on his face. "Hello." The smile leaves his face and is replaced with anger. "What do you mean? I'll call you right back." He hangs up. "Sue you're going to have to excuse me for one moment. Keep up the good work and keep me informed." He gets up, hurries to his office, and closes his door. Meanwhile, Sue continues writing her reports.

Harris calls his sergeant back. "Did you find it?"

"No, Sir. We did not find a single roll of 35mm film."

"Are you sure you did a thorough job of searching?"

"Yes, Sir. We've pulled out a good portion of the walls, ceiling fans, all the panels out of the automobiles. In fact, I recommend that we burn the place."

"No, not yet. The film still might be in there. If we get the girl, she might know where her husband hid it."

"What do you want us to do?"

"Just leave."

Harris hangs his phone up, puts it in the center of his desk, and shakes his head. "What am I going to do?"

A minute later Sue's laptop comes alive again.

It's Debbie calling from her land-line. "Dem men dat were there since yesterday, dey leaving now."

Steve's voice comes through the speaker, "Ok, you just stay away from there. You hear. Since the FBI's taken over I'm not even allowed on that property."

"Ok, Steve. When you come home for lunch?"

"I'll be there in about thirty minutes."

"Love ya."

"Love ya too."

As the computer is saving the information, Sue's face turns red with anger. She grabs her purse, walks out the department's door, and drives to Houma.

Harris opens his door and walks back to Sue's cubical to find her gone. He looks at the laptop and uses the mouse to replay the last message. As he listens to it, he realizes where she's headed to. He walks back into his office, closes his door, and calls his sergeant.

"Sergeant, this is Harris. Sue is headed down to Houma. I know that you are on your way back. Make sure that she sees you, drop off your team, and meet me on Lakeshore Drive in about an hour."

"She's figured it out. Hasn't she?"

"No, not yet; but she's putting it together faster than I ever imagined. We are going to have to misdirect her. See you when you get here."

Jacques calls Randy again while he is sitting on his back porch. "Hey buddy, what do you have on Billy Chauvin?"

"One week prior of the extraction, he was reported missing by his wife. Houma police department is investigating the disappearance, but they haven't come up with anything yet."

"Now, I'm stuck."

"What happened? Maybe I can help."

"She was attacked by five men. The only one she knew was Chauvin."

"Relax friend, do you have a computer?"

"Yeah, it's not too fancy, but it works."

"Good, I'll burn a DVD for you with a lot of mug shots of people in that area. Maybe she will recognize one of them."

"Randy, I don't have a DVD player. Can you burn CD's?"

"Yeah, it will just take more of them. I'll FedEx them overnight. Where do you want me to send them?"

"Send them to the Meraux, LA post office—zip 70075."

"If you want, but I could send them directly to your house."

"Randy, FedEx doesn't deliver where I'm staying."

"Ok buddy, you should get them tomorrow. Later." They both hang up.

1900 The enraged Sue Rodred returns to the FBI Field Office. She walks into Harris' office, where Harris is sitting at his desk. "I thought you were going to let me handle it! If you want to handle it, fine! I want to be pulled off! I can just put up with you on the Satinito case for another two years or however long before you retire!"

"Sue calm down. I think that I have some explaining to do."

"Explaining to do! Why waste your breath! I want a transfer!"

He stands up. "Come on Sue, I would like for you to meet someone."

"I told you that I don't want anything to do with the case. I don't want anything to do with you."

"Sue, things are not as they seem. Come on."

"What the hell? Ok, let's go meet whoever you want me to meet."

They get into Harris' automobile and drive down Lakeshore drive. Along the way, Harris stops and tells Sue to get in the back seat. With her face still red with anger, she gets out and gets into the back seat. As soon as she closes the door, the driver's side rear door opens; and his sergeant gets in. His sergeant is wearing a black suit with a black shirt, and he looks as mean as ever. Sue immediately can smell death written all over this guy. She puts her hand in her purse and grips her revolver. "That's the idiot that tried to run me off the road." He smiles at her. She can immediately feel his dislike for her.

"Sue Rodred, I would like you to meet Mr. Jones. He works for the CIA. He has a special interest in Mrs. Meyeaux. Apparently, Mrs. Meyeaux isn't as squeaky clean as she appears to be."

His sergeant looks at Sue's hand in her purse. "I think you can take your hand out of your purse. If I wanted to kill you, I would have done it a long time ago. If you are quick, you will only be able to get off two maybe three shots. I'll still have enough strength to kill you. I've been shot before Mrs. Rodred. You see, I welcome death. The trait is an asset in my line of work, because it allows me to take more risk than my adversaries." She pulls her hand out of her purse. In his sarcastic tone, he continues. "What do you think that you know about this woman?"

"Malynda Thibidoux, born in Quebec, Canada on January 29, 1964. Her father moved from Quebec to Meraux, Louisiana in 1979, and to Houma, Louisiana in 1980. She graduated from Terrebonne High School in May of 1982. She went to LSU and received a degree in Child Psychology in 1986. She married Scott Meyeaux in 1987. Both her mother and father were killed in a car accident in 1990. She gave birth to her daughter Celeste in 1996. She's actively involved with the church and highly liked by her community. What else do you want to know?"

"Tell me what do you think you know about her husband—Scott Meyeaux."

"Scott Meyeaux was one of Satinito's muscle men. He was born in New Orleans on September 15, 1963. Played linebacker for LSU from 1984 through 1986. Enough, where is this going?"

"Tell me, did Mr. Meyeaux work for Satinito before he got married or after."

"After. Why?"

He pulls out a black and white photograph out of his coat and hands it to her. "Do you know any of these people?"

She studies the photograph. "The one on the left is Omar something or other. He ranks pretty high on the terrorist most wanted list. I don't know who the other guy is."

Sue begins to let down her defenses and becomes interested in what Harris' sergeant has to say.

"Do you know where Satinito gets his drugs from?"

"Probably Florida. My investigation has been so restrictive I can only guess."

"Try Quebec, Canada. Can you guess from whom?"

"This other guy in the picture?"

"Frank, you really have a smart one here."

"Who is the guy in the picture?"

"That's Malynda's Uncle Leon Thibidoux. We have been following Uncle Leon long before the FBI was investigating Satinito. Do you know how much money it takes to finance terrorism? Try millions. The drugs come in through Southeast Asia, France, Quebec, then to Biloxi. The money then goes back through Quebec, France, and to somewhere in the Middle East. In fact, the only reason you have been building a case against Satinito is to allow the drug traffic to continue without being interrupted. You see, we needed the FBI to investigate Satinito to keep the local sheriff departments clear of his drug dealing. That's why you have been so restricted in your investigation."

Sue's temper flares, "I have been wasting a year of my life crawling through that nasty swamp on a case that you don't want solved. How come you didn't tell me?"

"It was on a need to know basis, and you didn't need to know." Sue has a betrayed look on her face. "Get your panties out of the knot they are in lady, and grow up. We all serve our country to do the bigger good. Because of your investigation, we know how much money is being transferred. Presently, we have located ten of the eleven cells that this money is going to. As soon as we locate the last one, we will send in surgical strike units and take them out at the same time. In the mean time, you will be allowed to take down Satinito. So you see, we still need you to keep track of the money."

"So what does Mrs. Meyeaux have to do with this other than she has an Uncle Leon"?"

"Once we find the other cell, the surgical strike units will be given the green light. We have a list of people that we will be simultaneously picking up. Near the top of the list is Mrs. Meyeaux. We believe that she has a roll of film that was sent to her by her Uncle Leon. We believe that the film contains evidence of involvement of foreign governments."

"Wait, you are the CIA. You can't pick up US citizens on US soil."

"Don't be so naive Ms. Rodred. Black operations are carried out every day in the US. We need you to find Mrs. Meyeaux, and we need you to find her soon. Mr. Harris please pull the car over here." He gets out and gets into another car that's waiting, and they drive off in different directions. Sue is still in the back seat. Frank looks in the rearview mirror at her totally lost and confused face. She looks as if her life has just been sucked out of her.

"Sue, I hope you understand. I am just doing my job."

"I now understand. This is a little much for me. If you don't mind, I just want go home, take a bath, and go to bed. I want to have some quiet time for all of this to sink in."

Harris pulls into the garage next to her automobile. As she gets out, "Sue, remember this is on a need to know basis. Your team doesn't need to know. Am I clear on that?"

"Crystal, Sir."

"I'll see you tomorrow." She waves as Harris pulls off before she even starts her automobile.

Harris is not out the parking lot, and he's already laughing. He calls his sergeant. "You were great. I can't believe that she took it hook-line and sinker. Where did you come up with the name Leon Thibidoux?"

Sounding highly sophisticated to impress Harris, "Leon Thibidoux is a real person. He's a small time arms dealer in Quebec. I just went into Sue's files on the main frame pulled up her information on Mrs. Meyeaux. I found out that she lived in Quebec for a period of time. I did a criminal check on any Thibidoux, and Leon's name popped up."

"Touché Sergeant, let's go have a beer and celebrate."

"Let's not. Rodred is smarter than you think. Did she take the bait, or did she pretend to take the bait? I would be more worried about her than Satinito."

"Maybe you're right. Maybe, we should keep our distance. I'm going to tell Satinito that we found the film. That forces him into a stalemate with me, and we can continue business. Maybe, I'll go and celebrate with him."

"Would you get your head out of your ass? Look up in your rear view mirror and tell me if you see Rodred."

"No. Why?"

"Because if she pretended to take the bait, she's probably tailing you right now. If not now, then tomorrow. You need to play it cool for a few days. Let's see how she reacts."

"All right, you win. I'm going home and celebrate by myself."

"Great, I'll talk to you next week." They both hang-up.

CHAPTER 22

▼

Saturday 1800 at Jacques camp, Malynda is sitting at the kitchen table looking at the screen of Jacques' laptop. Jacques is standing over Malynda's shoulder while she's going through the mug shots.

"Jacques, I've been looking at pictures of criminals for two solid days. I need a break."

"Ok, let's take a five minute break."

She pleads, "No, Jacques. I mean like for the rest of the night."

"Malynda, this is extremely important. Please, just ten more pictures."

"Ok, ten more pictures, and let's call it a night."

She goes through the ten pictures and stops. Jacques gets ready to fold up the laptop, and she says, "Wait, go back two pictures—to that kid with the wavy brown hair."

Jacques back spaces to that picture. "That's him—the one they called Cliff."

"Bingo that's all I needed from you." Jacques snatches the computer from Malynda and eagerly pulls up his information. "Clifton Broussard, DOB 02-15-1981, Sex: Male, Race: Caucasian, Height: 5'-10", Weight: 145 pounds, Distinguishing Marks: None. . Last known address:.........Houma, Louisiana. Arrest records: 07-04-1999 convicted of simple battery, suspended sentence. (End of Records)" From there he goes to the internet white pages, finds him and notices a different address. He pulls up mapquest and gets directions to both houses. From there he goes to terraserver and pulls up recent aerial photographs of the areas around both houses.

Malynda doesn't like the look in Jacques eyes. "What are you planning on doing? I'm not sure that he's the right guy."

"Relax, all I'm going to do is take some pictures." He gets up and heads out the front door, across the street, and into his boat. He pulls an old 35 mm camera out of the console of the boat. He looks at the 50 mm lens and thinks to himself, "A telephoto lens sure would be nice." He walks back into the camp and loads three days worth of gear into his ruck sack.

Malynda knocks twice on Jacques' door and walks in. She sees him packing his gear.

"Jacques you promised to take me to Mass tomorrow."

"Mass will have to wait."

"No Jacques, it won't. You promised, and I'm holding you to it."

"I'll get Mrs. Melerine to take you."

"Jacques, I don't want Jean to take me. I want you to take me. You promised."

"Ok, if it means that much to you; I can put this off till Monday."

She walks up to him and gives him a kiss on the cheek. "Thanks, Jacques."

Jacques just makes a face and continues packing.

The next morning, Jacques, Malynda, Celeste, and the Melerines are sitting in a pew at the back of the Church. The procession walks in. Père Andrew, kisses the altar and begins mass. "Bonjour"

"Bonjour"

As they make the sign of the cross, "Començons au nom du père, du fils, et de l'esprit saint."

The mass continues in French. After the reading of the Gospel, Father Andrew gives the homily in broken English.

"Today, like so many utter Sundays, I not tell you what you shouldn't do; but Old Père tell you what you should do. Today, I tell you about a bigger plan dat God has for each of you. You people live hard lives, but you live life to da fullest. You make every minute count. Imagine telling da city folk, dey need to be at mass at four-thirty in da morning." The congregation begins to laugh. "There be many a bad things in da swamp—da mosquitoes, da gnats, da snakes, dem alligators and dem sharks. And who can forget the smell with the Norwest wind. Many a bad thing a happen in dat there swamp—boats sink, dey get hit by lighting. Who can forget the hurricanes? How many people lost their Grand Père due to drowning?" About twenty-five percent of the congregation raises their hands. "Wit all those bad things, why you stay? Old Père tell you why—cause of the good things, cause your close community, cause the feeling you get when you bring in da grand catch, cause you wouldn't have it no other way. Da good feeling you get when you put in a good day's work. Da oneness with nature as you watch the sun come up over da bow of your Lafitte Skiff. God given you what you need—no'ting more no'ting less. God, He give you ability to fix t'ings, to make something from nothing. For sample, Crazy Leon. We know he got no'thing more." The congregation erupts in laughter. "He not have book smart, but he can get dat skiff in for dinner everyday. Man oh man, one day I see dat cooyon standing on da fantail of his skiff using a paddle as a rudder and a shoe-string working da throttle. A boat done pass. The wake done hit. He almost rolled off the back end, except for he hold on to dat shoestring to keep from fall-ing in da water. Da bow came up, and he held on harder to dat shoestring. Full throttle down Bayou Loutre, he dropped da paddle, waved his hand, and screamed at the parked boats to get out da way. He not so smart, but realized if he let go of da string the boat would stop. Leon, he got wet dat day." Even the priest began to laugh and gives time for the congregation to calm down. "Da point is dat Leon not need book smarts to get home." Father Andrew wiped a tear from his eye. "God, He pretty smart. He have a plan for each of you—from da day your born to da day you die. He knows da skills you need. It's no accident you know how to do these things. Now sometimes, God's plan, He a little differ-ent than yours. Sometime, you don't understand why He do da things He do—like taking a love one. Sometime you'll never understand until you reach heaven and ask Him yourself. For now just know He's got a plan, and it's a good plan. For, He is good." Father Andrew stood in silence for a while and then sat down. The mass continues and ends. Père stands behind the pulpit. "No one leaves just yet. It's time to get some volunteers. The Widow Black's roof is leaking. I need a couple of men to replace a few pieces of tin. Let me see a show a hands. Good. There's one other announcement. We are honored this morning to have the greatest poacher dat ever lived—Jacques Boudreaux. He say dat he has ethics now and abides by da rules. I not so sure dat Mr. Game Warden dat he put up on so many of those mud flats is so convinced." The congregation laughs. "Jacques, you stand up where everyone can see you so if dey need to give a description of you dey know what not to say." Jacques stands up and everyone is still laughing and applauds. "As many of us down here are hiding from da law. Jacques thought it would be a good place to hide his girlfriend for a while. Everyone welcome Mrs. Malynda Meyeaux to the land of hiding. Malynda, you stand up and show your-self. Let's us pray for both Jacques and Malynda and welcome them into the fold of outlaws. Now let's conclude dis Mass." Père gives the benediction.

After mass Jacques sits down in his boat behind the console. He thinks about Malynda. He knows that Malynda's bruises are still there, but she's doing a good job of covering them up with make-up. He can see that she's getting around pretty good, and her whole outlook on life seems brighter. For the time being, she's content on taking care of the womanly chores around the camp. Jacques realizes that she doesn't need a twenty-four hour baby sitter any more. He also realizes that he needs to throw the first punch. A sniper on the defense is not a good position for him to be in.

He enjoys Malynda spending much of her time with him. They talk about old times, have evening and morning walks, talking about their goals in life, and what's going to happen to their future. He knows that this little time of bliss is just the eye of the hurricane. The storm wall with its maximum fury is just ahead of them.

Jacques is in the boat checking on the equipment in the console. He removes everything out of the boat to make it as light as possible. He sees Malynda watching him through a window in the camp. She comes out holding Celeste's hand and walks down the steps. She leans over and whispers something in Celeste's ear, and they walk out on the dock. They sit down with their legs crossed near the boat. Neither she nor Celeste says a word. They just sit there and stare at Jacques. Finally, Jacques looks up, "What did I do this time?" There's no response. They just look at Jacques and the boat. Jacques catches on. "Ok, let's go for a boat ride. I need to visit an old friend of mine in Chalmette." Celeste puts on the biggest smile and starts jumping up and down. Malynda stays seated with that same look on her face. She looks at Celeste. Celeste then sits down and sticks her lip out.

"You could make it a little easier on me and just tell me what you want."

Celeste shakes her head "No."

Jacques moves close to them. "Ok, how about going fishing?"

They both make a face and shake their heads "No."

"How about going for a boat ride and going out to eat at a marina?"

They both shake their heads, "Yes" and get in the boat. Celeste looks up at Malynda and asks, "Momma, can I talk now?"

Jacques looks at Malynda. "Isn't she a little young to be learning that stuff?"

"It's never too early to teach her the way the world works."

Jacques laughs. "Let me get a tub of frozen bait—just in case. You get yours and Celeste's life vest on."

Malynda sits in the cushioned seat in front of the console and holds Celeste in her lap. Once they are situated, Jacques starts the motor, looks at the tachometer to make sure that it's running, and he casts off. They slowly motor through Bayou Loutre, past Shell Beach, and into the Ship Channel. As Jacques motors into the Ship Channel, he notes the time of 10:35. Jacques tells Celeste and Malynda to hold on, and he opens her up.

The motor cover project is one of Jacques more successful home projects. He has sound damping foam in a custom made motor cover and a muffler in the lower unit that makes the noisy outboard almost silent. At idle speed, the motor is difficult to hear. When it's opened up, just the vibration through the lower unit can be heard. It isn't perfect. The major drawback is giving up five mph because of the back pressure in the muffler. He considers the five mph well worth being able to hear the fiberglass hull cutting through the water.

It's a peaceful morning in the Ship Channel. The sun is up high in the sky. The Ship Channel has a three to six inch chop, which his boat cuts right through. He trims his motor out, and the GPS shows that he's making forty-two mph. He looks down at Celeste and Malynda and sees a true picture of happiness. He sees Celeste laughing and Malynda smiling. Their beautiful black hair is blowing in the wind, and their eyes are squinting to keep the wind out. Jacques trims the motor up a little more and bounces up and down to add a little more excitement for Celeste. She starts laughing every time the boat bounces. They motor eight miles up the Ship Channel when Jacques sees the Bayou Bienvenue Locks. He drives through them at a reduced speed. Once clear, he opens her up again. He sees the red reflector marking Eddie's canal and turns west into the smaller canal. Within a minute, he is at Mr. Eddie's boat launch. Jacques looks at his watch, which reads 10:50. He pulls up to the dock and ties off.

They get out of the boat and walk into the small building. Jacques opens the door and the girls walk in. Mr. Eddie looks puzzled when the girls walked in. As soon as Jacques walks in, Mr. Eddie smiles

"Jacques, where have you been my friend? You come in and take a load off." They have a Coke and some good conversation about the latest fishing hot spots and best baits. After they finish their Cokes, they walk outside with Mr. Eddie. Jacques questions him about an old wooden oyster lugger that is sitting up on fifty-five gallon drums. The vessel is forty-one feet long and is painted white. The booms and cables are rusted, and many of the boards are rotten. He moves a drum close to it where they can get in it and look around. Mr. Eddie stays behind. They climb on the deck and go into the aft mounted cabin. The cabin is in decent shape. The steering still has nylon rope to move the rudder, and the seats are nicely cushioned. Jacques looks over the roseau canes and sees the cars on Hwy. 47. He goes below and sees that the engines have been removed. They climb off the lugger and bid farewell to Mr. Eddie as they re-board his boat. Jacques starts her up and drives her to the nearby marina restaurant.

Jacques realizes that being seen in the marina restaurant is a real risk, but he figures it's the safest place to go and eat. It's a public place with plenty of people.

The boat's parked within twenty-five feet of the table and is visible to everyone in the restaurant. In fact, their whole path from the boat to the restaurant is clearly visible by everyone in the restaurant. As long as he does not repeat this same technique of going out to eat, he convinces himself that it should be all right.

He pulls up to the restaurant bulkhead and ties off to the dock cleat using a single side cleat on the boat. They take their life vests off and walk to the restaurant. Jacques opens the glass doors for the girls and follows them in. The hostess greets them with a smile and shows them to their table. They sit down and order drinks. Jacques scans the restaurant and sees two deputies having lunch a couple of tables in front of them. One is about twenty-five years old, and the other looks like he's just out of high school. He realizes the one scenario that he isn't prepared for. If the police are involved or if there's an arrest warrant out on them, the police can easily take them away. Jacques totally ignores them. The waitress returns with the drinks and takes their order. Celeste has a grilled cheese sandwich. Malynda orders the trout almondine. Jacques orders the seafood platter. Within a few minutes, the food is on the table, and they begin eating.

The two deputies finish their meal before Jacques' party is halfway through. They get up and walk straight to Jacques' table. They approach from behind Malynda. They surprise Malynda, and she jumps. Jacques immediately starts laughing, and Celeste laughs too. The deputies apologize. Jacques can see the fear build on Malynda's face. She too now realizes the danger they can be in.

Jacques looks at Malynda, "Honey, you sure are jumpy today."

The deputies laugh, "What's that thing on you motor? Is it some sort of super charger?"

"No, it is just an extra sound barrier. You know how noisy those outboards can be."

"Hey, that's a good idea. Y'all have a good day, and sorry about scaring you Miss." Malynda laughs, and they walk away.

As soon as they walk out the door, Malynda asks Jacques, "Do you think that they might be trouble?"

"If you would stop staring at them, they probably won't be. Let's finish eating and get ready to make a fast exit."

"Jacques, they are just sitting in their car."

"I told you to stop staring at them. Look at me, and forget about them. They're probably looking for us to do something suspicious—like hurrying up and leave, acting real nervous, or keep staring at them. Just sit back and enjoy your meal. Remember, we came by boat. In order for them to follow us they will have to get a boat or helicopter. Either one is probably at least 15 minutes away.

We are just 5 minutes from finishing our meal. So, relax and enjoy." The deputy's car drives off. Malynda sighs, "What a relief! They finally left."

"Don't go get excited yet. They might have left, but they might not be far. They also might have called someone else." Jacques looks at Celeste. "How about some ice-cream?"

Celeste just shakes her head, "Yes."

A few minutes later, the deputy's car returns in the parking lot, and a nervous look comes over Malynda.

"They are back. What are we going to do?"

Jacques tries to calm Malynda down. "Relax, they wanted to see if we were going to run off. Once they see that we are still here, they'll go about their business."

Sure enough, they just pull up to the restaurant and drive away.

"Now, let's pay the bill and get out of here." Jacques pays the bill and walks out.

While they are boarding the boat, Malynda asks Jacques, "Do you think they recognized us?"

"I'm not sure if they knew, but something made them suspicious of us. Let's face it, they came back to check us out. Let's not hang around to find out."

Jacques starts the motor. Once Malynda and Celeste are settled in, he casts off and motors away. Before long, they are running wide open again. Jacques, being a little paranoid, takes the long way home.

He leans over the console "Hey you two, how would you like some fresh trout for tonight's dinner? Instead of taking the Ship Channel back to Bayou Loutre, Jacques heads north in the Intercoastal Waterway. They stop at Chef Pass and try their luck.

"Nothing's biting here. I got a good idea." He looks at Celeste raising his eyebrows. "How would you like to go to a beach?"

She looks at her mother, "Momma?"

"That sounds like a good idea. Let's go."

They reel in their lines and put their rods in the holders. Jacques starts the motor, and they're off again. They continue up the Intercoastal Waterway, crosses the Rigolets, heads into the West Pearl River, crosses over to the East Pearl, and continue upstream to a large sand bar.

Once there, Jacques runs the boat up on the sand bar and sets the anchor on the beach. He sets the canopy up for Malynda, and Malynda objects. "The sun will be good for me."

"Malynda, I'm going to take my time going back to the camp. You are going to have to last all day. I really wish that you would try to take a nap."

Jacques digs a trenching tool out of the console and gets out of the boat with Celeste.

"Come on Celeste. We're going to build a sand castle."

Jacques and Celeste play on the beach for two hours. When Jacques returns with Celeste, Malynda is sound asleep in the shade on the floorboard. When they climb back aboard, they wake her.

Malynda jumps up. "What time is it? How long have I been sleeping?"

"Wake up sleepy-head. It's three-thirty, and the tide is just starting to fall. We better hurry up to make it to my favorite fishing spot."

Jacques prepares the boat while Malynda dusts the sand off of Celeste.

"Malynda, do you still remember how to operate a boat?"

"Of Course."

"Good, you get to drive us home."

Malynda gets behind the wheel and turns the key. She waits a few seconds and turns the key again. The motor makes an ugly noise because it's already running. Malynda cringes, and Jacques gives her a stern look. She puts it in gear, and they motor down the East Pearl River. Jacques is impressed. Malynda feathers her out just right—just to the edge of being dancey. When they reach the mouth of the Pearl, Jacques sits Celeste down and moves behind the console. He punches into the GPS go to way point No. 13. The GPS gives a compass bearing of 128 degrees and a distance to go of 11.7 miles. Lake Borgne is a little choppy, which is normally the case. It's a big body of water with the average depth of 9 feet. Malynda trims the motor down a little bit more to make the boat bite into the waves instead of bouncing over them. Making the bearing adjustments takes her a little time to master. Before long, she's adjusting throttle, trim, and bearing just a well as Jacques can. Twenty minutes later, they arrive on the south shore of Lake Borgne. Their path leads them right to the mouth of a small trenasse that opens into a small five foot deep bay. Jacques directs her to the east side of the trenasse, and tells her to kill the motor. She does, and Jacques drops the anchor. Once the anchor grabs, Jacques lets out another ten foot of rope and ties it off to one of the front cleats.

The water is swiftly rushing through the trenasse from Bay Boudreau to Lake Borgne. Once the water makes it out of the trenasse, its velocity slows. The trenasses act as funnels. They take a large amount of water, which carries bait, from the bay to the larger body of water. The fish feast just as the water slows. Bait fish are popping the surface of the water. Jacques picks up a pole with a florescent green sparkle beetle, a piece of shrimp, and an egg shaped cork. He sets the bait eighteen inches below the cork. He tests the backlash setting, and hands the pole to Malynda. Malynda goes right up on the bow platform and casts right in front of a swirl. Jacques grabs the second pole and starts to set it up for Celeste when he hears the drag take off on Malynda's pole. He looks up at Malynda. He thinks to himself that she knows exactly what to do—keeping the rod tip high, tension on the line, smoothly reeling it in. Jacques grabs the net and lowers it into the water right along side of the boat. Malynda expertly guides the fish into the net. Jacques picks the fish out of the water. It's a three pound speckle trout. Jacques takes the fish off the hook and re-baits the line for her. He gets the live well running and puts the fish in it. Before he can wipe his hands off, Malynda has another speck about the same size as the first.

Malynda shouts, "Jacques, one day I'm going to teach you how to fish."

Celeste starts laughing at Jacques.

"Oh yeah, one day I'm going to teach you to take your own fish off and bait your own hook."

Malynda laughs, "I'll hook them and cook them. You bait, un-hook, and clean them."

Malynda throws the line out again. This time it sits a while, which gives Jacques enough time to set up Celeste's pole. Jacques sits on an ice chest on the rear deck with Celeste in his lap. He casts out Celeste's line, pops the cork a couple of times, and the cork goes under. Jacques sets the hook and lets Celeste reel it in. Meanwhile, Malynda sets the hook on another fish too. Jacques helps Celeste get hers in and then nets Malynda's. Jacques baits the hooks again. Jacques is watching both corks in the water then he looks at Malynda.

She's just standing in the front of the boat working the lure. Her silhouette is just a beautiful as can be. The sun is behind her giving her an angel like glow. For a second it's as if they are teenagers again. Her laughter and smile brings a sense of easiness and comfort that Jacques has been missing for some time. If there's a perfect woman, it has to be Malynda. Jacques just blissfully stares at her thinking about how his life could be with her. He looks off in the distance and sees thunder clouds building to the south.

"There is no sense you two getting wet. We have a meal. Let's pick-up and go."

Jacques picks up anchor, starts the boat, and motors through the trenasse. He navigates through Lake Eugene, Bayou Petre, and back into Bayou Loutre. He pulls up to his dock and ties off. Jacques is confident that he is not followed because there were just too many stops for a boat to follow them and the long trip took too much time to be followed by air. Being tracked by a satellite is the only worry he has. If they did, there is nothing he could do about it. Celeste is sleeping in Malynda's arms, and Malynda is also tired. Malynda carries Celeste across the street and into the camp. Jacques secures the boat, gathers the fish, and goes to the cleaning table on the back porch.

After Jacques finishes cleaning the fish, he walks in and sees Malynda and Celeste sleeping on the couch. He puts an afghan on them, puts the fish in the refrigerator, showers, and goes to sleep.

CHAPTER 23

▼

0330, Jacques walks up to Malynda, who is still sleeping on the couch. He's carrying his ruck sack on his shoulder. He kisses her on the forehead, and her eyes open.

"I may be a few days. If you need anything, don't hesitate to call Mrs. Melerine."

He walks out the door, loads into his truck and drives off.

0620 Jacques arrives in Houma and continues to the address on the mug pictures. It's a beat-up old house with a 1988 Buick Regal in the driveway. "This is not a car for someone in their early twenties." He drives to the second address. It's the second to last house on the end of a dead end street. Jacques drives to the end of the street and turns around. He stops across the street from the house and looks at his watch—0645. Jacques gets a great idea. He grabs his clipboard and a screwdriver from the toolbox. He gets out of his truck and appears to be checking the water meter of the neighbor across the street. He opens the meter cover, and writes down the meter reading, the license plate number and description of both of vehicles across the street. One is a nice red F150 truck, the other is a new maroon Lincoln Navigator with tinted windows. As luck has it, Cliff walks out of the house and gets in the truck. Jacques sizes Cliff to be five-ten tall but a hundred and ninety pounds. He plays it cool and waves to Cliff good morning. Cliff returns the wave as he climbs in his truck. He drops it in drive and burns the tires.

Jacques quickly puts the cover on the meter, jumps into his truck, and follows him. Cliff stops at Highway 659 and puts his right blinker on. Jacques stops five houses back and checks another water meter. Cliff pulls out into traffic. Jacques gets to the intersection just seconds after, but the traffic is bad. He can see Cliff slowly disappearing in front of him. Finally, he gets a break and pulls out. Several trucks and a school bus are in front of him, and he looses sight of the pick-up truck. Wishfully thinking, he continues along Hwy. 659 hoping to find him in a parking lot or down a side street. After a few miles, he becomes frustrated and gives up. "My first tail and I loose the subject within seconds. Great. Just Great."

He makes a loop to Hwy. 24 and pulls into the hole in the wall diner and begins to calm down. He realizes that he knows where the kid lives, and he'll get another chance. He sits in a booth, opens his file folder, and studies the aerial photo around Cliff's house. As Jacques eats breakfast, he starts scheming, "He is the second house from the dead end. The whole subdivision is surrounded by sugar cane. Cliff's street runs North from Hwy. 659 and is the main street of the subdivision. There's a dirt road or fire brake that runs perpendicular to Cliff's street in the cane field a hundred yards to the north of the end of Cliff's street. The dirt road intersects with another dirt road that accesses Hwy. 659. I can hide at the end of the street and take the pictures. I will need a telephoto lens and a place to hide my truck."

0900, Sue Rodred is sitting at her desk in the New Orleans Field Office in a white blouse and blue pants. She just receives the final e-mail with the subpoenaed phone numbers from Violet Johnson's phone.

"That's it, I've got them all. Now, I have a hundred pages of phone numbers, dates, and times. It's going to take forever to cross reference them."

She gets up, refreshes her coffee cup, and returns. She spreads the papers over her desk; and with color highlighters, she starts to group the phone numbers. After an hour into the exercise, she becomes bored and thinks about the weekend that she spent with Danny. She continues for another half hour and starts to daydream. She calls Danny.

"Danny, how are you doing?"

"Great Sue, extremely busy, but great. I hope you're not calling me for another weekend. I still feeling guilty from the last time. How's Harris treating you?"

"Harris is treating me pretty good. He brought me a cup of coffee the other day."

"Are you sure it's Harris and not an alien replacement?"

"It's him. In fact, I'm working on a top secret case with him right now."

"If it is not Harris, what's got you so bored?"

"What's that supposed to mean?"

"There are only two reasons, well three reasons you call me. The first is to blow steam about Harris. The second is when you are bored."

She laughs and in a playful tone, "How do you know it's not the third?"

"It hasn't been long enough for that."

She laughs out loud, spins her chair around, and pleads into the phone. "I need a man. I need you, Danny."

"Yeah, right. Like I said, why are you bored?"

"I'm buried in over a hundred pages of phone numbers that I need to sort through. I really hate this part of my job."

"That's only because you don't know how to do it. Do you have the numbers electronically?"

"Some of the companies sent hard copies due to the court order. Some sent electronic, but they are pdf format. You can't sort them."

"Scan the papers that are not electronic, and E-mail it all to me. I have programs to transfer that information to usable electronic format."

"That can take hours. I thought you said that you're busy."

"Something this simple I can do during my lunch hour."

"You're the best. The next weekend we get together will be my treat."

"Naw, I was treated enough last time."

"Was I that good?"

"Sue! Stop it! You're going to get me feeling all guilty again."

"Like I said you're not married yet."

"Just send me the files, and I'll talk to you later."

After breakfast, Jacques visits several pawn shops looking for a camera with a telephoto lens with no luck. He goes to the local Super-Mart, and he refuses to buy a $300 dollar camera and a $200 lens. Finally, he thinks of buying a disposable camera and shooting it through the spotting scope. It will be hard but saves him $500. He thinks to himself, "That takes care of the camera. Now what about the truck? What if I park it on side of the road with a For Sale sign in it?" He continues to the hardware section and buys two For Sale signs.

In the parking lot, he sits in his truck with the maps and the aerial photo. The map has a scale of 1" = 1320', but it does not show the cane field road. The aerial photo shows the cane field road, but does not have a scale. "Next time, I'll modify the scale of the aerial photo to match the map." He takes out his calculator and he scales a map template. He makes the necessary conversions and concludes that he has to go 385 yards west of the first intersection on the road then 110 yards on a bearing of 218° through the cane field. He makes notes in his shooter's log and puts the plan into action.

Jacques has some time to kill. So he drives by the hospital again and almost breaks his arm by patting himself on the back for a job well done. Along the way to Cliff's house, he takes pictures of some beautiful houses and beautiful oaks with his disposable camera.

He stops at a gas station and changes into his BDU's. He then drives to the entrance of the cane field road, turns his truck around, and parks it facing the highway. He grabs his ruck, puts the For Sale Signs up in the windows, and starts hiking northward. The road is clay mud that is a little over ankle deep, which makes for a long walk in the hot sun. The road is one bulldozer blade wide with a wall of eight foot tall sugar cane on each side of it. It is almost as if he is walking in a tunnel. On this day, the wind is blowing and the leaves of the cane are making a racket. He makes the west turn and starts counting paces. Just before he heads into the cane, he removes the extra ten pounds of clay mud from each of his boots; applies his face paint; hand paint; and mosquito repellent. The cane is thick and difficult to walk through. Once in the cane, his visibility is cut down to just inches. He keeps taking compass readings as he continues to fight through the cane. He comes to the edge of the cane field and gets his bearings. He winds up directly in line with the street. He stays two yards in the cane, and he shifts over to the east twenty feet to get a diagonal view of Cliff's house and to see around the dead end barricade. Once he has a good field of view, he eases back another three yards from the edge and lays down. He can see nothing. Using his rose bush trimmers, he crawls on his belly and cuts a shooting lane. He keeps all the cuttings to camouflage the entrance of the shooting lane and his equipment. He takes out his canteen, data book, camera, and spotting scope. After everything is in place, he views through the spotting scope, selects a few more reeds that has to be cut and cuts them. Looking towards the southwest, Jacques has a perfect view of the front of Cliff's house.

Jacques begins to glass the area. In front of him is a cut grass area that is fifty yards wide. The dead end street barricade is next, and Cliff's house is two houses in. He estimates the lots are ninety feet wide. Jacques looks at the fences. The neighbor to the north has a six foot wooden fence. Cliff has a four foot chain link fence that starts three feet behind the carport on one side. On the other, the fence comes all the way to the front of the house. Almost everyone else has six foot wooden fences.

Cliff's house is a small, single story house made with hardy siding that is painted light blue with pale yellow trim. Jacques estimates the house to be twenty-one hundred square feet. It has a carport on the north side where a Navigator is parked. He zooms in under the Navigator and in front of it he sees a cat food bowl with food and water. He then looks around for dogs and does not see any signs. To kill time, Jacques begins to range things and draws on his range card. It isn't very challenging because everything is so close and so uniform. Within a short time Jacques is bored and starts sketching pictures of Malynda and Celeste. The whole day the neighborhood is dead.

1300 Sue's at her desk and her phone rings. She looks at Danny's incoming number and answers it.

"Hey, Sue. I got what you needed, but it's in raw format. I need you to close all your applications because I'm going to link your machine to mine."

"Ok, all my applications are closed."

"Don't touch anything. Ok, here comes the phone numbers. I compiled all the incoming and outgoing phone numbers into this one file. How do you want them sorted?"

"I want only the phone calls a week before and a week after July 29th."

Sue watches the total number of pages decrease.

"Ok, Danny there are still too many numbers. Can you eliminate all the numbers that appear more than twenty times."

"Yeah, hold on." Within a few seconds the number of pages decreases again.

"Ok, it's getting better. Let's try for less than fifteen times." The pages reduce to ten. "Ok, let's save that file."

"Wait I need to put the associated names and addresses with the phone numbers. I saved the file in your network directory. Is that all you needed?"

"Let's try one more time within five days and see what happens." The pages reduce to one.

"Is that all you need?"

"Thanks, Danny."

"Wait, tell me about this top secret case you're working on."

"It's nothing much. An international terrorist named Leon Tibodaux is under investigation. Actually, it's pretty exciting. The CIA's involved. I met the scariest man of my life yesterday. It was just like a James Bond movie. I'm riding in the car with Harris. He pulls over and tells me to get in the back seat. When I do, this CIA agent wearing all black takes my gun away from me and shoves me in the back seat. He gets in the back seat himself, and Harris drives off. He fills me in on the case as we drive on. It was the neatest thing that ever happened to me."

"No way."

"Way!"

"You mean to tell me that you let someone take your gun away from you?"

"Well, maybe he didn't take away my gun. Maybe he just got in the back seat, but it was the neatest thing that ever happened to me."

"Sue, I don't know about that. I know a few CIA guys. They aren't very nice people."

"Are you kidding? He was great. My boring Satinito case now has a purpose. My life is great again."

"Sue calm down, things might not be so great."

"Quit worrying Danny, everything is ok."

"Sue, are you on a secure phone?"

"Yeah, why?"

"I want you to do me a favor. Listen to me very carefully. I want you to go and get a post office box. I don't care where, but somewhere in New Orleans. Tell me where it is and mail me a key. Memorize the address—never write it on anything except the envelope. And only do that right before you put it in the public mailbox. I want you to keep a diary. Don't put it on a computer—hand write it. I want you to put who you are meeting with, who you think is a suspect, who you think is working for you and against you. Everyday, I want you to mail it to your post office box."

Sue laughs. "Danny, you've been reading too many books lately."

"Sue please, I know these type of people. Will you do this one thing for me?"

"Sure, but I'll just be wasting my time. This guy just seemed like an everyday law enforcement person—just a little scarier than most."

"Please, for me."

"Ok, mother hen. If it will make you happy, I'll start today. I got to run."

Sue hangs up, prints the files, walks over to the shared network printer, picks up her papers and returns to her desk. She scans the phone numbers, and all of them are 985 area code. There are a few 504 area codes. "Hello Mr. 281 area code. Mr. Jacques Boudreaux, Houston, Texas. What were you doing calling Mrs. Johnson the day before the disappearance? You only called her one time and stayed on the phone for a little over two minutes. A little too long for a wrong number. I think that I need to pay you a little visit." She picks up the paper and walks to Harris' office. Harris is scanning the internet for vacation hideaways when she appears at the door. He quickly closes the website as she knocks on his door.

"Mr. Harris, I would like to question Mr. Jacques Boudreaux of a little town north of Houston, and get a search warrant for his house."

"What for?"

"I think that he is the one that has Mrs. Meyeaux."

"Let me see."

"Well, it's not much; but this phone record ties him to the social worker. That should be enough to bring him in for questioning."

"Ok, use the same ERT that you used at the hospital and fly out first thing tomorrow."

Sue rushes back to her desk and makes the necessary transportation arrangements and speaks to the local sheriff to tell him that she's coming in town and to a local judge to get the search warrant.

1325, in Jacques' hide, he records, the postman coming.

1335: a bleach blonde comes out of the Cliff's house to check the mail. She's maybe nineteen years old, five-two and maybe a ninety-five pounds. She's barefooted and is wearing a short, maroon, silk bathrobe. He locks the spotting scope focused on the mailbox and puts the camera behind it. When he thinks he has a good picture, he snaps it. He winds the camera and snaps it again. He pulls the camera away and looks through the spotting scope to verify it's still on target. It is. He watches her thumb through the envelopes before she starts walking back to the house. The wind blows up her robe, and Jacques can see that she isn't wearing anything under it. The peculiar thing is that she does not even try to cover up. She keeps going about her business like it never happened. He follows the girl back until she disappears behind the Navigator. He records the information in his data book.

1643, the back door opens, Jacques sees the girl's head over the Navigator's hood. She gets in it and drives off.

1655, she pulls back into the driveway. Jacques notices how disadvantaged he is because from his viewpoint he does not see her until she's turning into the driveway. She gets out and heads inside. This time Jacques barely gets a glimpse of her. "The Navigator obscures too much of my view. It sure is a nice vehicle though. How can these kids afford things like that?"

1710, Cliff pulls up into his driveway; and he backs out all the way to the dead end street sign. He's fifty yards away. Jacques quickly makes sure the scope is on low power, focuses, and puts the disposable camera behind the spotting scope. Cliff jumps out of the truck and jogs towards his house. Jacques can't keep up with the spotting scope and the camera. Before Jacques gets off a single picture, Cliff is out of sight behind the Navigator. Jacques becomes frustrated again saying to himself that there has to be a better way.

1900, the back door opens again. Jacques can see Cliff coming out and goes into the back yard. In less than five minutes, Cliff reappears with the lawn mower. He has no shirt and is wearing a pair of baggy shorts that hangs down so low that his boxers are showing. He proceeds to start the mower and begins to mow the grass. The first pass is away from Jacques. The next pass is towards Jacques. Jacques can see this kid is fairly well built, or at least he has a good six pack stomach. He went away again on another pass. Jacques sets up the spotting scope where he thinks that Cliff is going to turn. Puts the camera behind it and snaps the picture when he turns. He tries this several times, hoping to get a good picture. Cliff finishes cutting the grass in no time. He edges and begins to sweep up.

2000 the girl comes out. This time she's dressed to kill. She's wearing a bright blue glitter tube top, stretch mini skirt dress with six inch spike heels. Jacques drops the camera and is working the spotting scope. For such a skinny girl, she has a really big rack; and she fills out the dress. She walks up to Cliff, gives him a kiss, gets in the Navigator, and drives off. Cliff continues sweeping and puts the two bags of grass on the street for garbage pick-up. Jacques looks at Cliff's left hand, and he can't find a ring "Was he living with this girl or is he married to her? Awe, it doesn't matter. He's going to die anyway." After Cliff finishes, he starts walking to his truck pulling out his keys. Jacques quickly focuses on the door of the truck and puts the camera behind the spotting scope. Cliff continues toward the truck. When he gets to the truck, he stops. For some reason, he stares a few seconds directly at the opening of the shooting lane. It's perfect face shot, and Jacques snaps the picture. Cliff gets in his truck, pulls it in front of his house, gets out, and goes inside.

2135, it's dark and the streetlights come on. There's one right at the end of the street and another about one hundred and fifty yards away.

2300, Cliff takes out the trash. He's in a hurry for some reason. Probably, he's worried about missing a program.

2330, the lights in the house go off, which is a good possibility that is a TV program.

0355, the Navigator pulls up. She gets out and goes into the house.

0655, Cliff comes out of the house gets in his truck and drives off.

0900, Jacques is hungry and stinks after lying in a heavily fertilized field for almost twenty-four hours. He's ready to go, but he decides to stay until at least the postman comes.

1310, sure enough, the postman comes.

1320, the girl comes out again in the same robe. Jacques gets his eye candy for the day and leaves. When he returns to his truck, it's just the way he left it. He gets in it and drives home. He also finishes the roll of film by taking pictures of some scenic views along the highway. Three and a half hours later, he is pulling into his shell driveway in Hopedale.

Before Jacques gets out of his truck, Malynda is already standing on the front porch holding Celeste on her hip. Jacques grabs his gear bag and heads up the stairs. Malynda walks up to Jacques to greet him and quickly backs off, "You stink!" Celeste is holding her nose. "You look terrible!"

Jacques just smiles. "Yeah, ain't life great. Nothing that a little soap and water won't take care of."

"You should throw those clothes away and burn them. Then you should hose yourself down before coming in the house."

Jacques just goes inside and ignores her. He takes off his clothes, puts them in the washing machine, and jumps into the shower. Being clean shaven and bathed, Malynda finds Jacques more tolerable. She asks him if he's hungry and continues to make conversation. Jacques tells her all he wants is some rest. He goes into his room and goes to sleep. He wakes up later that night. Celeste is sleeping, and Malynda is sitting on the couch watching TV.

CHAPTER 24

▼

Tuesday, 0900: Sue pulls into the driveway of Jacques' Houston home with the two Evidence Response Team Members in her rent-a-car. Two deputy's cars are already parked in front of the house. A cowboy hat wearing, tobacco chewing, middle-aged deputy is sitting on the hood of his car in the front of the house. A young deputy in a cowboy hat is standing with his back leaning against the door of his detached garage watching the back door of the house. Sue tells one of the agents to cover the back door with the deputy. She walks across the lawn to the front door as the middle-aged deputy walks up to meet her. They knock, on the door and there's no answer.

The deputy says in a slow Texas drawl, "You know what Judge Grant said. We need to go to the place he works. If he's not there, then we'll see about the search warrant."

Frustrated, Sue pulls out her phone. "I bet he's not there. How about a phone call? Will a phone call make you happy?"

"Ms. Rodred getting all excited is not going to help anything. Judge Grant just wants to make sure you federal people don't go walking over people's constitutional rights. I suppose a phone will work. Let's give it a try."

While standing in the entranceway of Jacques' house, she dials a number and the receptionist answers. She asks for Jacques' superior and finds out that Jacques has been on a leave of absence since August eighth.

She hangs up and calls Judge Grant. "Judge, I'm calling about getting that search warrant for Mr. Boudreaux. I'm at the house and he has been missing since August eighth. May, I please have a search warrant?"

"Let me talk to the deputy."

She hands the phone to the deputy. She watches the deputy nodding his head as he looks at Sue.

"Ok Judge, I'll take care of that. Here, he wants to talk to you again." And he hands the phone back to Sue.

"Ms. Rodred, listen to the deputy. I don't want you going in and breaking up stuff or disrupting that house. You are not allowed to take anything out of the house until it's properly catalog. You and your people are to be escorted by a deputy at all times. That means you don't get all split up and do things you shouldn't be doing. I told the deputy that if you give him any trouble, he's to handcuff the lot of you and throw you into the county jail. Yours truly will preside over your case. Am I clear on that?"

"Crystal, Sir."

"Good. Let me talk to the deputy again."

The deputy nods his head a few more times and hangs up the phone. The deputy has a grin from ear to ear as he hands the phone back to Sue.

Sue gives him a look that would kill most men. "You know, Texas is no longer a Republic."

"Miss, that all depends on how big of a stick you're holding. Right now I have the bigger stick; and if I was you, I'd watch that little attitude of yours."

Sue doesn't want to get off on the wrong foot so she waits for awhile. "Are you going to break open the door?"

"Nope, got a locksmith coming. Judge Grant said don't break anything—that includes doors." Sue makes a frustrated face and spins around in a circle.

The locksmith, arrives, opens the door, picks up his tools, and starts to head back to his truck.

Sue stops him. "You wait right there, we might need you inside the house."

Sue pulls out her pistol, and the deputy laughs. "Miss if this guy wanted to kill us, he would have done it a long time ago. You can put it up. He ain't home." They walk into the house. Sue immediately heads for the master bedroom's walk-in closet with the middle-aged deputy, and the other investigators head for the kitchen. Sue calls out for the locksmith. "There's a gun safe in here I need opened." While Sue waits on the locksmith, she looks at the shooting jacket hanging across from the safe. She then looks at the square impressions left in the carpet by the ammo cans. The other investigators are going from one trash can to another and then through the desk in his office. The locksmith gets the safe open. Sue looks inside to see the safe is empty except for a box full of insurance papers. From there she goes into the bedroom, scans the area, and takes notes. She digs through the nightstands on each side of the bed and then through his dresser.

The other team goes into the garage, and Sue goes upstairs. Sue goes back into the bedroom, pulls a picture of Jacques and his wife off the wall, and hands it to the deputy. "Deputy, I need you to catalog this." Everyone meets back in the kitchen, and they sit down at the kitchen table. The middle-aged deputy opens up the refrigerator and pulls out a can of Coke for everyone. Sue gives him a confused look as he hands her a Coke.

"Miss, he ain't going to worry about a few Cokes."

Sue looks at her note pad and starts. "What do you two have?"

One of the agents responds. "Someone beat us here. There's not a piece of scratch paper in the whole house, no garbage, and no phone or address books."

"I thought the same thing when I went through the night stands. What about the computer in the office?"

"It's just the docking station. There was a laptop there, but who knows where it is now."

"Let's assume that someone beat us here and took all the information that we normally look for." She lays out the eight by ten photograph in the center of the table. "What else do we know about Mr. Boudreaux from this house?"

"He left in a hurry. Arm fulls of clothes are missing out of the closet and entire draws are empty in the dresser."

"The gun safe is empty and all his ammunition is gone too."

"By the tire marks in the garage, he has a boat. Wherever he went to, he brought it with him."

Sue picks up the picture. "I've seen you before. Now where?"

"He also has a wife and a daughter, but they didn't go with him. Other than that we don't have much."

Sue looks at the deputy, "Do you mind if I question a few of the neighbors?"

"As long as they are willing to talk to you, I don't see any harm."

Sue walks to the dining room that sits in front of the house. She slowly lifts one of the wooden slats of the blinds and scans outside. She looks diagonally across the street and sees the shades in a window of a house move. "There's the nosy neighbor that I need to question. Come on Deputy let's go question the neighbor over there."

They walk across the street, walk up to the front door and a dog behind the door starts barking its head off. They ring the doorbell. A middle-aged woman holding a Yorkshire Terrier answers the door.

Sue speaks over the dog barking. "Ma'am, I'm Special Agent Susan Rodred with the FBI. I would like to ask you a few questions."

"Is Jacques in some sort of trouble?"

"We don't know yet. Jacques left a few days ago. Do you know where he went?"

"No, he drove up one day got his boat and left in a hurry."

"Was his wife and his daughter with him?"

"No, his wife and his daughter were killed in a car crash about two years ago."

"Do you remember what day he left?"

"It was about a week and a half ago."

"Do you remember what day? Was it a Saturday or Sunday?"

"No, it was a weekday."

"Do you remember what day?"

"I can't be sure."

"Did you do anything else on that day—like go to the mall or to the grocery store?"

"Yeah, I bought a new water filter that day."

"Do you still have the receipt?"

"Wait right here, I'll see." She closes the door and walks away. She returns a short while later. "Here it is. Why?"

Sue looks at the date on the receipt. "The day after the escape. Mr. Boudreaux is our man. Thank you very much. Since Mr. Boudreaux left, did you see anyone else recently come to the house."

"Last night someone was there real late. It was about two a.m."

"Were you up at that hour?"

"No, Killer wakes me anytime a car door closes."

"Did you see anyone?"

"They pulled all the way back to the end of the driveway. It was dark back there, but I did see one man."

"Did he have long black hair?"

"No, not this guy. He was bald."

"Mr. Jones. Thank you very much for your help." As she walks back across the street, "Deputy, I think I have everything I need. Thanks for your help and please thank Judge Grant for me."

"You have a nice day and drive safely."

They get back into the rent-a-car and drive away. The two deputies lock the house back up and leave.

That afternoon, Sue walks back into her cubical and immediately starts researching Mr. Leon Thibidoux. As soon as she plugs in the name, his criminal record comes up on the screen. She prints out several pages, but nothing links him to terrorism. Her next task is to research a Mr. Jacques Boudreaux. She finds that he has no criminal record. She begins to think to herself. He has a shooting jacket. Many high power rifle competitors have a military record." She goes into the military records and types in Jacques' name. The screen comes up with a request for a user name and password. She types in her user name and password, and a message comes up on the screen "ACCESS DENIED." Nothing aggravates Sue more than being denied access.

She calls Danny. Danny is sitting back watching another computer program crash when the phone rings.

"Hey, Danny, I need access to a file. Can you help me out?"

"Sue you know you already have more access than you supposed to have."

"Come on can you help me?"

"No, not this time. If you're denied access, see Harris. I could loose my job on this. You really shouldn't be in files that you don't have access to. You could loose your job over this."

"Ok, Danny, enough with the lecture. Just forget I called." She hangs up on him.

Sue sits back and thinks. "The password has to be used by several people in the government. It has to be simple to remember. Federal Government. What is common knowledge of the federal government—the presidents and their birthdays? She starts out with a few presidents, and she tries Harry S. Truman as user name and May081884 for the password. Her screen opened the file of Jacques Boudreaux. A grin comes over her face as she pats herself on her back for breaking the code. She starts reading the information on the screen. Jacques Boudreaux, born 1964, Meraux, Louisiana, graduated from high school in 1982 with honors, received a Bachelor's of Science from Louisiana State University in 1987 in Mechanical Engineering.

Frank Harris walks by her cubical and stops. "Sue what did you find at Mr. Boudreaux's house?"

"Only what you wanted me to find."

"What do you mean?"

"You know what I mean. You told your friend Mr. Jones about Boudreaux didn't you?"

"He's our friend, and yes I did."

"Well, he got there the night before; and he cleaned out all the evidence that I would have found."

"I'm sure he has his reasons."

"I thought you said that we were going to work as a team. If you want me working as a team, we investigate together. You don't send him in the night before."

"Ok, I'll ask him to coordinate a little better with you next time. Let's go have a beer and talk about it."

"You just betrayed me, and you are asking me to go have a drink with you. What's the matter, your spooky friend can't meet me in the office?"

"Sue, just in case you don't realize it. You're flaring that little temper with me again. I expect you to behave more professional than that. Also, let me remind you that he's not supposed to be working inside of US borders."

"Mr. Harris, with all due respect, today at five o'clock I'm blowing the hinges off the door. I'm going home and then for a jog."

"Ok, Sue. Maybe we can talk tomorrow when you have calmed down."

Frank walks away with a smile on his face. Sue turns back to her computer and her screen is blank. She tries to wake it up and finds that it is locked up. She re-boots and tries to get back into the military database again. She punches in the user name and password again and the "ACCESS DENIED" message appears. She tries again with the same results. "Great, now they locked me out of the file. Ten minutes to five...close enough." She closes her laptop, organizes the papers on her desk, packs her things, and walks out.

2130: A compact car pulls into a parking space in front of a two-story town house. Sue Rodred gets out of the car wearing sweat soaked running shorts and an oversized tee shirt, and she walks towards the door. She's carrying a drive through salad in her left hand and her black patent leather purse in her right. She gets to the door, puts the purse under her right arm, and digs her keys out. She's feeling good about herself after her workout. She sticks the key in the lock, and she has a difficult time turning the dead bolt. She jiggles the key a little, and the lock turns. She walks into the dark apartment, and turns off the alarm. She drops the food bag on the nearby desk and reaches to turn on a light. Before her fingers reach the switch, a gloved hand roughly covers her mouth and grabs her nose. Before he can wrap her up with his other hand, she instinctively reaches in her purse, grabs the pistol, crosses her body with it, points the pistol and purse under her left arm pit, and pumps two .38 Special rounds into her assailant. He lets go of her mouth, reaches around her face, grabs a hand full of hair, and spins her out away from him. The purse falls to the floor while she spins out. He tries to close the distance as she tries to add distance. She performs a standard body armor drill by pumping another two rounds into his chest and starts to level on his head. As she's bringing around her support hand, he grabs the cylinder of the pistol with his left hand before she squeezes off the round. She tries to squeeze the trigger with both hands, but she can't. He accelerates his momentum towards her and hits in the center of her chest with the heel of his hand. He uses his momentum to lift her off of her feet and drives her into the wall. She hits the wall with such a force that her support hand comes off the pistol. Having the leverage advantage, he quickly takes the pistol out of her hand; and she slides down the wall into a sitting position with her legs straight out. He jumps on top of her with his full body weight and his right hand tightly gripping her throat. She opens her mouth to gasp for air. With his left hand, he cocks the hammer back, and shoves her pistol up to the cylinder into her mouth. The entire room is filled with dark objects and shadows, except for glowing of her oversized eyes. Tears run down the side of her face, and the sound of uncontrollable whimpers come from around the pistol. She can see the man wearing black that is on top of her is still trying to catch his breath. She can hear him breathing. She can feel the pain of his knee digging into her thigh. She can taste and smell the burnt gunpowder residue on the pistol, but she's totally paralyzed. She realizes what is happening to her. She tries to move her hands to push him off of her, but her eyes are the only things that are responding to her wishes. The man finally catches his breath.

"Today, you were digging in some files that you shouldn't have been. I'm here to politely ask you to stop. If I find out that you're digging in them again, I'm going to black bag you. Do you understand me?"

She remains stiff with fear.

"Little missy, I don't care what kind of case you're building against him. Take my advice. Drop it and destroy anything that is associated with him. Do you understand me"?"

She still can't move any part of her body.

"Just remember. If I catch you in Boudreaux's files again, you'll be dead within twenty-four hours. There is nowhere you can hide that I can't find you."

The confusion in her eyes is obvious to him—even in the dark.

"Just say our country owes him, and I even more than anyone else."

He moans as he stands up and grabs the left side of his chest. He looks at Sue, shakes his head, drops the pistol at her feet, and walks to the door with a limp. He opens it and peaks outside. Sue sees her cocked stainless steel revolver at her feet and knows that there is one round remaining. She wants to grab it, tries to grab it, but can't move. She begins to take mental notes of her assailant standing at the door, but can't concentrate. He steps out and closes the door behind him. After he leaves, she begins to cry out loud and pulls her knees to her chest. She kicks the pistol away from her and continues to cry while sitting against the wall rocking herself for a period of time. She looks up at her purse, scoots over to it, pulls out her phone, and calls Danny.

In an elegant Washington, D.C. restaurant, Danny is sitting across the table from his soon to be fiancée. She's in a cream colored evening gown, and he is wearing a black tuxedo. As the waiter is placing the entrees on the table, he feels for the ring in his coat pocket. His face glows as he pulls it out, ready to get down on one knee, and pop the question. His cell phone vibrates. He pulls it out of the belt holder, looks at the number, and puts it back.

His fiancée asks, "Who was that?"

"Oh, it's not important. I can take care of it later."

Two seconds later it vibrates again. He looks at the number at the number again and puts it back.

"Maybe you should answer it."

"It can wait. Right now I want to tell you what a wonderful night I have planned for the future Mrs. Merrit." He gets down on one knee, pulls out the ring, and places it on her finger. As he starts to propose, his pager vibrates. He glances at the number, and sees Sue's number with 911 extension behind it. "Excuse me honey, this is extremely important. I need to make a phone call. Go ahead and start eating. I'll be back in just a minute."

He walks outside, dials Sue's number, and she answers. "Sue, this is not good timing if you know what I mean. Quit playing around." He hears her crying on the other end. "Sue, is it you?"

"Yeah." And he hears her crying. He's never heard Sue cry before. It's not like her. It's not in her to cry. Extremely concerned, he asks, "What's wrong?"

"I need your help. I got involved in something that I don't know if I can get myself out of. Please come as soon as you can."

"What did you get involved in?"

"I'm afraid to tell you over the phone. In fact, I probably shouldn't have called you at all. I'm sorry Danny. Just forget that I called, and go back to doing whatever you were doing."

"Wait Sue, these are secured phones."

"Not to these people."

"Just stay where you are. I'll be there as fast as I can."

"No, Danny. Not this time." Danny hangs up, and he runs back to his awaiting fiancée. "We've got to go. Something really important has come up." He pays the bill and rushes out the restaurant. He hails a cab and puts his fiancée in. She notices that he doesn't get in."

"What's wrong honey?"

"It's Sue. She's in trouble." She makes a snotty face. "I love you more than life itself. She's a friend, and she's in some serious trouble. If you love me, you'll understand." He gives her a kiss, and hails another cab. He holds up his badge and pistol drawn, walks up to the driver's window, orders him to get over, and he climbs in behind the steering wheel.

"This is an emergency. Start the meter."

Danny races the cab through the streets of DC as he punches four numbers into his cell phone and puts it to his ear.

"Listing please."

"Andrews Air Force Base."

"The number is......"

"Andrews Air Force Base, how can I help you?"

"This is Daniel Merrit with the FBI, I want to speak to the general in charge. It's extremely important."

"Hold while I try that extension."

He holds as he hears the phone ring. "General, I have a Special Agent Daniel Merrit with the FBI on the line. He says it's important."

"Mr. Merrit, what can I do for you?"

"General. What is the fastest mode of transportation you have to get me to New Orleans?"

"New Orleans, you better have a charge code sonny."

"I do, you can pull it out of our budget. I just need to get to New Orleans and do it quickly."

"I just put two F-15's on the tarmac. They're fueled and ready to go. Where are you?"

"I'm just pulling up to the guard house now."

"I'll have some MP's come pick you up."

He gets out of the cab and pays the cabby. Within seconds, a jeep with two MP's speed up to the guard shack, pick him up, and drive him to a locker room. He is being fitted with a flight suit as he explains to the general what's going on."

"Hell, I thought you said you had a charge number. Dang it, charge this to training. Boy you owe me big time, you here that."

"Thank you general, and I won't forget it."

"Shut your ass up and get on that bird before I change my mind."

An hour and a half later in New Orleans, Danny stops at the police barricades, gets out the car in his olive drab flight suit, and runs with his pistol drawn. He flashes his badge as he runs by the police standoff. He opens the door to Sue's apartment, and finds her still crying on the floor shaking with fear. He runs to her and embraces her. Ten cops enter with their pistols drawn.

Danny screams at them. "She's FBI, relax."

They search the apartment. One of the cops picks up the pistol that is lying on the floor. He opens the cylinder.

"Four shots."

He walks over to Danny and Sue. "Someone has a lot of explaining to do."

Danny screams at him, "Back off."

"I'll back off, but I'm going to have to write a report on it and you."

Danny jumps into his face and pulls rank on him. "How would you like to spend the rest of your life getting out of one federal investigation after another? All I have to do is make one phone call, and I can have three of them waiting on your desk in the morning. Now, pack your stuff and leave. This ain't a freak show."

The cop stands down, rounds up his men, and leaves.

"Sue, what happened? What did this guy look like? Was he white, black? How tall was he?"

"Stop it, Danny. I don't want to go after this guy."

"Sue, look what he did to you. You can't let him get away."

"Danny, this guy is bad news. I hit him in the chest four times with "+P's," and he didn't even flinch. He just kept coming at me."

"So he had a bullet proof vest on."

"Danny, I knocked the wind out of him, but it had no effect. Trust me, just let him go."

"What is it all about?"

"It's about me digging into the files today."

"Leon Thibidoux must be a pretty important man. How many times have I told you that you could get in trouble getting into secure files? You used the Truman password, didn't you?" She nods her head. "Truman formed the CIA in 1947. I told you that they are not the type of people you fool around with."

Her crying slows down. "It isn't Thibidoux; it's Boudreaux."

"Who's Boudreaux?"

"He was on the phone list you sent me. He's an engineer in Houston, but he has or had something else going on. I don't even want to know."

"He's your prime suspect with the Meyeaux case, isn't he?"

"She would be in better hands with Satinito than these people. I'm just going to drop it and forget that I ever heard the name Jacques Boudreaux."

"Sue, you can't do that. You're an agent for the FBI. It's your job to solve this case."

"It's my job to stay alive. I'm writing Mrs. Meyeaux off."

"What are you going to tell Harris?"

"Nothing, I'll just pretend I'm still working on it. We'll find her body sooner or later."

"I can't believe you are saying this."

"Believe it, Danny. These people have more power than any mob. Just drop it. You were right. Do you hear me? Just drop it."

They remain sitting on the floor holding each other throughout the night.

CHAPTER 25

▼

Wednesday morning, Jacques is sitting at the kitchen table and is still troubled about his inability to follow Cliff.

Jacques calls Randy.

"Jacques, how's James Bond doing?"

"Randy, do you have some electronic tracking equipment?"

"If it's worth having, I have it."

"Great, I need something to track somebody."

"I've got these micro transmitters that you put on their clothes. They're great. Just pick a fight with whomever you want to track or hire a pretty girl. Stick the pin in their jacket, and they will never know. As long as you stay within a hundred yards, you won't loose them."

"Randy, it's summer time. Not too many people in New Orleans wear jackets during August. Besides, I need something that has a few miles of range."

"Fear not old timer. I've got just the thing—Doppler transmitters. They have a five-mile range and are the size of a pack of cigarettes. They come with a magnet. You just attach it to the inside fender well or bumper."

"Great, it's just what I'm looking for. How much?"

"Hold on, that's the good news. The bad news is that you need an antenna and a receiver. This antenna's huge. It's like a thirty-inch flying saucer. You need to mount in on a frame in the back of your truck. The receiver plugs into your cigarette lighter. You get anywhere close to them and they are going to know that they are being tracked."

"Don't worry about it. How much?"

"I'll loan it to you if you promise to return it to me in good condition."

"Since you're in a generous mood, do you have a good surveillance camera?"

"Only the best. It's got a two hundred to six hundred millimeter lens that operates in infrared mode or daylight mode. The only problem is that you need to buy some IR film for the infrared mode if you want your pictures to come out right."

"Do you mind if I borrow it?"

"No, problem. I've got a back up."

"Ok, if I break it, I'll buy you a new one. Just mail it to the same address as before."

"It's on its way. Hey, one other thing, undo your dome light if you're thinking about doing surveillance. The little nasty light will give you away every time. What about the Virginia match?"

"Sorry Randy, don't look like that I'm going to make that one."

"Are you doing any shooting?"

"Always."

"Jacques, there'll be other matches. Take care of yourself."

"You too." They both hang up.

That afternoon, Jacques is paddling his pirogue in Bayou Loutre back to his camp. Celeste is in the front seat enjoying her daily boat ride. Jacques can see Malynda anxiously waiting on the pier. He gets closer and can see the Melerines under their camp. "Oh, no there is Père Andrew digging a fishing pole and ice chest out of the bed of his pick-up truck."

Celeste points with her finger and laughs. "Jacques, there's Father Andrew. He's as big as Santa Clause, and he talks so funny."

"I know." Jacques paddles to the pier.

"Bonjour, Jacques. Remember, I said you need purpose in your life. Today, you take Old Père fishing."

"Ok, Père. I'll take you fishing. Just let me get the pirogue out of the water."

"No, we take da pirogue today. I watch you nearly everyday paddling dis bayou with no purpose. Today, I give you purpose. Come on, Jacques, I teach you where to catch da fish."

Malynda quickly helps Celeste out of the pirogue while she laughs and shakes her head. "Don't look at me. It's his idea."

"Père, I'm not sure this pirogue can hold the both of us."

"Da pirogue, she be fine." Père hands Jacques the ice chest, which he puts behind him.

Jacques objects. "Wait, where's my pole? More importantly, where's your paddle."

"You not need a pole, and me, I not need a paddle. Come on Jacques hold the boat steady while I get in."

As Père gets in, the pirogue takes on about an inch of water. Père settles in his seat.

"Come on, Jacques, I want to get to the far side of Hopedale Lagoon. You need to get a move on if we going to catch a limit of fish before dark."

Jacques starts to paddle away as Père sits in the front like a captain. He waves to Malynda and Celeste. "Malynda, you fix up some fish fry. I show Jacques how to catch fish. We going to bring back beaucoup trout."

Malynda has a smile ear to ear, as she waves back, "No problem, Père. We'll have fish tonight."

Jacques gets to the mouth of Hopedale Lagoon and starts to cross the almost mile of twelve to eighteen inches of water. "Jacques, Old Père, he working up a sweat. You reach in dat ice chest and hand me a beer. You get yourself one too. We have a good time today you see. We have some time to tell some stories."

"Not much to say, Père."

"Melerine, he says dat you've been practicing twice a week, and you driving Malynda crazy wit shooting dat empty rifle at night. You drive all da way to Pascagoula to shoot a rifle. Why you do dat when you can shoot right here?"

Jacques is relieved that he wants to talk about shooting instead of moving back down to Hopedale. "It's the closest thousand yard range, Père. I need to be positive that my rifle is going to do what it's supposed to do."

"How you say you need practice? You shoot plenty good. What's da matter? Why so much practice? You don't know dat rifle by now."

"No Père, I know the rifle real well." Jacques reaches into his back pocket and pulls out his data card. "Here. Look on that card. That data took me years shooting in different conditions to develop. The data printed on that card is exactly what the rifle is going to do."

"You slow down. Come on, you can paddle while you talk."

"All right. The reason that I practice is to gain confidence in my wind estimation and guessing that nasty mirage that we have down here in the one hundred degree plus temperatures with one hundred percent humidity."

"Mirage, qu'est-ce que c'est?"

"Mirage is the bending of light due to the heat waves rising from the surface of the earth. When people look at an object in the distance, they are actually seeing the reflection of that object—not the object itself. The heat waves with the wind moves that image off the real object. Take that pipeline sign that is about eight hundred yards off. Today, we have a ten-mph wind blowing about forty-five degrees towards us and to the right, high temperature and high humidity. The real object is eighteen inches left and six inches high of the image you see because the wind is blowing the image to the right and down."

Père laughs. "I t'ink you done suck down too much beer. Eighteen inches—so what. I still hit the sign if I aim at it."

"The sign is eight feet wide. The average person is only twenty-three inches wide. That's less than twelve inches on each side of center of mass. You would miss a person. If you had the windage right, you could gut shoot them. It's a horrible way for a person to die."

"I can't believe dat."

"I'll show you one day. The most important reason that I'm practicing is I want to be confident that when I squeeze that trigger I know where the point of impact is before the bullet gets there. The only way to get that confidence is to get out to the rifle range and get out there often."

"Ok, Jacques. We here. Tie us off." Jacques pushes the paddle into the mud and ties off the pirogue to it. "You sit back, sip on dat beer, and Old Père will load up dis boat up until it sinks." Père baits his hook and throws out his line.

"Jacques not too many people know about this deep hole on the other side of Hopedale Lagoon. I take people here when I want a captive audience."

"Oh, no. Here it comes."

"Yep, dis is da perfect spot for a long sermon. Da water is only a foot deep, which is too shallow to swim back. Da gumbo mud bottom is like quicksand so you can't walk. Yep, you stuck with Old Père for a spell." Jacques thinks to himself that it's useless complaining. "Jacques today I start my sermon about that beautiful girl that the Lord put into your life. Then, I'm going to talk about your near future. Then, I try to convince you what's important in life. Ha! I got one." He pulls it in and throws it back to Jacques.

"Père, it's too small. I'm throwing it back."

"Jacques, you do no such t'ing. You put it in da ice chest."

"It looks like I'm going to be busy catching da fish. I think dat I change the order of my sermon. You tell me dat I know nothing about money. I tell you dat you no nothing about life. Before you decided to help Malynda, when's da last time you had an adventure? I didn't here you."

"I'm thinking."

"Go ahead and think."

"Ok, about two months ago, I helped pull someone out of a wrecked car."

"Was da car on fire?"

"Nope, but I could have saved someone's life."

"Don't count. You can't call it an adventure unless you risk harm to yourself. Let me ask you, do you do da things you want to do or are you doing what everyone else wants you to do? Do you get up early, come home late, and not spend anytime on da things you want to spend time on?"

"I have bills to pay. In order to pay the bills, I need to work."

"Cooyon, you are a slave to your style of living. You give up life itself to pay da bills. Ha! Old Père, he's got another one." He reels it in and throws it back to Jacques to take the hook out.

"Well Père, you're getting closer to being legal."

"Mon amie, you just put it in da chest. Jacques, I can see how much you enjoy dis place. It provides life to you. I want you to seriously consider moving back. Enough wit dat. Now, we talk about Malynda. Malynda, she seems like a real nice girl, and she can cook too. You ever thought dat God put her here to add purpose to your life. He seems to be fulfilling your need for adventure. Maybe, He provide you a good wife too, but she says dat you don't spend too much time wit her."

Jacques pulls out two more beers, opens them both, and hands Père one. "Père, don't go planning a wedding. I don't want to become too attached to her. To be honest, I don't think she's going to have a long life span. The people that abused her tried to kill her. They are some real professionals. Eventually, they will have another opportunity. I can only hide her for so long."

"Weh, you probably right. I'm sure dat you think da answer is in dat rifle of yours."

"Père, can you think of any other way?"

"Can't say dat I can. But you remember what happened after Colombia. For some people, it takes time to get over these ugly things."

"Père, it wasn't the killing that bothered me. It's not knowing whether I was working for the right side or not. I was young and stupid. I was looking at a free ticket to college. At the time, I thought that I was working for the government. Now, I'm not sure whom I was working for. I could have been working for the drug dealers themselves. I still don't know. This time I know which side I'm on."

"Do you really? I like Malynda. I think dat she's a wonderful girl, but you need to think how long it's been since you last saw her. Sometimes, people dey change, and sometimes dey don't. How can you ever be sure? It seem to me dat if dey wanted her dead, dey could have easily done it. Ha! Dis is going to be da last one." He reels another trout in and throws it over his shoulder. Jacques unhooks it.

"Wait a minute, Père. Just a second ago, you were trying to marry her to me. I'm not positive which side she's on, but I am sure the people I'm hunting tried to kill her." Jacques throws the fish in the ice chest. "Père, that's twenty-five fish and only one is a keeper."

"You put dat one in there wit da others. Dey all keepers. Come on let's get back before it gets dark." Jacques unties the paddle and starts back. Père continues his lecture. "Jacques, I can't tell you what to do with Malynda." Père laughs. "If God gives you something, it would be a shame to turn it down—like these fish. If she turns to be on da right side, it would be a sin letting her get away. How much time before it starts?"

"What do you mean?"

"Old Père, he's no fool. Me and Melerine, we see what you doing. First, you booby trap your camp. Second, you fix that old trapper's plank behind Bayou Loutre. Da only t'ing is da walkway no longer goes into da swamp. It now cuts out da bend in Bayou Loutre and da highway. It's a straight shot through da marsh. You cut off da mile by road to a little over two hundred yards. Da little dock you built looks more like a shooting platform. Amazingly you can see da bridge from da platform. How far would you say da platform is away from da bridge? Say seven hundred yards."

"Six hundred and twenty yards."

"Ha! Old Père, he not so stupid is he? Third, every day you go out to catch shrimp, but you try a different spot every time you go. You're relearning da marsh, and using Melerine's skiff to do it."

"I bring back more than almost all the other shrimpers. I pay for all the fuel and give Mr. Melerine all the money for the shrimp."

"You no dummy, Jacques, neither is Old Père. You have your honey holes, and dis year is a good year for shrimp. You hit your holes first light and fill da boat box. Den you take a boat ride. You're not doing it any more. Dat tells me you learned everything you wanted to.

"That skiff is perfect for shallow water exploring."

"I know how many times you put da game warden on dem mud flats. Now, you feel pretty safe. Your house is secured. You control da road and da bridge. You have your escape route or attack routes planned. You are ready for da ugly stuff. When is it going to start?"

"In a week or two. Listen, Père, these are some pretty bad people that I'm up against. If anything should happen to me, I want you to make sure that Malynda is taken care of."

"Jacques, if you make a comment like dat, you need to make a better plan. You keep making da plan until you don't need to make dat comment."

"Père, I'm going to take them when I want to and where I want. I pick the time and the place. I'm strictly offense. If I think that I'll need to go on defense, I just wait for another opportunity."

"Jacques, how much does Malynda know? Does she know what you are planning on doing?"

"She knows something is going to happen. I'm not sure she knows exactly what though."

"Maybe it's better you keep it dat way. Sometimes women, dey don't understand da way of da world."

"Père, how do you view me killing?"

"Jacques, dat's a difficult subject. You have to determine dat for yourself. You were brought up right. You only kill for food and survival. You live by those rules, and you sleep good at night. If you kill for any other reason, you don't sleep so good. Ah, we finally made it to Bayou Loutre. It's not far now.

As Jacques paddles down Bayou Loutre, Père is waving to all the people on the porches. They laugh and wave back. They pass a docked crew boat. There's an overweight forty-year-old man wearing a polo shirt and blue jeans standing on the bow. His skin is tanned like leather, and he has dark greasy unkempt black hair and wild beard. Père Andrew screams to him. "Johnny, you come to Jacques' and have some fish tonight."

Johnny laughs. "No thanks, Père. I don't feel like cooking for you tonight."

"We let Jacques' girlfriend cook for you. She can cook almost as good as your Aunt Jean."

"Jacques found a woman that can cook as good as Aunt Jean. I'm getting cleaned up, and I'll see y'all in half an hour."

They pull up to the dock, and Père almost flips the pirogue when he tries to get out.

"Jacques, you clean da fish, and we have fried fish tonight. Don't waste no time. Johnny will be here shortly."

Jacques watches Père walk across the street empty handed. Jacques pulls up the pirogue, empties it, and carries the ice chest to the back porch. While Jacques cleans the fish, he can hear Père inside bragging about how good of a fisherman his is. Malynda pokes her head outside. "Jacques the grease is hot. Do you have anything I can start with?" Jacques hands her a plate of fillets, and she walks back inside with them. He hurries with the last few fish and cleans his mess. He walks through the back door just as Mr. Melerine is letting Johnny in the front door.

The six adults sit at the table and Celeste sits in her mother's lap. Père says grace, and they eat. Near the end of the meal, Jacques notices that Johnny keeps staring at Malynda's chest; and Jacques makes a face at him.

"Malynda, is that the crucifix that Jacques gave you?"

"Yep, he gave it to me on my sixteenth birthday. I've been wearing it ever since."

"You know that I picked it out for Jacques."

Jacques laughs. "You're lying, Johnny."

"Ok, but I was with him."

Malynda asks, "Johnny, how long have you known Jacques?"

"Since we were twelve. Man, I can tell you some stories about this guy. We were running the swamp with flat boats long before we could drive."

Mrs. Melerine stops Johnny. "Your stories are going to have to wait until we clear the table and start da card game."

Mr. Melerine and Père go out on the front porch to smoke a cigarette. Everyone else pitches in and cleans the dishes in no time. Mrs. Melerine grabs the deck of cards and a margarine container full of nickels and quarters. Père and Mr. Melerine come back in. They play Booray, and Johnny tells wild stories of Jacques' younger days. 2200 everyone has had their full of laughter for the night and bid good night.

As soon as everyone leaves, Malynda takes a shower and goes to bed. Jacques tucks her in and goes to bed himself.

2200 in the suite of Satinito's Casino, all the members of Satinito's bunch are present, except for Mike. They are standing about in a festive mood wearing casual attire holding a drink in their hand. The suite is set up for a party with silver trays of hors d'oeuvres and food. Party music is blaring out of the stereo system. Joe is talking to Satinito, and Cliff is talking to Tony.

"Mr. Satinito, I still don't trust Harris. He's a huge liability."

"Joe, relax. Everything is under control. We're in a stalemate. We have equal power over each other. He can't do anything to me, and I can't do anything to him. He's a partner."

"He can still make off with a night's take and disappear. I want to move the collection spot."

"No doing, the spot is perfect. I tell you what, if you are nervous about Harris, I'll make sure he is here with me on collection night. He won't pull anything knowing he's within my arms reach."

"Mr. Satinito, what about the girl?"

"What about the girl?"

"She saw us."

"So what. She saw you. We haven't heard from her in nine or ten days. She's either dead, or she's doing the smart thing—hiding and keeping her mouth shut. Give Malynda credit, Joe. She's no dummy."

"Mr. Satinito, sooner or later, she's going to come out of hiding."

"I know. Where do you think is the first place she's going to go? Here Joe. Within a month, she's going to call me and ask me to pick up her and her daughter. I'm willing to bet this whole casino on it."

"You sound pretty confident. What makes you so sure that she's going to call you."

"She'll do anything to keep herself and her daughter alive. Sooner or later she's going to realize that she's going to have to contact me to ensure that. She's going to want to make a deal."

"No, I mean you sounded confident within a month."

"Malynda's a junky and is going to need her fix. Who is she going to call to get that fix? Me that's who."

Joe laughs. "Mr. Satinito, what are you talking about? Malynda don't do drugs."

"Are you kidding? She's one of the biggest junkies I know. She's not a drug addict, but she's a junky just the same. Her drug of choice is her expensive lifestyle. It's more addictive than any drug on the street, and it has been ripped away from her. She'll fight it for a while, but in the end she'll find out that she can't live without it. When the realization sets in, that's when she's going to call me. You see everything is under control. So, relax while I get this party started."

Satinito turns down the volume, walks over to Cliff, and hands him a credit card style key. His speech is a little slurred. "Cliff, welcome to my Mead Hall. Here's your key to a new way of life. A long time ago a group of men—no an entire culture of men—knew how to live. They were the Vikings. They would host large parties before important events, and they would host large parties after important events. Come to think about it, they would host large parties all the time." Everyone laughs. "They believed that they were all going to hell in the after life. So they partied their asses off in the present life. I've adopted their motto—Live for today because there's no tomorrow. We follow the customs of the Vikings. This is our Mead Hall. We have eight suites. Since you are the last man on the food chain, your suite is 605. We also follow another important Viking custom. The warriors, who we are, had wives and slaves. The wives were for providing children and a good home. The slaves were for pure sexual enjoyment. Oh sure, they waited on the warriors hand and foot, but we all know it was just to throw off the wives. What they really wanted was a good piece of ass." The main double door opened and six giggling and screaming barely dressed women come running in with Mike behind them. Satinito with a woman on each arm screams over the noise. "Cliff, meet the slaves." The music is turned back up, and they party.

Two hours later, Cliff sees the shirtless Tony walking off to take a leak. He walks up to Tony's girl that is totally naked and hands her two black temporary tattoos.

"Do you want to really turn Tony on?"

"I'm doing a good job of it right now. Why?"

"When you and he are alone tonight, surprise him. Put one of these on right under you bellybutton and the other in the small of your back. He told me that it drives him wild."

She looks at them with a puzzled look. "It's the number '2'." She giggles. "Ok." She starts to lick the temporary tattoo.

Cliff stops her. "Tony thinks it's weird. He don't want anyone else to know about it. You'll ruin it for him if you do it now."

"Ok." She walks over to her purse and puts them in it.

Mike grabs Cliff by the shoulder.

"What was that all about?"

"A little present for Tony."

"Tony don't like surprises. I hope you know what you're doing."

"Oh, he is going to like this one."

"Cliff, did I do a good job picking out your girl? I mean the live-in I got you is hard to top."

"Man, you did great. Big and plastic, just the way I like them. Mike, you did great."

Mike slaps him on the back and laughs. "I told you I could make a good match maker."

"I better get back to my girl. At the rate she's going, she's going to be so stoned that she'll be useless tonight."

The party continues for hours, and they break off and go to their separate rooms.

Cliff's date is stoned beyond belief, and he has a problem rushing her down to the end of the hall. Cliff watches Tony disappear into his room, and Cliff fumbles with the key to open his own. As soon as Cliff gets the door open, he runs into the bathroom and puts a black number "2" on each cheek of his face. He walks back out into the living room, locks the entrance door, then grabs the girl, runs into the bedroom, and locks the bedroom door.

The girl looks at his face with the twos on it. She giggles. "You're weird"

He laughs. "I have my reasons. It's going to be great. Go sit at the head of the bed and wait." Cliff turns on all the lights, places a lounge chair ten feet away from the bedroom door, and sits in it facing the door. The girl comes to him and kneels between his knees and starts unzipping his pants.

"No, believe me you are going to want to be over there."

"Why? I want to be over here."

Cliff is laughing. "Just do what I tell you. Tony is going to bust that door down in a few seconds."

The girl does as she's told and quickly gets bored sitting in the bed by herself. Cliff listens to her complain for a little over ten minutes, and they hear a wild man screaming and running down the hallway. The girl shuts up, and they hear the entrance door being broken in. The girl grabs the sheets and pulls them up to her neck. Cliff's knuckles tighten up on the armrests as he tenses up to get ready for Tony's fury. The bedroom door and part of the frame are completely blown out of the wall. Tony is standing there naked with a stainless steel .44 magnum revolver. The girl pulls up the sheet above her head. Tony sees Cliff, puts the pistol in the other hand, flies across the room, grabs Cliff by the neck and launches him into the wall. He puts the revolver to Cliff's face and starts pulling the trigger. He sees the 2's on his cheeks, drops him, and backs off.

Cliff makes spooky ghost noises. He raises his arms and wiggles his fingers as he slowly walks forward.

"I'm the number two, Tony, and I'm going to get you."

Tony levels the pistol. "No! Back off man! I'll shoot you! I'm not screwing around!"

Joe with a white towel wrapped around his waist and a snub nose pistol in his hand runs into the room. "What's going on in here?"

Tony responds, "It's Cliff. He's messing with me. I'm going to kill him. You better find his replacement, because I'm going to kill the little bastard."

"Cliff, what did you do? Tony, put the gun down. Nobody is going to kill anybody." Joe steps over the door on the floor, and sees the 2's on Cliff's face. "That's far enough, Cliff. If I hear about you messing with Tony about the number two again, I'll put a bullet in you myself."

Satinito walks in wearing a robe. "Joe, What's going on?"

"Cliff played a practical joke on Tony."

Satinito holds his finger out to Cliff. "Youngster, you better mature quickly. This type of horseplay is for kids. In the business we're in, we can't afford to have immature kids around. Joe, make sure that this kid grows up tonight or is found dead in the morning."

Joe interjects. "Mr. Satinito, I'll handle it."

"Fine Joe, I'll trust your judgment." Mr. Satinito walks out of the room.

Joe looks at Tony. "Tony, go back to your room."

"Not with that bitch in there."

"Take Cliff's broad, and tell the other one to take a hike." He roughly grabs the girl by the hand and drags her out of the bed. He looks her over, turns her around and looks her over again. "Let me see the bottom of your feet." She shows him. He sees that she doesn't have any tattoos, grabs her by the hand, and roughly drags her out of the room behind him.

"Cliff, you're a good kid but not very smart. You made me look bad in front of the boss. We need to work as a team. You need to understand that. Right now, Tony could kill you. Don't smile, he still might. This is your last chance. You screw up one more time, and I'm going to turn you over to Tony just like I did with Billy. You are not going to screw up any more are you?"

"No, Sir."

"To make you respect Tony, you're going to be his partner. Starting tomorrow, wherever he goes, you go. If he kills you in the process, he'll save me the trouble."

Joe walks out the door and leaves Cliff alone in the room.

CHAPTER 26

▼

Thursday 0530, Malynda wakes and looks for Jacques. She searches the front yard and sees that his truck and boat are still there. She goes out on the back porch and sees Jacques sitting in a chair looking over the marsh with his spotting scope. He's making notes in his shooting data book."

"Morning wild man." Jacques laughs but doesn't take his eye away from the scope. "What are you looking at?"

Jacques looks for a few more seconds and makes another note. He stands up and makes a gesture for Malynda to sit in the chair. "Here take a look."

Malynda gets behind the scope and looks through it. "It's two hills out in the marsh."

"They're Indian Mounds."

"What? Indians built hills out in the marsh. What for?"

"That's where they buried their dead. Look how plain and perfectly round the tops are."

"What so special about them? Why are you looking at them? They just look like two hills in the swamp."

"They're the high ground. One day we might have to cross that swamp to escape. If there's a sniper out there, that's where he'll be. That's why I'm studying them. I want to know what those things look like in the morning, in the middle of the day, at dusk, and in the moonlight. Do you know how to walk the marsh?"

"Yeah, you put your feet on the grass clumps."

"What happens if your foot misses a grass clump?"

"You sink past your knees."

"How do you break the suction on your thigh?"

"You lay down and use the grass to pull yourself out."

"Not bad. I'm glad you know about these things. It's going to make it easier if we have to escape."

"Jacques, you're beginning to scare me."

"Don't worry. In the sniper world, preparation is the key to survival. In a sniper dual, the one who spots the other one first wins. I've studied and made notes of every likely place that a sniper could hide."

"Jacques, last night, was Johnny telling the truth about all those stories?"

"All except those about the women. They were lies—all of them."

Malynda jumps up and playfully starts pinching Jacques. "Sure they were. Come on in and get some breakfast."

Jacques puts the case on the spotting scope and pulls it away from the chair. "Malynda, I need to talk to you." Jacques motions to Malynda to sit back down. "I think that you better sit down. If you are up to it, I would like for you to look at a picture. Do you think you can do it?"

She shakes her head, "Yes."

Jacques pulls the close-up of Cliff out of his pocket and hands it to Malynda. "Is this the guy that raped you?"

Tears start coming from Malynda's eyes. She nods her head up and down. "He's the one. I'm sure of it."

"Are you positive?"

She screams, "Yes, Jacques I'm positive. He's the one."

Jacques takes the picture from her and puts it back in his pocket. Malynda stands up, wraps her arms around his neck, and cries with her face in his chest. Jacques wraps his arms around Malynda's back and gives her a big squeeze. "Don't worry. He'll never hurt you again. It is going to be ok. Now, how about that breakfast?" They stand there for awhile holding each other, and then they walk in the camp.

0900, In Satinito's Casino Restaurant, Joe and Satinito are having breakfast together.

"Joe, so what have you decided to do with the kid?"

"I'm going to make him work with Tony for a while."

Satinito laughs, "The first time he screws up, Tony's going to kill him."

"Well, it will save me the trouble. Mr. Satinito, he's a really good kid. He's just a little young and has a lot of play in him."

"The decision is yours. Last night, I thought about what you said about Harris. Tonight, I want you to bring my nephew with you just in case."

"In case of what? If you think something is going to happen, we should move the collection spot."

"I'm not thinking anything is going to happen. I just think that he'll be good to have around. He's got one of those fancy sniper rifles. It's just added security, that's all. You should feel better knowing that someone is protecting your back."

"Maybe you're right. He did ok at the hospital, and we used him when we were dealing with new people."

"Good, I'll call him later today. Are you ready for tonight?"

"Everything's in place. We're not doing anything different than any other Thursday night. What about Harris?"

"Relax about Harris. I'll call Harris and make sure he shows up tonight."

They finish their meal and part their separate ways.

2000: Frank Harris is sitting on the couch alone in Satinito's Mead Hall. He hears the door latch turn, and Joe walks in with Mike.

As Joe walks to the bar, "Mr. Harris, turn on the TV. Switch it to channel one hundred fourteen."

Harris grabs the TV remote control and turns it on. The big screen is divided up into four panels of people gambling downstairs in the casino.

Joe laughs as he walks over to the bar. "Watching people throw their money away is more entertaining than anything the networks developed. We should tape it, put it on the air and call it—"Complete Idiots."

"Joe, where's Satinito?"

"He'll be up in a couple of minutes."

Before Joe fills his glass, there's a knock on the door. Mike opens it. Satinito walks in as usual with a woman on each arm. "Hello, Mr. Satinito."

"Hello, Mike." He winks at Mike. "Go downstairs and scare up some entertainment for our guest." Mike leaves the room. "Franky, how do you like what I've done to the Mead Hall?"

Harris makes eye motion to the women. "I told you never to use my real name in public."

"Relax, old boy. These girls hear nothing and see nothing. They're only here to entertain us. In their line of work, you get what you pay for. These girls are as expensive as they come, and they are worth every penny. To fully appreciate them, you need to spend a few days with them. They not only provide their normal prostitution services, but they provide companionship. Imagine having a woman 24/7, that enjoys doing everything you want her to do without you even asking her to do it. My life is great and these two beauties just make it better by the minute." The girls giggle. "Go get your sugar daddy a drink." They walk over to the bar, and Satinito sits in the lounge chair ninety degrees from Harris.

"Satinito, you double crossed me."

"Hey, double crossed are such strong words. The pictures are just an insurance policy. Now, we both have insurance policies. I don't like the look I just saw on your face. It said that you don't have the pictures."

Harris lies. "I have them. They're in safekeeping. Why don't you have yours?"

Satinito laughs, grabs the TV controls, and goes up one channel. All four panels are of Harris' sergeant. "Franky, what's this. We can't have a goon like that running around on the floor. He'll scare off all my business and make all my girls nervous. Invite him up. Let's face it; if you are worried that I'm going to do something to you, you would want him near you—not on the floor." Harris makes a face. "If you're not going to invite him up, then send him home. He's useless to you on the ground floor anyway."

Harris opens up his cell phone and calls his sergeant. They watch him answer it on the TV. "Sarge, this is Harris. Everything is ok. You can go home now." They watch the TV screen as the cameras follow him out into the parking lot, into his car, and off the property.

"Satinito, we still have a problem. Do you realize that Malynda Meyeaux is still alive? She could have evidence that can put you in jail for a long time. I know what kind of deal you could swing by fingering me. You're a huge liability to me."

"Like I said relax, I know this woman. She might even be dead by now."

"Listen to me, we need to find the girl."

"You mean with all of your resources you have at the FBI, you can't find her. I tell you what; you relax here for a few days. She will call me, I'll pick her up, dress her up, and hand her to you."

"What makes you so sure that she'll call you?"

"She has no one. Her family is dead. The rest of her relatives are in Quebec. She has never seen them. Do you understand that she's scared and alone? She can hide for a little while. Maybe stay with a friend for a little while, but eventually she'll feel desperate and call me."

"Satinito, I don't want to wait. I want to go to sleep and know my problem is solved. You know, friendship goes a long way down here. She could probably hide forever. Did you think about that?"

"I was just telling Joe last night, the woman has expensive taste. Just wait and see. She'll call. You got to give it some time. It has only been ten days. Even if she knows that she has the evidence, whom is she going to give it to? All the authorities are on the payroll, including you. Don't rule out, that someone else might want her dead too."

"Satinito, she's not dead. I think that you should take a couple of weeks off from the deliveries."

Satinito looks at Joe, "What's with you and Joe? You two need to understand that we are taking in between two and three million dollars a week. If we don't fill the need, someone else will. If that happens, we will have to either eliminate the competition or find new buyers. One is too much of a mess, and the other is too much work. Besides, do you realize if my boss starts asking questions and finds out about our little screw-up, we're all dead?"

"Can you at least change your pick-up days?"

"We have a smooth system in place. Nothing will happen."

There's a knock on the door. Joe lets Mike back in. He has two twenty-five-year-old, playful, giggling girls that are full of energy. They look like twins that just stepped out of the centerfold pages of Playboy. Their persona gives the impression that they know how to have a good time. They're wearing matching dark sequin purple micro-dresses that fit them like a tight pair of driving gloves. The dresses have a two-inch collar, no back, and a diamond cut out of the front to show their ample cleavage.

Satinito laughs as he sees Harris' jaw almost hit the floor. "Mike, I see you found the twins. Come on in girls."

Satinito looks at Harris. "This is my gift to you. Girls, this is my special friend (he winks at Harris)—Junior. I want you to take good care of him. Anything he wants, give it to him. Girls, he is a real tense guy. I want him leaving feeling like he doesn't have a care in the world."

They put on a big smile, giggle, and strut over to him. "Don't worry, Mr. Satinito; we know how to handle these tense guys. He's going to leave feeling like a new man." One girl walks behind him, loosens his tie and starts rubbing his neck and shoulders while the other one walks to the bar and fixes him another drink.

Mr. Satinito laughs, "Junior, here's to a great partnership. Take this card. It's a fifty grand credit. Now, what more could you ask for partner? You've got the casino's best suite, the best girls, and some gambling money. You spend a couple of days here and relax. I'll meet you downstairs in the restaurant in a couple of hours."

Satinito, Joe, and Mike leave the room laughing. Once outside Joe grabs Mike, "Why the twins? They'll probably kill that old guy."

"Boss, think about it. Could you pick a better way to go?" The three of them laugh.

Joe looks at Satinito, "What do you think are the odds of him making dinner tonight?"

"Maybe tomorrow night, but definitely not tonight. He'll be ordering in tonight. I'm sure that he's getting the massage of his life right about now. To be honest, I hope that I don't see him for the rest of his stay. He's getting real nervous. Nervous people do irrational things that screw things up for the rational team players. We need to find that girl and find her fast."

CHAPTER 27

▼

Friday Morning, Jacques wakes up bright and early, heads to his shed, and starts working on his ghillie suits. He has one for winter and one for summer. The winter one is mostly burlap color; whereas, the summer one is mostly green. The base is an XXL jumpsuit—one desert camouflaged and the other woodland camouflaged. The jumpsuit has netting sewn to it. Twelve to eighteen inch strands of burlap are tied to the netting. The burlap is dyed in various shades of greens and browns. Both ghillie suits have a boonie hat that is camouflaged the same way.

Sitting on the floor of the shed, he starts pulling apart the brown camouflaged one. He figures that one needs the most amount of work. After a couple of hours, he has the burlap off the jumpsuit netting. He then mends the rips and adds patches where the jumpsuit is worn.

He carries his mess of burlap to the back of the property where the marsh grass starts. He then separates the strands into five piles. The middle pile is about a third, and the other piles have less.

He half fills a five-gallon bucket with hot water and adds green dye. Using a paddle, he stirs it. He throws one of the small piles of burlap in it. After the dye has a good time to soak in, he pulls it out. It is much darker than the marsh grass. He throws a small pile of burlap in the bucket. He adds just a touch of yellow and tests it against some marsh grass. It needs a little more yellow, but he starts here.

He throws one of the other small piles in and dyes it. Pulls it out, rings it out, and lays it on the grass. It's a little darker than the nearby marsh grass. He adds some more yellow and tests it. It's almost an exact match. He throws the jump suit and hat in and lets it soak in the dye. After the jumpsuit, he throws in the large pile of burlap. He continues to add a little more yellow. He then adds the other two piles of burlap.

When he finishes, he has five shades of green that is going to be used on his suit. He hangs up the jumpsuit on the clothesline and spreads the burlap out in the grass to dry.

Jacques looks up and sees Malynda on the back porch in her robe drinking a cup of coffee.

"Are you doing laundry now?"

Jacques just laughs. "It is just a little project of mine."

"How about some breakfast?"

"Well, if you are up to it. It sounds good."

"Just give me five minutes."

Malynda heads back into the house.

He washes his hands and stretches his green suit out on the floor. It has a few worn spots and tears, but overall it's in good condition. He cuts patches from an old pair of BDU's and is about ready to sew them in when Malynda calls.

Jacques drops everything and heads in the camp. It's a simple breakfast—scrambled eggs, bacon, grits, and toast. Jacques grabs his seat while Malynda pours him a glass of juice and sits down. "Jacques, I want to wear something nice to Mass this Sunday."

"I don't see where that would be a problem?"

"Do you think we could go shopping and buy me a couple of new dresses?"

"Now, that's a problem."

Malynda begins to pout, "Shorts and blouses are all we have. How can we go to Church in shorts?"

"You did last week." She continues to pout.

"Give me your sizes and I'll…"

"How can you pick out something that will fit me right?"

"Malynda, you can't be seen in public. Have you forgotten that there are people that want to kill you? Do you remember the little scare that we had at the Marina?"

"Nothing happened. They probably stopped looking for me all together. It has been almost been two weeks. Can you please think of something? Please?"

"It's only been ten days. I'll try to think of something. Just give me some time."

They continue eating.

"Malynda, how about shopping in Baton Rouge or the Gulf Coast?"

"Baton Rouge is fine. We should be able to find some nice outfits there. We'll have fun you'll see."

"You and Celeste get ready and don't take all day. It is a pretty far drive."

Celeste starts jumping up and down, and Malynda quickly cleans the table. Jacques just shakes his head and thinks to himself, "How can a woman that I'm not even married to within seconds ruin a perfectly planned day? I just don't understand it. Oh well, such is life. The ghillie suits will be here when I return."

Within an hour everyone is being loaded in the truck, and the journey to Baton Rouge begins. Jacques does the mall thing. Not to his surprise, the shopping spree grows as they go along. The exponential rate of growth does surprise him. The one dress each turns into three dresses each. They need shoes to match the dresses, and purses to match their shoes. They also get a couple of casual outfits, a bottle of perfume, haircuts, lunch and dinner. The thousand dollars that Jacques brought should have easily covered two dresses. He looks into his wallet, and there is nothing except a five-dollar bill and a couple of ones. The hour is getting late, and Jacques determines it's time to go home.

On the way home, the girls are excited about their new purchases. They are giggling and laughing and discussing which ones they are going to wear tomorrow, the next day, and the day after. This is perhaps a little too much excitement for Celeste because before long she's sleeping. Malynda lays out a blanket on the rear seat bench and puts Celeste on it. She then moves closer to Jacques, wrapping her arm around his and snuggles next to him. "Jacques, I can't thank you enough for today." She kisses him on his cheek and falls asleep on his shoulder.

CHAPTER 28

▼

Saturday morning, Malynda wakes up and starts looking for Jacques. She finds him sitting on the floor of the shed tying the dyed burlap into his ghillie suits.

"Jacques, what are you doing?"

"Making some camouflage?"

"Come in and get some breakfast."

"I already ate. Went into town and made it back. I put some donuts on the counter."

"Well, are you coming in?"

"Malynda, I just need about another hour, and I'll be finished." She stomps her foot and runs back into the camp.

An hour later, she's sitting on the front porch in a rocking chair with Celeste in her lap drinking a cup of coffee. She hears the shed door open and gets up to see. She sees Jacques with his ghillie suit on. Malynda and Celeste laugh. Celeste points her finger at Jacques. "Jacques looks like the swamp monster."

"How do you two like it?"

"Jacques, I can think of a million better ways to spend the morning than making whatever you have on."

"Good, I have something for you to do." He walks to his truck, pulls out two bags, and walks up the stairs."

Malynda sees that Jacques is about to put her to work and runs inside, but Jacques follows her.

"Jacques, outside with that thing. You're shedding all over the floor."

"Wait just one minute. I bought you two a present. Their eyes light up, and a smile comes across their face." He pulls out two school backpacks and two plastic containers.

"Jacques that don't look like presents."

Celeste runs to Jacques and punches him in the leg. "Yeah, Jacques that don't look like presents."

"I need you to make grab bags."

"What's a grab bag?"

"When you are on the run and you need to escape quickly, the contents of this bag should be everything you need for three days. I have food and toothbrushes. I need you to fill in the rest. You need to have two sets of clothes—one short and one long. It needs to be as light as possible. So only put the necessities."

"Jacques, we are going to need more than that little bag for three days of stuff."

"That's the hard part. You need to determine what you really need and what you can live without. Come on, I want to see them by lunchtime."

They take the bags and go off into the bedroom. Jacques walks out the back door and into the swamp grass behind the camp. He takes his ghillie suit off and studies the color of it to the grass. He notices that it is about a shade or two lighter than the grass, which is perfect. Dark sticks out. He then takes it back onto his property, sprays it with scotch guard to keep it from soaking up water, and goes back into the shed to start on the second one.

It's almost lunchtime and Jacques has just finished spraying his second one. He goes into the camp to find Malynda and Celeste sitting on the couch watching TV. Celeste gets up and runs into the bedroom and reappears with her bag while Malynda stays pouting on the couch.

"That's good Celeste. Where's your momma's? She goes back in the room and gets Malynda's. Jacques puts them on the kitchen table, opens both the bags, and looks at the stuff inside. As Jacques goes through Malynda's bag, he can see that she's just waiting for him to say that it isn't good enough.

"Y'all did a good job, but you're lacking one thing—ziplock bags. You need to put everything in ziplock bags just in case it's raining or we have to take them swimming."

Malynda gets up off the couch and walks over to Jacques. "I was afraid that you were going to make me throw a lot out."

"If it fits in the bag, it's ok." Jacques breaks out the ziplock bags while Malynda makes sandwiches for lunch. They eat lunch and go for a boat ride that afternoon.

CHAPTER 29

▼

Monday morning, Harris and his sergeant are sitting on a park bench on Lake-shore drive. Harris has a file folder tucked under his arm.

"Sergeant, let's take them down this week."

"Why the sudden change of heart?"

"You're right about Sue. She suspects something."

"Great, so you come and have a public meeting with me."

"Relax she doesn't have any evidence yet. She knows that accusing a superior without a conviction would mean the end of her career. Even trying to get a wire tap without a conviction could be the end of her career. She's going to wait until she's one hundred percent sure before she tells anyone. I want you to make sure she's dead long before that."

"How come you're so sure that she doesn't already have the evidence?"

"Because I took your advice, I stayed away from Satinito, except for the nights that she's on her stakeout. The only evidence that could convict me would be the roll of film that we can't find."

"How do you know she hasn't found it yet?"

"Because I would be in jail instead of here talking with you." Harris pulls a map from the file folder. "Here's the set up." He points to the map. "Here's the hotel. Joe puts back-up east and west of the hotel." He points at the intersection of US 90 and Short Cut Road. "Here's a State Park. It's more like a rest area than a State Park. This is where he stages the drug dealers. They all have times that they are to approach the exchange site. Sue sets up at the hotel. She puts one of her team members on each of Joe's back-ups, one at the State Park, and one in a boat to pick her up. When the night's over her team meets at the East Pearl and

Hwy. 90 boat launch. Three miles east of the State line there is an abandoned weigh station. It's perfect for a stop and ambush. I figure you can ambush the three cars, drive back to the boat launch and ambush Sue's team."

"With all due respect, I would like to push it off another week. I would like to observe the operation once. Consider it a trial run. How wide is the East Pearl?"

Harris digs through the folder. "I don't know. Why?"

"Sue is our liability. I want to make sure that she dies. I want to hit her from across the river with the first shot. The rest of my team will clean up her team, but I want to get her on the first shot. If she smells something funny, she can wind up taking us down."

"I think you're over estimating Sue's abilities; but on your trial run, see what's possible. How you do it is entirely up to you. I'm just interested in the final results. An extra week would be nice, I'll get a chance at this little redhead."

"I can't believe you're thinking about a redhead at a time like this."

"Why not? The wonderful thing about delegating work is it gives me time to do what I want to do. Like I said before, I surround myself with dependable people. I'll depend on Sue doing exactly what she's been doing for the past year, and I'll depend upon you to do yours. Now, I have a little free time."

"What about Rodred? She now has another week to put this together?"

"I'll just occupy all of her time with wild goose chases." Harris has a grin from ear to ear. "See how easy that is."

The sergeant gets up, gets in his car, and drives off. Harris stays there overlooking the water.

1100, Jacques is in the same hide as before by Cliff's house and observes a quiet neighborhood. 1330 the postman comes, and ten minutes later little Miss Bleach Blonde comes out in the same outfit to get the mail. At 1645, she gets in the Navigator and drives off. She returns ten minutes later. At 1715, Cliff backs his truck up at the end of the dead end street, and goes inside. Jacques thinks to himself that this pattern is a good sign. It appears that they have a Wednesday routine.

Jacques pulls out his pellet gun and shoots out the street light that is at the end of the street. He then puts the pellet gun back into his ruck. He continues to observe. Cliff cuts the grass. Midway through, his girlfriend comes out gives him a kiss good by and drives off. After Cliff finishes bagging the grass, he heads inside—just like before. It gets dark, and the street light begins to come on. Jacques starts pulling out the pellet gun again when it burns out. Half an hour later, it's dark. There's light from the stars and the street light further up the street, but in the shadows it's black.

Jacques waits another half hour for his eyes to adjust, and starts packing his stuff. He changes from his woodland BDU's to black BDU's. He puts on his black knit hat and blackens his face and hands. At 2230, he checks his pockets one last time. He has a small roll of duct tape with the end folded over and handcuffs. With his black one and half inch diameter by two foot long wooden dowel in one hand and his ruck in the other, he comes out of the cane field ninja style. He proceeds to the dead end barricade, drops his bag off at the base of it, and continues to the house. Once at the house, he hides along the wall of the north side of the house between the carport and the fence. As soon as he gets in a comfortable sitting position, he realizes that he forgot about the carport light. He looks around the corner of the house and sees the carport light with a simple glass dome on it. He leaves his dowel on the side of the house, quietly walks over under the light, removes the dome, and loosens the light bulb. He quietly returns to his hiding spot, and starts rehearsing.

He hears the door start to open, and he stands up with his back flat against the wall. Jacques' heart rate goes up, and his breathing is dramatically increased. He begins to breath out of his mouth to cut down on the noise. He hears the trash can open, something being stuffed inside, and it closes again. He then hears the trash can being wheeled out towards the street. Jacques moves quickly; and with a single blow to the back of the head, Cliff falls. Jacques handcuffs him and duct tapes his mouth and ankles. He throws him over his shoulder and runs for the cane field. On the way by the dead end barricade, he picks up his ruck. The next hundred yards are rough moving with his Ruck in one hand and Cliff in his other. Jacques ruck arm is cramping, but his adrenaline rush keeps him going. Finally, he makes it to the dirt road. He drops the ruck sack and Cliff off of his shoulder. He put the ruck sack on his back and makes a run for the truck.

He reaches the truck out of breath, a little dizzy, and right on the edge of tunnel vision. He puts the truck in four wheel drive and goes. When he gets back to Cliff, he sees Cliff squirming in the middle of the road. Jacques stops the truck, grabs his dowel, jumps out and runs over to him. "Am I going to have any trouble with you? If I am, I should just kill you here." Realizing his helpless state, Cliff stops struggling. Jacques goes back to the truck and pulls out the mum bushes. He proceeds to help Cliff to his feet and loads him in the bed of the truck. He takes a piece of chain, wraps it around his neck, and locks it to the newly installed eyelet in the bed. He then proceeds to put the mum bushes on top of Cliff, and ties them down. Jacques realizes that he's home free.

Two hours later along a dirt road, Jacques stops at a cattle gate with a sign on it—"Horse Shoe Deer Lease, No Trespassing." He gets out, works the combination, and opens the gate. He drives another fifteen minutes down the dirt road. The road is rough, but Jacques intentionally hits every hole he can. He only hopes that his package would only suffer a few broken bones along the way.

He drives by a string of fifteen house trailers and campers, and he backs his truck under the skinning shed. It's summer time, and the deer lease should be empty. The skinning shed is a twenty foot by twenty foot concrete slab that's sloped towards a center drain. The structure is made with metal I-beam frames and a tin roof on top of it. The top of the arch is fifteen feet tall. The single pitch roof slopes down to twelve feet on the sides, and it has no walls. Directly above the metal grating drain is a sheave that a cable hangs from. At one end of the cable is a game gambrel. At the other end is a boat winch that is mounted chest level to one of the structure's I-beam columns. There's a double stainless steel sink with a stainless steel table at the edge of the concrete for processing the deer meat. Hanging on one of the I-beams near the sink is a rolled up, red industrial, one inch rubber water hose with an industrial one inch jet nozzle on it.

He gets out of the truck, turns the skinning shed's lights on, and walks over to the water pump house. He opens the door and notices that the pump switch is already in the "ON" position. "Either someone left the pump on, or somebody is up here." He intensely looks at the trailers. He then sees a light come on in Mr. Bubby's trailer. "I just hope that he doesn't have any company." Jacques continues tending to his business. He throws the mum bushes out of the truck, lowers the game gambrel to the bed of the truck, and ties Cliff's ankles to it. He winches Cliff's feet up and takes up all the slack in Cliff's body. He then climbs in the truck and unlocks Cliff's neck from the eyebolt, walks back to the winch, and cranks Cliff above the truck. Once Cliff's head clears the bed, Jacques can see that Cliff realizes that he is hanging upside-down in a skinning shed; and Cliff starts squirming to get free.

Jacques puts the mum bushes back into the bed of the truck and pulls the truck along side of his camper.

When he returns, he sees a seventy-six-year-old, overweight man standing there in a tee-shirt, denim coveralls, and a baseball cap. "Mr. Bubby, I'm glad it's you up here. Are you up here alone?"

"Yep, but that is one ugly deer you have there. You know that you are hunting out of season."

"There is no closed season on guys like this." Jacques digs in his wallet. "Here is some money to go town and rent a motel room. You might not want to be here tonight. It's going to get messy."

"What did this guy do to deserve this?"

"He raped and almost killed an old girlfriend of mine. You might have heard the story about that girl in Houma."

"The girl with the six-year-old kid?"

"Yep, that is the bastard that raped her. Tonight, he's going to tell me who the other's were."

"Wait here I need to go get something."

"Where are you going? You're not going to call the police are you?"

"Are you kidding? I'm going to get my Louisville slugger. Twenty-three years ago, a bastard just like this one raped my daughter. She hasn't been right since. All the years on the force, I dreamed about having a bastard like this in this situation."

"Do you have a banana in that camp of yours?"

"Yeah, what do you want a banana for?"

"Just bring it when you come back."

As Mr. Bubby disappears into the darkness, Jacques, using the winch, lowers Cliff so that his head is a foot above the drain. The foul smell of the drain should be almost enough to kill him. Judging by the size of Cliff's eyes, Jacques can see that the smell of the drain is the last thing on his mind.

Mr. Bubby reappears with the baseball bat. "Do you have my piñata ready?"

"Ok, Mr. Bubby. You can have a few swings at him, but don't hit him in the head. I still need some information from him. I need to go get some skinning knives out of my camper. Here's the money for a motel room. When I get back, I really need you out of here."

"Ok, I understand. Now, let me at him."

Jacques thinks to himself that he is glad that Mr. Bubby understands the fact that normal men don't want others to know how much of a monster they can become if they have to. To Jacques, there's never justification for a human to mutilate another. Society accepts the justified killing of a human but not mutilation. The whole concept of unspeakable torture dates back well before Christ. There are two types of madmen that perform torture—one that enjoys it and one that has a purpose. Normally, there are only two types of purpose—one is to make an example for others to see, and the other is to get information. Jacques thinks to himself that this one is to get information.

The wind is blowing hard from the south. Jacques sees flashes of lightning and hears the nearby thunder. It's fixing to rain. Jacques also hears Mr. Bubby screaming something, and then he hears the scream of Cliff. "Thank God the wind is carrying Cliff's screams into the twenty-five hundred acres of uninhabited woodlands. Jacques digs out a couple of skinning knives, a ball-peen hammer and a couple of golfballs. He hears the screaming has stopped. Shortly thereafter, he hears Mr. Bubby's truck driving down the dirt road towards the main gate.

After hearing the truck leave, Jacques walks back to the skinning shed with his hands full of equipment. He sees the yellow banana on the stainless steel table. He sees that Mr. Bubby tied the tag line from the gambrel to one of the I-beams and removed the duct tape from his mouth. Mr. Bubby didn't bust him up too badly because he is full of fight and is shouting obscenities at Jacques. Jacques pays no attention and lays his tools in front of Cliff. Jacques gets a few more things out of the truck.

Jacques takes a pair of bandage scissors and starts removing Cliff's clothes. He cuts the outside leg of the shorts. One snip of the cuff, and the bandage scissors ripped all the way to the waistband. Two more snips and through the waistband. He proceeds in the same on the other side. Within a few seconds, he pulls Cliff's shorts off of him. He starts on his polo shirt. He starts on the outside of the sleeve and proceeds to the collar. He then repeats the process on the other side. He then runs the scissors from bottom to top and removes the shirt. He moves to his boxers them in the same manner as the shorts. Jacques steps back to admire his work. Done within a minute, and there isn't even a nick. With no clothes on him, the red marks of Mr. Bubby's bat shows on his chest and back.

"Do you know why I brought you here?" Cliff does not answer. "Gee, just a little while ago you were shouting all sorts of obscenities."

Jacques walks to a nearby chair and sits in it. "Cliff, you can make this easy on yourself or you can make it hard. Either way, I will get what I want. Look around you. There is nothing here for miles. Nobody can hear you. So, what is it going to be?"

Cliff replies with a string of obscenities, saying that Jacques is a dead man, and he isn't going to talk.

Without getting up, Jacques reaches over to the hose and removes the jet nozzle. "You look like a tough kid. You look like you can take a lot of torture and still not talk. I'm going to speed up the process. Instead of giving you pain, I'm going to take a little something away from you—oxygen. He turns on the hose and almost drowns him. Finally, Cliff has enough and pleads for Jacques to stop.

Jacques places the towel full of butchering tools in front of Cliff, and opens it. Cliff shuts up and stares at the tools in front of him. Jacques grabs the banana and places it on the towel. "You probably know what the knives and saw are for, but I bet you're wondering what's the deal with the golfballs and the banana?" Cliff looks at Jacques as if Jacques just read his mind. "I bet you are not a deer hunter. The golfballs are used for skinning a deer. Look back behind you, and you will see an eye-hook embedded in the concrete with a rope on it." Cliff does. "It makes a skinning job extremely fast. You use a knife to skin the deer to the rump. You cover the golf ball in the skin, wrap the noose of the anchored rope around the skin so that the golf ball doesn't come out. You then crank the boat winch, which raises the carcass. Since the anchored rope pulls down on the golf ball while the carcass is being raised, the skin is pulled right off." Since humans are different than deer, I need a golf ball for each leg. So now are you ready to tell me who your friends are?"

Cliff starts pleading for his life, but he still is not giving any useful information.

"Since I'm not hearing what I want to hear, let's talk about the banana. Before you start skinning a buck, one of the first things you have to do is cut his pecker and balls off. With you, it is going to be a little different than skinning a deer. If I cut you like a deer, you'll bleed to death in a couple of minutes." Jacques picks up the banana and the fillet knife. "We are going to start at the base of your pecker like this. I'm going to push the knife between the muscles." Jacques pushes the fillet knife through the banana. "I am going to pull outward and up in one swift motion like this." He then pulls the knife through the length of the banana. The banana is now split in two. Jacques can see that Cliff's ready to talk, but just needs a little something to push him over the edge. He puts on his latex gloves.

Cliff starts nervously laughing. "You're not going to do that." Before he can get the words out, Jacques stands up and starts walking to Cliff with the fillet knife…

"Cliff, did you know that Malynda is an old girlfriend of mine. You raped one of my old girlfriends."

Cliff takes another look at the cut banana and starts screaming, "I'll tell you everything you want to know. Just don't do it man. I'll talk."

Satisfied that he is going to talk, Jacques lowers Cliff so that his shoulder and part of his back rests on the concrete. His legs and feet are still vertical. His hands are still handcuffed behind his back. Since his feet are still suspended, Cliff is still incapacitated from moving. Letting Cliff down also serves another purpose—it gives Cliff the illusion that he might actually survive the night. Cliff becomes extremely cooperative.

Jacques grabs his clipboard and started asking the questions. He starts off with questions that he already knows the answer to. This line of questioning is used to determine if he's lying.

"How many were with you?"

"Five"

"Who raped the girl?"

"I did, but I didn't mean it. I mean I didn't bust her up."

"Who did?"

"It was Tony. I tried to stop him, but I couldn't."

"Does this Tony have a last name?"

"I don't know it. You have to believe me. If we were caught, we couldn't rat on the others."

"What does this Tony look like?"

"He's big, I mean big. He must be at least six-four and weighs close to three hundred pounds."

"A man of his stature must have a special piece of jewelry. What is it?"

"He has a leather Ju-Ju bag that's always hanging around his neck."

"Where does he live?"

"Somewhere outside of New Orleans. I only went to his house one time."

"Is there anything that makes this guy distinguishable."

"Yeah, he sort of looks Mexican. He has a real dark tan."

"What type of car does he drive?"

"A black Chevy Impala SS. He's got it sup'd up."

"Where does this Tony hang out?"

"He's got a side job as a bouncer at the "Le Club de Belles Femmes" in New Orleans."

"Why would a guy on the payroll work for peanuts as a Bouncer?"

"He's got a girlfriend that works there. Her name is Tina."

"What does this Tina look like?"

"She's tall. I mean really tall like five-ten. She has long red hair and cold blue eyes."

"Does she have any tattoos?"

"No, she's clean, man."

"Who else was involved with the raid?"

"Billy."

"Actually, Billy is the one I wanted first. I looked for him, but I couldn't find him. Where did he go?"

"Billy knew the girl. He's the only link between the girl and us. When Joe found out that the girl wasn't dead, he threw a fit. We stuffed Billy in the trunk and buried him in the woods up I-59."

"Who else?"

"There was Joe. He's the boss-man. We all work for him."

"Where can I find him?"

"That one is easy. Every Thursday night, he collects the drug money in front of an abandoned hotel on Hwy. 90 somewhere near the Mississippi and Louisiana state line."

"What does he look like?"

"Older fellow in his fifties. He is a little overweight."

"What type of car does he drive?"

"A white Lincoln Town Car."

"Cliff, you are doing good. Let's see. We have you; a Tony; a Billy, who's dead; and a Joe. I only show four people. Who's the fifth?"

"That would be Mike, Joe's bodyguard. He is almost as big as Tony. He even looks just like Tony. They could pass for twins. Man, he is cut out of stone. If you find Joe, you'll find Tony."

"Why did you do what you did?"

"Man, she was going to die anyway. I figured, why not get a little in front of her old man before we killed her?"

Jacques gets enraged. "No. I mean, why did you hit that house!"

"Scott took some pictures that he shouldn't have."

"Where's the film? I don't know. I thought we had it, but we didn't. Joe said the police might have it."

"Well, I want to thank you for your cooperation."

Cliff starts smiling. "You don't have to worry about me. As soon as you let me go, I'm long gone—maybe Canada or Mexico."

Jacques walks to his truck and returns with his 45 and a black garbage bag. "I didn't say anything about letting you go. I just said that I was going to make it easy on you. Remember, you raped and tried to kill a defenseless good friend of mine. I take that personal." Jacques walks over, points the pistol at Cliff's face and pulls the trigger. He then loads Cliff's carcass on his four-wheeler and drives it deep into the woods. Since the trail is marked with bright-eyes, it's extremely easy to follow. At the end of the bright-eye trail there's a seven-foot long by three foot wide by four foot deep hole waiting. He throws the carcass in the hole, covers it with dirt, and the entire area with leaves. On his way out, he pulls out the bright eyes. He drives back to the camp, cleans his four-wheeler, picks up his tools, and thoroughly washes the skinning shed's floor. He spends the rest of the night in his trailer reflecting on the events that have just occurred.

CHAPTER 30

▼

Tuesday 2100, Jacques is stepping out of his bedroom with a pair of dress slacks and a polo shirt on. Malynda is sitting on the couch with Celeste watching TV. Malynda looks up at Jacques and starts giving him the third degree.

"Are you going to see an old girlfriend?"

"Nope. It's business."

"Business at nine o'clock at night, sure it is."

"I think that I have a lead on another one of the guys that killed your husband."

"Where's the camouflage? Where's your bag? Why are you so dressed up? When are you going to be back? Or can I ask?"

"I should be back before daylight." Jacques gives Malynda and Celeste a kiss on the forehead and walks out the door, gets in his truck and drives off.

He drives to New Orleans French Quarter, down Decatur Street, and parks on the street near the river and St. Peters. He walks up St. Peters and stops in Pat O'Brien's for a Hurricane to go. He continues to Bourbon St. and turns left, and takes in some of the jazz music and the sights as he blends in perfectly with the rest of the tourists. At Iberville, he turns right and there it is "Le Club de Belles femmes." He pays the cover charge and walks into the dimly lit classy nightclub.

He stops at the door and notes the layout of the establishment. The stage with a gold pole is in the center of the place. The stage is more like a model's runway that has tables with comfortable chairs around them. A long bar is located to the right. Jacques sees a group of guys getting up to leave. He walks to the open table near the stage and sits down. Before he's comfortably seated, a cocktail waitress greets him and asks him, "What are you drinking tonight?"

"Sam Adams." He drinks his beer and enjoys the entertainment. Everyone, except the bachelor party, is quiet and just sits back and enjoys the show. Even though he looks like he's enjoying life, he's uneasy because somewhere in the room is a man that he's going to do mortal battle with. He scans the room. There's a bachelor party having a great time, several tourists, and the frequent visitors; but he can't find the bouncers.

He scans the room again for the bouncers. They're there; they're just invisible. He uses a near-by table dance for an excuse to stare in one direction for any length in time. He just looks beyond the table dancer into the dark corners and shadows. Once his eyes adjust and he notices what to look for, he begins picking them out. He identifies at least three of them.

The dance routine is pretty simple. A girl's name is announced, and she comes out and does a dance to the first song in a dress. For the second song, she peels off all of her clothes except for her six to eight inch heels and a g-string. The stage names are pretty typical like Star, Lacey, Honey, Sassy, and Christy. As they dance, patrons walk up to the stage and slip dollar bills into the sides of their g-strings. The girls are pretty smart. They never take their eyes off of the tipping patron. If they are facing them it's simple. When they turned away, they're using the mirror in front of them.

The bachelor party begins to get out of control—a little too much alcohol and not too much sense. The announcer announces "Lets hear it for Christy." They start whistling and hollering before she even comes out on the stage. This five-four blue eyed, blonde in a full-length red dress comes out from the stage door. It's Cliff's girlfriend. She knows how to get audience's participation. Jacques can't see what all the fuss is about. She's attractive all right; but considering that all the dancers are, what made her so special? When she peels off the dress, she has what looks like a 38"DDD or more chest, 18" waist and 32" hips. She's playing the bachelor party pretty hard, and they're waiting in line to tip her. Jacques thinks to himself that this is going to be easy. One of these boys is going to do something stupid like try to touch the girl and get physically thrown out. They try but with all the alcohol they're slow, and her reactions are as quick as a bobcat. Each time a guy tries to touch her, she just moves away, smiles, and shakes her finger at him. It's obviously a game to her, and she's enjoying every minute of it. Needless to say the bouncers are not needed. After her song finishes, she covers her top with the red dress and moves over to the bachelor party to perform table dances.

Jacques for a moment forgets why he came there and starts watching the bachelors. The announcer announces, "And here is Amber." The music starts playing, and the blonde is giving the bachelor party a real good show. A shadow casts over Jacques as the stage dancer walks by. It's Tony's girlfriend. It has to be. She is tall and lean with long red hair. She's in her mid to upper twenties. Unlike Christy that is full of energy, she's a dancer that uses slow seductive movements. Jacques can tell that she's also experienced enough to give men what they want without really giving it to them. She does her first song and then moves to her second song. As soon as she moves out on the stage, Jacques goes up to tip her. She crawls to him on all fours. Her head is down with her hair over her face. She stops right in front of Jacques and kneels straight up. She stands back up and pulls the side of her g-string for Jacques to slip his dollar in. She takes her other hand and pulls her hair away from her face, looks down at Jacques, and says thank you. When she pulls the hair away, Jacques sees the bluest eyes he has ever seen in his life. They're almost scary because of the contrast of the red hair and light blue eyes. Jacques looks up to her. "I would like a table dance when you are through." She just smiles again and continues working the audience for tips. Jacques goes back to his table, orders another beer, and enjoys the rest of her show.

Everyone claps after she finishes. The music starts and the announcer announces the next dancer. Meanwhile, Amber comes out and personally thanks everyone for their tips. She pulls a chair next to Jacques and extends her hand. "Hi, I'm Amber. What's your name?"

Jacques answers, "Charlie."

"Are you in New Orleans for pleasure or business?"

"Business, but now it is purely pleasure. You have beautiful red hair and long pretty legs. Just how tall are you?"

"Five ten and with these heels I'm six four."

"Walking in those heels all night is got to be painful. How late do you normally work?"

"Normally, until 2:30 or 3:30. It all depends on how long the crowd is here. Sometimes I work till 6:00. Are you still interested in a table dance?"

"I just have a thing for tall women. You bet, I wouldn't pass an opportunity like this up."

She gets up and goes to the bar. She tells the bartender something and returns. In less than a minute, a thirty inch diameter platform the height of the chair is brought to the table. She turns Jacques' chair away from the table and places the platform between his knees. She climbs on top of it facing away from him and reaches all the way down to her ankles, grabs bottom of the long dress, and pulls it over her head. She turns around, faces him and gets down on all fours. She crawls on his chair arms until her head is above Jacques. Her long red hair makes a tent and her breasts are just inches away from Jacques' face. She makes a few movements and slowly backs her way back onto the platform. She stands up, turns away again, and reaches for her ankles. She pulls her chest all the way to her knees and smiles at Jacques.

Before Jacques reaches up to grab her, a thought passes through his mind: "I won't be able to help Malynda if I get just as messed up as her. Awe, what the hell?" With that he jumps up, wraps his arms around her, and falls back into the chair with her. She screams, and Jacques lets go. She jumps up and slaps him across his face. Right after her slap lands, he has four rather powerful hands on him. Jacques doesn't resist, and the two men roughly escort him out the door. The one with the leather pouch is definitely Tony. The other one is just as big and ugly as Tony. Once outside, the other bouncer holds Jacques; and Tony lands a good punch into his abdomen. Jacques immediately falls in the fetal position with the wind knocked out of him. Tony says, "If I see your face again, I'll kill you. Now, get up and leave." With that Jacques picks himself up and staggers off.

"I survived without any broken bones, and I have two hours to kill. A nice non-alcoholic daiquiri would be a good thing to have. I'll go sit on the river walk and enjoy a cool breeze for a while." He walks back down Bourbon street, stops in a daiquiri shop, picks up the daiquiri and continues to St. Peters. At St. Peters, he turns right and walks to Decatur. Once at Decatur, the decision of which way to go is difficult. Turn down river and grab some sugarcoated beignets with some chocolate milk at Café Du Monde or head up river for a great roast beef sandwich at Maspero's. Even though they use buns, instead of french bread; Maspero's makes one of the fullest and best tasting roast beef sandwiches available. It's always well worth the money."

He decides why not do both. He fattens himself up at Maspero's. He then walks along the river walk past the location where he parked his truck to Café Du Monde. Once at Café Du Monde, he orders three orders of sugar coated beignets and three chocolate milks to go. Jacques decides to take a chance on finding a parking spot on Iberville street. He walks back to his truck and drives to Iberville street.

The dimly lit street is a two car width, one way street with parking on one side of it. Sure enough, half a block past the club, there's an open parking spot. It's a tight fit, but Jacques manages to parallel park on the third try. His truck sticks out, but it's still legally parked. He adjusts his mirror to see the entrance of the club, slouches down in his seat, and waits. Once he gets comfortable, he realizes that sandwich might not have been a good idea. With his belly full, being motionless, and boredom; he begins to fight sleep.

0200, he's only there 30 minutes, and he's checking his watch every five minutes. The people begin to slowly filter out of the French Quarter.

0300, only extreme party animals remain in the French Quarter. Iberville still has a few cars on it. Watching the traffic thin out, Jacques wonders if his plan will still work. He's parked one parking spot from the stop sign. If there's no traffic, he will not be able to place the transmitter. Jacques' plan is a risky one. He figures that Tony parks his car in the parking lot across the street. With the one way street, his only way out is past where Jacques is parked. Once he sees them walking to the parking garage, he will slip under his truck. When they are stopped in traffic next to his truck, he'll use the telescopic pole and place the transmitter under Tony's car. The problem is that if there's no one in front of Tony. He will not stop alongside of the truck.

0345, some revelers walk by Jacques' truck, get in the car that's parked in front of him, and drive off. Jacques is just ready to take advantage of the opportunity and move the truck forward when he sees Tony, Amber, the other bouncer and another girl walk across the street to the parking garage. He thinks to himself. "It's too late to move the truck, but imagine all the risk being removed by pulling up one parking spot. Jacques quickly starts the truck and moves forward to the intersection, kills the motor, grabs the telescopic pole, gets out of the cab, and slides under his truck. Once under the truck, he turns the transmitter on, places it in the grips of the pole, and waits anticipating every car that comes along side of him. Finally, a black impala with a lot of exhaust work stops right along side of the truck. Jacques quickly tries to place the transmitter underneath the car by the gas tank. The car sits really low, and it's a difficult task. Finally, the magnet grabs something metal, and Jacques releases as Tony speeds away. Jacques is not quick enough with pulling in the pole. The car behind Tony's rolls over the pole. Luckily, Jacques is clear enough to be able to let go of the pole and escape without injury.

As Jacques is crawling out from under the car, a man's voice screams at him. "Stop right there, and keep your hands where I can see them." Jacques turns to his left and two New Orleans Police officers are running his way. They get closer and tell him to put his hands on the truck and assume the position. Jacques complies. One of the officers pulls out Jacques' wallet, hands it to the other officer, and continues to pat him down. The other one asks, "Jacques Boudreaux, you're a long way from Texas. What were you doing under that truck?"

"I was checking the starter. Sometimes, it vibrates loose."

"Do you own that truck?"

"Yes sir, she's treated me real good over the years."

"Let me see the title and registration."

Jacques opens the door and digs the title out of the glove box.

"Where is the registration?"

"It's on the windshield above the safety inspection sticker."

The officer looks inside of the truck when Jacques is getting the paperwork and sees the empty milk cartons and white powder sugar. "Looks like you've been sitting here awhile."

"I left my inside light on, and she wouldn't start. Sometimes if I let her sit for a little while, she'll kick over. She didn't do it this time, so I checked the starter. Sure enough, the wire vibrated loose from the starter. I wrapped it real tight. She should be ready to go now."

"What is that in the back of your truck?"

"It is a doppler antenna. In Texas, I'm a tornado chaser."

"Well, it looks like you check out. Have a nice day. If you are going to be chasing tornadoes, take my advice and get a new truck." The officers laugh and walk away.

Jacques gets in the truck, and it starts right up. He drives off and turns on the doppler screen. The antenna makes a full sweep and finds nothing. Jacques thinks to himself that if he couldn't keep a tail on a car with a transmitter, he better keep his day job. He's obviously not cut out for the detective life.

He drives around the French Quarter for awhile and finds nothing. He drives a grid search pattern and finds nothing. He gets on the interstate and drives to Metairie, drives another grid search pattern and finds nothing. He drives out to the lakefront and makes a pattern and finds nothing. "By this time they could be anywhere." The sun is up, and Jacques is tired. He gives up and decides to head home. On the way home, he goes through an after action review. "The difficult part is putting the transmitter on the car. It's on. It has a five-day life. I just need to hang around the French Quarter until he shows up again." With all the driving and concentration on the screen, he looses sight that he's almost out of gas. He stops at a gas station, fills up, and heads back to his fishing camp.

While driving to the camp, Jacques passes a donut shop. He looks at the powdered sugar and empty milk pints and feels guilty. He makes a U-turn and picks up some chocolate milk and beignets for Malynda and Celeste. As he continues to the camp, he's in a daydream thinking about the night's events. He replays what went right, what went wrong, and what he should have done differently. An ear piercing electronic beep suddenly wakes him. Jacques quickly turns down the volume and starts paying attention to the electronic screen. The little green dot is getting closer with every antenna pass. Jacques' mind draws a map of the area. This area of St. Bernard Parish is a narrow one-mile strip of habitable land. To the north is a twenty-two foot tall hurricane protection levee, which keeps the swamp water out of St. Bernard Parish. To the south is the Mississippi River with a twenty-two foot tall hurricane protection levee. There're two major roads—one that pretty much follows along the Mississippi River and the other is about midway between the two levees. Jacques is on the one that is midway between the levees. He's expecting the dot to start to move a little to the right or left of dead center, but the dot stays directly in front of him. He's right on top of the dot. Then, the dot is behind him and getting further away. Jacques realizes that the transmitter probably fell off the car. He circles back to pick up the transmitter. As he is making another pass, he turns up the resolution. The dot is a little to his south. He takes a right turn on the only available street, and slowly drives down the street. The street is typical for this area. It has houses on both sides and stretches from the middle road to the river road. The lots are sixty feet wide by one hundred and twenty feet deep, and the houses have ten feet between them. Right after the turn, the green dot is east of him. He passes it up again. Jacques has the location narrowed to one of the two end houses. He continues almost to the river road, turns around, and makes another pass. This time he's sure, the transmitter is in the second house from the corner on the east side of the street. The car has to be in the garage. To keep from drawing attention to him, Jacques decides to leave the area and continue to the camp.

Jacques pulls into the shell driveway of the camp. Malynda has made a morning ritual of drinking a cup of coffee on the porch to welcome a beautiful new day. This morning is no different. Jacques gets out of the truck, grabs the biegnets and chocolate milk, and heads up the stairs.

Malynda looks at Jacques with a smile. "Did you find who you were looking for?"

"I think so. I still need to confirm it."

"Who?"

"His name is Tony. I'm pretty sure that's the one that beat you."

"Where?"

"Fifteen miles up the road."

"Is he headed this way?"

"No, that is where he lives."

"Is that in Chalmette?"

"Nope, it is on this side of Chalmette."

Malynda hurries into the camp and starts closing all the curtains in the camp, "Jacques, I'm getting worried."

Jacques walks behind her reopening them, "He has been there the whole time, and we have been here the whole time. I still think that we are all right. You just need to be a little more careful, and I think we might want to stop the trips to town for a while. Here I brought you some beignets." Jacques heads for the shower. He re-appears with a towel wrapped around him, and he heads straight for his bedroom.

Malynda hurries to run after him before he closes the door, "Jacques, I want to talk to you."

"After I get some sleep, you can talk all you want." He closes the door and climbs into the bed.

CHAPTER 31

▼

Malynda walks into Jacques dark and cold room and closes the door behind her. She sits on his bed and begins to rub his bare shoulder.

"Jacques, it's eleven o'clock. I made some lunch for you."

Jacques can tell that something's up by the tone in her voice. He starts to get up, and she gently holds his shoulder down.

"Jacques, I need to talk to you."

Jacques feeling a little uncomfortable says, "Ok, let me get up, get some clothes on, and we can talk while we're eating lunch."

"I need to talk to you alone, and I can't wait any longer. I've been meaning to talk to you for some time. Every time I plan to catch you alone, you go out on one of your all night things. I can never find the right time to talk to you. I need to talk to you, and I need to talk now. The first thing I want to talk to you about is Celeste. If something would happen to me, I want to know that you are going to take care of her."

"Malynda, nothing is going to happen to you. If anything does happen to you, I'll raise Celeste as if she was my own daughter." Jacques knows this isn't the real reason Malynda is in his room, and he starts to get up again. "If that's it, let's eat."

"Wait. I have more. Who did you go see last night? Was it a girlfriend of yours?"

"No, and you don't want to know."

"How come you never talk about your wife? Are you still married to her? I know that I am digging into your private business, but I need to know? I had a talk with Jean, and she said that your wife passed away almost two years ago, but you are still wearing your wedding band. Is it true, did she pass away?"

"Yeah, she did."

"I'm sorry to hear about that, but just because she died doesn't mean that you have to die too. Jacques you have your whole life ahead of you. God gives you that. You need to take advantage of it." Jacques starts to get up again. "Jacques, I still have one more question for you. Do you still have feelings for me?"

"I have deep feelings for you. I always had and always will."

"I have been throwing myself at you for a month now with no response."

"It's only been sixteen days."

"What is with the days? Are you trying to set a record to see how fast you wrap this up and be done with me?"

"No, it's my way of staying focused. Every morning I get up and pat myself on the back that I kept you alive for another day."

"Jacques that's my point exactly. You're keeping me alive, but I'm not living. I need more than a robot keeping me alive. You closed your feelings off to me. I have emotions, and I know you do too. Jacques, my husband and your wife are gone. We need to get on with our lives. Do I grieve the loss of Scott? Sure I do, but we have now. We have an opportunity that is given to us again. I don't want to pass it up again."

"You've been talking to that crazy priest. He's got the two of us married already."

"Maybe he's right. Maybe this is a God sent. Maybe we should take advantage of it and see where it goes."

"Malynda, believe me. I love you dearly, but I need to stay focused. My head needs to be clear. Within the next couple of weeks, I am planning on doing some pretty terrible things. Things that I don't think you will approve of."

Malynda begins to tear up and stops him, "I understand that you need to do these things. I also understand that you are doing these things for Celeste and me. You have a dark side. Every man has one, but you do good with yours. Jacques, I am willing to put up with your dark side because you also have a good side. Do you understand what I am trying to tell you? I love you—all of you. Your good side and dark side."

"I love you too, but"

"No buts, Jacques."

"I can't believe that your husband hasn't been dead for a month and you're making a pass at me."

"Jacques, life is a limited gift. You need to take full advantage of it every day. Who knows, we might die tomorrow."

"You sound like Old Père."

"Père is right."

"But we are going through a traumatic time. After this is over and we still have these feelings, we'll do something about it. Who knows, I might be killed tomorrow. How would you like to loose two men that you love die in a short period of time?"

"What difference would it make? I have already fallen in love with you. You need to relax a little bit and enjoy life. You're so paranoid. We need to live for today. Tomorrow, we're going to have the same things to worry about. Why not just take off one day from planning and whatever else you have been doing? Just one day—that is what I am asking."

"I wish I could but I have something that I have to do, and I have to do it today. You say that I am paranoid, and you're right. Me being paranoid has kept me, as well as you, alive so far. I don't want to relax. I want to question every creak in this house. I want to question the sound of every car that drives by. One time that creak is not going to be normal or that car is not going to continue down the road. When that day comes, I want to be the one that surprises them and not the other way around."

"Jacques, you have provided me everything that I need but you're neglecting my feelings. Jacques, I'm human. I need to be hugged and held. I need to be touched. I don't know if I can be any more direct—Jacques, I need you. I want you. I have feelings for you. I have needs. What more do I have to do?"

"You are going to have to wait for another couple of weeks. Hopefully, it will be all over by then."

"I don't want you then. I want you now."

"Believe me. Just wait a couple of weeks."

Jacques gets up and gets dressed. Malynda wipes the tears from her eyes and leaves the room. Jacques emerges from his room, and they eat lunch. Jacques then grabs one of his ghillie suits, the camera and enough food and water for two days. "I'll probably be gone for two days. There is enough food and stuff here to keep you two happy."

"I need more than food to make me happy. Please, don't go." They embrace each other. "I have to. I'll tell you what. Write me a love letter for each day, and I'll do the same. Ok." Jacques pulls away from her and leaves her crying.

He drives back to Tony's house. He sees a wooded area with a grass covered clear cut on the north side of the highway. He uses the same "For Sale" trick with the truck. He parks his truck just out of sight of Tony's house in the highway right-of-way. He decides to set up with his back against a tree fifty yards into the wooded area across the highway from Tony's house.

The hide is a simple one—he puts his back against a tree and sets up Randy's camera on the spotting scope's tripod. He finds a nice pecan tree to rest against. His butt fits perfectly between the roots and the taper of the tree fit his back comfortably. From there he removes a few limbs and bushes to give him a view of the front of the house. He sits back down and rechecks his field of view, and it looks good.

This time Jacques has all the comforts of home. He has a camouflaged life vest to sit on and a small ice chest with soft drinks and food.

1300, Jacques pulls out his data book and scans the area. He's fifty yards away from the highway and five yards into the woods from the edge of a clear-cut. The clear cut is large enough to put a strip mall on. He looks to the south. He views the house diagonally across the clear-cut, across the highway, and across Tony's street. The front door is two hundred yards away.

Judging by the style of the house, it's probably built in the sixties. The house is white with green trimming. He has a double driveway but a single garage on the north front side of the house. The house to the north of his has the garage on the south front side. There's a community sidewalk in front of his house, and the front door is located in the middle of the house. It also has a storm door. The mailboxes are located across the street. There's the normal mercury vapor light at the intersection of the street and the highway. It's located on the same side of the street as Tony's house. The next street light is also located on the same side of the street as Tony's house and is five houses down. There are no trees down the whole street, just gardens in front of the dwellings. Jacques completes his scan for large items. He starts focusing on smaller ones. He finds a security home monitoring system sign in Tony's front yard, a lock on his mailbox, uncut front yard, weeds growing in the garden, and Christmas lights still in the bushes in front of his house. After Jacques makes notes about everything he sees, he quickly becomes bored.

The neighborhood is perfectly still. The noise of the highway is annoying at first, but it soon becomes repetitive and tranquil. He becomes sleepy, and his mind wanders. He then starts thinking about Malynda's conversation. He becomes quickly confused on what to do. Yes, he does love her and would do anything for her and Celeste. Was he ready to jump into another relationship? Was Malynda ready or was she just grasping the first opportunity? Is she the same person that he knew a long time ago? Does he want to complicate his basically simple life? Jacques wishes the conversation never happened. Then again, he's glad to know that she still has feelings for him.

1500, A westbound maroon Lincoln Navigator turns south on Tony's street and breaks his concentration. It stops in front of Tony's house. Six people get out—four guys and two girls. He quickly gets behind the camera and zooms in. He starts taking pictures. One of the guys is Tony. He's as big as ever. He has a tan muscle shirt that is ready to rip from any quick movement. The two older guys are wearing polo shirts, shorts, and dock shoes. The fourth guy is just as big as Tony. He's wearing shorts without a shirt. He recognizes Amber, who's wearing short green shorts, a green bikini top, and sandals. The other girl is dressed similar with khaki shorts, purple bikini top, and white tennis shoes. They both have their hair pulled back in ponytails. Amber's hair reaches midway down her back, but the other girl's reaches a little past her shoulders. They run to the front door. Amber must have to use the restroom pretty bad because she's dancing around at the front door, and everyone is looking and laughing at her. Tony sticks the key into the door, and they go inside. After they are inside, Jacques looks at the counter on the camera. It shows twenty-two pictures, and he decides to put another roll of film in the camera. He thinks to himself that he has a full-auto camera that cycles faster than a full-auto weapon.

Jacques turns the camera towards the Navigator. It's parked in the street facing away from him. He takes a picture of the license plate and writes the number down. The number looks familiar. He flips back through his data book. The number does not match Cliff's.

1520, the front door of the house opens, and everyone emerges from the house. They're joking and laughing. Everyone has a bottle of beer in his or her hand. They open the back of the Navigator and pull out fishing gear. Jacques starts taking selective pictures of the people. They pull out a large 128-quart ice chest, and put it down right behind the Navigator. Tony walks away from the crowd and disappears along side the house. He returns a few seconds later with a short piece of timber that he places under the backside of the ice chest. The chest is full of five to six pound speckle trout. The fish almost stretched from one side of the ice chest to the other. When Jacques sees the fish, a million thoughts race through his mind. "Two favorite spots to catch big specks like that are Black Bay and California Bay. California Bay is in Point-a-la-hatche. If they went there, they would have returned by the river road. They had to go to Black Bay. The easiest way to get to Black Bay is through Hopedale Lagoon. The way to get to Hopedale Lagoon is through Bayou Loutre. They could have passed right in

front of the camp. If they saw Malynda, there's nothing I could do about it now."
He goes on to complete his mission.

The girls peel off their shorts to reveal their thong bikini bottoms. Jacques can
see that they are a little sunburned. In fact, everyone's a little sunburned. Tony
breaks out a camera, and they start posing for pictures. Jacques thinks to himself,
"How thoughtful of them." The first picture is one of the older guys kneeling
down along side of the ice chest. Tony takes another one with the same guy with
both girls and the fish. The old guy then holds up a fish in each hand and a girl
on each arm. "The way they're playing this guy up, Jacques thinks he must be
Joe. Jacques zooms in as close as he can and snaps the best pictures he can get.

It's the guy's turn. Tony pulls off his shirt. Jacques concludes that they're
probably steroid abusers because of their lean muscle mass. These two guys are
cut to the point that Jacques could see the striations of the muscles in their chest
and shoulders.

The two older guys just step back and drink their beer. The first picture is of
the two muscle bound guys behind the ice chest, then on side of the ice chest.
Amber grabs the camera and backs up to take the pictures. She obviously doesn't
know how to stoop. She bends at the waist with knees locked and her back parallel with the ground. The older guy nudges Joe and points at the girl's rear and
says something. She hears him, smiles, crosses her legs, wraps her hands around
her ankles, bends all the way over so that her upside down face with a smile from
ear to ear is next to her knees. Her long red ponytail is on the ground. The next
picture is the guys along side of the ice chest with the fishing poles. They muscle
up for that one, and Jacques gets a good picture. It's then Tony and Amber's
turn. The other girl takes the camera and tries to top Amber's little show for the
older guys. With Amber standing next to Tony, Jacques begins to size him up.
Tony posed for a picture with Amber's head on his chest. His arms are bigger
than Amber's head. His chest width is more than twice the width of Amber's
shoulders. The little neck he has is as wide as Amber's waist. Jacques comes to the
conclusion that Tony is just one big dude. Next up is the other couple, and
Amber continues photographing. Apparently, everyone is having a good time,
because there's a lot of laughter. Amber hands the camera to Joe's friend. Both
couples pose for the pictures with the ice chest full of fish. After the picture taking
is over with, the two older guys stay outside with Tony's friend. The girls go in
the front door, and Tony goes around the side of the house. Jacques camera runs
out of film again, and he reloads the camera.

The girls return with more beer, and Tony returns with an ice chest and a
towel. Tony pulls the fish and ice out of the ice chest. There's something else in

there—blocks of ice. Jacques is straining to see, but he can't make out what it is. Tony reaches in the ice chest and starts pulling out five-kilo packages of cocaine. He wipes them off and throws them into the back of the Navigator. Joe starts to protest, but his friend calms him down. After Tony finishes loading the Navigator, he pulls the privacy curtain on the cargo area and closes the rear of the vehicle.

1600, Joe, Joe's friend, Mike and Mike's girlfriend load up in the Lincoln. Tony stands there with his arm on Amber's shoulder waving to them as they drive off. Tony and Amber go inside. At this point in time, Jacques wants so badly to get back to Hopedale to make sure everything is all right with Malynda. If he leaves now, he'll have to wait another week to set up again. He prays for the best and continues his recon.

1700, the first neighbor pulls in her driveway. The rest of the neighbors begin to trickle in. Jacques makes notes of the vehicles, houses and times.

1830, all the neighbors are home.

1915, Tony's garage door opens. The black impala SS rolls out the driveway. It's headed southbound on his street. Jacques figures that it's time for Amber to go to work. Shortly there after, the neighborhood is lifeless again. Darkness falls; Jacques knows that he cut a small shooting path. If he moves a little bit he would not see the obstructions until he's ready to take a pictures. He makes notes of when the streetlights come on and when the lights go out in the houses. He goes to infrared mode on the camera. In Tony's yard is an infrared light beam that comes out of the alley between the houses, across the front of his yard, and back into the alley on the other side of the house. It's an infrared fence. Tony has an electronic warning device inside of the house. Jacques makes a note of it and takes a nap.

2200: Joe, Mike and Tony are in the Mead Hall sitting on the couch and chair looking at the TV. They're laughing at the people loosing their money on the casino floor. Joe looks at his watch. "Tony, where's the kid?"

"I don't know."

"What do you mean, you don't know? What did you do to him? Did you kill him?"

"No boss. The last time I saw him was the exchange night. I haven't seen him since then."

Mike holds his hands up, "Hold on. I'll straighten this up." He pulls out his phone and dials a number and puts a big smile on his face. "Hey, baby. Where's that well endowed boyfriend of yours?" He looses his smile. "He's not with us. When was the last time you saw him?......Wednesday night was over a week ago.

You didn't think about calling us?......No, you didn't think. Go see if he took any clothes...What? His truck is still parked in front of the house......Your boyfriend is missing for a week and his truck is parked out front. You're not concerned?......Yeah, he was supposed to work with Tony, but he never did...Go check his clothes...All of his clothes are there. Thanks for nothing."

Mike looks at Joe and starts to explain.

"Mike, I heard enough to fill in the bimbo's part of the conversation. Tony, one more time, what did you do with the kid?"

"Nothing, Boss. I'm serious." Fear comes across Tony's face, and he starts rubbing his Ju-Ju bag.

"Look if you killed him, I'm Ok with that. Just tell me."

"I didn't kill him."

"What's wrong with you?"

"Boss, remember last week. He had two number two's on his face."

"Yeah, I remember the two's saved his life not took it away from him. If he didn't have that crap on his face, you would have killed him. Relax, Tony, there is no number two associated with today or tomorrow. Come on snap out of it. I need you tomorrow."

The door opens and Mr. Satinito makes his entrance as usual. One of his girls fixes him a drink, and he makes a toast.

"Joe, where's the kid? Did you decide that he couldn't cut it?"

"Mr. Satinito, I think he flew the coop."

"He knows our whole operation. Now we have two liabilities. Either one can bury this operation. Joe in the past few weeks, you really screwed up. I think that we need to make some changes around here. This week continue as usual. Put Tony on the west side of the hotel. Your east side will be open."

"What about your nephew? He could cover our east side."

"He stays with you. Next week, I'll get some real muscle from back home. For tomorrow, you need to operate without any protection on the east side. If we are moving the collection spot, we might as well get rid of Harris too."

Thursday 0400, a car pulls in front of Tony's house. Amber get's out and heads inside the house through the front door.

0500, Tony comes back home.

0515, the sun starts coming up.

0530, Tony emerges from the alleyway. He's putting out the trash. He takes pictures of Tony as before. Tony disappears again in the alleyway.

0615, the first neighbor drives out of their driveway.

0630–0730, the neighborhood empties.

0800, Jacques sees enough. He packs his gear and rushes back to the camp to find Celeste beating Malynda at Booray.

Later that day, Jacques drives back to town and picks up groceries for the camp. His first stop is at a one-hour film processing shop to process the three rolls of film. He pays for the pictures, reviews them, and walks over to the enlargement and copy center. He carefully picks out the useful pictures, crops them, and makes eight by ten pictures from them—except for one that he makes an eleven by fourteen. He puts the pictures in a folder and pays on his way out. From there he walks to the grocery store. Malynda is getting a little better with the list and is being a little more acceptable with the omissions and substitutions. He drives back to the camp and spends the rest of the day making minor repairs to the camp. After dinner, Jacques goes on the Internet and gets aerial photos of the stretch of highway on Hwy. 90 so he can start putting together a plan that night.

CHAPTER 32

▼

2200 in the Mead Hall, Satinito is sitting on the couch and holding a conversation with Laura Lee, while both of his girls are making coke lines at the bar. All the women are wearing sequence micro party dresses. The door opens and Harris walks in.

Satinito turns around. "Junior, welcome. Is this the little piece of candy you asked for?"

The girl stands up and giggles, and spins around for him to see. In her Alabama accent, "You like?"

"Satinito, this partnership is working out just fine."

"My man, fine is what's standing in front of you. Come on girls, I have a feeling this guy and red have something to talk about." Satinito gets up, his girls grab each one of his arms and he walks out of the Mead Hall.

The young redhead struts over to the bar. "Junior, what'll you have?"

"Bourbon and seven."

"Me too."

"You too."

She laughs. "What's your hurry? We have all night, and I'm going to make sure you enjoy every minute of it." She brings the drink to him. "Here's to the best night in your life." She toasts him.

At the same time that Harris is getting toasted, his sergeant slithers with his rifle westward through the roseau canes towards the east shoreline of the East Pearl River. His team is located three miles east on Hwy. 90 at the truck weigh station. He works his way near the water's edge and sets his bipod. He scans across the East Pearl River to the boat launch's parking lot. The parking lot is lit by three mercury vapor lights—one on the end of the four boat concrete back-down and two in the clamshell parking lot. He looks for Sue's man in the roseau's. From the pictures, he is located on the south side of the parking lot. He studies the movement of the canes in the wind. His fourteen power scope sees a shadow along the cane line, it's an opening. The reeds are not moving on either side of the opening. He tries to see through the reeds to spot Sue's man—no luck. The sergeant mils a few objects to confirm his range. He looks for Satinito's man and can't find him.

0245, the sergeant sees Joe's town car drive across the bridge into Mississippi followed by Tony's black impala.

0330, a van pulls up with a boat trailer. When the van pulls up, the guy in the roseau canes comes out with a camera in one hand; and he uses his other hand to swat the mosquitoes. He jumps in the sliding door.

0345, a flatboat pulls up to the back down ramp. Sue gets out of the flatboat and onto the dock. She's wearing a one-piece black Speedo swim suit and is hold-ing a bottle of lime colored sports drink in her hand. She's soaking wet. After she ties off the boat, she stands straight up and stretches with her hands above her head. She opens the plastic bottle and drinks almost all of it. The sergeant can hardly resist taking advantage of this target of opportunity. He pushes the safety forward. As soon as the safety clicks to the off position, Sue stops drinking and looks directly at the sergeant. "I can't believe this woman. She can't see me. She can't hear me. Why is she looking right at me?" She cups her hand over her eyes to block the glare from the light on the dock and scans the distant shoreline. "I still can't believe this woman. You live today, but next week I'm going to drill you right between those big tits of yours." Shortly after, the van backs the trailer down the backdown ramp. Sue unties the boat and the driver of the flat boat drives the boat on the trailer.

Once the boat is out of the water, the whole team gets in the van. The van sits there for fifteen minutes. The sergeant assumes that they are having an action review.

0415, the van starts up and takes off.

The sergeant gets up and walks back to Hwy. 90. He looks around. He sees a nice place to park his van. "We'll use silenced weapons. My team has forty-five minutes to hit Joe and get the van here. They can wait here in darkness. When I see the flatboat, I can send the van across the bridge. When the van makes it to the other side of the bridge, I'll nail Sue. Standing on that dock in the light, she's an easy target. My men can finish off the rest of her crew. We'll load the bodies back in the van, drive it to the weigh station, and scatter the bodies about. By this time, I'm sure Satinito will have taken care of Harris. I'll divide the money amongst the men."

CHAPTER 33

▼

Friday Morning Sue drags into the office half asleep and half an hour late. She sneaks by Harris' office, and he says nothing. She gets into her cubical and sets up her laptop. She looks up and sees Harris with a smile from ear to ear standing in her entrance way.

"How much money was transferred?"

"I'm estimating about two point two."

"Anything else."

"One of the guys was missing."

"Which one?"

"The new kid."

"I suppose that Cliff just couldn't handle it."

"I suppose not. This is quickly becoming a blood bath. We need to break this up."

"Sue, all I need is another month. Can you just give me another month?"

"Sure, another month."

"I tell you what, take the rest of the day off."

"What about the two o'clock report?"

"Is there anything else that happened last night that didn't happen any other night?"

"No."

"Well, I'm giving you the day off."

She gets excited. "Really." Harris nods his head, and she reaches to shutdown the laptop.

"Whoa, Sue. I'm giving you the day off on one condition, you take it off—no files, no laptop, no work."

"Wait, what if a phone call comes through?"

"I'll check on it from time to time. If anything seems interesting, I'll call you." She gives Harris an *I don't trust you face.* "Go ahead, I'll log you off before I leave tonight."

Sue grabs her purse and rushes out the door before Harris changes his mind.

She gets into her car thinking how she's going to spend her three-day weekend. The light bulb goes off in Sue's head. "I'm so stupid. I left my computer on and unlocked to the man that has made my life miserable for the past year." She turns the car around in the parking lot and roughly stops in the first available parking spot. She opens the door, gets out, walks back to the elevators, and pushes the button. While she's waiting, she reads the names in the glass covered building directory. She stops on Clifton A. Wallace. "Cliff, how did he know the kid's name? I didn't even know it." The elevator door opens, and she does not get on it. Her mind is working in a furious pace. "If Harris is dirty, this whole drug set up is making him filthy rich. He's using us to keep tabs on Satinito's bunch. Wait, all he was worried about this morning was the amount of money. He's probably using us to make sure that he gets his cut. I don't know how I can prove this, but I don't want him to have access to my computer." She pushes the elevator button again. The elevator doors open, and she gets in. On the way up, she changes her mind again. She rides the elevator back down, gets back in her car and drives off. As soon as she's out of the parking lot, she calls Danny."

"Danny, this is Sue. I need a big favor, and I need it in a hurry."

"I'm kind of busy, Sue."

"Can you monitor what happens to my computer without anybody knowing you're monitoring it?"

"Yeah, sure. Why?"

"I think Harris is dirty."

"Sue, watch what you're saying."

"I know what I'm talking about. I just need some evidence, and I know exactly how I'm going to get it."

"I hope you know what your doing. I'll start tracking your computer right now."

"Thanks, Danny. Putting Harris behind bars will be the fulfillment of my dreams. Talk to you later." Sue drives home to her townhouse and starts putting the pieces together.

0900 Jacques takes a ride to New Orleans Map Company and purchases a topo of Hwy. 90 near the Mississippi/Louisiana state line. Jacques mounts his GPS to his dashboard and takes a ride to Mississippi via Hwy. 90. Before I-10, Hwy. 90 was the way to the Mississippi Gulf Coast. The area that he is most interested in is between US 190 and the Mississippi—Louisiana state line. In this location, US 90 runs almost due east—west. There's a borrow canal on the south side of US 90 with a small levee on the south side of the canal. On the north side of US 90 is a mixture of roseau canes, slews, and oak groves. As he passes US 190 outside of Slidell, he starts paying more attention to details. He's looking for possible drug dealing locations within this three and a half mile stretch of un-populated highway. Even though Cliff told him that the spot is in front of an abandoned hotel, Jacques doesn't want to rule out the possibility that Cliff lied to him. He wants to investigate all possibilities.

At the intersection of US 90 and US 190, there's a picnic area. The picnic area has two entrances fifty yards apart on US 190 and none on US 90. He pulls in and starts stretching and walking about. "This could be a decent spot. It has US 90 east and west and US 190 that goes back to Slidell. The sight has potential, but it also has a serious fault. There's no line of sight along the roads. The picnic area is located in several bends of the roads. A vehicle can easily surprise them."

He next comes across the old abandoned White Kitchen restaurant. It's close to the intersection of US 90 and US 190. He pulls into the shell parking lot and appears to be checking his tires as he scopes the area. This is another good spot, but he remembers that many fishermen meet here. It probably has a lot of traffic early in the morning.

Half a mile east from US 190 is the bridge over the West Pearl River. It has a boat launch and plenty of trucks with boat trailers parked at its base. The bridge is a drawbridge type that is manned twenty-four hours a day. There's also a house to the east of the bridge near the boat launch. He decides that it's not worth stopping for.

Driving another mile and three quarters further is a bridge that crosses the Middle Pearl River. It too has a small dirt boat launch. It's a fixed concrete bridge, and the area is isolated. He pulls over and walks up to a man that is fishing from the bank. Jacques asks how's the fish biting and continues to carry on a conversation while he scopes that possible location out.

Three quarters of a mile further, he sees the abandoned hotel with a parking lot. This spot is ideal. He pulls over and opens the hood of his truck. He looks under the hood and then crawls under the truck. While he's under the truck, he takes pictures of the area without looking obvious. He then gets up and appears to take pictures of the truck from all sides; however, the truck is for the most part out of the scene. The hotel has a large parking lot that can probably fit a hundred automobiles. The parking lot is made of concrete, and it's in fair condition. The hotel is positioned two hundred yards from the highway. The borrow canal that parallels US 90 is fifty yards behind the motel. On the north side of US 90 is a wooded area with large oak trees. This spot has good visibility. He can easily see a quarter mile to the west and half a mile to the east. He lowers his hood, gets back into the truck, and continues towards the state line.

The state line is just another three quarters of a mile. There's a small convenience store. The largest single selling item is probably Louisiana lottery tickets. He stops in for a Coke. The store is set off the highway fifty yards. It has two gasoline pumps in front. If it's not manned twenty-four hours a day, it probably has some sort of burglar alarm.

The East Pearl River marks the state line. At the East Pearl River boat launch, the East Pearl River is nearly two hundred and fifty yards wide. The bridge is the turret type that is also manned 24 hours a day. Just to the south of the bridge is a four boat, concrete, back-down ramp with a large parking area for boat trailers on the western shoreline. He pulls over. This is a popular spot for the fishermen. This location probably has too much activity for drug dealers to operate. While sitting in his truck drinking his Coke, he makes notes of everything he saw that day. After writing the notes, he starts the truck up and heads back to Hopedale. As he passes the abandoned hotel, "It appears that Cliff was telling the truth about the hotel, but what did he lie about? More importantly, what did he leave out?"

On the way back, he sets an Icon in his GPS at every probable location. After he passes the picnic area, he imagines that he's a drug dealer, and analyzes each spot for it's advantages and disadvantages. He stops at a one hour photo shop and gets the pictures developed and heads back to Hopedale.

1800, Sue is in her townhouse in a large tee shirt and a pair of running shorts. Her phone rings, and she answers it.

"Sue, it's Danny, I think you should know that they are downloading your hard drive. Do you want me to stop them?"

"No, let them do it. I don't have anything on there that they don't already know about. Can you tell who's doing it?"

"No, as far as the computer is concerned, you are."

"Ok, keep me posted."

Sue calls the senior ERT that helped her with the Meyeaux case.

"I need a favor. Tonight at midnight, I need to meet you at the elevators of the office."

"Ms. Rodred, you sort of brushed me off on our last trip."

"Don't get your hopes up. It's work. Bring your equipment. I want to lift a few fingerprints."

"Yes, ma'am. I'll see you tonight at midnight."

"See you then."

2100, Jacques grabs all of his maps, notes and pictures and goes into his shed. He knows that there are five men he's hunting. Joe killed Billy, and he killed Cliff. Tony, Joe and Mike are the only three left.

Jacques begins talking to himself. "Mike is Joe's bodyguard. So wherever Joe is, Mike will be. Tony's a wild card, but he's easy to find. I can take Joe and Mike at the drug dealing spot, and Tony at his house." Jacques has several eight by tens pictures and one eleven by fourteen. He separates his information into two stacks—one with Tony and Tony's house; and the other with Joe, Mike, and the drug dealing spot.

"Let's start with Tony." He hangs the eight by ten pictures on the wall. "I can set up like before and instead of a camera, I'll have a rifle. A headshot from the sitting position at two-hundred yards is a piece of cake. Having Tony headshot might spook Joe and Mike. If I want to get them all, it's going to have to occur all on the same day. I can shoot him up close with a pistol, but it will be noisy. What about using a silencer? I will still attract attention from the news media, which will alert the other two. Tony just has to disappear without a trace. I got it. I could drive by early in the morning and ask him for directions. When he comes up to the truck, I could shoot him with a silenced pistol, jump out of the truck, throw him into the back, and drive off." Jacques looks at the pictures of Tony. "This guy weighs close to three hundred pounds. Picking him up is out of the question. If I'm going to cart him off, I'm going to need a winch or someone to help me. Mr. Melerine, he can help me." Jacques looks at the pictures again. "No, shooting you is just too easy of a death for you. I want to make you suffer. Just in case your soul escapes hell, I'm going to make sure that you live it first. You're going to get 'six poles.' Now, all I have to do is find a way of capturing you." Jacques looks at a close up shot. "You look like Grendel. How can I capture Grendel? The garbage can with the wooden stick worked fine for Cliff. I guess it will work for Grendel. I'll use a galvanized pipe instead of a wooden dowel. I can't charge him because if he sees me, I'm dead. Can I get him in the alley and wait for Mr. Melerine to come with the truck? The alley is like walking into a dead end. It's ten foot wide with a redwood fence at the end of it. It has a concrete floor with brick walls on both sides. If Grendel doesn't go down on the first blow, there's nowhere to hide and nowhere to escape." Jacques looks at his sketches of the house and surrounding houses. He then looks at his bird's eye view drawing. He looks at his pictures again, and he notices there's a small garden in the alley along the side of Tony's house. The garden stretches out as far as the overhang. "Tony has to bring out the trash through the alley. The garden forces him to walk away from the overhang. I can get him from the roof." Jacques looks at his plan view again and the pictures. "The roof of the house to the north should make a nice shadow on Tony's roof." He takes a straight edge and draws a line from the street light to the roof to the north and to Tony's house's roof. "It should start where the fence is. Even if the moon is out, it will be hard to see a person in all black lying down on the roof. I can get on the roof by using the red-wood fence, wait there until he puts out the trash, jump him, and call for Mr. Melerine with a radio. He can back the truck right up to the alley. We throw him in, and off we go. The only problem is that it will be a daytime operation, but we have half an hour. It should work, I just need a piece of pipe."

To the right of the pictures of Tony and his house, Jacques hangs up the eleven by fourteen. He thinks to himself, "I should have made a poster size of it." To the right of it, he hangs up the pictures of the motel. He hangs up the Topo map next to them, and pictures of Joe and Mike next to the Topo. He looks at the pictures of Joe's friend and wonders what to do with them. He decides that it isn't his fight. He just wants the ones, who did wrong to Malynda and her husband. He puts them back on the table. He puts a circle on the Topo where the motel is and steps back to think. He begins talking to himself again. "If I'm a drug dealer where would I expect an attack from? How do I protect myself from the police? Where would I think is safe and why? Obviously, the road is the biggest vulnerability. A car traveling at sixty miles per hour could be on them in seconds. If I'm smart, I'll have lookouts at the bridges on each side. If I get in trouble, the lookouts could act as the calvary. The only other way in or out is through the swamp. A person would have to be desperate to make it through swamp. He would have to use multiple vehicles. He would have to use a four-wheeler through the woods, a pirogue through slew, a boat in the river, and walking that marsh is no piece of cake. So let's say a person uses the swamp to get there. He holds them up. Now, he has to carry the money and the drugs out. He radios a car to pick him up. The goons at the bridge seal off the highway, and the robbers meet a slow death." Jacques moves over to a good facial of Joe. "What would you do? How can I give you the surprise of your life?" Jacques studies his face. "You're pretty clean cut. You look like one of those guys that gets their hair cut every other day. Clothes color coordinated. Even your fishing clothes are pressed. I see that collar." He looks at another picture that's a full body shot. "Look at those shorts. I bet they're dry clean only, maybe even designer name. Doesn't matter how good your clothes look; you are still going to die. I'm going to figure out a way. It will just take a little time."

There's a knock on the door, and Malynda walks in. "Jacques, are you in here?"

"Yeah, but you shouldn't come in here." Jacques realizes his mistake. Women always have a predictable trait—they will always do what you suggest them not to do. Malynda is no exception. She comes in and looks at the pictures of Tony. "He's the one that beat me." She passes over the eleven by fourteen with a smirk. She looks at the pictures of Joe and Mike. She points to Mike. "This is the one that held Scott against the wall." She then points at Joe. "Who's this? He wasn't there. The other guy has a bald spot."

"Are you sure this wasn't him?"

"I'm sure Jacques. This wasn't him."

Jacques turns the pictures over that are on the table. "Is this him?"

"That's him. He was giving the orders and laughing at me as I was being beat."

Jacques is a little puzzled because at Tony's house the whole group was playing him up. He was like a client to them, or he was like a boss to them. Jacques takes down the pictures of the strange man and replaces them with Joe's. It's not his fight.

"Jacques, I hope you'll take care of them; and do it soon. We need to get back to living a normal life." She walks back to the eleven by fourteen and points to it. In a snotty tone, "Who's this? Your new girlfriend?"

"That's the girl I went to see the other night."

"Yeah, sure. Who is she?"

"I told you."

"She might be a contortionist, but she has a wide derriere."

"She's just fine the way she is. The camera makes her look wider than she is. Isn't that what all women say?"

Malynda runs over to Jacques in a playful mood poking at him, "Men! That is not what all women say." They play for a little while and Malynda wraps herself in Jacques' arms. There's a moment of silence as she looks up at him, and he down at her. "Jacques, I'm afraid that you might get hurt or even dead. Let's turn this over to the police and let them handle it."

"Can't do that. The only way that I know that you will be safe is when I see mud being thrown on top of their gravesite. Besides, I'm going to keep my distance. It will be ok—trust me."

Malynda buries her head in Jacques' chest and gives him a big squeeze. "What is going to happen when this is all over with?"

Jacques softly replies. "I'm not sure. First, let's just get it over with. Now, I need some time to think. Don't you have some womanly things to do?"

Malynda makes a face on the way out. "I guess I could clean the camp for the hundredth time today."

Jacques tells himself that she doesn't understand. He has used up all of his vacation, and he's raiding his savings account to keep going. He can't keep this up much longer. "There's a bright side. Where there're drugs—there's cash money with nobody's name on it. Maybe, it's enough to get Malynda a new start. If I'm lucky, it might even be able to get me a new start. I just have to find a way to steal it without getting killed."

Jacques looks at the picture of the front of the motel, and begins talking to himself. "The motel is in terrible shape. It's obviously caught on fire at least one time and has seen many hurricanes. It was probably built before I-10 was. It's a four story straight building with an outdoor stairway on each side. There's probably an internal elevator in the center with a single hallway on each floor that stretches from one outdoor stairway to the other outdoor stairway. Rooms are on each side of the hallway. Most of the windows are entirely missing or at least broken. I can set up in one of those rooms and snipe the whole parking lot. With making a few holes in the walls, I can shoot; relocate to another room; and shoot again." He looks at the pictures again. "The entire first floor is sealed off with steel plate. The stairways are open, and there's access to the roof on one side. There's a few major problems with sniping from the motel. First, there's no escape route. The roof is big, but eventually I'll be rushed. Second, I'll be in the bald ass open getting to the motel. Third, it's an obvious hide." He looks at pictures around the parking lot. "The area to the east is sparsely populated with grass in areas. The area to the west is a wooded area. He figures that it's too open on the east side, and he'll have to get too close on the west side."

Jacques gets back to studying the map. He looks at the picture of the hotel and then the aerial photographs. He draws a grid on the aerial photograph using the width of the highway as a basis and starts putting dimensions on it. "The hotel is fifty feet wide and three hundred feet long. It's set off the highway right-of-way by three hundred feet. The borrow canal is a hundred feet wide and the space between it and the hotel is a hundred feet. The highway right-of-way is fifty feet on each side of the highway. The parking lot stretches from the hotel to the highway right-of-way and has a concrete entrance over the right-of-way on each side. On the west side of the hotel, the parking lot is a hundred and fifty feet wide and on the east side is fifty feet wide. I could set up on the south side of the borrow canal. There is a small levee." Jacques looks at the aerial photograph. He picks a point on the levee and using a straight edge and draws the boundary of his view. "If I set up on the eastern side of the motel, I have a clear sight of almost the entire parking lot because the barren ground that is east of the hotel will not obstruct my view. I can adjust by sliding along the levee. Just a small portion of the parking lot near the structure will be obscured." He does the same study on the western side of the motel. "The western side option view is much more limited because of the wooded area west of the small canal. The structure and the wooded area bound my lines of sight. This sight does have an advantage—there is a forty-foot wide canal that stretches from Hwy. 90 to the borrow canal. It must have been for fishermen. The motel probably at one time had a back down ramp."

"The only other option is the wooded area on the north side of Hwy. 90." Jacques looks at the pictures. "The highway right-of-way is clean cut. The highway is four feet above the wooded area. I can use a climbing deer stand and set up." Jacques laughs to himself. "That would make a nice present for a counter sniper team—fifty yards into the woods up a tree. No thank you."

He continues talking to himself. "The borrow canal levee looks like the obvious choice. Even though I have a better view of the parking lot from the eastern position, I like the western position better. If something were to go wrong the wooded area would offer cover for my escape. The small canal also offers me some protection. He looks at the aerial photograph and compares it to the picture of the front of the motel. "What's missing from my obscured view. Within a hundred feet of the structure, there's trash, oyster sacks, and rather large pieces of broken concrete scattered about. All the debris pushes them closer to Highway 90." He looks at the pictures and tries to locate the debris on the aerial photograph. "The edge of the piles of debris almost makes a straight line from the northeast corner of the motel to where the small canal meets Hwy. 90." He continues the line to the small levee on the east side of the hotel. "This will be a perfect spot. I would have a clear view of the usable portion of the parking lot." Something troubles him about this location. He can't explain it, but he doesn't like the spot for some reason. He looks back to the location he picked on the west side of the hotel. "I have more cover here, and escape is much easier. The debris pushes them so far north that they'll be in clear view from this position anyway."

Jacques looks at the lines of sight on aerial photograph. "The far east side of the parking lot is my only problem. Other than a small trash pile close to the highway and the access canal, there's nothing." He looks at a picture with the levee. "It looks six feet tall." He looks at the debris. "Highest pile is between three and four feet tall. I can shoot over the debris. If I set up where I can't see them, I'll just have to adjust along the levee to get a better view."

"Just two more things—approach and escape routes. To keep the area sanitized, I want to come in from the south." He looks at the Topo and finds a small bayou half a mile south of the motel. "Half mile stalk, that's seventeen hundred and sixty pulls. It's a long stalk through the marsh. It will take some time, but I've done this before. Ok, so that is my way in. My way out needs to be faster. I'll have to go through the woods on the north side of the highway." Jacques goes back to the aerial photo. "The woods are only three quarters of a mile deep, then a hardwood swamp, and then a marsh grass swamp. Once I get to the Middle Pearl, I can ride it out to the highway. I'll put my truck there. Wait, the goons could be there. There's another boat launch on the west side of the West Pearl. The launch is at the back of a subdivision called Indian Creek Village." Jacques looks at the map again. "Man, that's a long haul. I'll have to have my boat waiting for me in the Middle Pearl. Now, I have a way in, a hide, and a way out." He picks up a tablet of paper. "It's time to start making a list of what can go wrong."

2400: The door of the shed opens and Malynda walks in, "I think you are spending too much time with your new girlfriend. It's time to give it a break. You can finish in the morning."

"You're probably right." Jacques turns out the light and heads back to the camp with Malynda.

"What are you doing in there that is taking so long?"

"Making a plan so that I don't get killed or caught."

"I still think that we should go to the police."

Jacques looks down at Malynda and shakes his head.

For the rest of the night Jacques can't sleep. He keeps playing the plan over and over in his mind. He's trying to figure out what can go wrong, and how he can react to it. "The swamp is one nasty place. I have to deal with snakes, spiders, alligators, goons, gunfight, getting lost in the woods, and getting lost in the swamp. I'll divide it up into two categories of trouble—one that I have control over and one that I don't. The ones that I don't are snakebite, spider bite and being attacked by an alligator. Now, to solve the other ones that I have control over. Gunfight is easy—kill everybody without exception quickly and from a distance. If I can block the road to keep the goons from getting to the scene, I will have more time to escape. I could use tire rippers that magically appear on the road when all the commotion starts. What if I launch the rippers from a cata-pult—a remote control catapult? Well, maybe not a catapult, maybe some type of cannon. Getting lost in the woods isn't a big deal. I just need a compass, stay calm and search for the next available landmark. The best way to stay alive is to hit hard and fast and disappear just as fast. I'm going to need help on this one. I'm going to have to get Mr. Melerine involved."

At midnight at the FBI Field Office, the young clean cut investigator with too much after shave on is waiting for Sue outside the elevators. Sue walks in full of sweat wearing a baggy shirt and shorts. No make-up and her hair is a mess. She tells the young agent. "I want you to search my cubical for bugs, and I want you to dust my entire cubical for fingerprints—starting with the computer. I need you to do this—no questions asked."

They get on the elevator and ride up to her floor. He quietly crawls in her cubical on his hands and knees. He searches the bottom of her desk and reference table. He stands up, searches the cubical, and finds a small microphone placed in between the cubical partitions. He motions to Sue and points to it. He completes scanning the office for bugs, and the one is all that he finds. He slowly lifts the laptop screen, looks at the keyboard, and shakes his head. He sees another bug hidden under the keys. He looks closely at the keyboard and the desk near the computer. Closes it and walks out. He motions for Sue to follow him. They walk down the corridor near Harris' office. He whispers to her. "Are you under inves-tigation?"

She shakes her head "No."

"What are you involved with then? There are two real expensive bugs in your office. You can see that the fingerprints on the computer are smudged and there's a trace of fine powder on the keyboard, I'm assuming that he used latex gloves with powder in them. I suspect he put the gloves on before he came into your cubical and took them off after he left. The trail stops there. Do you want me to pull the bugs?"

"No, they'll just replace them. Besides, miss information is a powerful tool." Sue looks into a nearby trash can. "It's got trash in it. Great, the cleaning crew hasn't taken out the trash. Let's find the pair of gloves."

"What for? The rubber stretches so much that you won't be able to get a good print. Face it, this is a dead end. Don't pass go, don't collect your two hundred dollars."

"That's it—a pass." She pulls out her phone as they walk out to the elevators. She sees the disappointment on the young agent's face. "Oh, you're so sweet." She leans over, gives him a big hug, and a kiss on the cheek. "Thanks."

Sue calls Danny.

"Danny can you get me a list of people that left the building after they were finished downloading my computer?"

"Sure, just a second. They finished downloading at 1820. There were only ten people that left the building's parking lot from 1820 till you entered the parking lot. Here, I'll read them off. See if you recognize them."

"They all seem legitimate. Do me a favor and e-mail me the list."

"Sue you sure are a slow learner. They could have set up a recorder in your computer. Quit being so lazy and write down the names."

"Ok go ahead." Sue begins to write down the names. "Wait, I can no longer use my computer. Danny, I'm going to have to have you pull up their dossier and fax them to me." She sees the young agent to the elevator, and she walks back to the shared fax machine on her floor.

"Sue, what if someone sees them?"

"Danny, it's midnight."

"Ok, give me half an hour or so."

"I'll be waiting at the fax machine."

Sue anxiously waits at the fax machine. Twenty minutes later the fax machine rings and pages start coming through. The fifth dossier comes through, and it is of Harris' sergeant. Sue sees the black and white picture and picks it up. "Well, Mr. Jones, what are you doing in this stack?" She reads the second page as it comes off the machine. "So you're not CIA, you're just an entry team leader that is assigned directly to Mr. Franklin Harris. This is interesting." She waits for the other faxes to come through and calls Danny to verify that he's complete. She picks up the stack of fifty pages and heads out of the building.

CHAPTER 34

▼

Saturday 0700, in Jacques' camp, Jacques wakes to the smell of French toast. He gets up and heads towards the shower.

Malynda stops him. "No, you don't. You don't have enough time. Sit down and eat your breakfast first. I never saw you sleep this late. What's the matter?"

"Didn't sleep to good last night. I had a lot on my mind."

"Please take the day off. You've been going day and night. It has to be taking a toll on you. Jacques, please. Just lounge around the camp in your tee shirt and boxers today—just for today."

"You're right. A day of rest and relaxation would probably do me some good. I have some paperwork that I can do."

"As long as you don't have to go outside! Today, I want you to relax inside in the air conditioning."

After Jacques and Malynda finish their breakfast, Malynda starts on the dishes and Jacques takes a shower. Jacques shortly re-appears in a white tee shirt and boxers. He goes into his room and comes out with a pencil and an engineering tablet. He makes himself comfortable on the couch. Malynda isn't far behind him. She lays her head in his lap as he starts designing the catapult.

He brainstorms for a while. He finally comes up with something that will launch the tire rippers on the road. He plans on using a three pound coffee can, a piece of PVC pipe, and a rubber inner-tube. He starts out with a five foot section of eight inch PVC pipe. He draws a three quarter inch slot almost the entire length on each side of the PVC. He makes a note on the drawing to punch a hole in opposite sides of the coffee can near the bottom and through the bottom on each side of the coffee can. He plans on putting the can in the pipe and thread some copper wire through the holes in the can forming loops. He can then drill a hole in front of the slot. He can use some more copper wire to form loops. He can cut the inner tube in long strips and tie it between the loops on the pipe and the loops on the can. He can add a few sheet metal screws at the end of the PVC pipe to stop the can from coming out. For the trigger, he draws an "L" with a little notch on the bottom. He decides to use a piece of one-eighth inch aluminum plate and cut a one-inch thick "L" that's three inches tall and two inches wide. On the lower leg of the "L," he extends a small piece into the pipe so it just penetrates the PVC pipe. He can drill a hole in the PVC with the can in the set position and cut a three-sixteenth inch groove that is only half of the wall thickness deep for the "L" to stand up in. He can then drill a hole in the top of the "L" for the control arm to tie into, place the "L" on the pipe, and tie an inner tube around leg of the "L" and the pipe. The inner tube will automatically reset the trigger. For a safety, he can drill the PVC pipe and install a piece of quarter inch round bar in front of the can. For the remote control, he can mount it on a small piece of two by four that screws into the PVC pipe. He'll fill the can with tire rippers and use a plunger to push the can pass the trigger. With the remote control unit, he'll hit the switch. The can will be violently launched forward, come to an abrupt stop at the sheet metal screws, and the tire rippers will continue out the device in a shotgun pattern. To give the tire rippers a little trajectory, he decides to mount a piece of two by four on the muzzle end, and he decides to drive a one inch diameter wooden stake through the pipe behind the can in the set position to anchor it. For camouflage, he'll paint it brown and cover it with old oyster sacks.

Jacques puts the tablet down on the coffee table and starts to get up. He looks at Malynda, "Don't you need something from town?"

"No Jacques, you're taking the day off."

"I know, but I just have to run some errands—that's all. It won't take me long. It is just a quick trip into town and back."

"I don't know why I even try. Just make it a quick trip."

Jacques dresses, gets in the truck, and leaves. He drives out to town where he knows of a hobby shop that specializes in radio-controlled airplanes and boats. He walks in the glass door and a chime rings. The hobby shop has racks of models and parts and hanging from the ceiling has several completed airplanes and boats. A young fellow with wild red wiry hair and an un-kempt beard comes from the back room to the sales counter. "Can I help you?"

"I'm looking for a radio control unit with two receivers and a two-day battery life."

"You might be able to hook up two batteries together in parallel. You would extend the battery life that way. I'm afraid that the receivers are only sold with the transmitter."

"Can one transmitter operate two receivers?"

"It should be able to, as long as you buy the same brand and the same frequency. We can test them out before you buy them."

"Thanks. What about the range?"

"They say that they can operate up to three miles. I've only tried a mile and a half, and it works fine."

"What about servos?"

"The servos come with the package. A package comes with a transmitter, a receiver, receiver batteries, servos, and a charger."

"I'll take two of the same type, and I need some control linkage."

"How many channels do you want? They come in even numbers from two to fourteen." Jacques looks at the salesman with a puzzled look. "Channels are the number of different servos that you can operate from the same transmitter. If you want range, the least I recommend is six."

"That'll do. Do you have any control linkage?"

The salesman walks away and comes back with some control linkage. It's a piece of flexible yellow plastic hose inside a semi ridged blue plastic hose. Jacques looks at it. "Do you have anything ridged?"

"You really want to use this stuff because it doesn't involve soldering." Jacques just makes a face. "I think I have some of those old ridged connections somewhere." The salesman starts digging in a box of obsolete equipment. "We keep this box of old stuff in case someone has to repair an old plane or boat. Nobody uses this stuff any more. Here we go, a pack of six. It is adjustable on one end by a threaded linkage and the other end you cut to fit and solder the linkage on. Will that be it?"

"Did you include the extra batteries?"

"Sure did."

"How much?"

"The units are $220 each, batteries $25 each, control linkage $6. With 8.25% tax, it comes up to $536.92."

Jacques pulls out the cash and gives it to him. He carries the stuff out and puts it in the truck.

His next stop is a building supply place. He purchases all the materials and the tools necessary to build the cannon. His next stop is a dive shop, where he purchases a pair of fins and a good fitting mask. The last stop is at a police supply shop for the tire rippers.

Jacques walks into what looks like a jewelry shop. An elderly fellow greets him as he walks in the door, "Can I help you?" Jacques can see that this guy is ex-police and probably ex-military.

In a friendly tone Jacques replies. "I'm looking for something to stop poachers at my deer camp. They cut the barbwire fence on this pipeline right-of-way, drive on the property at night and shoot all of the deer."

"Have you called the game warden?"

"Yep, sure did. The problem is that I think he might be one of them. It is the summer time, and there is no one up there. They raid our camps and destroy our stuff."

"Where did you say this was?"

"In Mississippi."

"I don't believe a Mississippi Game Warden is involved. It's probably a bunch of kids. Do you know how much of a problem it is to arrest a minor, and how much paper work that needs to be filled out? After you do all of that, they're out before they're formally charged. It's the judges, I tell you. The judges are the problem with the justice system today. They're too soft. With all the brutality charges, can you imagine what would happen if you put your hands on a minor?"

"I don't want to hurt them. I just want to give their ATV's some flat tires."

"Have you tried roofing nails? They work just fine."

"I'm afraid that they'll just use plugs to fix the tires. I want the tires destroyed. I want to make a statement."

"I might have the exact thing that you are looking for. They're called tire rippers. They are like four little metal knives that are connected in the center. When they are thrown out on a road, one of the little knives always point up and the other three support it. It can't land upside-down. Police use it for roadblocks."

"Can you sell me that? I mean, I don't want to get in trouble with the law."

"I don't see why not. You can buy it off the Internet. They're expensive."

"How expensive? I won't have to take out a second mortgage will I?"

"Let me see. I think that I have some back here." He pulls out a ten pound flour sack. "Here they are." He carefully puts them on the glass counter and opens the package. Jacques looks at them. Each blade is an inch long and a quarter of an inch wide and a sixteenth inch thick. The ends are brought to a point and beveled. "I can let you have the whole bag for." He paused for a second. "Say $80."

"How about I buy two bags for $150?"

"I guess that will be ok."

Jacques looks into the glass counter, "These handcuffs look real strong. What's the deal? Regular handcuffs not good enough anymore?"

"A couple of years back, some deputies arrested one of those oyster fishermen. He was a big fellow on PCP. To make a long story short, he was handcuffed in the back of the police car; and he broke the chain of the handcuffs and began to rip the cage out of the car. The cops abandoned the car and kept him inside with drawn pistols. They had to wait to get one of those tazers on him. They double cuffed him and left the tazer in him until he was behind bars. Ever since, they have been carrying these hinged cuffs."

"How much?"

"$80"

"Ok, I'll take them." As Jacques is pulling out his money. "Is everything in here $80?"

The salesman smiles. "Nope, I just figured that someone that just spent $150 on tire rippers could afford $80 handcuffs." They both laugh. Jacques thanks him and walks out the door.

Jacques gets back in his truck and starts driving back to the camp. He thinks to himself. "The lucky part of the trip is that he's got everything. The unlucky part of the trip is the time. I've been gone for over five hours, and I still have over an hour drive back. Malynda is going to be fuming. On the way home, I'll buy a DVD player and pick up a chick flick and buy her some flowers. I think that should smooth things over."

He makes it back, and as soon as he walks in the door, Malynda lets him have it. "I was planning on spending some time with you. I wanted a relaxing day with no worries. I feel safe when you are around, but you haven't been around very much lately." She continues and Jacques can see that she's in hormonal overload. He hands her the flowers. The flowers work all of a few seconds, and she starts again. He continues to unload the truck and set up the DVD player. He hands Malynda the two movies, which apparently works. Jacques strips down to his boxers again and sits down on the couch.

"I'm sorry Jacques. I've been cooped up in this camp. I need to get out. I'm like a prisoner. You made some good choices for the movies. Let's do movie night tonight. For now, I just want you to be near me."

The rest of the day they lounge around and watch TV. After they eat dinner, they go for their afternoon walk. When they return, they pop popcorn, turn out all the lights, and put the first movie in. It's a Disney movie. They watch it; and after the movie, Malynda puts Celeste to bed. Jacques loads the second movie and starts it. Malynda goes into the kitchen and pours two glasses of wine. Jacques is sitting upright in the couch. Malynda snuggles up to him with her head on his shoulder, both her hands holding Jacques' arm, and her knees are bent with her feet on the couch. Fifteen minutes into the movie, Jacques is in a deep sleep. Malynda wakes him and walks to his bedroom with him. Jacques tells her good night, goes into his bedroom, and she goes to hers.

An hour later, she returns to his bedroom. She crawls on top of the covers and lays next to him. "Jacques, do you still have feelings for me."

"Of course I do. I just need some time."

"I am worried about me and Celeste. How are we going to make it?"

"Don't worry about anything. You are welcome to stay with me as long as you like."

"I don't want to stay with you. I want to be with you." She moves her head closer to his, and they passionately kiss. Malynda lays with her head on Jacques chest. "How much time do you think you'll need?"

"At least until this is behind us."

"I'm satisfied with that for now." She puts a smile on, gets up, and leaves his room.

CHAPTER 35

▼

Monday morning, Jacques gets up early and starts working on his cannon. He reads the instructions on the radio control units. There's nothing special, but they require twelve hours initial charge on all the batteries. He starts charging first thing. By 1100, he's in his shed testing out the first cannon out. He puts it on one side of the shed and points it to the other wall. The inner tubes are tight. Using a broomstick, he sets off the trigger. It goes off, but the trigger is too heavy. It jumps a foot off the ground and slids two feet forward. Jacques pulls out the trigger and files it back a little bit. He tests it again. This time it goes off without a problem. He resets it with the rippers in the can. He sets it off and the rippers are launched into the wall twenty feet away.

Jacques walks into the camp and Malynda confronts him. "Jacques you need to do something with the trash. It smells terrible. Burn it or do whatever, just get rid of the smell."

Jacques walks over to the burn barrel and Malynda is right. The smell is coming from shrimp heads. Jacques walks back to the house trying to get the stink out of his nose, "Where did the shrimp come from?"

"Jean gave me forty pounds a couple of days ago. I de-headed them and put them in the freezer. I didn't think they were going to smell this bad."

"Ok, do you have any other trash before I start the burn?"

"No, start the burn. The smell is getting in the house. It's awful!"

Jacques goes back outside grabs the gas can and just before he pours it on the shrimp heads he gets an idea. "What if I use these heads to keep Joe and Mike out of the east side of that parking lot?" Jacques shovels the heads into a double plastic trash bag and puts the bag in the bed of his truck. He starts the burn and goes inside to clean up. Washing his hands does not due the trick. The stink soaked his clothes. He removes his clothes and puts them in the washing machine.

"Malynda, I have an errand to run. I'll be back in a few hours." He gets in his truck, drives to the abandoned hotel, pours the shrimp heads out of the bag into the parking lot, and drives back.

When Jacques returns, he heads straight for the shed to go over his plan again. He's still looking at the pictures on the wall of his shed. Mr. Melerine walks up behind Jacques and puts his hand on Jacques' shoulders. "Is it time?"

"Thursday. Mr. Melerine I'm going to need some help on this one."

"What's your problem?"

"I have a plan, but I need someone to drop me off and pick me up."

"No problem Jacques, I can do dat."

"I also need a hand with this one." He points to Tony's picture. "I'm planning on bringing him to six poles."

"Six poles, dat's serious. Jacques, dat's not like you. Why not just put a bullet in his head and get it over with."

"The problem is timing. Thursday morning, I need this guy to disappear without a trace. If I put a bullet in him, the news will spread and his friends will know that I'm coming for them."

"Ok, what do I have to do?"

Jacques points to a map. "Just wait right here with the truck. When I call you on the radio, come and help me load this lug into the truck. We take him to six poles. After that, I need you to take the Miss Jean, drop my pirogue off here, and then drop me off here." Jacques continues to explain his plan.

"Where're you planning on parking your truck?"

Jacques points to the map. "Right here."

"Jacques, I think you are leaving yourself in the open water too long. Look right here. There's an old abandoned Church on Hwy. 190. Behind the Church is a small ditch that leads all da way to the West Pearl. Dat's where you want to go. You can hide your truck real good behind dat church."

"Thanks, Mr. Melerine."

"Jacques, why don't you let me help at the hotel? I have a good 30–30 with an octagon barrel. She shoots straight."

"Thanks, but no thanks. I appreciate the offer, but this is not going to be a picnic. I'm going to have a rough time myself. Besides, I'm going to try to keep three hundred yards between me and them. At three hundred yards, your 30–30 has a trajectory like a rainbow. I'm afraid it's not going to be much help."

"The offer is still there. Just say da word."
"I tell you what, if you help me with Tony, that will be plenty enough."

CHAPTER 36

▼

Tuesday morning, Jacques knows this is his last day to prepare. Tomorrow, it starts. He knows that he'll not be able to stop until it is over.

First light, Jacques drives down to the pipeline canal that leads to six poles with a small flat boat on a light trailer. He pulls it off the trailer and fifty yards into the marsh. The twelve foot flat boat is fairly light. The only thing in it is a portable metal six gallon gas tank, and a ten horsepower motor on it. It's high tide and the water is in the grass. Being next to the road, the marsh is fairly hard and easy to walk in. In no time, he reaches the pipeline canal. He walks back to the truck, unhooks the trailer, and stashes it in the nearby marsh grass. He then heads back to the camp, gathers all of his equipment, and heads to the shed.

Jacques lays out all of his equipment on a table. He starts putting some of the equipment that he's not going to be using on the floor. He puts the equipment that he absolutely needs on the end of the table. These items include his rifle, his pistol, his ghillie suit, grease paint, scissors, rose bush trimmers, a lock-blade pocket knife, topo, his hydropack, transmitter, and compass. His next stack is items that are almost necessary, which includes an athletic bag, fins and a mask, and insect repellent. The next stack included things that would be nice to have like breakfast bars, yard guard, his spotting scope, poncho, and food. Jacques puts the spotting scope and poncho on the floor. The next thing that he looks at is the amount of ammunition that he would be taking. He has to kill two people, which only takes two rounds. His rifle holds three rounds. He figures three would be good enough. One full pistol clip for his 1911 should be plenty. He reminds himself. "I'm not there to stand toe to toe with him. If things go bad, I'll escape and evade." He puts as much as he can in ziplock bags and then all of this equipment in a small school type of backpack.

He works the catapults until he's certain that they will not malfunction. He then charges the batteries of the receivers and the transmitter.

He breaks down his pistol, cleans it, and lubes it. He proceeds to clean his rifle. He finds three of the most perfect rounds he can put his hands on, and chambers each round to make sure that they feed into the rifle.

He is not sure why, but he feels a need to pack his web gear harness. In his fanny pack he puts three days supply of food in a plastic container, two sixty round plastic containers of rifle ammunition in ziplock bags, his poncho, and G.I. cleaning kit. On each side of the fanny pack, he puts a full one quart canteen—one with the metal cup and one without. On his left side, he puts his bayonet. In front of it, he puts an M-16 mag pouch that he filled with eighty rifle rounds in two ziplock bags and tops it off with fifty pistol rounds in a ziplock bag. In front of the M-16 pouch, he adds a four pack of 45 clips. On the right side, he places another M-16 mag pouch with first aid supplies, trip wires, and other survival supplies. Between that pouch and the canteen, he leaves room for his pistol holster. He puts the pistol and pistol holster on the belt and puts it on to balance it out. It weighs twenty-five pounds, which he considers more than acceptable. He adjusts the straps so that the weight is evenly distributed. He moves around to make sure everything is tight and doesn't make any noise. Once he is satisfied, he takes the pistol and holster off and puts it back in the backpack.

He picks everything up off the floor and stuffs it into his ruck sack.

He starts rehearsing everything that he's going to do with all of his equipment on. He realizes he needs a garbage bag to stuff his ghillie suit in because if it gets wet it will weigh over a hundred pounds. He also realizes that he needs something to keep the bore of his rifle dry. He digs around in his rifle maintenance center and pulls out a small balloon. He'll expand a case in the chamber before he leaves. The boots take too long to put on after he makes the swim. He needs some swim shoes that will fit inside of his fins. The fins take too long to put them in the pack. He decides to drill a hole in each one so that they could hang on in a carabiner attached to his belt loop.

He does another mock rehearsal, and he decides it's good enough. He hopes that he plans for all the little unexpected things that will happen. It's lunch time, and Jacques knows that he has to leave his equipment alone. The longer he goes through it, the more weight he'll add. It's heavy enough, and it has everything he needs.

He looks at his clothing selection next. He's going to need several sets of clothes. The first set is Black BDU's, the next set is Woodland BDU's, and the third set is a pair of shorts and polo shirt for the ride home. He loads everything into the truck, except for the black BDU's.

As he walks into the camp Malynda is just putting sandwiches out on the table. She looks up and sees that Jacques is just in time, and they sit down and eat.

"Malynda, what about going for a boat ride after we're finish eating?"

Celeste's face lights up and a worry face comes over Malynda's.

"What if we run into them out on the water?"

"I doubt that would happen. Come on, we all need to get out?"

"Ok, but I am still a little nervous about it."

They load up into the boat and go for a ride. That afternoon the tide is falling pretty good, and Jacques decides to try their luck with fishing. Jacques anchors near the outflow of a trenasse. The poles have the classic set up with the florescent green egg cork with one clear and one florescent green sparkle beetle hanging from it.

Jacques is fishing, but Malynda can tell he's a million miles away. She can feel his tension, and realizes that something big is going to happen soon. They catch a dozen speckle trout, and they head back to the camp.

When they get back to the camp, Jacques cleans the fish; and Malynda gets the fish fry ready. They eat in silence as the TV plays in the background. Not paying attention to the time or the TV, Jacques just misses the weather. He walks out the door without saying a word. He climbs into his boat and listens to the marine radio. "This forecast is for the Louisiana Coastline east of the Mississippi River and out thirty miles and west of the Mississippi and out thirty miles. A high pressure is sitting over southeast Louisiana and will remain in place for the next forty-eight hours. Winds are expected to be light and variable. Seas are expected to be one to three feet, calm in protected bodies of water. The extended forecast: a front is expected to move through on Friday. A small craft advisory is expected to be in place. Wind will be out of the southeast twenty to twenty-five knots, seas expect to be four to six feet. At the Rigolets High Tide is at six p.m. Low tide is at six a.m. Range two point three feet. At Venice......At Chandeleur Island........." He turns the radio off.

When he turns the radio off, he sees Malynda standing at the end of the pier.

"Jacques, what is your problem?" He looks up, and his eyes say everything. "When is it going to happen?"

"It starts tomorrow night." Jacques is fooling with some of the electronics on the dashboard of the console.

Malynda jumps into the boat, walks up to him, and hugs him. "I had no idea that it was so soon."

He looks down at her, and she up at him. Their eyes meet, and they begin to kiss.

Malynda pulls away, "Why do you have to do it? We can live happily down here." Jacques looks at Malynda with a stern look. "Ok maybe not down here, somewhere else then. I have relatives in Canada. Let's move to Canada."

"Malynda, I'm not one to run away from a fight. I want to be able to sleep at night without the worry of waking up to find out that you're killed." After Jacques statement, there's silence and an awkward feeling comes across them. Jacques turns out the lights in the boat, and they head back up to the camp holding hands.

When they arrived in the camp, Malynda sits on the couch. Jacques goes into his room, grabs some sleepwear, and heads to take a shower. After Jacques finishes taking his shower he's hoping to come out and talk to Malynda some more; but all the lights are out and Malynda must have gone to bed with Celeste. He goes into his room hoping she's there waiting for him, but he disappoints himself. He closes his door, climbs into the bed, and gets his mind back on the mission.

Thirty minutes later, he hears footsteps in the kitchen and hears the cabinet open. Jacques gets up and sees Malynda getting a glass of water. She has a pair of his boxers on with a white tee shirt. He slowly walks up behind her and kisses her on her neck. He nibbles on her ear while he strokes her shoulder. She makes a slight sigh and turns around. They embrace and kiss. Jacques lifts her body and carries her into his bedroom closing the door behind them. Jacques opens the curtains, and they make love in the light of a full moon.

CHAPTER 37

▼

Wednesday 0700, Jacques wakes to Celeste knocking on Jacques' bedroom door. The sun is already up, and Jacques jumps up. Malynda gently puts her hand on him and tells him to lie back down. She puts on her tee shirt and boxers and walks out of the door. She greets Celeste with a big smile, picks her up, and walks into the living room with her. "Jacques and I have some grown up talking to do. While Jacques and I talk, I need you to stay in here and color me some pretty pictures."

"Ok, Momma. Are you and Jacques married?"

Malynda laughs, "Not yet honey. Not yet."

Malynda returns to the bedroom, and climbs back into the bed with Jacques.

"What did you tell her?"

"I told her that we had some grown up talking to do." They enjoyed being close to one another.

"Jacques, do you believe in angels?"

"What kind of question is that?"

"Do you?"

"I suppose so, why?"

"That terrible night, I sent one to you. I don't know why to you, but I did."

Goose bumps cover Jacques body. "She got to you, didn't she?"

"Something happened that night. Can't tell exactly what. But something happened. If you have another, you might want to make sure that she stays with me tomorrow."

"Jacques, please consider Quebec. They speak French and everything."

"No Malynda, this is my home." Jacques can't believe what he said.

Celeste interrupts them by knocking on the door, "Momma, I'm hungry."
Malynda looks at Jacques, "I think it is about time we get up."
They get up and get dressed. They're both tired from the night before, and
Jacques knows it's going to be a long night. They eat breakfast and for most of
the day, Jacques and Malynda lounge around the camp. They take a nap lying on
the couch together. Jacques wakes an hour later and thinks to himself. "If I get
killed tomorrow, I'll die a happy man many times over. However, I would like to
have a bowl of ice cream before I go." With that thought, he gets up and fixes
himself and Celeste some ice cream. He looks at Malynda sleeping there looking
so comfortable.

Jacques sits at the kitchen table and writes a letter, folds it, and stuffs it in an
envelope.

Malynda wakes up about supper time. She warms up the left over fish from
the night before.

2100 in the Mead Hall, Joe, Mike, and Tony are sitting on the couch and
enjoying a drink.

Joe looks at Tony, "Tony, I need you tomorrow. Come on. What's your problem?"

"Boss, you know I'll do anything for you, but not tomorrow. Tomorrow is the
twenty-first..."

Mike chimes in, "Yeah, Tony, it's the twenty-first."

"Y'all don't understand. At midnight, it turns to the twenty-second. On the
twenty-second, I'm just going to stay in my house surrounded by my protection
potions and candles."

"Tony, as it is, we lost Cliff. I have no back-up at the state line. With you not
there, I have no protection from the west. I'm dealing with Satinito's nephew
too. This whole thing is getting a little creepy. I don't like to be covered by people I can't trust."

The door opens, Satinito walks in as usual with a woman on each arm. He is
followed by three three hundred and fifty pound bouncers with no necks.
"Where's the music? Come on in boys. I'll like to introduce to my new body-
guards. Joe, Mike, and Tony meet Tank, Half-track, and Two Ton."

Joe can't believe what's going on. "Mr. Satinito, I hope you don't pay those
guys by the pound." Everyone laughs.

Satinito puts his hand on Mike's shoulder. "Mike take Half Track and get
some women for us." Mike and Half Track leave the room. "Joe, how do you like
the beef? You shop for ex-football players. I shop for Pollocks from Chicago."

"Mr. Satinito, I think that we need to call off tomorrow night. We have a little problem."

"What's your concern?"

"We don't have any protection on the east side, and I can't convince Tony to come out tomorrow night. That leaves both the east and west open. It's too risky."

"No problem, we can use Half Track and Tank for backup." Joe doesn't like the idea, and his expression tells Satinito. Joe thinks to himself. "With the goons on each side and Satinito's nephew as a sniper, I could get killed right there."

"Relax Joe, it's nothing permanent. Just until Tony overcomes his issue and until you find a replacement for Cliff."

"Ok, Mr. Satinito. I guess I could use the help."

Mike and Half Track walk in with the women. Mr. Satinito turns on the music and the party continues into the night.

Before Jacques realizes the time, it's 2100—time for him to get ready. He dresses in his black BDU's. He puts the handcuffs in his front right pocket and a two foot section of rope in his cargo pocket. He almost forgets the walkie-talkies, goes back into his bedroom, and digs them out of his ruck sack.

Jacques is ready. He kisses Celeste on the cheek and passionately kisses Malynda. He tells them good-bye, and he'll see her in a couple of days. He hands Malynda the envelope and tells her not to open it unless he does not return by Saturday night. He kisses her one more time and leaves. He looks back at the camp to see Malynda holding Celeste on her hip and tears coming down the cheeks of both the girls. Mr. Melerine is waiting in Jacques' pick-up. "Come on Jacques, it's not going to get any easier. Let's go." Jacques jumps in the passenger seat, and Mr. Melerine drives off.

Jacques and Mr. Melerine reach the boat ramp on the state line. They turn around and drive back a hundred yards to a spot on the highway that has no shoulder and a steep embankment. Jacques gets out, grabs a catapult and the burlap sacks "Mr. Melerine, take the truck back to the boat ramp. I'll call you on the walkie-talkie when I'm ready to be picked up."

Jacques carefully places the catapult on the highway right-of-way to cause the greatest spread of rippers, and he hammers down the stake to secure the catapult. He makes sure that all the rippers are in the can. He turns on the transmitter, makes sure that the trigger's set, covers it with the burlap sacks, and removes the safety. He calls for Mr. Melerine.

Mr. Melerine picks him up, and they drive to the Middle Pearl River. They turn around and repeat the same process. The next stop is Tony's house.

CHAPTER 38

▼

0200 Thursday morning, Mr. Melerine stops on the highway two hundred yards short of Tony's street. Jacques points out the area to park the truck across the highway. Jacques gets out and moves stealth like through the neighborhood. Remembering the location of the electronic gate, he runs into the alley next to Tony's house. He opens Tony's neighbor's gate, goes into his neighbor's back yard, and closes the gate behind him. He climbs on top of the redwood fence, and then onto Tony's roof. He notes where the shadow from his neighbor's roof forms on Tony's roof and makes sure he stays in it. He lies as flat as possible on the roof. The only problem is the pipe. The roof slopes from Jacques' left to his right, and Jacques is right handed. He can't hold the pipe for hours. If he puts it down, it'll roll down the roof. He has to put it on his left side. Jacques get his body as comfortable as possible and waits.

0430, Tony pulls into his driveway and into his garage. Jacques is lying on the roof with his ear on the shingles. He can hear Tony and Amber talking in the garage. Jacques thinks to himself. "Now, I'm going to find out how really wild Amber is in the bed." To Jacques surprise, they're arguing over chicken feet? He hears the inside garage door close and still hears them arguing. He hears an interior door slam close. Jacques moves into position. He begins to think about the wonderful night that he had with Malynda. Thinking about it kept him awake and alert.

0450, Jacques hears the inside garage door open. He grabs his pipe and quietly gets on one knee. The side door opens and Jacques' heart is racing over two hundred beats per minute. At this moment, a memory flash hits Jacques—Grendel had a spell put on him so that no sword could cut him. Jacques wonders if it applies to galvanized pipes. He hears the trash can open, and he can hear Tony putting something in it. He then hears the wheels of the can start to roll. Jacques looks down and behind him. Tony is naked with a towel wrapped around his waist. He's walking past Jacques when Jacques sees that Tony senses that something's wrong. Jacques thinks, "Too late" and jumps out. Tony is quick and steps towards him. Jacques misses him with the pipe, but on his way down he manages to wrap his left arm around Tony's neck. Jacques just barely brings him to the ground. Jacques is ready to hit him in the back of the head when Tony flips over and grabs Jacques' hand with the pipe. Jacques knees him in the balls several times, but it just pisses Tony off. Tony punches Jacques in the face and throws Jacques over his head like a light rag. Jacques lands on his side but still maintains control of the pipe. Tony is instantly up on his feet, charging Jacques. Jacques is getting up on all fours when Tony goes to plant a foot into Jacques' ribs. From the kneeling position, Jacques swings with all of his might. He catches Tony in the left knee just as he's coming forward with his right foot. Jacques misses the tissue and hits something solid. So solid that it feels like he hit another pipe. It hurts so badly that the pipe drops from his hands. Tony falls hard holding his knee. Jacques picks up the pipe and finishes him off. He rolls the big guy over and handcuffs his hands behind his back. He then ties his feet so that he has twelve inches of rope between them. Out of breath, Jacques calls Mr. Melerine to come pick him up.

Mr. Melerine is there in no time. He backs the truck to the alley and helps Jacques load Tony in the bed. Once in the bed, Jacques takes the tire chain; wraps it around Tony's neck; and locks it to the pad-eye that he previously installed. They both jump into the truck and drive off. Half a mile down the highway, they pull over. Jacques gets out, wraps Tony a few more times with the pipe, covers the bed of the truck with a tarp, and gets back into the truck. Jacques is still breathing hard. "Mr. Melerine, that was a stupid idea. I almost got myself killed. I should have taken your advice and just shot him." Mr. Melerine just laughs as they continue to Hopedale. "Jacques, you know the old saying—if it don't kill you, it will just make you stronger." They both laugh.

They pull up to the pipeline canal and offload Tony. Jacques cuts a section of the tarp, makes some air holes, and ties it over Tony's head. Tony's knee is the size of a cabbage ball. Jacques takes the pipe, and Mr. Melerine grabs the 30–30. They slowly walk Tony to the boat and push him in. They sit Tony in the front. Mr. Melerine sits in the middle seat with the rifle on Tony, and Jacques drives the boat. As they come to the end of the canal, they can see six timber pilings that are sticking ten feet out of the water. The stench becomes almost unbearable.

Four of the piles have full skeletons hanging from them, one has a partially decaying body on it, and the second one has a partial skeleton of one hand and the forearm hanging from a chain. Jacques turns the boat to that one. Jacques jumps out of the boat into waist deep water. He wades to the front of the boat, grabs the chain that's still wrapped around Tony's neck and pulls him overboard. Jacques picks him up and walks him over to the pole. As he walks him over, Jacques can feel bones breaking beneath his boots. He wonders if Tony has any idea what his bare feet are getting cut on. Jacques pulls the bones of an arm out of the handcuff and gets his lock out. He backs Tony against the pole and Mr. Melerine takes his pocket knife and cuts the tarp near his mouth. Mr. Melerine tells him to open his mouth, which Tony refuses. He rams the rifle muzzle into his teeth. He tells him to open his mouth again, and he does. He shoves the rifle muzzle in his mouth, and tells Jacques that he can undo the handcuffs. Jacques undoes one hand, and orders Tony to place his hands high above his head. He complies. Jacques locks his other hand in back into the handcuff and uses the chain that is already there to lock the handcuffs into position. He then unlocks the chain from around his neck and uses it to attach his feet to the bottom of the pole. Once he's secured, Jacques pulls the tarp off his head. Tony immediately spit on Mr. Melerine. Mr. Melerine catches the side of Tony's face with the barrel of the rifle. Tony spits on him again. Jacques sees that Mr. Melerine is ready to swing at him again. "Mr. Melerine let him go. You know what awaits him."

"You and I might know what is in store for him, but do you mind if I tell him? First, the crabs will start eating on you. The sun is going to bake your skin off. The mosquitos are going to gnaw on you all day. This afternoon at dusk, the gnats are going to drive you crazy. All night long, you are going to be eaten alive. You might die of dehydration, craziness, or just lack of blood; but you are going to die just like the guys next to you." Tony spit on him again.

He wipes the blood and spit from his face. "What's those chicken feet doing around your neck?"

"They're for protection. Marie Laveaux is going to protect me, and I'm going to come back and kill the both of you."

"Sonny, you're as dumb as you look. Those chicken feet are a symbol that you're a coward, and Marie Laveaux is a Catholic. What you did to that girl, I doubt that she's going to help you." Tony spits on him again. Mr. Melerine wipes it off of him, and Jacques starts the boat and pulls away. Shortly into the journey back to the truck, Mr. Melerine spots a water moccasin sunning itself on the bank. He tells Jacques to stop the boat. "I've got one more thing for that bastard." Mr. Melerine grabs the paddle and uses it to catch the moccasin. He gets back in the boat holding the snake by the head. "Head back to our friend. I've got a little something extra for him." This time they do not even get out of the boat. Jacques just drives it right into Tony's chest. Mr. Melerine puts the snake close to Tony, and Tony starts violently screaming. Mr. Melerine takes the snake and forces it to bite Tony in his chest. Once the fangs are set in, Mr. Melerine milks all the poison out of the snake into Tony and pulls the snake away. Mr. Melerine waits for Tony to stop screaming. "God was pretty smart when he put venom in moccasins. This poison is very interesting stuff. It is divided up to work in three ways. First, it affects your central nervous system. This is important because it stuns whatever it bites. After the snake bites something, it can't have its prey running off. Second, it causes internal bleeding. This is what kills its prey. Third, it causes decay to aid in the digestive process. You can probably relax. The poison is going to do all of that stuff to you, but because it was designed for small animals. It probably isn't enough to kill you. Normally if you could get to the hospital within forty-eight hours, you will probably live. You'll be dead from other things by that time. On top of everything else, you are going to start by running fever. The fever is going to make you feel like you are going to freeze to death. Then you are going to start throwing up. Then the diarrhea is going to hit. You are going to feel sick and weak. You might even go into convulsions." He places the snake on top of Tony's head. Tony starts violently screaming again. The snake immediately bites Tony in the forearm and is hanging from him. Eventually, the snake lets go and falls in the water. As they leave, Tony continues shouting obscenities at them.

They reach the other end of the canal near the truck. They pull the boat to the road, then the trailer out of the grass, and drive back to the camp. Jacques backs the flatboat under Mr. Melerine camp and waves at Malynda standing on the porch. They unhook the trailer and Mr. Melerine follows him to the old Church off of Hwy. 90. Jacques pulls behind the Church, puts the truck in four wheel drive and drives into the woods behind the church. He turns and faces the vehicle where it's pointing towards the road. They cut some bushes and camouflage the truck. Jacques looks at his watch. "Come on Mr. Melerine we're running behind schedule." They load in Mr. Melerine's truck and drive back to Hopedale. They arrive at Mr. Melerine's house to see Père Andrew waiting in the Miss Jean with the pirogue already loaded in the skiff. Jacques grabs his gear out of the shed, and they motor off.

Jacques looks at the pirogue. "Père, where did the electric trolling motor come from?"

"I borrowed it from Snake. Since you got so tired so much da last time you took me fishing, I figure you can use it."

"Thanks."

They cast off and head across Lake Borgne and into the Middle Pearl River. Jacques keeps looking at his watch and shaking his head. Mr. Melerine starts to head into the canal, and Jacques stops him. "Mr. Melerine, I don't have enough time." Jacques scans the cypress tree line a mile across the marsh grass and points to the biggest tree. "This bayou runs right along that tree line. You see that big cypress tree that has the broken limb hanging from it."

"Yeah, I see it."

"Put the pirogue right next to it. I'll find it. Let's get to the drop off point."

Mr. Melerine backs up the Miss Jean, and they are underway again. They get to the drop off point, and Jacques checks his gear one more time. Père Andrew stops Jacques. "Jacques, you gots your rosary."

Jacques makes a face at Père. "No, Père. Not today, I don't have the time."

"You better make time. I was like you, Jacques. Old Père, he lost his faith. I was twenty years old almost freezing and starving to death with bullets flying over my head in a foxhole in Korea. A stranger gave me dis rosary. Told me dat it would protect me. Told me dat it would bring happiness back into my life. Just as old Melerine gave dis rosary to me so many years ago, I give it to you. Here Old Père, he wants you to take it wit you."

Jacques smiles and puts it in his shirt pocket. "Thank you Père." Jacques pulls his ghillie suit out of its bag, stretches it out on the boat's deck, and hoses it down with Yard Guard. He puts the grease paint on his hands and face. He smiles and makes a face at Mr. Melerine, "Go ahead and stash the pirogue real good. I'll see you in a couple of days."

He strips down to his boxers and eases himself into the water with the Ghillie suit slung over his shoulder. He walks in crotch deep water into the seven foot tall roseaus and puts his ghillie suit on. Mr. Melerine and Père motor away. He walks through the roseau canes for two hundred yards. At the edge of the roseau canes, he stops and overlooks the grassy marsh. It's waist high and thick. He can see the mum bushes on the levee six hundred yards in front of him. He can also see the motel. He pulls out his compass and takes a bearing towards it. He knows once he's down in the grass his visibility is only going to be inches in front of him. If he pops his head up and someone is on top of the hotel who knows what he's doing, he's busted. At a half of a yard per pull, it's twelve hundred pulls through the marsh. This will take two to three hours at five yards per minute with breaks.

The grass is bent over due to the wind. Jacques stretches his left arm forward. He then slightly picks up the grass in front of him and slides under it. Stalking in the marsh is fairly easy because he can grab the grass and pull himself along. The difficult part is the itching caused by the mosquitoes, grass, and saltwater. It's enough to drive a man crazy—like Tony.

Except for the bug bites, the stalk is basically uneventful. He makes it to the levee at 1400, and he has plenty of time to make himself at home. He misses his mark and winds up on the east side of the hotel. Once at the levee and behind the mum bushes, he peers through the mum bushes for a little over half an hour looking for any sign of movement. There's none. He eases back to the hidden side of the levee, takes a break, eats a breakfast bar, and changes the vegetation of his ghillie suit to match the mum bushes.

As if he's being watched, he eases westward along the backside of the levee to get to his shooting position. As he pushes westward he looks for items that do not belong. He finds an old peppermint candy wrapper. A little further, he finds a small piece of burlap. He then crosses over a well-used alligator slide. From there on he's more worried about the nearby alligator, the heat, and being seen. Before he crosses over to the front side of the levee, he observes for a while again. He also thinks about the items he found on the backside of the levee. He's two hundred and fifty yards from where his targets will be. He starts to ease into his shooting position when it dawns on him—he might not be the only sniper here. The candy wrapper, the piece of burlap, the slide, and the placement of the concrete debris in the parking lot begin to tie together and make sense. He pauses and eases back off the top of the levee. He has to make a decision to go through with it or back out. He figures that he can't turn around now and risk being seen by the other sniper. He knows that the sniper is going to set up on the east side of the hotel, and he knows how he's going to get there. He has to stay. He decides to move fifty yards further west on the levee to a place past where the canal teed. It's a defensive movement. The small canal that runs out to Hwy. 90 has plenty of cover on each side of it. The small canal has high grass on the parking lot side and the thick woods on the western side. He comes up to the top of the levee just west of the small canal. He eases over the top and into a shooting position, which is three feet back in the mums. He's further west than he planned. He lost more of the view of the northwest corner, but gains more of a view closer to the front of the motel. He prunes the mum bushes to make a shooting lane. Once he's comfortable in his position, he covers the scope of the rifle and his head with his veil. He takes the transmitter out and turns it on. He looks at his watch, which reads 1500. The waiting game begins.

He thinks to himself. "If the opportunity presents itself, how can I make it work? I know where the other sniper is going to set up. I can slide along the levee and kill the other sniper, but he probably has a radio and checks in. Besides depending on his size and training, the stunt could get me killed. The original plan was to shoot, swim across the canal, run through the parking lot to the cars, grab the money, and run. What if I would swim into the small canal that runs to Hwy. 90? I would shoot. He would not see the muzzle flash because he would be concentrating on the drug dealing. He would hear the shot though and would be looking for me." Jacques looks eastward. Forty yards to the east of him, is part of a rusted steel barge that is pushed into the levee and sank in the canal. Jacques continues mumbling to himself. "If he is on the other side of that barge, he'll not be able to see me without getting on this side of the barge. I could shoot, slip into the water and swim underwater into the small canal. I can swim to the end of the canal, run fifty yards, grab the money, and continue. One big problem—I'm going to have to swim forty yards underwater and a hundred and twenty-five yards once I am in the canal. It will take me at least thirty seconds to make it across and another two minutes in the canal. Two and a half minutes is plenty time for him to reposition. If he repositions, he would have to line up directly with the canal to see me. Well, I have two things going for me—he won't know if I'm looking for him, which may cause him to hesitate repositioning, and I will only be exposed for fifty yards. I can cover fifty yards in five seconds. I can use the car as cover and run across the highway. He'll have to lead me by two feet. It looks possible, let's see how much money we're talking about."

He mil's a fifty-five gallon drum that is close to where he thinks they'll set up. It ranges two-hundred and seventy five yards. He dials in his elevation of three point seven MOA and zero windage. He assumes that by nightfall the breeze will stop. He puts his scope caps back on, sweats, and waits.

2000, his hydropack is just about empty. A car pulls up and drops someone off. It's a sniper that has a ghillie suit on. He watches him through his veil. He gets out of the car carrying a rifle, and he runs to the hotel. As he approaches the building, Jacques loses sight of him. Jacques' adrenaline is rushing. "Stay in control and be confident of your camouflage. Don't move. Don't retreat. Just stay until after the sniper leaves." Jacques keeps looking—hoping to catch a glimpse of him. Finally, he sees him. He's heading up the stairs on the west side of the hotel. He goes all the way to the roof where he exits the stairway, and Jacques looses sight of him again.

Jacques is not happy with himself for not planning for the sniper, but realizes that he's pretty safe and relaxes. He knows where the sniper is, and he doesn't have to worry about being out flanked. The sniper is on top of a four story building a hundred yards away from him. For the sniper to see Jacques, he'll have to be looking almost straight down from the edge. The third and most important concept is that the sniper is in front of him. If the sniper's doing his job, he should be focused on the drug dealing in front of him and not behind him. Jacques thinks this is all good. He'll have to just sit and observe tonight, but he'll live for another opportunity.

Dusk comes at 2045, and the gnats are unbearable. Jacques ghillie suit is completely soaked with his sweat. He's hot and miserable. To top it all off, he drinks the last drop from his hydropack. The gnat's terror only lasts for thirty minutes and mosquitoes take over. The gnats can't penetrate his wool gloves, but the mosquitoes penetrate his ghillie suit. Obviously, his yard guard has worn off.

Jacques looks towards the scene and only the far parking lot entrance mercury vapor light comes on. He looks at the near entrance light and sees that it has been shot out. The full moon is out, and it gives him ample light to see around him. From his vantage point he can see the whole front of the parking lot. Everything is easily within three hundred and seventy-five yards.

2200, a car that is heading west pulls into the parking lot. It parks parallel to the highway facing west six feet off the road. It's the Lincoln Town Car that dropped off the sniper. Jacques estimates that it parks twenty-five yards further than the fifty-five gallon drum that he ranged earlier. Jacques tunes his parallax adjustment. He tries to see into the car's windows, but they are tinted. Being on top of the levee, he is level or slightly higher than the roof of the automobile.

Ten minutes later an eastbound car pulls in the parking lot. The driver eases within ten feet of the parked car. Two teenagers get out with a tan envelope in their hand. The driver of the parked car gets out and levels his MP-5 on the teenagers. Jacques looks at the driver; it's Mike. A few seconds later, the front passenger gets out. No surprise, it's Joe. Joe holds a white package the size of a shoebox. Joe puts the white package on the hood of his car. The teenagers give Joe the envelope. Joe opens it, looks in it, and gives them the white package. The teenagers ease back into their car and drive off. Meanwhile, Mike and Joe get back into their car. Twenty minutes later the same thing happens, then again twenty minutes after that. Jacques thinks to himself. "This Joe is pretty smart. He spaced them out twenty minutes apart so that he'll not have to deal with a crowd or line. By having them spaced out, the whole transaction takes less than a minute." Jacques continues watching. Some of the kids only have one envelope, but most of them have two or three.

CHAPTER 39

▼

In Jacques' fishing camp; Malynda, Mr. & Mrs. Melerine, and Père Andrew are playing Booray on the kitchen table. They are waiting on Malynda to deal. "I can't believe y'all are playing cards tonight. Do you realize Jacques could die tonight?"

Père Andrew tries to ease her nerves. "Playing cards passes da time. It gives us something to do while we worry. Jacques, he's no fool. He only fights battles dat he can win. Come on and deal da cards."

Everyone throws in a nickel in the pot, and Malynda passes out five cards each and turns up her last card to be the four of spades.

Mr. Melerine talks up, "Malynda are you in?"

Mrs. Melerine slaps her husband on the shoulder. "Can't you see dat da girl is worried sick about Jacques?"

He laughs, "She should be worried about other fools. They are the ones that are going to have a rough night tonight. When I dropped off Jacques, he was just fine. I saw his plan, and it's a good one. He'll do just fine."

"Mr. Melerine, you don't know these people. Jacques don't know these people. What if something goes wrong? Jacques doesn't have real experience, he just does toy soldier stuff. This is real. Père, you know I'm right."

"Te Fe, like Melerine said, I don't think you need to worry about Jacques. He has more experience at doing dis type of thing than he tells you about."

"But what if Jacques gets killed tonight? It'll be my fault."

Père Andrew holds his finger to Malynda. "Jacques, he likes doing these things. Jacques, he's a true warrior. Shakespeare the playwright, he had da best definition of a warrior. He say dat a coward dies a thousand deaths, but a warrior only dies once. Jacques, he only dies once. That's da way he wants it. Jacques, he moved to Houston; and I saw da life drained from his body. He moves back down here, and his life is worth living again. Jacques, he lives for da adventure, and you give him dat. Since Jacques moved down here, his life has purpose. He lived more in da last two weeks than he lived in da past ten years. Some people, dey never take chances and take too good care of themselves dat they don't live a day of their lives. Some people, dey take chances and enjoy life and die young. Who lives more?"

"But, I don't want Jacques to die. I hope he'll take me as his wife."

Everyone at the table starts laughing and clapping their hands.

Mrs. Melerine deals out the cards when everybody annies up a nickel. "Malynda, just pray dat Jacques comes home safely and everything is going to be all right."

"I want to go check on him."

Mrs. Melerine says, "Child you do no such thing. Jacques has everything planned out. You let him be. If we interfere, it will be worst dan doing nothing. Take some good advice and just pray. If it's Jacques' time, it's Jacques' time. There's nothing you can do about it."

Père looks at his watch. "It's ten o'clock. Praying sounds like a good idea. I think I'll head back to the Church. Maybe, He'll hear me better there."

Mr. and Mrs. Melerine get up. "We better be going too."

Mrs. Melerine gives her a hug and a kiss on each cheek. "You go to sleep; and Jacques, he be back in da morning. If you like I stay here wit you."

"I appreciate the offer Mrs. Melerine, but I think that I'll be ok."

"You sure child?"

Fighting back her tears, she shakes her head "Yes."

"You change your mind, you call me. You hear. You don't worry about da time. You just call, and I'll be right over."

Malynda gives her another hug. "You're wonderful people. Thank you." Malynda walks them out and wishes them good night. She returns inside, changes into her sleep wear, and cleans the entire camp. She's tired and tries to go to sleep. She lies there in the bed with Celeste and tosses and turns, but she can't go to sleep. She gets up to get a glass of water and sees one of the prayer candles is no longer lit. She sees the envelope that Jacques left her on the counter. She opens it and turns on a light.

Dearest Malynda,

If you are reading this something terrible has happened to me. I want you and Celeste to carry on. Do not hold yourself responsible for my mistakes. I knew the risk, and I took my chances. If I had the choice to do it again, I would. You would not be able to stop me. Even though I did not make it back, I hope I have accomplished my mission; and you and Celeste can once again live peaceful lives. You must carry on for yourself and Celeste.

Here is my bankcard, credit cards, and my computer access codes. All my banking is done electronically. If you keep paying the bills, there should be enough money so that you can live undetected for years.

I will always look over you and Celeste.

Love,

Jacques

She starts crying, thinks about Mrs. Melerine's offer and picks up the phone.

CHAPTER 40

▼

0130 at the abandoned motel, Jacques continues observing the transactions in the parking lot. A gold charger burns into the parking lot. The car has some horsepower. The tires spin for nearly a hundred feet before the car's acceleration can catch up with the horsepower. He jams on the brakes, spins one hundred and eighty degrees, and stops. They burn rubber again towards Hwy. 90, slow the car down, and pull right in front like the others. Two guys in their mid twenties get out. They're scrubby looking—sloppy beards, long hair, and look as if they haven't bathed in a week. The driver and passenger run towards the hood of Joe's car and beat on it with their hands, as if they're playing the drums. After they're done, they point both of their index fingers at the driver and spin around in unison. These guys are high on something. Even while standing still, their feet are still moving. Joe and Mike stay in their car. The passenger goes back to the charger, reaches into the charger's window, and pulls out a brief case. Jacques hears something off his left side and feels something going over his left elbow. Without raising his cheek off his rifle he looks down and sees a moccasin under his veil with him. The snake continues under his rifle and through the right side of the veil. Jacques breathes a sigh of relief and continues looking through his scope. One of the wild bunch walks back to the front of Joe's car, holds the brief case up, and opens it. When he does, the driver's screaming, "Who's the man? Who's the man?" The passenger is laughing as he's waving the brief case side to side like he's teasing a kid with a piece of candy. Jacques moves his scope to sixteen power to get a better look at what's inside of the briefcase. With each wave, Jacques is saying, "Just a little more wave, where I can see what's inside." Finally, he turns the brief case towards himself to close it. Jacques gets a good peek at a brief case full of banded money. After he closes it, he puts it on top of the Lincoln; and Mike gets out. The boys back off as Mike levels his MP-5. Joe gets out with an athletic bag. They make the exchange, and the boys slowly drive off. Joe must have told them something about their driving habits. After Jacques sees the brief case full of money, he's determined to make it work and starts working on a plan.

As the next car drives up, Jacques leaves his rifle and transmitter in position, eases himself backwards to the other side of the levee, and removes his ghillie suit. He reapplies mosquito repellent to his hands, face and neck. He tightly rolls up the ghillie suit, and quietly puts it in a plastic trash bag. He pulls out his fins, mask, and athletic bag from his backpack. Stuffs the ghillie suit on the bottom of the backpack, then attaches a carabiner to one of his belt loops of his BDU's. He takes off his boots and puts them in the backpack. Then he tightly rolls up the athletic bag and sticks it on top. He put his fins on over his swim shoes and eases back into position behind his rifle with his mask in hand. When he gets back to his rifle, the car is just pulling off. After five minutes, Jacques realizes how much protection the ghillie suit gave him against the mosquitoes because his sweat drenched BDU's offered very little protection. He blocks out the torture of the mosquitoes by thinking of Malynda and the money. He has to come up with a plan. He thinks of and plays out various scenarios, but the answer keeps pointing to escape and to live to fight another day.

Another two cars come and go. After the second car leaves, Mike and Joe stay outside of their automobile. Jacques can see Mike putting a walkie-talkie to his mouth, and both guys are looking at the motel. A couple of minutes later, Jacques sees the sniper emerge from the motel stairway walking towards Mike and Joe. Jacques' heart begins to race, but he has to think straight. "I have three shells and three targets. It's just an every day speed drill. Shoot quick. Shoot true. The light will have to stay lit. Shoot, transmit, throw the rifle on my back, pack on my stomach, mask on my face, in the water, swim, remove fins, emerge from water, get bag, get money, and run like hell." He plays the scenario over and over. All he needs is an opportunity. Jacques adjusts the power ring of his scope to minimum power and follows the sniper in the cross hairs. Jacques can't believe his eyes. In front of him is a two for one shot. The sniper and Joe's heads are perfectly aligned. Safety off and fire. Jacques knows that he pulled to the right and chambers another round. Mike starts spraying in a hundred degree arc into the wooded area. While the rifle is on its way down, Jacques opens his other eye to keep track of Mike. He can see Joe and the sniper are down, and Mike moves in close to them. Jacques acquires Mike. He fires and this time the rifle rockets back perfectly. He re-chambers and takes out the mercury vapor light. He leaves the spent cartridge in the chamber. He then hits the transmitter.

It's time to move. He can see his two shinny pieces of brass six inches to the right of the chamber. Quickly getting into the kneeling position, he picks up the two spent shells and puts them in his pocket. While he's in his pocket, he pulls out a balloon and puts it over the muzzle of his barrel. He folds the bipod, throws the rifle over his neck and shoulder in an upside down position, puts the back-pack across his chest, puts his mask on, takes ten really deep breaths, and silently slips into the water. Once in the water, he follows the contour of the bottom of the canal by feel. He surfaces when he swims into some shallow water. He's in the smaller canal but still has a long way to go. He corrects his bearing and submerges again. The next time he pops up, he only has another twenty-five yards to go. He submerges again and just overshoots his mark. He swims to the marsh grass on the shore into inches of water and catches his breath. He removes his fins and attaches them to his carabiner on his belt loop. He draws his pistol, turns the safety off, and charges for the car. It's an ugly scene. He sees Mike on top of the sniper, who's lying with his face into the front wheel. Joe is desperately trying to crawl away with only the use of his left arm. Jacques knows what has to be done. He runs directly to Joe and puts a .45 slug into the back of his head. He turns and head shoots Mike and the sniper and holsters his pistol as he opens the rear passenger's side door. He unzips his pack and stuffs the envelopes in it. He then grabs the four brief cases and runs across Hwy. 90 into the woods. A hundred yards into the woods, he stops and empties the brief cases into his athletic bag. He's having problems fitting all of the money in the bag. "I should have brought a larger bag." He tries to stack the money to fit more, but he still has to leave nearly a full brief case behind." After the athletic bag is full, he fills his backpack and leaves the rest behind. Jacques did not plan for the weight of all that paper. The fact that it's green paper makes carrying the stuff a little more tolerable. He re-situates his gear by carrying his rifle, putting his backpack on his back and ath-letic bag over his shoulder. He takes a compass bearing, and starts jogging north-ward through the woods. After a quarter of a mile, he comes to a small bayou that's fifty yards wide. In the darkness, he sees the shadows of a couple of alliga-tors in the water. He waits for them to pass, eases in, and uses the breaststroke to get to the other side. Half mile later, Jacques reaches the slew and takes a break. He's out of breath and thirsty. He's surrounded by water, but it is the undrink-able brackish swamp water. He starts into the slew, eases off the throttle, and begins to pace himself. The slew is above ankle deep mud and knee to waist level water. He continues across until he comes to a grassy marsh. At the marsh line, he lets his eyes adjust and looks for the lone cypress tree where the pirogue is stashed. Jacques becomes confused because everything looks different in the dark. He's also viewing the trees from the slew and not from the open marsh. He starts walking west along the marsh line. The big trees become scarcer. After a couple of hundred yards, he turns around and heads east. He retraces his first two hundred yards, and continues another hundred to the east. He comes across the small canal and follows it to a large cypress tree. He finds the pirogue upside-down on the east side of the cypress tree. He flips it over and to his surprise added to the equipment is a small ice chest. He opens it to find six cans of cold beer. Jacques opens and drinks a beer as he laughs to himself, "That's seven good things you gave me Père." He carefully places everything in the pirogue, mounts the trolling motor, and begins paddling over a mile to the Middle Pearl. Once in the Middle Pearl, the water is deep enough to run the trolling motor. As he heads north with the trolling motor running, Jacques decides to open another beer, relax, and enjoy life. As he makes it to the bayou that connects the Middle Pearl to the West Pearl, he hears police sirens and lots of them. "How could they have known so soon? Maybe a passing motorist got snagged in the tire rippers? Maybe some how they were involved?" Right now the only thing Jacques can think of doing is putting as much distance between him and them as possible, and he begins paddling to assist the trolling motor. By the time he makes it to the West Pearl, there is a helicopter with search a light. He continues on the western shore southward in the West Pearl to keep from being seen. He sees the small ditch that's marked by a beer can that is hanging from a string that is attached to a tree limb. The ditch goes westward into the woods on the west side of the Pearl. Jacques lifts the trolling motor and paddles two hundred yards before he runs out of water. He pulls the pirogue out of the ditch and hides it a hundred yards in the woods. He leaves the ice chest, paddle, battery, and trolling motor with the pirogue. Jacques follows the ditch for another half mile through the woods. There is a mercury vapor light in the back of the Church's parking lot. Once he finds the parking lot he gets his bearings and goes to the truck. He reaches the truck out of breath, off loads everything, and strips down. He loads everything except the rifle in a black garbage bag and throws it in the bed of the truck. He pulls the carpet back from under the back seat and throws the rifle under it. He folds the back seat to the upright position. He walks to the back of the Church, finds a garden hose and bathes. Upon returning to his truck, he verifies that all the grease paint is removed, puts on a pair of shorts and a polo shirt. He removes the camouflage from the truck and drives through the woods, through the gravel parking lot of the Church, and west on US 190—towards Slidell.

0615, Jacques only travels five miles before he's stuck in traffic of a police roadblock. It's a pretty simple roadblock that Jacques can easily run. There's a sheriff's car on the side of the road with its lights on and two deputies flagging down cars. They don't stop most of the cars; they just flag them through. As Jacques approaches the officers, he rolls down his window. The deputy holds up his hand to stop, and Jacques complies.

"Can I see your driver license, and can you tell me where you're coming from?"

Jacques hands the deputy his driving license. "I was visiting some friends in a subdivision that's a few miles up the road. I'm getting an early start back home. What's going on?"

The officer looks at Jacques attire and peeks inside the truck. "There is a mass murderer loose in the area. Be real careful and don't pick up any hitchhikers. Have a safe trip back to Houston." The officer flags him on.

After the roadblock, Jacques turns the radio on and listens to the reports. Most of them are the same—"A mass murderer killed at least three, probably more, along Hwy. 90 this morning. The police are not releasing any information; however, they say drugs are involved. Hwy. 90 is closed between US 190 and the state line. The police have this area sealed off. If you live in this area, close and lock all your doors and stay indoors. Repeat. A mass.........stay indoors. We'll get you more information when it becomes available." Jacques continues to flip through the stations on the way home. After a half hour with nothing new to report, each station has experts giving their opinions. Jacques is amused about how someone can be called an expert, give an opinion, and never visit the sight of the crime. He's glad when he pulls into the camp's driveway. He thinks to himself. "Very successful mission—I'm alive, I got the girl, and I got a whole bag full of money."

Jacques is a little surprised that Malynda is not waiting for him on the porch like she normally does. No matter, he walks into to the camp feeling proud of his accomplishment and once again is dead tired. He opens the door and steps in. "It's finished; it's all over with." Malynda is sitting on the couch with Celeste in her lap. They are wearing their Church dresses. The expression of Malynda's face looks as if her best friend had died. Her eyes are all watery, and there's a tear rolling down her cheek. Before Jacques can ask what the problem is, he's hit from behind and driven to the floor. Once on the floor, Tank and Half-track repeatedly kick him until he's in a helpless state.

The short period of abuse stops—Celeste is crying and screaming. Satinito walks out of the front bedroom. "So, you are Jacques...I don't know whether I should congratulate you, condemn you, or both. You did me a great service getting rid of that bad bunch. I couldn't control them anymore. Malynda is a real sweetheart. She really should get an academy award for this performance as Sister Malynda." Satinito laughs. "She hasn't been to Church in years. Jacques, she led you on; and you took it hook, line, and sinker. Now that the job is done, she doesn't need you anymore." Another tear begins to run down Malynda's face. "Come now Malynda, no since crying about it now. Your plan worked perfectly. You got rid of your no-good husband, and I got rid of a bunch of bad apples. Now, you can start your life over. You see Jacques. A little over a month ago, she came to me because she caught her husband fooling around on her. I told her that I would take care of the problem, but she would have to help me out and get rid of that bad bunch of mine. I asked her if she knew of anybody that could help me, and that's when your name came up. Oh the hospital, that was her idea. I thought that it was too risky, but she said that would be the only way you would help her." Jacques looks up at Malynda. "You slept with her—didn't you? You're a sucker because that is the oldest trick in the book. You fell for her—didn't you? The way women can play with men's emotions is so cruel—isn't it?"

Malynda's crying and shaking her head, "Stop it!"

Satinito holds his finger up to Malynda. "Malynda, remember our deal. Jacques, you need to realize that she's a professional; and she's very good at what she does. She has that way about her. If I was you, I wouldn't worry about her because I'm going to take good care of her—just as we planned it. I'm going to dress her up in only the finest dresses that money can buy. Jacques, too bad for you that you are just too good; otherwise, I would put you on my payroll. You have little things that will just keep getting in the way like morals and being a gentleman." Jacques looks down at the floor, and Tank grabs him by the hair to make sure he's looking at Satinito. "Come on Jacques, you didn't think that the girl could live happily ever after with you. Did you? Get real. She always had and still has an appreciation for the finer things in life—the things that you could never afford."

Jacques thinks to himself that Satinito is right. He thinks about the mall experience, and how fast she went through the money. He could never afford her in high school, and he can't afford her now. It was all a performance. His face turns red with anger as he reflects on the killings that he performed for her. He was used as a puppet, and he was stupid enough to fall for her act.

Satinito sees that the message sunk in. "Jacques, I hate long good-byes. Thanks Jacques and so long. I hope you understand—it's just business. Come on Malynda. Grab your kid, and let's go. Tank and Half Track drag him out back."

He points to Tank, "I want you to put a bullet in his head." He points to Half Track, "and I want you to put a bullet in his chest."

They both reply. "No problem boss."

Satinito roughly grabs Malynda by the upper arm and leads her out the front door.

She starts screaming. "You said that you weren't going to hurt him! You promised!"

As they're picking Jacques off the floor, Tank picks up Jacques' rifle. "This will be a nice addition to my collection." The two men drag Jacques out the back door and down the stairs. The goon stands the rifle up against the bottom of the stairway. Jacques turns his head and sees a Camaro and two Lincolns pull into the driveway. The driver of the Camaro gets into the last Lincoln. He sees Celeste is carried to the last Lincoln and Malynda gets into the near Lincoln with the gray haired bastard. Half Track backhands Jacques. "She don't concern you anymore. Let's get this over with." Jacques can hear two cars leaving.

Satinito stops his car two hundred yards down the road, he rolls down his window, and dials Harris' number. There's no answer. He calls the hotel main line and connects to Harris' room. The phone rings and Harris answers it.

"Franky, wake up. I told you everything would be ok. I've got Meyeaux's wife, and listen to this." He holds the phone out the window.

Jacques is still in a daze from physically being beaten and mentally worked over. Half Track shoves Jacques into a kneeling position facing the marsh in front of them. Jacques is making his peace with God as he hears the gun go off. He feels no pain, but his whole body goes numb. A million visions run through his mind. Then, he hears the second shot.

Harris hears the two shots. Then, he hears Satinito order his driver to head home.

"Franky, did you hear that. That was our hero taking two bullets. We are going to celebrate tonight."

"How come you didn't call me on my cell phone?"

"I did, you must have turned it off."

"No, I must have left the ringer off. This time I agree with you. It's time to celebrate. I'll see you when you get back." He laughs and hangs up the phone.

Harris finds his phone and sees that there are six messages from Sue and two from his sergeant.

Jacques is confused because he still has his senses—no blackness. Nothing has changed. Somehow the second shot sounded different. One of the goons falls on top of him, and Jacques realizes that he's not dead. He pushes out, away, and turns around. There, in front of him lay the two goons. Both of them headshot. He turns, looks, and sees Mr. Melerine coming out of his camp. "Now, what do you have to say about my 30–30."

Jacques gets up, runs for his rifle, and then to the boat. Mr. Melerine is right behind him. Jacques gets on the radio and changes it to channel 13. "Mrs. Dee, this is Jacques. Open the bridge now and get out."

"What for? I caught some nice speck's last night. You want some?"

"Mrs. Dee, you need to open the bridge now, get in your car, and drive away. Do it now."

"Ok, ok, and I don't want to know."

Jacques grabs a hand full of ammunition out of the console. "Mr. Melerine get my gear out of my truck and put it in the boat. When the shooting stops, come pick me up with my boat—not before. Do you understand?"

Mr. Melerine shakes his head. Jacques slides over the side of the boat with the rifle in his hand. He swims across Bayou Loutre holding the rifle out of the water. He's blinded with anger as he swims across Bayou Loutre to the levee. The anger builds as he runs along the trapper's planks behind the levee. He crosses the levee and gets in a good prone position on the platform that he built. As he opens the scope caps, he's determined that everyone is going to die. He can see only one of the Lincolns in front of the bridge. He takes off the reticle caps and dials in twelve and a quarter MOA elevation and one MOA left windage. The waiting game pursues. Finally, the driver gets out of the car. Through the twenty-power scope, Jacques can see that the driver is waving his hands as he walks to the bridge. He's walking back to the car when Jacques has a moment of opportunity. The person in the back seat rolls down his window and sticks his head out. It's the gray haired bastard with the ponytail that was doing all the talking. Within a second of him sticking his head out, Jacques fires. A second later, gray matter covers the front windshield. The rifle rockets straight back and then up. Without looking where the first round lands, he works the bolt. The rifle lands back on the bipod with another round in the chamber. The driver knows what's going on and starts running directly away from Jacques. Jacques acquires the second target, quarters it, and squeezes the trigger. Two seconds after the first shot impacts, the driver gets hit in the back of his chest with the second round. He chambers his third and final round and searches for his next target. She did not immediately appear. He figures with her new boyfriend's brain splattered all over the inside of the car, she would have come out screaming. Maybe she's in shock, maybe she's hit, or maybe she knows what's waiting for her as soon as she shows herself. Jacques just waits.

Malynda is crying as she sees the driver fall. She looks around at the pink mist still in the air of the automobile and the lifeless body of Satinito next to her in the back seat. The mist clears as she still looks around at the interior of the automobile. She tries to pull herself together. "They have Celeste. The only way I'm going to get her back is to face Jacques. I'm going to have to take a chance."

Jacques is intensely watching the vehicle. Wishing for her to show herself. He sees the passenger's side rear door slowly open, and Malynda emerges. Jacques positions himself so that the cross hairs quarter her. In a fit of rage, he squeezes the palm bag to gut shoot her. He keeps the cross hairs on her as she moves to the rear of the car. "Why is she giving me an easier target?" He watches her kneel down with her head bowed. She's quartered towards him. He moves the cross-hairs to her left breast and is ready to fire. She kisses her crucifix, makes the sign of the cross, and looks as if she's praying. She keeps herself perfectly still. The wind dies to nothing. Jacques becomes sympathetic. He takes off the windage to half a MOA, and moves the cross hairs to her head. "I don't gain anything by making her suffer." He gets his heart rate down, breathes in, exhales, blinks, sees no movement in aim point, touches the trigger with his finger, and stops. He can't go through with it. He watches her through his scope for a few seconds. She picks up her head, looks around, and starts running full speed back towards the camp. Jacques stands up. He hears Mr. Melerine coming around the bend, and he now can see Malynda running with his naked eyes. Mr. Melerine pulls the boat to the platform.

Jacques gets in the boat, puts his pistol on, and runs the boat towards Malynda. When they get close to one another, Malynda runs out on a dock, and Jacques lets her jump in. Before she's all the way in, Jacques grabs her by the hair and forces her down in a face down lying position. "Keep your hands where I can see them!"

"They got Celeste! They got Celeste!"

Jacques pays no attention to Malynda. He's pushing his knee into her back with his full weight upon her. He's mashing her face into the deck of the boat with a hand full of hair.

At this point, Malynda forgets about Celeste and starts worrying about her own life. Her face hurts, and she can hardly breathe with his knee in the middle of her back. She can feel Jacques roughly running his hand down her back and sides. She's roughly rolled over, and he moves his hand to her throat. Fearing the worst, she closes her eyes. She feels his hands pass over her front side. Then the abuse stops.

Jacques sees the terror in Malynda, but he doesn't care. He's still not satisfied if she has a weapon on her. Jacques tells Mr. Melerine to head towards the bridge. Mr. Melerine pulls up to a dock near the bridge as Mrs. Dee is returning. She screams across Bayou Loutre at Jacques. "Jacques, every time you ask me to raise da bridge; you shoot somebody." Jacques just waves at her. "Mr. Melerine do you mind cleaning up the mess."

As Mr. Melerine is getting off the boat, "How about another car that ran off the road into the canal accident sound?"

"Look for a black athletic bag. If it is in the car, grab it. Head home, and I'll meet you there in a couple of days." He draws his pistol and points it at Malynda. "Sit on the bow deck and don't move!" She complies. He pushes full throttle, and they are in the Ship Channel in no time. "I'll get Celeste, but I'm still not sure you'll make the full journey."

CHAPTER 41

▼

1000, the abandoned hotel is a scene of multitudes of law enforcement people walking over one another. A FBI trailer is the center of the chaos. Sue Rodred in a olive drab jumpsuit is standing in front of the trailer coordinating the effort. A helicopter landing nearby on the highway interrupts her.

Frank Harris gets out of the chopper in an extremely bad mood. He walks directly to Sue. "I want to talk to you in the trailer—now!" He sees Sue still giving directions to people. "I said now!" Sue and Frank walk into the trailer. "Everybody out of here." Frank waits for everyone to leave. "Why did you let this happen? Sue you were here. Why didn't you take this psycho down? I want this case solved before the General Crimes Section is brought in. Do you understand me?" He makes a face of disgust. "Why are you not in proper attire?"

"Sir, this guy knew what he was doing. I don't think he is your classical psycho."

"Well, what do you have besides that he knew what he was doing and that he is not a classical psycho?"

"Look at these pictures. Look at his equipment."

Frank picks up the pictures. "You had time to take pictures, but you couldn't shoot him."

"Sir, it was pitch black dark. All I had was a pistol. Shooting a pistol at over two hundred yards at a moving target in the dark is just a waste of time. The only reason I got these pictures was because of the infrared camera lens."

"What about back-up? The area should have been sealed and back-up should have been no further than a couple of minutes away."

"Sir, we only had one vehicle; and it's being towed as we speak. He used an electronic transmitter to cover the road with rippers and escaped through the swamp."

Frank begins to get loud, "Do you realize how much heat I've been taking from the local police departments? Each time these guys want to throw Satinito's bunch in jail, I tell them hands off because we have a federal case ongoing. This investigation has been going on for the past two years. The District Attorney almost lost the election because of this case. For what? One nut case blows it all in a single night. Would you look at that rifle? What kind is it?"

"It's a custom. It was definitely a magnum—probably 300, 338, or bigger."

"What else do we know?"

"He is a male between five—eight and six feet tall, is between twenty-five and forty years old, weighs two hundred pounds, size ten shoe, has a receding hair line, and drinks cheap beer. He is a good shot, extremely fast with working the bolt, in good shape, a good swimmer, efficient in getting the job done, and can travel the swamp with ease."

"Cheap beer, is that a joke? How much money did he get away with?"

"I'm estimating two point three million."

"Well, we don't have to worry about this guy living too long. Satinito will have his head on a silver platter. Do you think this guy is military or maybe SWAT? The local law enforcement knew what was going on and were told to stay away. Do you think that he could be one of them?"

"Maybe Special Forces or mercenary, but definitely not SWAT. Whoever he was, he spent a lot of time with that rifle. I'm guessing he is some sort of competition shooter."

"What do you mean?"

"He easily got off three well placed shots within fifteen seconds, and hit a street light at over three hundred yards with one of those shots. SWAT mostly practices at small targets at a hundred yards and closer. Military practices at larger size targets at three hundred yards and farther."

"I'm not as easily impressed as you are with his shooting abilities. Obviously, you haven't seen our sniper teams."

"Sir, I use to be a sniper—remember."

"Yeah, I forgot. Wait, I thought you said there were three shots."

"Yeah, he shot Joe and the sniper with the first shot. The second shot hit Mike, and the third took out the light. Mike and the sniper were dead instantly. Joe was hit in the face and was pretty much paralyzed except for one of his arms. Everything was quiet for two minutes. Out of the grass emerged this guy with his pistol drawn at a full out run. He shot Joe in the head, and then put one into each of the other two. He opened the door, grabbed the money, and disappeared on the other side of Hwy. 90. I called for back-up, and Tim reported back about the rippers. It took me half an hour to get a helicopter out here. We used the St. Tammany Parish dogs to track him down. He crossed a bayou four hundred yards back. The dog handlers would not let their dogs cross it because the number of alligators in the Bayou, and it was too deep for the four-wheelers. We went around and picked up the trail again. We followed it into a slew, and we lost his trail in there. We started again where the slew met the marsh. We picked up his trail again and followed it to a beer can and a fresh pirogue slide. We haven't picked it back up yet. The local trackers think that he spent a lot of time in Louisiana swamps. They said that his path was carefully planned. He used a wooded area to put some distance between him and the scene. He crossed an alligator infested Bayou that would have turned back most men. After he crossed the slew, he got lost, which meant that he's comfortable without using a GPS. He only moved at a pace that the land allowed, which was evident because he didn't trip, stumble or fall. He surely wasn't in a hurry because he stopped to drink a beer where he had the pirogue stashed."

"If he was a local, do you think that one of the local police could have intentionally let him through the roadblock?"

"Maybe. Around here friendship means a lot. Besides, the way they see it—he did them a favor."

"So we have a sharp shooter, who is not afraid of the Swamp Monster, running around in the middle of the night. How do you plan to catch him?"

"He is either still in the swamp, or he is outside of our roadblocks by now. We are still searching for him. We have choppers in the air, and..." The door of the trailer burst open and interrupts Sue. An Agent runs in.

Once in the ship channel, Jacques trims the motor. Jacques can see that Malynda is frightened as never before. Jacques screams over the roar of the wind, "Face me and slowly take off all your clothes. Keep your eyes on me, and keep your hands where I can see them." He points with his pistol. "Start with your dress. Take it off and toss it overboard." She does. Jacques pointed the pistol right at her. "Now your bra and panties, and I mean slowly." She hesitates. "So help me God. I will fill with holes and let the crabs feast on you. Now, take them off and throw them overboard." She does and sits back down in the front of the boat trying to cover her nakedness. "Stand up, put your hands above your head, and slowly turn completely around." She does. "Sit back down and stay there without moving." Malynda sits back down trying to cover herself. Jacques empties the chamber of the pistol and holsters it. Jacques, while watching Malynda the whole time, slowly reaches down into the console and pulls out a rain suit. He reaches out over the console and hands it to her. "Put this on and sit in the front seat." As she's putting on the rain suit, Jacques reaches into the console and pulls out a pair of swim shoes. He hands them to her. "Put these on and stand next to me."

Once she realizes that she's going to live, her attention focuses back on getting Celeste. "Jacques, we got to get Celeste. They got her."

"I know. It takes thirty minutes by car to get to Bayou Bienvenue. It only takes fifteen minutes by boat. They probably have a five minute head start, which gives us ten minutes to set up."

Malynda starts explaining and pleading to Jacques.

"Malynda, I don't want to hear it. Just save it. I'll get your daughter back for you."

Jacques turns the boat south through the locks and into Bayou Bienvenue. From there, he turns west into Mr. Eddie's Canal and runs the bow of the boat on the marsh near the boat launch. He reaches in the console and grabs a pair of walkie-talkies and pulls his ghillie suit from his backpack. He slings his rifle over his shoulder and pulls out a shotgun from under the bow. Jacques grabs Malynda by the hand and runs towards the small lugger that's on top of fifty-five gallon drums. Jacques hoists Malynda on top of the pre-placed drum. "Get in the cabin. When you see them, use the radio to tell me which car it is." Jacques runs out to the highway, puts his ghillie suit on, and backs two feet into the roseau canes. Five minutes later the radio comes alive with Malynda screaming, "They're coming! They're coming! It is the silver car." Jacques rises to the kneeling position with the shotgun shouldered. As the silver Lincoln drives by, Jacques shoots out the front passenger tire and dives to the prone position behind his rifle.

Malynda watches the car lose control, go on the emergency lane, then into the grass, then back on the emergency lane two hundred yards away from Jacques. She watches as both the driver and passenger get out to examine the tire. Both of them stoop down and are talking to one another. She hears the rifle go off and sees the furthest one fall. She hears a second shot and watches the second one fall. She sees Jacques run to the car, grab Celeste, and a black bag and is running back towards her. She gets out of the boat and runs out towards the road. As she rounds the corner of roseau canes, Jacques almost runs over her. She rips Celeste out of his hands, and they both run to the boat. Once in the boat, Jacques slams the throttle full open. Once she's in the seat with Celeste, everything becomes a blur. She's crying and babbling as she rocks Celeste. Malynda looks back at Jacques and can see the fury still raging in him. She knows it's not over with, and she knows that she's in a hopeless state.

CHAPTER 42

▼

Back at the FBI trailer, the agent screams, "He did it again, two more guys shot. On State Hwy. 47 just a few minutes ago."

Sue grabs him, "Go get that chopper fired up. I'll be there in a minute. You can fill me in on the way there."

Frank stops Sue, "Wait a minute. That's my helicopter. You have no right to use it without my say so. Use the search chopper."

"Sir, he still might be in the swamp. Even if he is not, we still need evidence that he left behind. Let me use your chopper and let the search chopper continue searching. Remember this guy moves fast. If I take the extra fifteen minutes to drive down, he has another fifteen minutes head start. This guy is an amphibian. We can't catch him by car or boat. We need a helicopter. Come on Harris for once, be a team player!"

"Rodred, I'm going to let you use my chopper this time. When we get back to the office, we are going to talk about your team player attitude. One other thing, I'm going with you." Frank, Sue, and a young agent boards the chopper. Once aboard, Sue asks the agent for the situation report.

"He shot out the front tire with a shotgun then two head shots."

"That's our guy. Any witnesses?"

"No. The owner of the boat launch was there, but he said that he didn't see anything."

"How did he get away?"

"We don't know."

Sue communicates with the pilot, "Circle back around. I want to pick up one of those dogs and a trainer."

Sue then picks up her walkie-talkie. "I want your best dog and handler. We are going to put down on the highway so block it off."

The pilot circles around and lands on the road. The dog trainer is a hefty man. The pilot records the trainer's weight and dog's weight on the manifest. He looks back to the passenger compartment. "One of you will have to get off. We're overloaded." Everyone looks at Harris, and he reluctantly gets off. Ten minutes later, they are landing in the boat launch's parking lot. Two agents in suits run towards the helicopter. "Ma'am, we found the place where he shot from."

"Good, get the dog over there. I what to know how he escaped."

They quickly get the dog out and are running him over to the hide when the dog picks up the scent. He runs over to the lugger, then to the hide, then to the car, then back towards the helicopter, then to the water's edge. There's a boat slide. Sue runs to the boat launch store. The owner greets her with a bright smile. "Would you like a Coke?" Sue looks at him and turns on her charm. "That would be great. Do you have any local fishing maps?"

"This is a boat launch. Of course, we have fishing maps. Here let me show you some." The owner pulls the whole stack of organized maps out of the box and scatters them out on the counter. Sue finds one that covers a large portion of southeast Louisiana.

Sue grabs the young agent. "Go get the Coast Guard onboard. Get their helicopter searching the mouth of the Mississippi River Gulf Outlet and Breton Sound. We need to contain this maniac. Get me one of the local deputies that knows these waters."

A deputy comes over to Sue. Sue motions to the young agent to get in the helicopter. "Get in front with the pilot. She and the deputy get in the back. She puts on the headset. "Fly north following the Intercoastal Canal towards the Pearl River and keep your eyes peeled for any boats in the area." The chopper takes off.

The deputy looks at Sue with a dumbfounded look. "Mrs. General, there is going to be hundreds of boats out there. It's a Friday during the summer. There are thousands of square miles of marsh. He could be anywhere. You might as well give up now. If he knows the swamp, you stand zero chance of finding him."

"I'm not a general, my name is Rodred. If we can't find him in the water, let's find out where he is going to come out of the water. He can't stay out there forever. So tell me where's a likely place for him to come out?"

"Well, Rodred. Let's say he doesn't have a camp or is headed for a camp. You know people leave them open for people to get out of the weather. He could have come out right there at Bayou Bienvenue or could be as far as Grand Isle."

Sue holds up the map. "Show me."

The deputy laughs, you need a bigger map—like a state map."

"Well, let's put people at launches."

The deputy laughed harder, "You don't have enough people. Besides, do you even know what type of boat you are looking for? Do you have a description of this guy?"

Sue shakes her head, "No".

Sue radios back to the boat launch. "Do you have anything to report?"

"Sue, he has an accomplice this time—a female with black hair that weighs a hundred and ten pounds. From her stride, she's five—four. They are also carrying a package or something. He was carrying it from the car to the launch's parking lot, and she carried it from there to the boat."

"Any idea what it was?"

"No."

"Anything else?"

"The boat's a tri-hull."

"Appreciate the fast response. This guy is going to get away again unless we get more manpower in the water. Get all the sheriff departments, Coast Guard, whatever you can get within a sixty-mile radius. Get them on the water and let's start doing some random safety inspections. Get some land units at as many launches as possible. We might get lucky."

Sue has a big grin from ear to ear and looks at the Deputy, "Ok hot shot, we got a description of the boat and one of the people on the boat. How do we find them?"

"What do you have?"

"It is a tri-hull, the suspect is a female, black hair, one hundred ten pounds, five foot four."

"We will set up a road-block at the intersection of Hwy. 300 and Hwy. 46. That will seal off Hopedale and Delacroix Island. Also, contact the Ostrica locks and give them the description. You will have to initiate the response in the other parishes. You want to get a boat in Orange Bayou. If he is heading south that is probably the path he is likely to take. It probably won't help, but you can also call Port Eads at the mouth of the river. If he is going the long way around, he'll probably refuel at Port Eads."

"This is Coast Guard Chopper calling for Agent Rodred come in, over."

Sue picks up the walkie-talkie. "This is Agent Rodred, over."

"We found a vehicle in the Mississippi Gulf Outlet with the coordinates…, over."

"Air Coast Guard, do you have us on your radar, over."

"Affirmative, over."

"Give us a bearing, over."

"From your position, bearing 172º, over."

The FBI pilot replies, "I've got them dead ahead."

Sue calls Harris on her cell phone. "Sir, he's got an accomplice. She's five four, black hair, and one hundred ten pounds."

"That's impossible. That's Malynda Meyeaux. They probably have her daughter too. You're looking for three suspects. Malynda Meyeaux, five-four, one hundred fifteen pounds, shoulder length straight black hair. Her daughter, Celeste Meyeaux, six years old, looks just like her mother. I'll get a fax sent over to you. Do you have anything else?"

"Air Coast Guard, found a car in the Mississippi Gulf Outlet. It's probably nothing, but we're on our way to check it out."

As they approach the hovering Coast Guard Chopper, they can see a silver Lincoln stuck on the rip-rap. The pilot sets the helicopter down on a shell pad a hundred and fifty yards away. Sue, the other agent, and the Deputy get out and run towards the car. The car is in waist deep water. As Sue wades to the car she can see it's Satinito. Satinito's cell phone is ringing. She quickly locates the phone in Satinito's coat pocket. It's a Government issued secure phone. She looks at the incoming phone number and recognizes it to be Harris'.

CHAPTER 43

▼

Jacques turns into Bayou Loutre where he has to cross a pleasure boat's wake. He cuts his speed in half and cuts the wake close to the other boat. Malynda and Celeste bounce, and Celeste's teddy bear flies out of the boat. Celeste immediately pitches a fit, "Mommy, I promised Daddy that I wouldn't loose it."

Malynda gives Jacques the puppy dog eyes, and he turns around. As he passes near the bear, he leans over and roughly picks it up. He gives it to Celeste. "Hold on tight to it. I'm not turning around again." Despite the No Wake Zone, Jacques keeps full throttle. He pulls up to his dock, ties off the boat, and tells Malynda to run in the house with Celeste. Jacques scrubs and hoses down the whole inside of the boat trying to remove any traces. He then started a trash fire in his burn drum and throws his ghillie suit and gloves in it. He continues to unload the boat and brings his stuff inside.

As soon as he walks through the door, Malynda starts hysterically babbling to him as she tries to wipe the blood off the cuts on his face and head. He can hear Celeste in the bedroom crying. Jacques looks at Malynda with his broken heart. "Calm down, and go take care of Celeste. It's been a long night for everyone. We have plenty of time to talk later." She begins to profusely thank him, and he just raises his finger and points towards Celeste. Jacques has a million thoughts going through his head, and hundreds of questions he wants answers to. Jacques is running on fumes; he only wants a hot shower to get the swamp water off of him and a bed. He washes the blood and dirt off his body, wraps a towel around himself after he finishes. He's surprised to see Malynda sitting at the kitchen table crying and waiting for him.

She pleads to him. "Jacques, we need to talk."

"I think that you need to attend to Celeste."

"She's sleeping"

"Well, you are going to have to wait until after I get some sleep, because right now I am still ready to put a bullet in you."

"I didn't have anything to do with it. I only agreed to go with him because he promised not to kill you. You have to believe me."

"What I did today was for that little girl—not for you. Tomorrow, I want you out of here. Just pack your things and leave."

"How can I do that? I have nowhere to go. I have no money."

Jacques grabs the athletic bag and throws it at Malynda almost knocking her off her chair. "Here, now you have more than enough money. Just go."

Malynda starts crying hysterically, "I opened your letter and didn't know what to do. I knew that Mr. Satinito could have stopped the whole thing. All I had to do was call him. Ok, I knew Scott was doing something illegal. I just did not want to believe it. I had no idea it was this bad."

"So you lied to me the whole time."

"No. There was no plan with Mr. Satinito. I loved my husband. He made all of that up. I agreed with him to save your life. He said if I cooperated, he wouldn't hurt you."

"I don't care. Just take the money and leave."

"Jacques, I want you—not your money. You have to believe me."

"I'm not sure what to believe. We'll talk more after I can think straight."

Jacques leaves Malynda crying at the table. He goes into his bedroom and locks the door behind him. He puts on a set of BDU's, and cleans his rifle and pistol before the saltwater damages them. As soon as the rifle and pistol are cleaned, he loads the pistol and puts one in the chamber. He pulls the duct tape off the booby trap switch and makes sure there is nothing on top of the trap door in the floor. He loads his AR-10 and leans it against the headboard. He lays in the bed with the pistol in his hand and tries to relax. It's a useless effort. He tries to straighten everything out, but everything points to the fact that Malynda betrayed him.

CHAPTER 44

▼

Sue puts the phone in her pocket and quickly points to a wire and screams. "It's booby trapped! Run!" The two other back off and head back to the chopper. On the way to the chopper, the other young agent pulls Sue to the side. "I saw what you pulled off of Satinito. What are you going to do about it?"

"How long have you been an agent? Are you really sure what you saw? How much training have you had? Do you really know, how the FBI really works? Are you ready to throw away your carrier?" She calls the Deputy over, "Let's get this straight. We walked up to the car and saw Satinito and his bodyguard. I saw the car was booby trapped, and we pulled back. Nobody saw the cell phone. You got that. Nobody saw anything else. Let's get back into the chopper and continue our search."

They get back into the chopper, and Sue orders the Pilot to continue the search. She then communicates with the Coast Guard Chopper and tells them to do the same. She calls Harris' cell phone. "Sir, we found Satinito in his car, dead."

"That's just great. We don't have a case anymore because all the suspects are dead. Did you find anything else?"

"No, we couldn't approach the car because it's booby trapped. I'll get a bomb squad on it right away."

"Did you put the call in yet?"

"No sir, I'm going to do that right after I get off the phone with you."

"I want you to handle this personally. Swing back around and blow it up yourself. Do I make myself clear?"

"Sir, I don't have anything to blow it up with."

"I have some C-4 in the luggage compartment of the chopper. Make sure you use enough, if you know what I mean."

"Ok, if you say so."

Sue orders the pilot to return to the automobile and land back on the shell pad. The three of them get out, get the C-4, and tells the pilot and Air Coast Guard to clear the area. Sue's pilot said that he's running low on fuel and has to go back to Lakefront Airport to refuel. She acknowledges him with a hand wave. Sue asks the Deputy and the young Agent if they have experience with C-4. The deputy says he does.

"I need you two to blow the car. It's not booby trapped, but I'm setting one. I need you to go through Satinito's car and see if you can find anything. Make it look like you are wiring the car. You need to be fast. People are watching us. I'm going to make a phone call. When you finish, run the wire over this levee, and we'll blow it."

The deputy and the agent go to the car with the C-4. Sue goes to the detonation location and calls Danny.

"Danny, I need a favor, and I need it quick. If I don't get the information soon, some really bad stuff is about ready to come down. I finally got Harris. Malynda Meyeaux and Jacques Boudreaux have a roll of film that Harris wants badly. I'm guessing that it has some incriminating pictures of him and Satinito."

"Sue, slow down. How do you know this? You better be sure before you make any accusations."

"We just found Satinito's body with a secure FBI phone. It was ringing when I found it. Guess who's number was the incoming call."

"Harris."

"Yep. He's dirty. I just need to find Boudreaux before he does. Get me a phone number in Southeast Louisiana."

"Sue, how much time do I have?"

"None. Call me when you have something. Later." She hangs the phone up.

Sue calls one of her team members at Mr. Eddie's boat launch. "I need you to search Scott Meyeaux's house in Houma. You're looking for a roll of film. Hurry up."

"Have you talked to Harris lately?"

"Yeah, why?"

"He is pretty upset and is bringing me a fax right now of Malynda Meyeaux. In fact, he is using your search chopper to do it. He has to refuel before he gets over here. He is also assembling an Entry Team. They are on their way down here too."

"An entry team that is so Frank. We don't know where this guy is. When he hits the ground, stall him. Get someone to search the Meyeaux house again. I'll call you back in fifteen minutes."

The deputy and agent come over the small levee with the wire spool in their hand. They hook up the detonator and blow the car up. When the pieces start landing around them, they realize that they either used too much C-4 or aren't far enough away. Sue gets on the radio and calls the chopper back. The pilot tells her it's going to be at least another ten minutes. She calls Danny again.

"Danny, what do you have? I'm running out of time."

"Your guy was so easy to find. I would say he is a pretty good shot. He is one of a few civilians that competes in sniper competition, and he always places within the top five. In fact, he even beat you two years ago."

"Did you find any links to Louisiana?"

"Be patient and let me finish. He grew up in St. Bernard Parish. He married and moved to Pearl River. He then moved to Houston. I went through his bank account, and I found he wrote a monthly check to a Mrs. Jean Melerine. Melerine and Louisiana? I pulled her personal information. Guess, where she lives? Try Hopedale, Louisiana. I went into her bank account, and she pays two monthly electric bills, phone bills, and water bills. She only has one residence. She pays hers and her next-door neighbors bills. Her next door neighbor has been dead for over thirty years."

"I love you. What's her address, and what are the two phone numbers".

He gives them to her, and she writes them on her arm.

"Which phone number doesn't match her home phone?"

"The second one."

Sue looks at the Deputy. "As quickly as you can and without using the radio, I need you to get an unmarked van down to Hopedale and pick this guy and woman up. Put him in a safe house that the FBI doesn't know about. Get them on the road now. I'll give them the address as soon as we get it. Just make sure that they don't use the radio."

The deputy picks up his cell phone and dials a number.

Sue calls the number Danny gave her.

The phone ringing wakes Jacques. He picks it up, "Hello."

"Jacques Boudreaux?"

"Yeah, who is this?"

"My name is Susan Rodred. I'm a FBI agent. I know you have Malynda and Celeste. Don't run. The people you killed are only half the problem. I'm afraid the other half is too big for you to take on. We have a van on its way to pick you and Mrs. Meyeaux up. The roads and waterways are blocked. It is only a matter of time before you are found. There is an entry team on its way. I know you can take them out, but don't. So far, all you have killed are a bunch of no good drug dealers. It will be hard to get a jury to convict you on that. On the other hand, if you kill FBI agents doing their job that's different story."

"Why are you doing this?"

"You and Malynda have a roll of film that may incriminate some dirty agents. I need you and Malynda alive. For now, let's leave it at that."

"I want everything expunged from the records."

"Mr. Boudreaux, I don't have the power to do that."

"Do you know what those guys did to Malynda and her husband? I want everything expunged from the records or no deal."

"I don't have the power to do that. I can talk to the DA. I tell you what. If we can't work a deal with the DA, I'll give you forty-eight hours head start."

"I'm keeping my gear with me at all times. Do you understand that?"

"Ok Mr. Boudreaux, anything you want. I just need to get you out of there before the Entry Team arrives. How do I get to you?"

"I'm one point three miles past the bridge in a yellow camp. We will be waiting four camps before it. It's painted a rust color. I'll put a Coke can on the mailbox flag. Have your driver back into the driveway all the way under the camp."

"Mr. Boudreaux, I got it. A Coke can on the mailbox, one point three miles from the bridge. Hurry, Mr. Boudreaux you have to move now."

"What's your phone number?" Jacques gets a pen and writes it on his hand.

"My number is 504-555-1212."

"I'll call you if anything should happen."

Sue hangs up the phone and relays the information to the Deputy. The deputy makes the call to the van.

Sue calls her team member at Mr. Eddie's boat launch. "What is happening on your end?"

"The Meyeaux house burnt down this morning—arson. The entry team van drove by ten minutes ago. I tried to call you, but your line was busy. Oh, one other thing, Malynda Meyeaux just made the top ten most wanted. She is also considered a threat to national security. She is being linked with overseas terrorist operations, and she must be taken at all cost. The emphasis is put on "all," if you know what I mean. I don't know what you are doing, but you better pick up the pace because Harris just landed in his helicopter. Gotta go. Talk to you later."

Harris gets out of helicopter and walks towards the agents. Harris shows them a couple of pieces of paper, "Here is a picture of Malynda Meyeaux and her daughter Celeste. Did Sue blow the car?"

"She blew it good, Sir."

"How come I can't get in touch with her?"

"I was just on the phone with her."

Harris dials Sue's number. "Sue, did you blow the car?"

"Yes sir, the car is toast."

"Did you find anything else?"

"No sir, I'm just waiting on my chopper to resume the searching. The lead on the girl should help a lot."

"Sorry about that sport. We had to refuel the search chopper. The search chopper hit the pad just as mine was finished fueling up. We should be able to cover a lot more area with two choppers anyway. Yours should be on the way shortly."

A deputy interrupts Frank, "I got a deputy that said that he saw the girl. He said they were in the marina a couple of weeks ago. I told him to come over. He'll be here in a couple of minutes."

"Sue, I have a deputy that saw Malynda in the marina. He should be here in a couple of minutes. I'm going to stay here and interrogate the deputy. When you get your chopper, I want you to start looking over Delacroix. I'm going to look over Hopedale. He has to be in one place or the other."

"Ok, I'll start looking over Delacroix as soon as my chopper returns."

Sue looks at the deputy. "How much longer? Harris is going to start looking over Hopedale. You need to tell them to hurry."

"They're a few minutes from the bridge."

The sheriff's car pulls into Mr. Eddie's boat launch parking lot. A young deputy gets out and reports to his sergeant. The sergeant walks him over to Harris."

Frank holds up a piece of paper and starts with the questions. "Did you see this woman?"

"Yes sir, she was real elegant and friendly looking. My knees turned to rubber when she smiled at me."

"Junior, do you realize that she's considered an enemy of the state and has been connected to overseas terrorism? She has probably killed hundreds with that little smile that turned your knees to rubber. Who was she with?"

"Her husband and a little girl."

"Her husband is dead. Did you see what type of vehicle they were driving?"

"They were not driving an automobile. They came to the marina with a boat. It was blue and white, center console tri-hull. It was set up real nice for fishing. The guy had some sort of silencer on the motor that made the motor look twice as big as it really was."

"Did you speak with this guy?"

"Sure did, he was a real friendly type too. He explained all about the motor."

"Well, that real friendly guy just killed five people." Harris just makes a face at him and boards his chopper.

Sue is sitting on the shell pad waiting on the helicopter and looking at her cell phone. It rings. It is one of her team members at Mr. Eddie's launch. "Harris just got some information on the description of the boat. He is in the air headed your way. He should be there in less than five minutes. I also saw the entry team drive by."

"There is not much I can do now. We just have to let it play out."

Sue looks at the deputy, "Where are they?"

"They are just pulling up. They don't see anyone. Wait...there is a note. It says that he decided not to do it this way. He'll get in contact with you."

"Tell them to get out of there quick. All hell is about to break loose."

The deputy relays the message to the van.

Sue covers her head with her hands. "What have I done? He's going to set a trap and kill them all. I just know it."

Harris' helicopter flies over Bayou Loutre. Harris spots Jacques' boat within seconds, and Harris calls in the Entry Team. Frank tells the pilot to circle the area and look for vehicles on the road. Frank sees a van heading back to town. He calls his sergeant. "There is a red van heading south two miles in front of you. Stop it, and search it."

"WilCo on searching the van."

Frank grabs the headset. "Get back over the house with the boat." The pilot complies.

The entry team parks their van perpendicular to the road. Since there's a six-foot deep ditch on each side of the road and the road has no shoulders, the road is completely sealed off. The ten-man team is already dressed for entry in their black body armor and MP-5's on their chests. They stop the van and thoroughly searched it. The sergeant radios back to Harris, "It was just one deputy driving the van. The van is clear. What do you want us to do with the driver?"

"Let him go. He's probably still in the camp."

"WilCo."

Sue calls for her pilot. "Where is my chopper?"

"Bad news. I should be in the air in fifteen minutes."

Sue radios Harris, "Mr. Harris, I need you to pick me up. My chopper is going to be another fifteen minutes."

"Relax, this whole thing is going to be over in a five minutes. I'll pick you up on the way back, and we can celebrate."

"If you insist." Sue starts to question herself about what is the right thing to do? Should she alert Harris that they are walking into a trap and lose her job, or should she keep quiet and hope for the best. She realizes that Jacques has plenty of time to wire the house and find a hide. He can blow the house and shoot any survivors that appeared outside of the house. From there, he'll stand no chance in front of any DA or jury. Sue looses all evidence in the case, and the case will be closed while the real criminal repeats the offences with a different set of puppets."

Within a few minutes, the entry team exits the van in front of the camp. Four team members stack up at the bottom of the stairs at the rear door, four-team members stack at the bottom of the stairs at the front door, and two team members stack at the shed door. Harris is watching the whole thing from the air. He gives the order, "Sergeant, go." Two team members from each side run up the stairs, break the door down and each roll flash-bangs in the house. After the flash-bangs are rolled in, the other team members are heading up the stairs. The flash bangs go off right before the team coming up the stairs enters—perfect timing. They shoot all possible targets in the kitchen and living room. From there they roll flash-bangs into each of the bedrooms and washroom and enter. They call out, "Clear." As soon as they called clear, the sergeant radios Harris. "He's not here. Should we look for evidence?"

"No, there is nothing there. Burn it all to the ground."

"WilCo."

They cleared the house and set it and the open shed ablaze.

Harris grabs the map that Sue left in the chopper. "Sergeant, let's seal off the area. Set a roadblock up at the other side of the bridge. I'll get the Coast Guard to set up an inspection point in both places that Bayou Loutre enters the Mississippi River Gulf Outlet. In the meantime, we'll increase the reward and see how many arrests, we can make before someone gives us some information. If we have to, we'll go door to door. We can't let these suspects get away. Sergeant, I've got a good idea. Leave his boat alone. We will seal off all exits except Seven Dollar Bayou. I want you and your men to commandeer a boat and wait for him there. He'll probably try to escape tonight. When he passes, I want you to cut this maniac to ribbons."

"What about the woman and the girl?"

"No witnesses—no survivors. After the job is done, burn it all. Am I clear?"

"Crystal, Sir."

Five of the ten-man team commandeer a Coast Guard Rigid Hull inflatable with a 30 mounted on the bow. Two set up a roadblock on the other side of the bridge. Three start patrolling the highway. The boat team drives a quarter mile down Seven Dollar Bayou and backs into a small dead end cut. The sergeant tells his men, "Put your weapons on full auto. This is going to be like shooting ducks on the water." He then orders three of them to spread out on the shoreline. The sergeant is behind the wheel and the other agent is on the 30. Once the ambush is set, they hide and wait.

The sergeant using his binoculars scans the marsh. He sees the Indian Mounds to his northwest and takes an interest in them. His phone rings, it's Harris.

"Sergeant, how are your men situated?"

"Two on the roadblock, four with me, and three patrolling the highway."

"I want you to go take care of Sue. She's in the middle of nowhere. I'm bringing you my chopper."

In less than a minute, Harris' chopper hovers next to the boat. Harris jumps into the boat, pushes the man off the 30, and stands behind it. Everyone in the boat is shocked by this display of immaturity. Harris looks at the sergeant. "Go do what needs to be done. I'll take over here."

The sergeant boards the helicopter. He gets in and grabs the map. They land on the highway, pick up the three guys patrolling the highway, and take off again. As they are flying over the marsh, the sergeant looks at the map, and how they have Hopedale sealed off.

Sue is looking to the northwest waiting on her helicopter to arrive. She can hear it but can't see it. She finally spots it, but it's coming in from the east southeast with the sun directly behind it. She tries to radio the chopper, but there's no response. The chopper makes a straight in approach, instead of circling. It flies in hard and fast. It breaks below the sun, and she realizes that it's not her search chopper. It's an olive drab military one. It flares back and sets on its skids hard. Four men wearing woodland BDU's and black masks jump out holding AK-47's. The deputy draws his pistol and is immediately shot in the leg by one of the bullets of a three round burst from an AK-47. The two FBI agents and the deputy raise their hands.

One of the men screams over the sound of the helicopter. "Susan Rodred, come with me." She walks towards the armed men, is tackled by two of them, and is pushed face first into the dirt. They pat her down and remove anything of value. She sees the young FBI agent make a move to rescue her and is stopped by the spray of automatic gunfire at his feet. Sue is handcuffed with her hands behind her back and hooded with a black hood that they fastened around her neck. They pick her up by her jump suit, run her to the chopper, and throw her face down on the floor of the chopper. The guys climb in behind her and put their boots in the center of her back crushing her breast and making it difficult for her to breathe. She hears the other two climb aboard, the turbine of the chopper winds up, and feels the chopper take off. For the next twenty minutes all she can hear is the loud noise of the chopper. The chopper lands again, and they get out by stepping on her. They grab her by her jump suit, drag her out of the chopper, reach under her armpits, carry her with her feet dragging across some concrete, and throw her into a van. The van takes a short ride and stops. She hears the sliding door of the van open, and she can hear that she is at an airport. Two men grab her and drag her up some stairs. She hits her head on something and feels a hand push her head down and her body forward. She's thrown into a vinyl seat and someone puts a seat belt on her. A few moments later she hears jet engines start and realizes that she is on a jet. She feels it taxi, hears the engines roar, and feels its acceleration as it takes off.

After they are in the air, she begins demanding answers. "Who are you? Where are you taking me? What do you want?" Complete silence is the only reply she gets.

An hour into the flight she starts complaining again. "I need to use the bathroom. I need something to drink."

She feels a person sit in the seat next to her. "Ms. Rodred, I advise you to shut your hole."

She recognizes the voice. It's the same guy that attacked her in her town house, and she looses control of her bladder. She feels him getting out of the seat.

"I'm glad to see you are scared of me. It just might save your life. Do you know a Daniel Merrit?"

"Yeah, what did you do with him!"

"Nothing yet. It all depends on your story to see what we are going to do with the both of you."

"Look, we're trying to help Jacques Boudreaux—not trying to arrest him."

"Go on."

"I'm almost positive that he has a roll of film that will be enough evidence to put my boss behind bars for a long time."

"It seems your story checks out."

"Frank Harris is trying to kill Boudreaux. Why don't you just kill Harris and be done with it?"

"We would like for you to handle your own spats. We just watch from the sidelines. As far as Boudreaux, I'm confident he can take care of himself. When we tried to train him for this type of terrain, he was the instructor; and the instructors became his students. I can guarantee you that he'll make it out alive. I can't guarantee that he won't kill a few of your agents doing it."

"Then, why did you kidnap me?"

"Because Harris is not only trying to kill Boudreaux, he's also trying to kill you. We intercepted a message from him to his sergeant ordering the hit. You would have been sitting ducks waiting for that chopper. It would have occurred in the middle of nowhere without witnesses. They would have just blamed it on Boudreaux. Now, what kind of deal could Boudreaux make if he's framed for killing you? We are going to drop you off somewhere, and you're on your own. We're not a babysitting service. Watch your back because we're not going to interfere again."

"What am I supposed to do?"

There's no response.

With the conversation, she lost track of time. Thirty minutes later she hears the landing flaps lower and the landing gear lower and lock. The plane taxies for awhile and comes to a stop. Her seat belt is released; two men grab her jump suit above her shoulders, and jerk her to a standing position. She is then manhandled out the door, down the stairs and into another van. Thirty minutes later, they grab her and force her into a squatting position with a man holding her down from each side. Her handcuffs are removed, the van stops, the door opens, and she is shoved out. She lands on her left shoulder as she hears the van speed away. She pulls off her hood, and the van is gone. She's in an upscale neighborhood wearing a olive drab jump suit that stinks of urine. Next to her is another hood. She picks it up and sees that it has all of her personal items that they took from her. Her cell phone rings, she looks at the number, and she answers it.

"Danny, are you ok?"

"Yeah, Sue. I'm all right. I told you those CIA types are not so nice."

"Quit preaching. Where are you?"

"I don't know. Where are you?"

"I don't know either. I'm in some up scale neighborhood."

"Me too."

"Danny look around and tell me what you see. They probably dropped us off in the same neighborhood." Sue gets up and walks to the center of the street.

"Sue, I can see you. Turn around."

She can see Danny running towards her in the middle of the street. They embrace, when Danny pulls away from her. She can see that his glasses are broken, and he has a busted lip.

"Danny, I'm so sorry I got you involved."

"I'll survive. Let's find out where we are and get out of here."

They find a newspaper and figure out that they're Northfork, VA, and call for a cab.

The sergeant's helicopter circles the wounded deputy and the young agent. The sergeant sees that Sue is not on the ground. He looks out into the sky and sees another chopper at tree top level to the north side of the Ship Channel flying away from them. He tells the pilot to pursue the other helicopter, and he calls Harris.

"Sue has been picked up with another helicopter. Do you want me to intercept?"

"No, I want you back down here. She's toothless without that film. We'll take care of the film first, then we'll take care of her."

"Roger that." He tells the pilot to break off and get back to the car site.

"Do you want me to pick up these two?"

"No, let them fend for themselves." The sergeant laughs at Harris' comment, and tells the pilot to get back to Hopedale.

"Mr. Harris, look to your northwest. Do you see those two hills?"

"Yeah, I see them."

"I want to set up on them. Have my ghillie suit and rifle ready when I get back."

"The hunter is coming out in you. Good."

The helicopter lands on the highway and lets the three agents out to continue patrolling the streets. It takes off and hovers next to the boat where Harris has the 30 in his shoulder. One of the sergeant's men hands the sergeant his rifle and his ghillie suit. The helicopter flies to the highway and drops the sergeant off on the highway a hundred and fifty yards south of the Indian Mounds. The pilot takes off again and continues the search.

Jacques and Malynda climb aboard the Cajun Runner. It's a one hundred and forty-five foot aluminum crew boat that makes runs out to Breton and Chandeleur Sound with people, equipment, and supplies. Jacques opens the rear hatch door and calls inside. "Captain Johnny, can you stash me and my lady friend for a short period."

"No problem, just get below and stay below."

They walk in and close the hatch behind them. The inside of the cabin is set up to transport personnel. It has several tables and bench seats like booths in a restaurant. Johnny is sitting in a booth watching TV.

"Jacques, you're causing a lot of problems for the people down here. Eventually, they are going to get tired of you and turn you in. Do you know that?"

"Well, I need to get out of here tonight. Can you do that for me?"

"I have a water run out to Block 24 that I'm supposed to make tonight, but where are you going? I mean, I can drop you off at an unmanned platform, and you could probably live forever if I kept suppling you food. Malynda looks real refined. Bathing with firewater might be a little rough on her."

"You would be surprised what Malynda can put up with."

"Yeah, look she is putting up with you. What can be worst than that?"

"I would appreciate if you can get me back up to Bayou Bienvenue."

Malynda and Celeste are playing checkers, and Jacques and Johnny are involved in idle conversation when they hear the flash bangs go off and automatic gun fire. Over the radio, they hear that a camp is on fire. Someone calls the fire department, and Johnny runs up to the bridge. "Jacques there goes your camp. You might as well stay down here, listen and wait."

Half an hour later there's all kind of radio traffic—mostly the Coast Guard boarding vessels. Johnny switches back to Channel sixty-eight to see if he can pick up any chatter. It sounds like Hopedale is sealed up. Johnny comes down from the bridge with a hand full of maps. He rolls out a map of Hopedale on the table in front of Jacques.

As Johnny listens to the chatter he starts marking on the map with a black marker. He puts one more "x" on the map and looks at Jacques. "If I could get you out I would, but this place is sealed off, Bro. They're taking their jobs serious this time. It looks like Seven Dollar Bayou is your only out. Commercial vessels can't go in it. We're supposed to use the Ship Channel. You need a sport boat." Johnny goes back up to the bridge. "Hey Jacques, your boat is still tied up to the dock."

"Johnny, it's a trap. They know only sports go down Seven Dollar Bayou. Look at it. The Bayou is a death trap. It is one long bayou without any openings to the marsh. Death trap? Death trap, that is an interesting concept. Do they want to capture me or kill me? They still think that we have the film. They're destroying all the evidence behind them. He gives a dirty look to Malynda, "Where's the film!" She starts to fear Jacques again and terror fills her eyes. "Celeste, you and Captain Johnny play checkers while me and your momma go to the galley and have a talk. Come on Malynda let's go!" Fear is written all over

Malynda's face, but she complies. They descend the stairway into the galley, and Johnny closes the hatch behind them. Malynda sees the dinette and sits down hoping to keep the table between her and Jacques.

Jacques grabs her by the shoulders and begins to violently shake her. He begins to scream. "Ok, where is the film, and what else are you withholding from me?"

She pleads. "I don't know about any film. I told you Joe took the film. Jacques, you have to believe me."

"Ok, so what do you know? Who else is involved?"

"Jacques, I don't know anything. Trust me. If I knew anything, I would tell you."

"You didn't want to leave me because you knew that they are still hunting you. You knew if they found you that they would kill you and Celeste. You knew that it wasn't over—didn't you?"

"No Jacques, I had no idea. Believe me!"

"Do you have somebody's money stashed away?"

Malynda in a frighten tone, "Jacques, I don't have any money stashed. I don't know anything." She then goes hysterical.

"Ok, I believe you. Just calm down. We will figure it out. Just answer me truthfully."

"Jacques, I'll tell you everything."

"Who was the gray haired bastard that I killed?"

"Mr. Satinito. He was a friend of my husband. He use to get us free stays at the Casino's on the Gulf Coast."

"Who was he?"

"Jacques that's all I know. He just entertained us."

"Was he an important man?"

"I guess so. He entertained a lot of people. Many times, we would have dinner at huge banquet tables with a lot of important people. I didn't know any of them. My husband use to point them out to me."

"Give me some examples."

"Well, there were actors and actresses. There were politicians. There were casino owners, and famous chiefs. There were a whole lot of people. I was more interested in Celeste than the people sitting at the table."

"On the night you were beaten and your husband was killed, what happened?"

"You know what happened!"

"No, I mean before. What happened on that day? Did your husband mention anything about a lot of money?"

"No! Jacques. Wait, he did say something about a big commission on a sale that he was about ready to wrap up."

"He must have hid the film because they would have found it by now if it was in the car. Where would he have put the film? Recall everything that happened that night."

Malynda recalls the whole afternoon.

"Malynda, the only time missing is the time he spent with Celeste. Let's go talk to Celeste. I'm going to let you question her. Remember, we are looking for a roll of film."

Jacques and Malynda go back to the crew area. Jacques fills Johnny in on what's going on. Malynda pulls Celeste to another table.

"Celeste, do you remember when Daddy came home?"

Celeste shakes her head and says, "Un huh."

"Did Daddy give you a roll of film?"

She shakes her head side to side.

"Did Daddy give you anything that he told you to take special care of?"

"He gave me my teddy bear and told me not to let Rex chew it up."

"Think real hard sweetheart; it is very important."

"No Momma, Daddy only gave me my teddy bear."

Malynda takes the teddy bear and squeezes it. She does not feel anything. Malynda walks over to Jacques and Johnny carrying the teddy bear. "I'm afraid there is nothing. The only thing that Scott gave her was this teddy bear."

Johnny and Jacques look at each other and then fight over which one is going to rip the teddy bear apart. Jacques grabs it first. He carefully squeezes it and feels nothing. He squeezes it harder, and he feels a hard object in the head. He takes out his knife, cuts the back of the head open, and pulls out the roll of 35mm film. "This is it." Everyone is celebrating, except for Johnny.

"Ok, you found the film. So what. You still have to get out of here alive. How do you plan on doing that?" Silence falls over the cabin.

"What if we make it to the Ship Channel? Can you pick us up on the shore?"

"Water is too shallow for me to get in, and my freeboard is too high for you to climb aboard. It would be nice if you could make it to a channel marker."

"Johnny, that's a great idea. We can walk across the marsh, swim to a channel marker, climb on it, and you can pick-us up. Great."

"All of this illegal planning that could take away my pilot's license and throw me in jail is making me hungry." Johnny looks at Celeste. "How about you?"

With a big smile, Celeste shakes her head up and down.

"How about peanut butter and jelly?"

Celeste screams, "Yeah, do you have strawberry?"

Johnny looks at Malynda, "Would you mind making the sandwiches while I talk some sense into Mr. Optimistic here?" Johnny waits until Malynda and Celeste make it into the galley and continues in French. "Man, you're crazy. The Ship Channel is a dangerous place. Do you know what kind of current you are going to be fighting? Also, we have a hard southeast wind with a falling spring tide. The Ship Channel is going to have four foot breaking waves. Not to mention the sharks that venture up that thing at night. If that isn't enough, there is the little matter of a FBI and at least one Coast Guard helicopter circling this entire area."

Jacques answers in French, "I don't have a choice. It is the only way."

"Ok, but I hope you have your affairs in order."

Malynda and Celeste come up from the galley with peanut butter sandwiches for everyone. Malynda in French, "Here are your sandwiches."

Jacques' and Johnny's faces light up with surprise. Malynda in English, "I heard every word you two said. Jacques is right. If we stay here, they'll find us and kill us. At least this way, we stand a chance. Besides, I'm a good swimmer."

Jacques looks at Malynda. "Malynda, I need to see your grab bag. Bring Celeste's too."

Malynda hands Jacques the two packs, "What is going on?"

"We are going to make that journey tonight. I need to lighten your load."

Jacques empties both packs on the table. There are three sets of clothes each, feminine products, make-up & perfume, child games, food, notebook and paper, colors and a coloring book, hand cream, soap and shampoo, toothbrushes and toothpaste, three sets of utensils, two rolls of toilet paper, a curling iron, and a couple of brushes.

"Malynda, we got to get rid of one set of clothes, pick the two you want to keep. Celeste, tonight we are going to play soldier, and we can only take one game. Pick the one you like the most."

"Can I take the coloring book?"

"Yeah, the coloring book and one other toy. Johnny, we are going to leave the generic things like toothpaste and shampoo on the boat. What do you think you can get away with?"

"I'll have problems with any of the kid games or toys, the clothes, the curling iron and definitely the make-up and perfume. You are going to have to take them with you or throw them away."

"Malynda, what is really important here? We need to get rid of some weight."

Malynda starts putting the stuff back into the backpack. "I'll carry it. It isn't going to be that heavy."

"Wait, I need you to put everything in Ziplock bags. We are going swimming with this stuff."

Jacques starts going through his ruck sack and pulls out a child size set of woodland BDU's, and makes eyes at Celeste. He then pulls out a small size woodland BDU and makes eyes at Malynda. "You two are going to be dressed in style tonight." He takes a trash bag and loads everything else he has in it. He hesitates with the spotting scope and decides to put it and the tripod in the ruck sack. He walks out on the deck, reaches into the life jacket box, pulls out two life jackets, and stuffs them in the ruck sack. He also grabs thirty feet of three-eights inch rope and puts it in the ruck sack. He gives the trash bag and his ghillie suit to Johnny. "Burn it."

"Man, that is some good stuff you want me to burn. Let me keep it for you, and you can come back to get it."

"Burn it."

Johnny starts his burn can and throws all the items in it.

Johnny walks back into the boat. "Well, my guest, there is nothing to do except wait. What do you think—an hour to make the walk."

"Better make it two hours."

"Jacques, I'm leaving at 2400, that makes your leave 2200. It's only 1800 now. Why don't you go below, grab a rack, and get some rest?" Jacques shows Malynda the berth and watches them climb in a rack. He heads back up the stairs to the passenger room.

"Jacques, what gives? You're operating on fumes: you need to get some sleep."

"I still need to get transportation once we get to Bayou Bienvenue."

"Bro, don't worry about it. Old Johnny will take care of it. Now, go below and get some sleep."

He takes Johnny's advice, goes below and he quickly falls asleep.

2130 Johnny walks into the berthing room. "Hey bro, it 2130 rise and shine."

"Johnny, how's it going?"

"It goes good for me, and perhaps not so good for you."

"What do you mean?"

"Whatever you have on that film must be pretty important because they declared martial law in Hopedale. Your place is totally destroyed. It's nothing but smoldering ashes. They started kicking in doors and arresting people left and right." Johnny laughs. "That didn't last long. As three of them came out the fourth house, they were met with thirty guns. They took their weapons, threw them in the back of a pick-up, drove to the bridge, threw them out, and told them to stay on the other side of the bridge."

"Johnny, they're just going to bring in reinforcements."

"Speaking of reinforcements, the parish decided to stay out of this one."

"We still have the guys on Seven Dollar Bayou."

Johnny laughs again. "Those guys are in for a surprise if they try to travel that bayou tonight. Crazy Leon and a few others stretched gill nets with the top line four foot above the water."

Jacques slaps Johnny on the shoulder. "God, I love this place."

Jacques grabs his BDU's and leaves the girls below with theirs. He goes to the passenger cabin and changes. The girls stayed below and change. When the girls finish, they come to the passenger cabin. Johnny and Jacques go below to make sure that the boat is purged of all signs of them being there. Once they are confident it's clean, they both come up to the passenger cabin.

Malynda strikes a modeling pose, "What do you think?"

Celeste imitates her mother, "Yeah, what do you think?"

Jacques replies. "Well, you both look beautiful in camouflage, but we need to make a few modifications. First, tie Celeste's hair in a ponytail. Second, remove your earrings. Now, I need to add some make-up." Jacques pulls out his camouflage compact and paints both of their faces and hands. "The next thing I need you two to do is drink two full glasses of water." They do, and Jacques paints his face and hydrates himself. "Ok, we're going topside and across the street. Once we're across the street, we will spray ourselves with the mosquito dope."

Johnny goes up to the cabin. He sees the FBI chopper to the south and the USCG chopper to the north. The radio comes alive. "Mayday, Mayday, Mayday. My boat is on fire. I'm three miles east of Breton Sound Island. I'm taking on water, and I'm sinking. Mayday, Mayday, Mayday." Johnny watches the USCG chopper head towards Breton Sound Island. Johnny comes back down and sees them out the hatch. "You should have at least a couple of hours. Good luck."

CHAPTER 45

▼

Jacques in a bent over position and rifle in his hand runs across the highway and under a camp across the street. He takes one knee. He looks back at the boat, flags Malynda to cross, and watches her cross the street with Celeste on her hip. When she gets close, he signals her to get down. He rests his rifle on top of a fifty-five gallon drum, flips up his scope caps, turns the scope to full power, and studies the Indian Mounds that are lit by the full moon.

After Malynda finishes applying the mosquito dope to herself and Celeste, she slowly moves closer to Jacques. "What are you looking at?"

"I'm looking at the Indian Mounds. If there's a sniper out there, that's where he'll be. The Indian Mounds are the high ground. I'm looking for the one imperfection." Jacques continues to glass the mounds for five minutes. "There you are."

Jacques sees the sniper on the Indian Mounds, and studies him for a while.

"Jacques, we need to get moving."

"Not yet. There is a sniper on the Indian Mounds."

Jacques ranges him to be four hundred yards with a thirty-knot head wind. He studies the movements, to make sure that center of mass is where the person is under the ghille suit is. He weighs his decision to himself. "If I shoot, they might even hear me in the wind. What about the consequences of shooting a federal officer? What if he has a partner that I can't see? Not this guy, it wouldn't be sporting of him. No, he's alone. I guess I stand a better chance alive than dead." He puts a round in the chamber. "Malynda, you and Celeste hold your ears and close your eyes." They do. Jacques gets his breathing down, turns his safety off, and puts the cross hairs on the center of the head portion of the clump. It moves again. "Something looks wrong, he's moving too much." He puts the safety back on, digs his spotting scope out the bag, and sets it up.

"Jacques, we need to get moving. We can't stay here. What have you been preaching about the wind? Isn't it hard to hit a person in the wind?"

He looks at Malynda's hair blowing in the thirty-knot wind. "Even with the thirty-knot wind, we're almost directly downwind. At four hundred yards, we're easy pickings." He looks through the spotting scope. "Just wait a minute, something's wrong with that sniper. There might be two of them up there." He zooms in to forty power and studies the moonlit sniper some more. The movements have a pattern to them. He waits for it to move again and notes where the movement is coming from. He focuses and studies the area. He sees it. It's a stick under the sniper that goes into the marsh grass. "Malynda, it's not a sniper; it's a puppet. The sniper is in the marsh grass. This guy is good. He wants me to shoot the puppet. That way he can replace it with himself midway into our journey."

"If you don't shoot the puppet, he won't replace it. Come on Jacques we are going to miss Johnny."

"We have plenty of time. I can't take the chance. He can climb up on the Indian Mounds at any time. If he gets up there while we are walking across the marsh, we're dead." Jacques packs the spotting scope back in the bag, takes the round out of his rifle, and sets it down on the bipod.

"Jacques what are you doing? We can't give up now."

He pulls out his bayonet. "We're not. I just need to take care of a little problem."

Malynda says nothing, but her face says it all.

"Don't worry, I'll be back in fifteen minutes." Jacques runs in the darkness under the camps until he is in line with the Indian Mounds. He picks out a star in line with the Indian Mounds. He only has to crawl a hundred yards in the marsh to get there. He gets on his hands and knees and starts slowly crawling towards them. He gets to the south side of the mound, gets on his belly and slowly works his way around the west side. He slowly slides the bayonet forward and moves the grass out of the way for him to see in front of him. He then pulls himself half a yard. He moves the grass and this time he can see the sniper three feet in front of his bayonet. The sniper is lying on his back, looking up into the night sky, and hoisting the stick up. Jacques pulls his knees up under his chest, and the sniper freezes. The sniper remains motionless trying to hear, but with the wind blowing the grass it's difficult. Jacques looks at this guy again, and thinks to himself. "This guy looks like he's been trained by the best. He'll probably just take the knife away from me and stick me with it." Jacques goes back to the full prone position, slides the knife back into the sheath, and pulls out his 45. He stretches out and points it directly at the side of the sniper's head. He turns the safety off. The sniper hears it, and looks directly at Jacques.

Jacques says, "Don't move."

"Relax partner. I'm not going to do anything."

"Put the stick down, put your arms over your head, and slowly turn over face down." The sniper does exactly as he is told. Jacques stands up, kneels down beside him, puts the muzzle of the pistol in the center of sergeant's back. He grabs the sergeant's pistol and throws it into the marsh. He then grabs his radio and throws it into the marsh. He takes out the sergeants handcuffs.

"Jacques, we can work this out."

"I don't think so. Shut up."

"You know that I can take you, because you can't fire that weapon without my team hearing you."

Jacques aims for the scope on the rifle and discharges the pistol, and waits for the ringing in the sergeant's ears to stop. "If they even heard it in this wind, they're not sure what they heard. Even if they knew what they heard, they were expecting it. Before they even think about using the radio, they need to hear at least two more shots. Now, move your hands where I can get these cuffs on you. Come on, palms out."

"You're a smart fellow. How come you don't just kill me? You know it's going to come down to that. Either you kill me, or I kill you. Once the hunt starts, it doesn't end until one of us dies. It's the rules of the game."

Jacques puts the handcuffs on him. "Let's just say that I have my reasons."

The sergeant laughs.

Jacques feels under the back side of the sergeant's belt, and he pulls out an extra key. He takes off his boots and throws them in the marsh. He systematically goes through all of the sergeant's pockets and throws their contents out into the marsh. He empties the rifle, throws the bullets in one direction and the rifle in the other.

"Are you finished, Mr. Boudreaux?"

"Not quite." Jacques pulls out a short length of cord and hog-ties the sergeant's feet to the handcuffs. "Now, I'm finished."

"I hope you enjoyed yourself tonight because I won't underestimate you again."

"You shouldn't have underestimated me in the first place."

"I'm truly going to enjoy killing you."

Jacques leaves without saying a word and runs back to Malynda and Celeste.

When he gets back to Malynda and Celeste, "Come on, let's get started." He reaches for Celeste.

Malynda pulls her back. "I'll carry her."

"Malynda, it's going to get tough. I think you should let me carry her, and you carry the life jackets."

"I said that I'll carry her."

"Ok, have it your way."

They start out into the marsh, and Jacques sees that Malynda is having a tough time from the start. He knows the marsh is hard near the road and just gets softer the further out they go. Nearly every step, Malynda misses the grass clump and sinks in the foul smelling mud to her knees. They make a hundred yards into the swamp, and the swamp becomes very soft. He sees that she is sweating bullets and is already out of breath. Malynda takes a step and sinks to her crotch. She tries to use her other foot to free herself, but it sinks too. Before Jacques can get to her. She drops Celeste and falls face first into the gumbo. Jacques picks up Celeste and carries her to a grass pile. When he returns, he can see that Malynda has been fighting to get out and is now up to her waist in mud. Jacques helps Malynda out of the hole, but the vacuum pulls both her tennis shoes off. As soon as her legs come out, the muck refills the holes. Jacques carries Celeste, and he watches Malynda fall over two more times. "Malynda, it's time to take a break."

They find a thick grassy area and sit down. Jacques looks at Malynda crying. She's covered in mud and uses her hands to wipe away as much of it as she can. Jacques thinks to himself that he should have taken her out in the marsh weeks ago. "Malynda, we need to slow down. You need to take your time and step on the grass clumps. It is the only you are going to stay afloat."

"Jacques, I can't see what's grass or water. It's nighttime. Let's turn around. I'm ready to give up."

"The only thing back there is death. We need to keep going."

He takes her pack, carries Celeste, and holds her hand to help her along. She still falls, but not as often. He can't complain, because he falls more than a few times himself. It's slow and rough going. They take breaks whenever they find a dry spot, but for the most part it is a walk of living hell.

Midway into their journey, they come across an old ten-foot wide ditch with no water. "Malynda, we have to cross this alligator style. It's the only way. Just get on your belly and keep your hands and feet moving. It's half swimming and half crawling. Just don't stop moving forward."

Shortly there after, they are within two hundred yards of the Ship Channel. The marsh grass is getting thicker, which makes the walking easier. Jacques makes the sign of the cross, because he knows that Malynda should be able to walk in the thick grass. He looks at Malynda and sees that she is no longer wiping the mud off of her. She is no longer itching the mosquito bites on her hands and face. Sweat is pouring out of her body, but she has the chills. By the way she is moving her head, he can see that she is having tunnel vision. He realizes that fatigue is taking over her. They sit and rest, but Jacques knows that the clock is now working against them. After a short break, he takes her pulse. It's 190 BPM. He waits another ten minutes and takes her pulse again. This time it's 165 BPM. It is not as low as he would like it, but it'll have to do. He urges Malynda on. She makes another twenty-five yards and nearly passes out. Jacques catches her and tells Celeste to climb on top of his fanny pack. By shear determination, he carries Malynda and Celeste the next seventy-five yards. They reach the shoreline of the Ship Channel. By this time, Jacques is exhausted himself.

Once they reached the water's edge, Jacques puts Malynda down, lets Celeste off of his back, removes his web gear, and lays down on his back. Malynda walks to the water's edge and sits down on a piece of driftwood. In the moonlight, the Ship Channel is a violent scene. There are four-foot crashing waves. The current is rushing out to sea at a good ten knots and the thirty-knot wind is trying to force the water back in the opposite direction. The result of the two opposing forces of nature causes utter chaos.

Malynda looks fifty yards out to the channel marker. It's a wooden tripod structure with pile clusters for legs and a small platform seven feet out of the water for the light's the battery pack. She screams over the howl of the wind, "There is no way. There is just no way that you are going to take Celeste and me out there. If we survive the swim, how are we going to climb up on the platform? It is just impossible. If we attempt this, we'll perish."

Jacques looks at the waves crashing into the structure. He grabs Malynda. "Calm down Malynda. The water is rough. We knew that. We brought life jackets, and we will tie off to each other. We won't get lost. We won't drown. We will make it. We will walk upstream some and just drift to the platform. Once we reach the platform, we will climb up and wait for Johnny."

"Jacques, I'm worried. I'm a good swimmer, but I'm not sure about going in that."

"Malynda, you are going to have a life vest on. The worst thing that could happen is that we miss the platform and drift out to sea. Come on. It's getting late. All you have to do is steer yourself to the structure."

They head a hundred and fifty yards upstream of the structure. Before they slowly walk into the water, Jacques secures everything in his web gear and makes sure Malynda's small pack is properly fasten. They put the life jackets on and tie off to one another. Jacques picks up Celeste and tells her to hold on tight to his neck. They slowly start walking into the water. Near the shore it's calm and warm. As they ease out further, the rip current gets worse. They can feel the cold water of the depths. They soon get swept into the fury of the rip current and waves. The violence is worse than Jacques imagined. Even with the life jacket on, he's fighting to keep his head above the water. Celeste is in a violent rage. Since the crashing waves have no regular patters, the rope that's attached to Malynda keeps tugging him and Celeste under, as it does the same to her. He keeps getting disorientated and is constantly looking for the flashing green light.

He sees the structure, and it's coming fast. There's a galvanized ladder that stretches into the water. He steers himself to it. He screams at Celeste for her to climb over his shoulders and on to his back. She does; and not a second too soon. He crashes into the ladder. The force of the water pins him to the ladder. He screams at Celeste to climb. She quickly does so. She's able to climb higher than the next wave could reach, but she runs out of rope. Malynda misses to the channel side of the ladder and the structure. The rope between Jacques and Malynda goes taunt. It starts to pull Jacques off the ladder. He's holding on to the ladder with all of his might, and he can hear Malynda's cries of pain with every jerk of the rope. He looks up at Celeste. The waves are just clearing beneath her. Jacques has to make a decision. He can't hold on to both of them. He pulls out his bayonet and cuts the line between him and Celeste. "Celeste, climb to the platform." Celeste climbs up and gets onto the platform.

Jacques puts the bayonet back in the sheath. The line goes taunt again. As soon as the load lets off, he takes the slack out of the line. He pulls in four feet of rope and ties it off with a slipknot. Another wave crashes into him and smashes his face into one of the rungs, and he begins bleeding from the forehead. He pulls the bayonet out and cuts the rope close to his waist, and puts it back in the sheath. He wraps the free end around one of the rungs a couple of times and ties the end of the rope to the rung below. He unties the slipknot knot. Each time the rope goes slack, he pulls the rope that's attached to Malynda with his left hand and uses the wraps around the rung to hold her position with his right hand when the rope goes taut again. Each time he pulls in two to three feet of rope. Since both of his hands are working the rope, each time a wave crashes through, he gets busted up. His arms are burning and feel like jello. Finally, he sees Malynda. She's screaming. She pulls herself around the barnacle covered pile cluster cutting her hands and arms. Three more pulls, and he reaches over the back of her head and grabs her life vest. He pulls her under him to protect her from being crushed by the wave. He cuts her rope, and he tells her to climb. Jacques waits for the next wave to crash and then climbs up the ladder himself with the bayonet in his mouth.

As he tops the ladder, he sees Malynda sitting on the platform holding tightly to Celeste. Malynda's still coughing up water, and they are crying. Malynda gives a look towards Jacques like a mother bear protecting her cub that clearly tells him to keep his distance. He can see that they are shivering from the wind that is cutting through their wet clothes. The shivering is approaching hypothermia. Jacques takes off his web gear and pulls out his poncho. He wraps Malynda and Celeste in the poncho and wraps himself around them. Jacques keeps looking to the west praying that Johnny isn't much longer.

Finally, he can see the Cajun Runner. Johnny motors past the structure and backs up to it from the downstream side. Because the wind is blowing in the opposite direction, handling the boat is tricky. Jacques knows exactly what Johnny is doing, and stands on the corner of the platform.

The boat eases back and the public address speaker comes alive. "I'm only going to be able to make one pass." The boat lightly bumps the stern on the structure one time. Johnny is a good pilot. Jacques can hear the throttles being worked to make the stern dig to keep it at a good level for Jacques to jump. Just as the boat touches the structure, Jacques jumps and grabs the handrail on the rear platform. Johnny repositions the boat for another pass. This time when he bumps the structure, Malynda hands Celeste to Jacques. Jacques gets Celeste in the cabin as quickly as possible, and makes it outside by the time Johnny is in position again. The boat makes another pass and Malynda jumps on board. Jacques tries to rush her inside, but she throws her arms up and runs away from him. Jacques rushes behind her, grabs her and Celeste and throws them into the shower with their clothes on.

Ten minutes later Malynda and Celeste reappear in dry clothes. As Jacques passes Malynda, she makes it clear that she's not speaking to him. Jacques goes below and showers himself. Five minutes later, Jacques starts heading up the stairs to the pilot house, and he sees Malynda sitting in one of the booths with Celeste in her lap. Malynda is holding her hands crying. He stops and turns back around. "You might want to come below. Maybe some antibiotic ointment might help those little nasty cuts."

They go below and find the first aid kit. Jacques looks at Malynda's hands. There's no blood coming out of the cuts, but he knows the poison from the barnacles is burning her. He rubs some ointment in the cuts, and she puts a bandage on his head. Jacques looks at the beat up Malynda. "And you didn't think that we would survive." She's not easily amused. Jacques goes below, picks everything up, and puts it in a black garbage bag. For the rest of the journey out to Block 24, they ride in silence in the pilot house. As they see the platform coming into view, they go below and wait. After thirty minutes of off loading water and loading the platform's trash, Jacques hears the engines go full throttle again. They come up to the passenger area. Malynda and Celeste lay down in one of the booth seats and try to go to sleep, and Jacques goes back up to the pilot house.

"Johnny, how's the return trip looking."

"Looks clear. There're not stopping traffic in the Ship Channel—just in and out of Bayou Loutre."

"Did you find me a vehicle?"

"Yep, sure did. You owe me five hundred dollars."

Jacques pulls out his wallet and hands over five one hundred dollar bills.

"Jacques you might want to smooth things over with Malynda. She's been through a lot."

"That's next on my list." Jacques descends back down from the pilot house into the passenger area. He sees Malynda lying down on a booth bench with Celeste lying next to her side. He lies on the opposite bench from Malynda and Celeste and looks under the table at Malynda. She lies there with her eyes open.

In a soft voice, Jacques asks, "Malynda, how are you doing?"

"Jacques, you could have gotten us killed tonight. The whole idea was stupid. Celeste is only six years old. I can't believe you cut the rope that connected you to her and let her climb that ladder by herself."

"I had trouble with that decision, but it was the only way that I could have saved you."

"When did you determine that I was telling the truth?"

"I haven't come to that conclusion. It still fits together too nicely."

"Then, why go through all this trouble with me? Why didn't you just cut my rope?"

"I remember a sixteen-year-old girl that gave me the best advice of my life—don't ever make a rash decision. Always sleep on it."

Malynda can remember that day and smiles. "I know there's nothing I can say to make you believe me. You need to come to your own conclusions. I just hope you come to the right conclusions. I need you, and I hope you give me and Celeste a chance." She reaches for her crucifix and notices that it's missing.

Jacques pulls the rosary out of his shirt pocket and hands it to her. Malynda clutches the rosary in one hand and holds Celeste with the other. She closes her eyes and falls asleep. Jacques lies there and finds comfort looking at Malynda and

Celeste sleeping across from him. He watches the crucifix of the rosary swing back and forth, and he drifts asleep.

0515, the change in engine speed wakes Jacques. He looks out the window and sees that they are pulling into Bayou Bienvenue. The boat backs up to a wharf. Johnny uses the engines to hold her position and goes out to tie her off. Johnny walks back in.

"Bro, it's all clear. Get your stuff and let's go. Jacques shakes Johnny's hand. "I owe you—big time."

"Don't mention it."

Malynda gives them a big hug and a kiss on the cheek, "Thank you so much Johnny."

"You don't owe me anything. Anytime this bucket-head mistreats you, give me a call."

Malynda laughs. "I'll do that."

They walk out into the predawn to see Père Andrew standing by his truck waving at them to come on. Jacques carrying their gear and Malynda carrying Celeste run over to the truck.

"Hurry up and get under dis tarp. They still have da marina blocked off."

Malynda puts Celeste down on the tailgate and looks under the tarp at a nearly missing floor board of the truck's bed and makes a face at Père Andrew.

"Dat bed is fine. You hurry."

She lets Celeste crawl in and crawls in behind her. She watches as Jacques climbs in behind her. Then Père closes the tailgate. As Père pulls off, Malynda is uneasy about seeing the ground below the truck and the exhaust fumes filling the area under the tarp. The truck comes to a stop, and she can hear men talking to Père. She looks at Celeste and holds her finger to her lips to make sure Celeste stays quiet. She sees Jacques in the shadows with his pistol out.

"Good morning, Father."

"Dat it is."

"You have a nice day."

"Thank you." He drives on and begins to pick up speed. As he does the exhaust fumes become almost unbearable. Jacques carefully picks up the corner of the tarp to let some fresh air in. Five minutes later the truck comes to a stop, and she hears the driver's door open, and Père talking to someone. The tarp flies back, and there is Mr. Melerine looking into the bed.

Jacques stands up on the best metal he can find and sees that he is between I-10 and the Ship Channel on Hwy. 47. "Where's the vehicle that Johnny got?"

As Père Andrew helps Malynda and Celeste out of the truck, he laughs. "Dis is it."

"Père, you're charging me five hundred dollars for the use of your truck?"

He and Melerine laugh. "Jacques, Melerine had a five hundred dollar bet dat you wouldn't make da channel marker, and Johnny be searching half da night looking for you in da Ship Channel. I guess he lost da bet." Jacques hurries Malynda into the cab of the truck.

Jacques looks over the truck. All the tires are bald, except for one that the steel belts are showing. The inside of the truck is worse than the outside. The seat has exposed springs. The dashboard has large holes in it and so does the floorboard. Jacques is a little concerned about being able to see the passenger's front wheel from the driver's seat. To his surprise when he turns the key, it starts right up and belches a big cloud of white smoke.

"Jacques you take good care of me truck. Every so often, you pull over and add da oil. I bought a whole case for you."

"Père, do you think that the truck will make five hundred miles?"

"If you bring enough oil, she'll give you five hundred miles."

"That's all I need."

He thanks Père and Mr. Melerine, puts it into first gear, and they pull out onto the highway heading north. They drive until they're heading north on I-59. He stops at the first Super-Mart they come across. While he goes to gets the film developed, he tells Malynda to get supplies for three to four days. He drops off the film and heads for the camping section. He picks out a double burner propane stove, several bottles of propane, a hurricane lantern and oil, a large ice-chest, a machete, ten water containers, a case of oil, pots and pans, and utensils. He then heads to linens where he finds a couple of cheap blankets, sheets and pillows. He searches the food section to find Malynda, and she isn't there.

He immediately panics and thinks that she's caught. He calms down and realizes that she's probably in the clothing section. He does a quick search of the store and finds her in toys. While she's picking out a toy with Celeste, Jacques looks through her basket of food. He thinks to himself that Malynda did a nice job on her selections. "I thought I would find you in the clothing department."

"That is our next stop."

"Make sure that you get yourselves some bathing suits. The place where we are going has a nice swimming hole."

Jacques continues to look through Malynda's basket and starts making notes of things that she's missing—like laundry detergent, dishwashing detergent, toilet paper, soap and shampoo, and towels. He transfers the contents from his basket into hers. He takes the full basket, gives her some money, and tells her that he would meet her at the truck. Jacques gathers the missing items, fills the ice-chest halfway with ice, pays for everything, and picks up the pictures. He can't wait to look at the pictures, and opens them on the counter. All of the pictures are of the same group that he took at Tony's house. The only difference is that there're no girls, and they're dressed in suits. They're standing behind a black van with the rear doors open. The inside of the van is stuffed with drugs. Jacques shakes his head in disbelief and thinks to himself. "I already have pictures of this." He puts the pictures back into the envelope, pays for them, and leaves.

At the truck, he puts the refrigerated items in the ice chest; ties it off; and carefully stacks the other items into one corner of the truck bed. He can see Malynda and Celeste are on their way. They're both smiling again, which brings a good feeling over Jacques.

They load up in the truck and head out. The next stop is to fill up the truck. Malynda asks to see the pictures. She looks through them and agrees with Jacques. Jacques tops the tank off and buys a few drinks for the trip. He gets back into the truck and re-enters I-59 north. Malynda keeps looking at the pictures over and over again. "We're missing something. What are we missing?" She continued to flip through the pictures. "Jacques, stop the truck! I found it. This is a government van. If you look closely at the license plate, you can see it's a government license plate."

Jacques pulls off to the emergency lane, and Malynda hands him a picture with the van rear door open and the license plate at an angle. It's difficult to see. Jacques stares a little longer. "That's it. It sure is government. That means one of these guys works for the government and he is—I mean was—supplying drugs to Satinito." Jacques hands the pictures back to Malynda.

Malynda pulls her hair back into a pony tail. "Jacques, it's hot in this truck. How much further? Where are we going anyway?"

Jacques looks at the beads of sweat developing on Malynda and Celeste's face. "Malynda, when this whole mess started; I always had a fall back position. I use to hunt this beautiful piece of property near Pachuta, MS. It has clean fresh water and a wooden structure that we can sleep in. What makes this place so special is that I know it like the back of my hand. If someone decides to try to take us there, they're in for a rude awakening."

Malynda's attitude flares, "I don't care where you take me. Just get me there soon."

They pull off the interstate, travel a few country roads, and come up to a cattle gate. Jacques gets out, works the combination, opens the gate, drives through, and locks the gate behind them. They continued for another half mile on a dirt road and pull up to a twelve by sixteen wooden structure.

It's made of scrap plywood and has a tin roof. There're no windows, but it has a door on each side. In front there's a tin cover that they can park the truck under. He opens the door and there's a bunk bed, a small plastic patio table with plastic chairs, a small counter top that has a sink, and the biggest rat Malynda has ever seen running around inside the structure. Malynda screams and runs out the door with Celeste. Jacques opens the other door and chases the rat out. He walks outside to find Malynda inside the truck with the windows up. He opens the door of the truck and coaxes Malynda out.

"Yep, I have plenty of fond memories of this place."

"Jacques, there's no electricity, or running water. There are weeds growing inside of it. There's even a rat living inside of it. This is not going to work. We need to stay at a motel."

"Malynda, relax. There is plenty to do up here. All we're going to do is eat and sleep here. The rest of the time you will be swimming, hiking, and enjoying nature."

"Sleeping is the problem. How do you expect to get any ventilation in here with no windows?"

"We leave the doors open. The cross draft will be just fine. Let's get our bathing suits on and take a dip in the creek to cool off."

Malynda and Celeste change into their swimsuits, and Jacques leads them down this trail to a sandy beach and a clean running creek. The water in this area is only a couple of feet deep. Jacques gets them situated and starts to walk off. Malynda stops him. "Please Jacques, let the rat have the camp. Let's get a motel room. Please."

"In the twenties, people lived like this all across America. Just pretend like it's the twenties. We won't be staying here for long, and you might even grow to like it. You and Celeste stay here. I'll unpack the truck and clean the place up. It'll be Ok. You just wait and see."

"It's not the twenties, and I won't grow to like it."

Jacques just shakes his head and walks back to the camp. He weeds it; sweeps the floors; and scrubs the table, the bedding, and the counter top. He sets up the ice chest, the stove, and hangs up all the clothes. He goes out back and hangs up a clothesline. He thinks to himself. "It doesn't look that bad." He pulls the shower board out from behind the camp and sets it up outside by one of the doors.

At the creek, Malynda finds a nice shady spot and lies down. She watches Celeste playing along the water's edge. Celeste points upstream and screams. "Momma, look." Malynda jumps up to see two deer crossing the creek and run into the woods. Malynda lies back again and begins to appreciate the beauty of the woods. She's surrounded by magnificent white oaks with a few pin oaks mixed in. Further up the creek, she sees birch trees. Before long, the animals become adjusted to their presence and begin to come out—first the birds and then the squirrels. This place is becoming so very peaceful to her.

She hears Jacques walking back down the trail. In a soft voice, "Jacques, come lie beside me." He lies right next to her. "I can see why this place appeals to you so much. You can easily forget about the whole world."

"You're just starting to see. Give yourself some more time and your mind will open to a whole new way of thinking."

"Jacques, how old are those trees."

"They're probably close to five hundred years old. They were breaking ground when Columbus was looking for the Americas. This creek was probably here before that. It's a lot to take in one day. We need to start heading back to the camp. It gets dark fast in woods." They pick everything up and head up the trail.

They get back to the camp just in time. The condition of the inside of the camp surprises Malynda. It's clean, and it resembles an old wooden cabin. She watches Jacques throw a big pot of water on the stove. He keeps checking the temperature of the water with his finger. "It's just about ready." He grabs a plastic Mardi Gras cup. "It's time for a shower."

She laughs. "Where do you expect us to take a shower?"

"Right outside. Just strip down, use the cup to wet yourself down, soap yourself, rinse, wash your hair, and rinse. I call it a pot bath."

Malynda strips Celeste and walks outside with her. Celeste thinks it's fun. She brings Celeste back in wrapped in a towel. Jacques heats up another pot of water. "Ok Malynda, it's your turn." She walks outside and starts to bathe. Celeste keeps poking her head out the door, looking at her Mother, and laughing at her. After Malynda finishes, it's Jacques turn. Jacques hurries because darkness is almost upon them.

As soon as he comes in, he lights the hurricane lantern, and starts to warm up some can food. They sit down and eat, Jacques cleans the dishes, and they get ready for bed. Malynda asks Jacques, "Where is the bathroom?"

"The out house is right out back. Go ahead and take the light."

She walks out side. A few minutes later Jacques and Celeste hears Malynda, "Whoa! look at the sky!"

Jacques grabs Celeste and heads outside. Jacques walks straight to Malynda and turns out the hurricane lantern. He tells Malynda and Celeste to close their eyes. A minute later, he tells them to open them. Their eyes adjust to the darkness. Celeste points to the sky, "Look momma, that cloud is glowing." Jacques points out that it's the Milky Way that they're looking at. Jacques points out some of the other constellations. He then sets up his spotting scope. He shows Malynda and Celeste the rings of Saturn, the moons of Jupiter, the moon, and the Great Nebula. Even Jacques is impressed at the quality of the image through his spotting scope.

They're tired and go back into the camp, and they say their prayers. Jacques helps Malynda and Celeste into the top bunk, and he climbs into the bottom bunk. Malynda protests. "We should have the bottom bunk. Why do you get the bottom bunk? It's not fair."

"You'll be better off up there. Just trust me on this one and go to sleep."

0200, Jacques wakes to a noise in the camp. He slowly rolls over to see a coyote in the camp. He jumps up screaming, and chases it out. Malynda grabs Celeste and screams. Jacques walks backs in. "Do you still want the bottom bunk?"

"No, I want to sleep in the truck."

"Think about it. There's just as many holes in the truck as in this camp. Good night."

Sunday morning, they sleep in late and wake to the noise of a couple of sparrows that fly through the camp. They get up and eat breakfast. Jacques decides to take Malynda for a little hike through the eleven hundred acre property. It's hilly and has clear cuts, young pines, mature pines and oak groves. Jacques mentions the hiking idea to Malynda and Celeste. To his surprise, they're both willing to go. They get dressed and go north on the camp road. Jacques throws Celeste on his shoulders. They turn into the woods almost at the gate they entered from and find themselves in a beautiful oak grove. They sit on top of a hill. Six hundred yards in front of them is another hill. A hundred and fifty feet below them is a small creek that is two feet wide. The oak trees are full and the sound of the water running in the creek is relaxing. Jacques looks at Malynda's expression of awe. "Jacques, I can't remember seeing anything so beautiful."

"This used to be one of my favorite places to hunt. It hasn't produced much deer, but it's a place where I can find myself. Just wait. I have some more to show you." Jacques urges them on, and they continue their hike. They follow the creek all the way around to the swimming hole and then back to the camp. It's 1500 and past everyone's lunchtime. They eat lunch and lounge around the swimming hole for the rest of the afternoon. The rest of the afternoon's activities are almost rehearsed. Celeste takes her bath, then Malynda and then Jacques. Due to the long walk, they go to sleep that night without any problems.

CHAPTER 46

▼

Monday morning, Malynda wakes Jacques. "Do you mind watching Celeste? I want to go back to that oak grove."

Jacques can tell that Malynda is beginning to grasp the beauty of the outdoors. "No problem. If we are not here when you get back, we will be at the swimming hole."

Malynda gets dressed, heads up the road, and then into the woods. Before long, she's at that same little spot in the woods. She walks a quarter of the way down the hill and sits with her back against a tree. She's just below the canopy and has a spectacular view. She pulls out Jacques' rosary and begins to pray. While she is praying, she's still and begins to blend in with Mother Nature. The little creek is fifty yards away, and she can hear the water trickling over the little log jam that is made of sticks. She can hear the breeze through the leaves of the trees. She can smell the clean country air, and she begins to notice every little movement in the woods. She no longer looks at the oak trees but into them. "If they can tell stories of their many years, what would they say? Maybe they are telling their story through the wind." She looks at a squirrel that is running in the branches. She wonders what's going through its mind. The beauty is too much for her and her eyes began to water. The longer she stays and becomes absorbed, the more it plays on her emotions. She tries to see where she fits in this ecosystem, but she can't figure it out. The more she ponders the concept, the more she realizes that it's probably better off without her. She starts to question herself, who she really is? Before long, tears are rolling down her face. She wants to stay, but her emotions can no longer take it. She gets up as quietly as she can. As she leaves, she can hear every oak leaf crush under her feet. She crosses over the hill where it turns into a pine forest. She finds a dirt road and follows it for a while. Then she comes upon a recent clear cut. She finds a comfortable place to sit and looks over the five-acre wide clear cut along the road. Grass is just starting to grow in the near barren land. It's as if she's looking over a graveyard of trees. She looks around the corner of the pine tree wood line and sees that the clear cut seems to go on forever. Her emotions go from a feeling of bliss to a feeling of sadness, and she begins to cry again. She fights the tears, but they keep coming. She gets up and follows the road back to the camp.

She looks around the camp and sees no one. She starts to walk down to the swimming hole, but she hears a voice to the east. She looks around, and she sees Jacques waving at her from the second hill in front of the camp. She walks over the first little hill, and then up the sides of the second hill. When she gets there, she sees Celeste and Jacques full of mud and sweat. "What on earth are you doing?"

"I'm digging a little house." Jacques wipes the sweat from his forehead and can see that Malynda has been crying. "What's wrong?"

"Nothing is wrong." Her face began to blush from embarrassment. Jacques knows what happened.

"Why don't you take my little helper to the swimming hole? I think that she needs to cool off. I'll only be an hour behind her." Jacques is proud of his spider hole, and he asks Malynda if she's going to check out his new accommodations. She agrees and climbs into the two-foot diameter opening into a four by four by four dirt room. She looks through one of the loopholes for a minute and comes out.

Malynda laughs. "Well, you have your own play camp that is complete with a bed so that you can spy on us when we bathe."

"I'm afraid that it's more serious than that. I'll talk to you tonight. Now, take this little girl swimming; and I'll see you in an hour."

Jacques goes back to work and Malynda carries Celeste down the hill.

Two hours later, Jacques shows up full of dirt at the swimming hole. He falls belly first in the water and makes a big splash. Malynda screams at him. "I hope you brought a bar of soap." Jacques reaches down in his pocket, pulls out a bar of soap, and holds it up. Jacques scrubs himself good, gets out, walks up to Malynda, and shakes himself dry. She screams and Celeste laughs.

"Jacques lie down here beside me. I want to talk to you." Jacques lies down on his side facing Malynda, and she rolls over to face him. "I saw this place where they cut all the trees down. Why did they do that?"

"You found the clear cut. You have to understand that this piece of property is a tree farm. They grow trees and cut them down. The problem is that they cut down fruit bearing trees like oaks and pecans and replace them with pine trees. The only thing that has protected the oaks on this property is that they grow in wet soil conditions. It's too much work to get to them out, or there is just not enough trees per acre to bother with."

"Why pine trees then? Why not replace with like kind?"

"Remember trees are a crop. Oak trees are very slow growing. This white oak is probably three hundred years old. The pine tree right on the other side of the creek that is the same size is probably only fifty years old."

"I don't think it is right."

"Right or wrong, it is the way it is. I just stopped in to cool off a little bit. I thought that you looked a little jealous that I have a clubhouse and you don't. So I decided that I needed to build one for you too."

"You're joking?"

"Nope, I got to get it done. I'll see you at the camp tonight." Jacques gets up and walks off.

CHAPTER 47

▼

Tuesday morning, Malynda can't wait to get back to the creek. Jacques tells her that he has to go on a little hike before it gets too hot, and then he's going to pick up some things in town. Jacques gets in his truck and drives to Meridian. He stops at a Super-Mart to pick up a few things, including twenty rolls of aluminum foil and a few propane space heaters. He looks around and finds a little hill a mile away that looks interesting. He decides to see if he can get close to the hill with the truck. He drives around on a few dirt roads. On the backside of the hill, he's able to get within a half mile. He hikes up the hill and looks around. From there he can see a good portion of the town. He has a good view of the gas station, Super-Mart, and the local motel. Jacques jogs to the phone at a service station and makes a collect phone call.

A woman's voice answers the phone. "Special Agent Rodred"

"This is Jacques Boudreaux. I think we need to talk."

"Do you have the roll of film?"

"Yep. The question is, which side of the law are you on?"

"I would hope on the good side, but sometimes the law is not black and white. What's on the roll of film?"

"I have some pictures of a government vehicle that is loaded with drugs. In the pictures there're three men. Two are dead, and I don't know who the other is. He is short and a good dresser. He has sort of a round face and has salt and pepper hair."

"Mr. Boudreaux, I think that the other person is an FBI Agent. If he's who I think it is, nothing in my career would be better than to nail this guy. We need to arrest him, not kill him. Killing him will be letting him off too easy. He needs to go to prison. He needs to become an example that no one is above the law. I need the evidence that you have to do that."

"What's in it for me? I need a pardon or something? I played by your rules in Hopedale. I could have easily wasted all of them."

"Mr. Boudreaux, I have already talked to the Attorney General's office, and they agree to dismiss all charges and have everything expunged for all the crimes that you may have committed. It's like a full pardon. They even agree to go to the press and make you and Malynda heroes. In turn, you have to quietly hand over that roll of film."

"Sounds like a trap to me."

"You have my word it's not. We like to take care of our problems internally and quietly. We do not want to lose the public's confidence. Make no mistake, the person that is in the pictures is a traitor to the bureau and will be punished. Mr. Boudreaux, you can't get a better deal. You have killed at least five people, and we are giving you a full pardon and going to make a hero out of you. Let's look at the facts. You're on the run. You're at the top of the FBI's most wanted list. You have a half a million dollar reward on your head. It's only a matter of time before your name hits the obituaries."

"It still sounds like a trap, but I can't take on the entire FBI. Ok, let's meet and make the exchange."

"Great, when can you get to the New Orleans Federal Building?"

"Not a chance. You are going to come and meet me on my territory and my conditions. I pick the place and the time. If I walk into the federal building, I am going to be toothless. Through this whole process I want to be armed. Do we agree?"

"Dismissing murder charges is a big deal. You haven't been arrested and charged with anything. How can we dismiss criminal charges without even formally charging you with something?"

"If you want your evidence, you'll figure out a way. Until we get all of this legal stuff handled, the only person that I want to see within a hundred miles is you. Am I clear on that?

"Ok Mr. Boudreaux, but I am going to have to bring a representative from Attorney General's office to walk you through the paperwork."

"One guy. He needs to be physically fit, but make sure that he's not some commando type. If I smell a trap, I'll kill you both. Do I make myself clear?"

"Perfectly clear Mr. Boudreaux. Mr. Boudreaux one more thing, what did you do with the money? It was a fairly sizeable amount. This pardon that we're going to give you don't protect you from the people that you took it from."

"It was under the floorboards of the camp. You can check it out for yourself."

"I'm afraid that won't help you. We will work that out later. What are your terms?"

"I want you and that attorney to fly into Meridian tonight and rent a car. I want you to stay at the local motel. Don't bring any jewelry or fancy clothes. I'll call you at 0430. When I call, you need to be ready to go."

"That is not a lot of time. Having the paperwork drafted up takes some time. It needs to be approved by several people. I'm not sure we can have it done by this afternoon."

"Are you not sure you could have the paperwork done or you not sure if you could locate me and kill me by that time?"

"I see your point, but you have been on the phone long enough for me to locate you."

"I didn't tell you anything that I didn't want to tell you. Remember that I pick the places. I'll call you tomorrow morning 0430. Good-bye." Jacques jogs back to the top of the hill and watches the service station for a full four hours.

Harris' phone rings, and he answers it.

"What do you have for me Sergeant?"

"Rodred nailed you and maybe me. I got the whole thing on tape. I told you she was going to figure it out. Do you want us to intercept Boudreaux?"

"No, he is long gone by now. Play the tape for me." Harris listens to the tape. "Sergeant, drive your team to Meridian. Make sure that your men stay away from that side of town. This guy's smart. If he smells trouble, he'll vanish again. Tonight, I want you to get a beacon on Rodred's rent-a-car. I want you to be real careful. This guy will probably be watching Rodred from the time she leaves the airport. Keep me updated."

"If we see him, do you want us to take him."

"No, wait until you have Rodred and Boudreaux together then take them both—no evidence and no witnesses. When you find Boudreaux, you will find the girl. She would be stupid to leave him now."

At the hunting camp, Jacques is making human dummies with sticks and aluminum foil. He goes up on the roof and pulls a piece of tin off the roof. Malynda comes screaming out of the camp when he pulls off a piece of tin.

"Jacques, what are you doing?"

"Giving you a sky light. I need you to make another grab bag for you and Celeste."

"Jacques, I thought you told me that they are giving you a pardon."

"I did, but I still don't trust them."

He climbs off of the roof and kisses her good-bye. "I'm going to watch them tonight. When I get back tomorrow morning, I need you to be ready to go."

"Ok Jacques. You be careful."

2200, Jacques gets in the truck and heads for his observation hill in Meridian. At 0415, he heads down the hill and he calls the motel. "Agent Rodred's room please."

"Agent Rodred"

"Rodred, I want you to go to the local Super-Mart and purchase a new pair of white tennis shoes—the ones with the big check on the side of them. I also want you to purchase orange jump suits. I want you to change your clothes in the store and leave your old ones in there. The only thing that I want you to walk out with is your badges and identification cards. When you get back in your car, I want you to wait in it for thirty minutes and then drive south on I-59. At the mile marker 105, there is a list of instructions. Follow them and don't try anything funny. I'll be watching you. What kind of car are you driving?"

"It is a green Taurus. How am I going to know it's thirty minutes?"

"There's a clock that can be seen from Super-Mart's parking lot. Park where you can see it. You have till 0500 to finish your shopping and till 0530 to start driving." Jacques hangs up the phone, goes up the hill, and sets up his spotting scope.

By the time he gets to the hill, Rodred and the attorney are walking towards the entrance of Super-Mart.

The sergeant calls Harris. "Mr. Harris, Rodred and the Attorney went into the Super-Mart twenty minutes ago."

"Good we've got him trapped. Let's go in and get him."

"You don't have him trapped. He is not in that Super-Mart. He is probably looking at me right now. I'm going back to the airport and monitor the beacon."

"Twenty minutes is a long time. I think that you should storm the place."

"Wait, you are not going to believe this. They just walked out of the Super-Mart with florescent orange jump suits. They're getting in their car, but they're not moving. They are just sitting there. I knew this guy was smarter than that. He's watching the parking lot. He wanted to see if we would storm the Super-Mart. I'm going to have to wait at least half an hour after Rodred leaves to make sure that he doesn't see me. A lot can happen in half hour. This guy thinks that he is pretty smart. We need to do it right, because we're only going to get one shot at this guy."

"Ok Sergeant, do what you think is right."

Sue waits until 0530 and drives off. She has a little over half an hour drive ahead of her. Meanwhile Jacques relocates off the hill and makes it back to the hunting camp. He takes Malynda and Celeste to the cave that he dug out. "Stay here until I call for you. Do not come out unless you hear the code words 'strawberry jelly'." He returns back to the camp and puts the aluminum foil dummies in the camp and closes the doors. He dons his ghillie suit, goes to his observation point, and sets up his spotting scope. He looks at his watch—0545. His vantage point is on top of a hill on the east side of I-59 near milepost one thirty five. He can see miles in each direction. Just south of his position at the bottom of the hill is a small creek that crosses under I-59 and winds through the deer camp property. To the west are pastures that are broken with small tree lines. He scans to the south and looks as far as he can see. There's nothing. He then scans north, there's only one car that is three miles out heading south. At this time of the morning traffic is light. He focuses on the car; it's the Taurus. He lets it drive by, takes out his data book, and made notes of every car that passes after it. He knows that he has at least an hour before she makes it back.

Sue drives to milepost 105, gets out, and finds a ziplock bag with a note. She opens it and reads it as the attorney waits in the car. "Drive back north to exit 142, then back south to milepost 134. There will be another set of instructions there." Sue gets back into the car and drives again.

Jacques is carefully observing vehicles in both directions.

0653, the Taurus passes again.

0708, it passes for the third time and stops four hundred yards away from Jacques in the valley between the two hills. Jacques watches as they get out the car and go for the note. He tries to size them up. "The attorney shouldn't be a problem. This guy probably hasn't been in a scrap for over thirty years. He's tall and thin. He's probably six-four and a hundred and seventy pounds. He's in his late fifties or early sixties. He has thick wire framed glasses, and his white hair is cut in a flat top. "Old guy with a flat top hair cut is a good sign. There're normally straight shooters with no-nonsense mentalities." Jacques never underestimates women, and he sizes up Sue. "Sue's tall for a woman." He recognizes her from the sniper match circuit. He watches her walk over to the mile post marker and pick up the next note. She reads it and starts looking around. She stares right at Jacques, gives him the bird, and starts walking for the pastures across from Jacques. Jacques watches as they chase from one note to another. Jacques is amused at Sue struggling to keep the Attorney moving. He sees that they're nearing the end of the paper chase. He runs down to the camp, turns on the propane heaters and both burners of the stove, closes up the structure, and heads down to the creek where it crosses the interstate. He hides himself on the east side of I-59 such that he can see under the Interstate to the west side. He watches them come and pick up the final note. Sue reads it, and immediately the attorney starts complaining about something. Sue says something back to him, and they remove all of their clothing. They walk under the bridge in the sand of the creek towards Jacques. The attorney is trying to cover himself up and carrying a brown legal size file folder. They get thirty yards from Jacques.

"That's far enough. Stop. I want at least ten yards between you. Move apart." They comply. "Mr. Attorney put the file folder down and step away from it."

"Mr. Boudreaux, I represent the attorney general's office. There's no need."

Sue looks at him. "Mr. Boudreaux is doing this for his own protection. If he wanted to kill us he could have done it hours ago." She looks at a stack of clothes twenty yards away from them. "The sooner we get this over with, the quicker we get to put those clothes on."

Jacques steps out of the bushes with his 1911 drawn and his rifle on his shoulder. "You, Mr. Attorney. Put your hands high in the air. Open palms. Slowly turn around." He does. "Turn around facing away from me and show me the bottom of your feet." He does. "Ok Ms. Rodred, you're next." She turns around and faces him. "Lift your arms higher." She lifts her arms and pulls her shoulders back. "Good enough. Show me the bottom of your feet." She does. "Turn away from me." He walks up to the lawyer. "Turn around Mr. Lawyer. Open your mouth and stick out your tongue. Lift it. Ok, you can move over there and put on those clothes. Now, your turn Ms. Rodred, turn around and stick out your tongue. Ok, you can move over there and put on those clothes. He watches them walk over to the blue jump suits and rubber boots. As they start to dress, he walks over and picks up the file folder. He thumbs through the papers and throws the attorney's pen in the creek.

"That's a hundred dollar pen, you just threw into the creek."

"I made it perfectly clear not to bring anything of value. Come on hurry up."

"Look, we're here to help you. You're treating us like animals."

"I'm doing what I need to do to stay alive."

Sue looks at Jacques. "Have you been winning any matches lately?"

"Just keep your trap shut and keep this on a business basis. I don't want to make friends with people I might have to kill. Come on and follow me." Jacques leads them through the woods. They come up the backside of a hill and see the entrance to Jacques' spider hole. Sue looks around and makes mental notes. Jacques pulls the poncho back. "Get in." It's crowded in the small area. Jacques climbs on the shooting platform and sets up his rifle and lays out some extra ammunition. He looks at the sweating old man. "Mr. Attorney, there's water and food in the bag; and you're welcome to it."

"Mr. Boudreaux, I told you that we didn't set a trap. You can relax."

"I didn't say you two set a trap. I said that it looks like a trap. Just wait here for a couple of hours, and we'll see. Ms. Rodred, if you want, you can set up that spotting scope and watch." Sue gets behind the spotting scope.

"Jacques, you've got a good spot picked out for the spider hole. Your looking to the west with the morning sun behind you. It'll be really hard to out flank you. To the north is an enormous briar patch that no one in his right mind would go through. On the hill that's five hundred yards behind us, I saw your second hide that's already built. To the south, they would be coming up four hundred yards in the valley between the two hills. What makes you think that we would not try to take you right now?"

"What makes you think that there is nobody in the hide behind us? If I was you, I would make sure that I am the first one to walk out of this hide."

"What is on the other side of your second hide?"

"Why do you ask?"

"You want them looking into the sun. I know that you have another fall back point."

"You're pretty smart. There is a five hundred yard clear cut with a barbwire fence in the middle of it."

"So your second hide is not a hide. It is just set up to give you enough time to cross the open clear cut. What makes you think that they will follow you in the open?"

"We are in a finger of woods that is surrounded on three sides by a clear cut. If they want me, they are going to have to get out in the open. Hopefully, it's not going to come to that."

The attorney reaches for the stack of pictures and starts going through them. He can barely see in the subdued light. He holds a couple of them at angles at the light coming in from the loopholes. "Agent Rodred, we've got all the proof we need. Frank Harris, who would have guessed? He was so close to retirement. Mr. Boudreaux, Ms. Rodred is right. You can relax. I have all the pardon papers in this folder. I am representing the Attorney General, and I am authorized to dismiss all charges and expunge yours and Mrs. Meyeaux's records for all acts committed within the past few months."

Jacques looks at the bruise on Sue's face. "Where did you get that from?"

"One of your friends. You can tell them that they don't have to be so rough on a person that is cooperating."

"What friends?"
"Your friends in the CIA."
"Are you sure they were CIA or well financed individuals?"
Sue thinks for awhile. "I can't say for sure."
"Ms. Rodred, when you figure it out; I would appreciate you telling me."
They sit there in silence.
They hear a large helicopter fly by. It's low and flying fast, but they're unable to see it. Jacques checks his elevation and adjusts his windage, "Mrs. Rodred, I listened to you last time. This time I'm doing it my way."
Fear comes over Sue's, "How did you know that we were not involved?"
"I'm still not sure. Last night at a quarter after two, I saw a two-man team put a beacon on your car. The first possibility is that you knew that I would be watching from a distance, and you staged the placement of the beacon. This possibility will make me think that you are not involved when you are actually involved. The second possibility is that you truly didn't know about the placement of the beacon, and you're marked to be killed with me. Either way, the results are going to be the same for the entry team. Your survival all depends on what the entry team does."
"Jacques, where is Mrs. Meyeaux and her daughter?"
"She's in safe place with the negatives." The attorney looks in the film pack and tells Sue that the negatives are missing.
"Wait a minute, that was not part of the deal."
"Don't worry, you will get them after I get your paperwork."
Sue studies the structure through the spotting scope. "You've got a trap set for them. You cleared a fifty yard kill zone all around the camp house. At four hundred and fifty yards, they are sitting ducks for a guy like you. If I had my cell phone, this would be all over by now. I have a team already set up to rush Harris' office. All I need to do is give them the word. Besides, they're never going to fall for your trap. We're a little more sophisticated now. We have little things like thermal vision. They're going to see that there isn't anyone in there and then try to hunt us down."
"Let them charge the hill. It'll take them more than a minute to get here. Do you realize how many will not make it here? As far as your sophistication, people rely too much on the new technology. I know a little something about thermal vision. I know that if you wrap dummies in aluminum foil and point a small heater at them, they will look something like a person. I know that if you remove a piece of tin off the roof and let the sun hit the aluminum foil it will look like a person. If someone has time to study it, they'll easily know that it wasn't. I'm bet-

ting that there's a bunch of shooters in that chopper that just flew over. They made a quick pass, saw what they thought were bodies, set down near by and are going to attack it."

The attorney gets up and looks at the structure. "Jacques, I don't know if I can give you a pardon for this. This is plain murder."

"Ms. Rodred, what is standard entry procedure?"

"They'll throw in a couple of flash bangs and charge the building. They'll kill anyone who resists them."

"Well Mr. Attorney, what if they threw in live hand grenades? Would it be murder then? Before you answer, remember that you are supposed to be in the structure."

"If you put it like that, considering the fact that there's an overwhelming, unlimited funded government rogue force that is heavily armed against you, I guess I could see it as self-defense."

"Mr. Boudreaux, before you light them up, let's wait and see if they follow procedures." The attorney sits back in the spider hole and remains silent.

"Sounds fair to me." Jacques hands out some earplugs.

Sue says, "You are pretty confident in yourself."

They wait for a while longer in silence.

Jacques taps Sue on the shoulder. "Look alive. I count two columns of five coming up behind the camp. I love how those black ninja suits blend in with the green surroundings."

"Not to mention, bringing MP-5's to do battle with a sniper. It's like bringing a knife to a gun fight."

They stop at the end of the trail before they enter the kill zone and take a knee. The sergeant raises his scoped rifle and studies the camp.

"Mr. Boudreaux, that is a EM scope. Your little trick is not going to fool them. What are you planning to do if your trick don't work?"

"It will work. People have learned not to question technology. People's minds work funny. Sometimes they want to see something so badly that they do even though in reality they don't."

The sergeant lowers the rifle and motions to his team to advance. They circle around to the front. One team is at eight o'clock position and the other team is at the four o'clock position. They bring their MP-5's up to their shoulders and level them.

Sue is looking through the spotting scope. "Mr. Boudreaux, it all looks good so far. Now, one is going to throw…" Automatic gun fire interrupts her as they start emptying magazines into the structure. After everyone is empty, they change out. One guy pulls the door open and two guys run by and throw in hand grenades. "Ok, I was wrong. Why aren't you shooting?"

The entry team rushes the building and there's some more sporadic firing coming within. Jacques picks out the sergeant and is ready to drill him. He imagines a tennis ball in the center of his head and keeps his cross hairs on the tennis ball. The sergeant takes off his helmet, and his battery backpack. He puts the pack and the rifle on the ground. He opens his cell phone and punches in a number.

"Jacques wait. The one with the phone, get him first; but don't fire until he hangs up the phone. He's probably updating Harris."

"I'm already on him."

Jacques can see the smile on the bald headed man as he talks on the cell phone. The entry team opens the door and throws the aluminum foil dummies out. He watches the smile leave the sergeant's face. The sergeant spins around facing the dummies. He turns back around and looks at his rifle on the ground and the cell phone in his hand. He looks around for the nearest cover. Jacques can see defeat is written on his face. The sergeant lowers the phone to his waist and starts scanning possible hides as his team gathers around him.

"Jacques, he knows it's a trap! What are you waiting for?"

"Patience. I want to look into his eyes when I nail him. He's not going to bolt until he can pick a direction. He can't pick a direction until he finds me." Jacques checks the wind and his natural point of aim one more time. The sergeant looks right up at the spider hole. Before he can react, Jacques drills him.

"Half inch left of the nostrils."

Before anyone realizes what has happened, Jacques works the action and fires again. This time he takes out the man to the left of the sergeant.

"Right Eye."

They now know what's going on and start scurrying for cover. He works the action and clips one in the hip as he's running for cover.

"Right hip."

He grabs three more cartridges and loads them. Three of them lay cover fire and four try to charge the hill. Four try and three die. The fourth runs for cover. Jacques loads again.

"You have one behind the structure, one behind the truck, one behind the fifty-five gallon barrel, and the wounded one on the road."

Jacques waits.

"What are you waiting for? Shoot through the barrel!"

"The one behind the barrel is not going anywhere, and I can take him anytime. It is the one behind the structure that I need to get next. He is the one that can circle behind us."

They can see the one behind the structure hand signaling for the one behind the barrel to go help the wounded one. The one behind the structure lays out cover fire as the one behind the barrel runs out from behind the barrel to help the fallen agent. The cover fire does not even come close to the loop holes. The agent that's laying cover fire steps out just a little to far and gives Jacques a head shot opportunity, which he takes full advantage of.

"Right under the nose."

The agent that's helping the wounded one raises his hands to surrender. The one behind the truck does the same. Jacques is taking a bead on one of them.

"No Jacques. It's over. It's over."

Jacques puts his rifle on safe, and gives Sue his pistol. "Well, are you going to arrest them or what? I'll cover you from up here."

At the New Orleans' Field office, Frank Harris is sitting in his office with the door closed. He is listening to the sergeant on the phone and his sergeant goes silent. He hears the crack of a bullet and then a distant rifle going off. He hears the next crack and the rifle again, and again. Men are screaming and the sound of automatic gunfire is coming through the speaker of his phone. He realizes what is going on. He hangs up the phone, gathers some papers, his car keys, and opens the door of his office. He sees a stranger at the end of the cubical corridor. He pokes his head out and looks towards the elevators. There is another stranger at the elevators. Panic overcomes him. He retreats back into his office and locks his door. Frantically, he begins stacking furniture against his door. He pulls out his pistol, sits in his chair, and levels the pistol towards the door.

At the hunting camp, Sue climbs out the spider hole and jogs down the hill. Jacques witnesses the arrests and climbs out himself. He helps the attorney out of the spider hole, and they walk down the hill together.

They get down the hill and can see Sue has the sergeant's phone straining to listen. She holds her finger up for them to stop. "They're making the raid. He's trapped in his office, and he barricaded himself in. They're ready to bust in." A look of disgust comes over her face. "Harris took the easy way out. He just blew his brains out. It's all over now."

Jacques reaches down to his cargo pocket and pulls out his walkie-talkie. "Malynda, Strawberry Jelly!, Strawberry Jelly!, Strawberry Jelly! Sweetheart, it's all over now. You can come out. We'll meet you on top of your favorite hill. We have some papers to sign."

The attorney asks Sue. "Who's involved with the entry team?"

"I'm not sure, but they are not part of the Bureau. They don't have any identification papers on them."

"Is that Bureau equipment that they have?"

"Sure is. We will find out more when we question the three that survived."

Jacques walks the attorney to Malynda's hill. She's sitting down with Celeste in her lap waiting for them. Jacques sits down next to Malynda and gives her a big squeeze. He has a smile on his face. "It's over with. It is finally over with." Malynda grabs Jacques hand and smiles back at him.

The attorney sits down, and pulls out a stack of papers. "Gee, this is a beautiful place. Mrs. Meyeaux, I am an Assistant Federal Attorney acting directly on the behalf of the Attorney General of the United States of America. We are truly sorry about the loss of your husband and your house, the danger that your life was put in, and for the inconveniences that you experienced. I can assure you that justice has been served—the rogue agent has killed himself. The FBI takes pride in the personnel that it hires. They are brightest individuals in law enforcement. They go through an extreme amount of schooling, and they also go through an extensive background check. The FBI only selects the best of the best. Events like this one are almost non-existent. We'll study how this slipped through the checks and balances and make the necessary adjustments so that it will never happen again."

"The sad part of this is that you and Mr. Boudreaux had to break several laws in order to protect your own lives. Mr. Boudreaux held up his end of the bargain and turned over the evidence needed to arrest Mr. Frank Harris, Jr. Our part of the bargain was to grant a comprehensive and unconditional pardon for all acts committed in the recent month. These papers are the pardons. These pardons will excuse you from any criminal activity you may have participated in during this time period. Please sign here." There are four sets of papers to sign. He shows them where to sign.

"This second document that I am going to ask you to sign is a confidentiality agreement. This document protects you as well as the United States Government. The pardon protects you from criminal charges; the confidentiality agreement protects you from any civil cases that might be brought against you. In this document you are signing that the events that occurred within the past few months have become classified as Top Secret. You may not divulge any of these events to anyone—even under court subpoena. Since you will be sworn to secrecy, it will protect the Government from embarrassment. Please sign here." He shows them where to sign.

"This third document is a hold harmless agreement. It basically states that you will not hold the United States Government responsible for the actions of its representatives for the past few months. Please sign here." He shows them where to sign.

"This fourth document is a document that shows that I gave you the ten thousand dollar whistle blower's reward check. Please sign here." He shows them where to sign and hands over the check.

"This fifth and final document is a Certificate of Appreciation signed by the President of the United States for the hardships that you went through to make this country a better place to live."

"Mr. Boudreaux, I understand you made away with a rather large sum of money that you said burned up. I hope that is the case, because the Government doesn't make a pardon for income tax evasion. I have a sneaky suspicion that you will be watched for a long period of time, and income tax evasion is a felony with severe penalties."

They hear a large helicopter land near the camp. "Well, Mr. Boudreaux and Mrs. Meyeaux, it was a pleasure; but I think that is my ride. Do you have the negatives for me?"

Jacques reaches into Malynda's grab bag, pulls them out, and hands them to the attorney.

"Thank you, Mr. Boudreaux."

Jacques tells Malynda to wait there while he walks the attorney to the camp. When Jacques arrives at the camp, he sees a small task force load the black body bags on the helicopter. He sees Sue, and she walks towards them. She screams over the noise of the helicopter. "Mr. Boudreaux, thank you for your help. Your pick-up truck took some scrap from the hand grenades. I don't think that it will run any more. You can take my rent-a-car." She hands him the keys. "When you're finished with it, just give me a call. I'll send someone to pick it up. We need to get together later and talk about how you planned all of this out. You moved way too fast for us to keep up, and we need to learn more about how to counter that. Maybe, I'll see you at your next match."

"Maybe, we can team up. You make a hell of a spotter."

"That sounds like a plan." They shake hands and Sue boards the chopper. Jacques waves as they take off.

Jacques walks back to where he left Malynda. "Come on Malynda. They're gone. If we hurry, we can pack and leave tonight."

"Can we stay one more night, and leave in the morning? This place is starting to grow on me."

"Sure we can, but we might want to sleep by the creek tonight, because the camp is pretty messed up."

Malynda has a smile of contentment on her pretty face. "Jacques, we'll make do."

They head back to the camp, perform their daily rituals, take some blankets, walk to the creek, and go to sleep.

CHAPTER 48

▼

The next morning, they pack and leave. Jacques drives back to Hopedale. Malynda asks Jacques, "I thought we were going to Houston?"

Jacques smiles. "I left something very important in Hopedale." He drives back to his camp, and to his surprise a new camp stands in its place. He parks the car, digs a trenching tool out of the trunk, and swims across Bayou Loutre. Twenty minutes later, he swims back across to see Père Andrew holding Celeste and his arm on Malynda's shoulder. They are all laughing. Jacques climbs out of the water with a black athletic bag. Malynda's eyes light up. Père Andrew sticks out his hand to greet him.

"Jacques, I was just telling Malynda how I got the volunteers to rebuild your camp. I first asked nicely like I always do. Jacques, you must have made plenty people mad, because no one volunteered. I closed da Church doors, turned off da air condition, and ask again. Man, within ten minutes, I had more volunteers than I knew what to do wit. I'm going to try dat some more. Where is me truck?"

"Père, your truck didn't make it."

Père Andrew shakes his head and a lost look comes over his face.

"Père, don't worry about it. I'll get you a new one. How much do I owe for the camp?"

"Cooyon da people, dey volunteer. The materials are Church money."

"How much?"

"Nothing Jacques. You and Malynda need to start a new life. I don't want an IOU. I tell you what, you owe me and da people da consideration of moving back down here. Come be part of our family."

"Père, after what I put these people through. I doubt that they would appreciate me living down here."

"Nonsense, you're a hero. You brought beaucoup excitement wit you dis time. People are still laughing about da film Crazy Leon made. He video taped those federals running into the gill nets. He even wanted to mail it in to one of dose video shows, but I convinced him dat might not be such a good idea."

Jacques unzips the bag and pulls back the black trash bag far enough for Père to see what's inside of it. "Père, you don't understand."

"Now I do. Hopedale needs a new water tower, you owe Père a new truck, and you owe da Church ten percent. Da ten percent comes first."

Everyone laughs.

Père hands Celeste to her mother and wraps his other hand over Jacques' shoulder. They walk across the street to the new camp. "Jacques, now dat was an adventure dat you and Malynda can tell your children about."

Malynda smiles and laughs and Jacques stops. "Now, wait a minute we're not married yet."

"Now, why you do a fool thing like dat."

"A fool thing like what?"

"Not be married yet. As much as you to put up wit each other dis last month, you'd be a fool not to marry each other." Malynda just keeps smiling. "Jacques, Old Père, he needs to know a date where he can get da Fais Do Do planned."

"Père, it's not appropriate to marry her so soon."

"I'd tell you what inappropriate—not taking full of advantage of everyday the Lord gives you. Dat's inappropriate."

Jacques thinks about what Père just said. In his soaking wet clothes, he stops, takes Malynda by the hand, and drops to one knee. "Malynda, will you marry me?"

She starts crying and jumping up and down. "Yes. Yes. A thousand times, yes."

"Yoohee, we have a party tonight. Weh?"

Mr. & Mrs. Melerine come out on the front porch of their camp to see what's all the racket about. Père screams out to them. "Melerine, you owe me twenty dollars. We have a wedding to plan."

Both the Melerines scream and applaud as they come running down the stairs. Mrs. Melerine is crying. She runs to Malynda and gives her a big hug. Mr. Melerine comes and shakes Jacques' hand.

Malynda hands Celeste to Jacques and starts running towards the camp.

Jacques screams at her. "Where are you going?"

"I have to call Debbie and tell her the good news."

Mrs. Melerine screams, "There's no phone in there. Use mine."

Malynda turns and runs to the Melerine's camp.

Mrs. Melerine takes Celeste from Jacques. "Come on little perch. Let's go inside. You men come in too."

Jacques has a smile from ear to ear as Mrs. Melerine puts her arm on his shoulder and walks him in.

Mr. Melerine puts his hand on Père's shoulder and holds him back. "Did you tell Jacques about the Coast Guard rescuing that one off of six poles?"

"Melerine, let's not spoil a good day. We have plenty of time to tell him. Da Cooyon only stands a slim chance of living to begin wit. Even if he do, dat congo poison will probably make him a vegetable. Let's get inside and celebrate and forget about da utter one."

Mr. Melerine and Père follow Jacques and Mrs. Melerine into the Melerine's camp where the celebration begins and this story ends.

Glossary

BDU or BDU's. Military Battle Dress Uniform

BPM. Beats per minute.

Beaucoup. Cajun for a lot or plenty.

Bienvenue. Cajun for welcome.

Boo. Cajun for honey, sweetheart.

Bore guide. A straight plastic tube that is used for cleaning the rifle. When it is inserted into the chamber, the plastic tube extends beyond the action. The end of it is trimmed to fit the chamber and on that end it has an o-ring to keep fluids from spilling into the action. To use it, remove the bolt and replace it with the bore guide.

Borrow Canal. A canal that is dug to get soil to build a road or levee.

Bright eyes. thumb tacks with reflective tape on them.

Butterfly Nets. Nets on metal rectangular frames that extend on both sides of the boat to skim the shrimp that come to the surface at nighttime.

Champagne. An orange plastic round basket that is slightly larger than a clothes hamper. It is used to transport shrimp from the boat to the dock. On an average, it holds approximately 50 pounds of shrimp.

Cooyon. Cajun for foolish, stupid.

Couvoun. A common fish meal made with a spicy red gravy. Unless specified otherwise, the fish would be red fish.

Drag Bag. A padded, cloth, rifle case with netting sewed to it to add natural vegetation. A sniper normally drags this bag behind him during a stalk.

ERT. Evidence response team.

Fais Do Do. Cajun for a family party.

Game Gambrel. A butchering device used to spread the rear legs of an animal's carcass while it is hanging upside down.

Ghillie Suit. Sniper camouflage suit, made with strands of burlap, netting, and natural vegetation.

Gnats . Blood sucking creatures made by the devil. They are the devil's improvement to the mosquito. It is a small insect about 1/32" long that attacks in swarms. They get into eyes and noses. They even have been known to clog carburetors on outboard motors.

Hand Sock. A sock filled with sand or rice that goes under the butt plate of a rifle and is squeezed by the non-trigger hand for minor adjustments in elevation.

Lagniappe. Cajun for a little something extra.

Lazy Line. A rope that stretches from the trawl board to the pocket. This rope allows the trawler to pull in the pocket without bringing in the whole net.

Mais. Cajun for Well

Mamoos. Like butterfly nets without the bottom half of the frame. They are a 10' x 5' rectangular aluminum pipe frame that a net is attached to. They attach to the boat approximately 1/3 to ½ back from the bow on each side. They stretch out on both sides of the boat to skim the water.

Mon Dieu. Cajun for My God.

Mum Bushes. Wax myrtles

Muzzle Break. A device that is mounted on the muzzle of the rifle. This device reduces the recoil by the redirecting the high-pressure gasses 90° outward or somewhat towards the shooter.

The Parish. St. Bernard Parish.

Piddle Pack. A small bottle with a hose that allows the sniper to urinate without leaving his position or getting urine on himself.

Pirogue. A small water vessel like a canoe. It is much narrower and has lower sides. A canoe mostly stays above the water with plenty of freeboard. A pirogue sits low in the water with minimal freeboard. Pirogues are known to float on wet mud.

+P's. Commercial high power shells for .38 Special. Pistol should be rated for +P's to use them.

Rifle maintenance center. A work station that the rifle sets in for cleaning and maintenance. Normally there are two V's that are spaced apart with a tray between them.

Rip Rap. 6" to 24" rocks, stone or concrete blocks used to control erosion along a shorelines.

Roseau Cane. A saltwater cane that grows to ¾" in diameter, heights greater than 8' tall, and in very thick patches.

Ruck or Ruck Sack. Slang for ALICE pack, which is a 1 to 3 day backpack used by the military.

Ship Channel. Local lingo for the Mississippi River Gulf Outlet.

Spider Hole. A comfortable hide that a sniper uses for long periods of recon or shooting. It is normally dug in from the backside of a hill, and it has a rather large living chamber. The front side normally has two loop holes for the sniper and spotter to view from.

Stokes Litter. A wire mesh litter used to transfer injured personnel to and from boats and helicopters.

Trenasse. A small ditch that connects two large bodies of water.

Weh. Cajun for the French Oui which is English Yes.

Lagniappe—A Technical Discussion on Long Range Accuracy

The topics covered in this section are meant to provide information to improve a shooter's ability to engage targets. The topics include: safety; qualities to look for in a rifle; qualities to look for in a caliber or ammunition; qualities to look for in optics; exterior ballistics; interior ballistics; ranging; wind estimation; shooting basics; trajectory goals; break-in in procedure; and cleaning. My shooting card is located on in my website. It's made specifically for my rifle. Other rifles will have different data, but the reader can get an idea of direction and magnitude of the adjustments. The following discussion is purely the author's opinion. Like all opinions, many people will disagree with part or all of them.

Safety is the most important part of shooting. A shooter should treat a weapon as if it is always loaded. It is only to be pointed at something that a shooter wants to kill. Eye and ear protection is a must. Reloaders should always stay within acceptable charge limits. The inside of the rifle chamber reaches pressures over 50,000 psi. The only thing holding the pressure from coming out of the bolt is a thin piece of brass—called the case.

What to look for in a long-range rifle? Unless a shooter is purchasing a match grade semi-automatic rifle that guarantees a ½ MOA, he should look at purchasing a bolt action rifle. A bolt action is the most accurate rifle type and has the least amount of moving parts. It is also less fowling than semi-autos. In a hunting situation, there is rarely time for a well-placed second shot. A word of caution, AR-10's do not qualify as NRA service rifles. They are considered match rifles and will have to be fitted with space age, target style sights to competitively compete in NRA service rifle competition. A long barrel is another quality to look for because each 1" of barrel length adds approximately 50 ft/s to the bullet's velocity. Most standard bolt action barrels are running between 22" and 24". The barrel of a bolt action rifle should be free floating. A dollar bill should slide between the barrel and the stock all the way to the action lug. Some heavy target barrels are glass bedded an inch in front of the action lug to provide additional support for the barrel. A good glass bedding job almost always improves accuracy and only costs approximately $200.

A stainless steel barreled action with a fiberglass stock or carbon steel barreled action with a beautiful wooden stock is a matter of preference. A stainless steel barrel will hold the pattern longer, but it rapidly falls off towards the end of its life. The accuracy of steel barrels gradually fall off throughout their life. If the rifle is cleaned regularly, either will out live the shooter. A good example is the carbon steel, WWII M-1 Garands that are still in service.

Adjusting the trigger lighter than the factory setting is a dangerous adventure. In semi-automatics light trigger pulls can cause slam fires. In bolt actions, factory triggers that are adjusted light will inconsistently break at weights other than their set points. The inconsistent break will cause flyers in grouping and cause a lack of confidence in the shooter's rifle. If a shooter wishes to have the pull less than the factory set point, he should invest in a trigger designed for that purpose. The NRA service rifles' minimum pull is 4 ½ pounds. In sniper competition, many of the competitors with custom triggers have them set at 2 pounds.

Choosing a caliber is another matter of preference. A shooter should stick with popular hunting calibers like .243, .270, 7mm, 308, 30–06, and 300. Ammunition for these calibers can be found at nearly all sporting goods stores. A hunter that is shooting larger game like elk and moose should stay with a 30–06 or above. For shooting bear, nothing is too big. In a vacuum, bullets with smaller diameters are more accurate than bullets with larger diameters because the bullets are not balanced and wobble when they spin. The smaller the diameter and the lighter the bullet, the less the wobble will be. Also with the smaller calibers, the recoil is less; therefore, the rifle moves less while the bullet is traveling down the barrel. Bullets that weigh more are less effected by the wind, and are better for long distances because of their momentum. Inside of 200 yards, the smaller diameter bullets have an advantage over larger diameter bullets. Outside of 500 yards, the opposite is true. There is one exception—the 6.5–06. It shoots a 6.5mm, 140 grain bullet with a ballistic coefficient of 0.62. It has the same trajectory as my 30 caliber, 200 grain bullet. A shooter that wants a long barrel life should limit his muzzle velocity to 3000 ft/s. Anything over 3000 ft/s causes excessive barrel wear.

Bullets for hunting should be the expanding types. Bullets for competition should be match bullets. Match ammunition does not expand. Most commercial brand of hunting ammunition is a combination of expansion and retained mass. There are a few special designed ammunitions that are made to expand the entire mass of the bullet. Some specialty bullets expand in the front half and the rear half stays whole. Other bullets have plastic inserts to increase accuracy and help expand the bullet. Trajectories of different bullet types in the same caliber are not the same. The trajectory of each bullet type that a shooter uses needs to be recorded. The shooter needs remember that <u>nothing</u> kills better than a well-placed shot.

Optics should be rugged, fog proof, and waterproof. The glass should be multicoated. A general rule in optics is the better the glass the higher the price.

Unless the shooter is strictly looking for a target scope, a variable power scope is recommended. Hunters want a low power of 3 or 4 and a high power of 10 to 14. Target shooters want a 6x20 or 8x25. Some target shooters go up to 40 power. The advantage of having a low power is a wide field of view, which makes for easy target acquisition. Hunters should always have their scope set on the lowest power. Increasing the power can be done after acquiring the target and if time permits. The advantage of high power is the ability to more accurately place a shot. The reason that target shooters want to adjust their power below 16 is because of mirage. On a day with heavy mirage, seeing the target is easier with the scope adjusted to a power below 16. Mirage will be discussed later, but it is the bending of light waves. It makes the target fuzzy on a clear day.

The glass is probably the most important part of a scope. When shooter looks through a scope, he wants to see a crisp and bright picture. This crisp and bright picture is a result of the quality of glass in the scope. All glass is not the same. Like diamonds, glass has scratches on the surface and imperfections within itself. These scratches and imperfections reflect light. The fewer imperfections that the glass has, the better the picture. Multi-coating is a procedure of coating the lenses to help the transmission of light through the scope by not reflecting the light off of the surface. On a normal un-coated lens, approximately 4 1/2% of the light is reflected off of each surface, which equals about 92% transmission per lens. On a coated lens about 1 ½% of the light is reflected off of each surface, which equals about 97% transmission per lens. On bright days, the light reduction is negligible because the shooter's pupil dilates to compensate for a lower light condition. During low light conditions, it is more noticeable because the shooter's pupils are already dilated. The reflected light off the inner lens surfaces or imperfections can cause ghost images.

The type of reticle is another important decision. For a hunting scope, the duplex reticle is the reticle of choice. The duplex reticle gives the shooter the advantage of thin cross hairs for shot placement and thick bars for low light situations. Target shooters want thin cross hairs. The thin cross hairs do not work well in low light situations, but they do not cover much of the target. Battery powered reticles are not recommend because in the time of most need the batteries will fail.

Scope adjustments are normally in increments of ¼ minute of angle (1/4 MOA). 1 MOA is 1.047" at 100 yards or approximately 1" at 100 yards, 2" at 200 yards, 3" at 300 yards, etc.

Parallax adjustment is adjusting the focal planes so that shooter is looking straight through the tube. On scopes that have a fixed parallax, they are normally set at 150 yards. On high power, long scopes; parallax becomes critical because of the small depth of view. On long scopes, the parallax settings change with temperature due to thermal expansion of the scope. If the shooter has an adjustable parallax scope, he should adjust the parallax until the target is focused. Once the target is focused, the shooter slowly moves the parallax adjustment while slightly moving his head up and down or left to right. When the cross-hairs stop moving with respect to the target, the scope's parallax is set properly.

Shooters should test their scopes, even the expensive ones. The tests should include clear sight picture, reticle movement, and impact movement due to changing scope power. With the scope on high power and the rifle sand bagged, the shooter takes three shots. He then aims at a second target and takes another three shots. He then zooms out to the lowest power and takes another three shots on another target. The points of impact should be the same, but he should expect the group size to open when the scope is set on low power. With the scope returned to high power, the shooter then checks the memory and that the movements of the reticle are properly calibrated. Memory is the scope's ability for the reticle to return to the same place after being moved. After the shooter has the rifle zeroed, the shooter moves the reticle 2 MOA up and 2 MOA right. He takes 2 shots. He moves the reticle 4 MOA down and takes 2 shots. He moves the reticle 4 MOA left and takes 2 shots. He moves the reticle 4 MOA up and takes 2 shots. He moves the reticle 2 MOA down and 2 MOA right and takes 2 shots. At a hundred yards, the paper should show a four-inch box with two holes in the center. When group testing a rifle, a shooter should allow 2 minutes between each shot.

If the shooter is unsure about which scope to purchase, he should go to a rifle range and ask someone if he can look through the scope. If possible, he should set several scopes side by side and compare. Most of the people at the range would probably like to know themselves how their scope compares to the other brands.

Exterior ballistics is external factors that affect the bullet flight once the bullet leaves the muzzle. The first effect on the bullet as it leaves the barrel is the rifling lands. All the lands have to end at the crown. If one land is longer than the others are, the bullet will favor one side as the bullet exits the muzzle. Another critical point is when the bullet clears the barrel and the gas expands behind the bullet. If the crown is not polished, the gas will expand unevenly and will have a negative effect on the bullet. The rifle's crown needs to be polished and without dings. If the lands are properly trimmed and the crown is polished, the first millisecond of bullet flight will be true.

The next effect on the bullet is flight stability. The bullet is spinning like a football. Too much spin and it wobbles, not enough spin and it wobbles. By adjusting the bullet's velocity, the shooter can find the sweet spot. My target rifle shoots a 200-grain bullet at 2950 ft/s with a 1–10 twist. The spin rate is approximately 212,400 RPM. It probably doesn't matter to hunters; however, this correct RPM verses speed is critical for target shooters. Buying a different brand of commercial ammunition, different weight bullets, and changing the charge of the bullets can change the bullet velocity.

Gravity is the next effect the bullet encounters. Bullets can't defy gravity—everything falls at an acceleration of 32 ft/sec^2. The best way to determine the bullet's trajectory, is by zeroing the rifle at 100 yards. Without adjusting the elevation of the scope, a shooter then shoots at 300 yards and measures the drop. My target rifle is zeroed at 100 yards, and it shoots 11" low at 300 yards. Using a ballistic program, the bullet's velocity can be back calculated by varying the velocity until the field data matches the program's data. Once the velocity is known, the ballistic program can be used to determine drops at different distances. Once the trajectory is calculated, it needs to be verified at the range. If a ballistic program is not available, ballistic charts will do.

The resistance of air density is the next effect the bullet sees. Air density is easy—the heavier the air, the more resistance—the more resistance, the more the drop. The colder the temperature, the denser the air is. (See Weather Conditions on my shooting card.)

As the bullet travels to the target, wind can blow the bullet in all directions. Many ballistic programs can account for wind. The basics are if the wind is blowing left to right, the bullet will hit right of the point of aim. If the wind is blowing towards the shooter, the bullet will hit high. If the wind is blowing down range, the bullet will hit low. A good example is at 100 yards with a 15 mph crosswind, the bullet should impact about 1/2" downwind. For hunters, being off ½" will not make a difference. For a target shooter trying to shoot a ½" circle, it does make a difference. A 10 mph crosswind at 500 yards pushes my bullet off 15", which could make for a bad shot on an animal if the wind is not compensated for. A 10 mph wind at 1000 yards pushes my bullet 67". The only way to know how to adjust for wind is by shooting in the wind and recording the data. A mistake commonly made is that shooters only account for the wind at the target or near themselves. When shooting a 1000 yards, the wind will not be constant through that distance. The shooter needs to account for the different winds from the muzzle to the target. A good tip for shooters is to shoot when the wind is blowing the hardest and aim slightly downwind of the center of mass. If the wind slacks off, the bullet will drift back into the center of the target. Many target shooters will aim at the ten ring on the downwind side of the bull's-eye and shoot during the highest wind. If the wind drops off, the bullet will drift in the bull's-eye or the ten ring on the other side of the bull's-eye.

Mirage is the bending of light waves due to wind, heat, and humidity. It is the heat waves rising from the surface of the earth. Mirage is normally coupled with wind. Mirage can be seen in a scope by looking above a light colored surface. It looks like little pulses running across the bottom of the image in the scope. The good thing about these little squiggly lines or pulses is that they can be used to predict wind speeds and wind directions. To read mirage, many target shooters will set their spotting scopes so that they are focused at three-quarters the distance to the target and then point them at the target. This will give a true mirage. If the scope is focused behind the target, the shooter will see a reverse mirage. The bad thing about mirage is that it moves the image of the target off the actual target. In reality the shooter sees the image of the target, not the real target. On a hot summer day at a 1000 yards, the image could be six feet off of the actual target. In Pasagoula, MS, the standard rule is adjust ½ the calculated wind value for the first sighter. Pasagoula is a place of high temperatures and high humidity. In Oklahoma, a place of low humidity; mirage is seldom more than 12" at 1000 yards. For grins, next time you go out the range on a hot windy day; lock your rifle down in a work-mate; and watch the target dance. The rifle is not moving; the image of the target is moving—the higher the power of the scope—the more the effect of mirage. In a crosswind, the image will be displaced downwind of the actual target. With a wind blowing towards the target, the image will be slightly elevated from the actual target. With a wind blowing towards the shooter, the image will be slightly lower than the target. If the wind is a wind blowing at forty-five degrees left to right towards the target and the shooter aims dead center of the target image, the bullet will impact the actual target high and right. To become proficient at reading mirage, a shooter must get at the shooting range at dawn; set a target up and his rifle in a work-mate or other vise like apparatus; and record the location of his cross hairs on the target. At timed intervals, the shooter should record the wind, humidity, temperature, what the pulses look like, and the location of the cross hairs on the image. One other piece of advice is never shoot in a boiling mirage. A boiling mirage is when the little squiggly lines are vertical or the pulses stop. The reason not to shoot in a boiling mirage is that the image will soon change location, and the shooter *will* miss. On the 1000-yard line, many of the better shooters will record up to six different mirages in their data book for that day. They wait until they recognize a mirage, hold off to compensate, and fire. Welcome to the complexity of shooting a 1000 yards.

Magmus effect is the displacement of the bullet due to the spinning of a bullet. On my target rifle, it is 3" right at 600 yards. A shooter can test this early in the morning on a calm day.

Interior ballistics is the effects on the bullet prior to leaving the muzzle. The goal of the shooter is to have the bullet leave the muzzle in the exact same spot, the exact same velocity, and pointed in the exact same direction as the previous shot. A 30 ft/s (1%) change in velocity with a 200-grain bullet at 2950 ft/s makes a 7" difference in impact at 1000 yards. If the shooter is aiming at the center of mass of a target smaller than 14", he can easily miss it.

Interior ballistics is easier explained as a sequential event. The shooter squeezes the trigger. The primer goes off. The bullet jumps out of the brass case and is forced into the rifling lands. The powder is ignited. The pressure causes the brass case to expand and seal in the chamber. The bullet is also deformed to the shape of the inside of the barrel. The lands actually cut into the bullet. The powder continues to burn forcing the bullet to accelerate down the barrel. Force equals mass times acceleration. Since the bullet is accelerating away from the shooter, there is an equal but opposite force that causes the rifle to recoil towards the shooter. This procedure must be consistent.

Much of this discussion is on reloading. Remember all the basic safety limitations still apply. A good idea would be to re-read them before modifying the loads.

The primer goes off. For those people that reload, match primers are the way to go. The additional cost is for consistency. The shooter wants the initial case swell and the amount the bullet is forced into the rifling to be consistent. All primer pockets should be uniform. The primer pockets should be trimmed with a deburring tool on the interior and cleaned externally. The case should be the same thickness from one case to another. Most reloaders use weight to determine consistency of the thickness of the cases.

The bullet jumps out of the cartridge and into the rifling. In my opinion, this is where most of the error occurs. The bullet takes the shape of the interior of the barrel. If the bullet is not pointed directly down the barrel, it will lodge in the rifling at a slight angle. Also, there is clearance or slop in the chamber that allows the cartridge to load into the chamber. If the cartridge is sitting on the bottom of the chamber and the chamber has 35/1000" clearance on the diameter, the bullet has to jump up half that distance to get into the rifling. How can the bullet jump up without lodging in the rifling wrong? To minimize this jump, target shooters fire form their cases. Fire forming cases is the process that the shooter fires the cartridge and slightly resizes the case so that the slop in the chamber is reduced. In semi-automatics or hunting scenarios, the shooter wants some clearance for feeding the next cartridge quickly. Say, an elk hunter has all fire formed cases. The temperature is 10 degrees F. He sees an elk on the next ridge 450 yards out—easy shot. He dials in the elevation and wind. He realizes that he forgot to load his rifle because he has been sleeping on a rock with no level ground in minus degree temperatures for the past 10 days. He takes a cartridge out of his coat pocket and puts it in the feed ramp. It won't chamber. He realizes that the cartridge is not fitting because it is slightly larger than normal. It is the same temperature as his body, which (even on this cold day) is somewhere well above normal. The rifle's chamber is slightly smaller than normal because it is at 10°F. Instead of forcing it, he does the smart thing by pulling the cartridge out and letting it reach the same temperature as the rifle. Once that is done, he re-chambers it and bags the elk.

The next error in bullet jump is the length of the jump. Most people measure the overall cartridge length, not the ogive length. The ogive length is a measurement taken from the base of the bullet to where the bullet is no longer the caliber or where it starts to taper. The overall lengths of bullets out of the same box are not the same; however, the ogive lengths are the same. The lands in the rifling will grab the bullet at the ogive. If there is a variation in the bullet ogive distance to the lands, the bullet will seat differently in the rifling each time. A word of caution, never seat the bullet out so far that the bullet is touching the lands.

The necks of the cases should be uniform. All lengths should be identical, and the neck should be equal thickness. If the neck of the case expands unevenly or differently than the cartridge before, the bullet will seat differently in the lands. The only way to get a uniform neck is by turning and trimming the necks.

After the cartridge is put together, the concentricity of the cartridge should be measured with a case tool. By putting the dial indicator on the tip of the bullet and the case on the supports. The out of roundness can be measured by turning the bullet. Concentricity of the bullet is a function of the concentricity of the neck. The concentricity of the neck is formed in the resizing die. To solve concentricity issues, buy a good set of match dies.

One other thing that affects the proper seating of the bullet in the lands is the trueness of the bolt face, action, and barrel. The bolt face has to be parallel with the action and perpendicular with the barrel. A gunsmith has to do this. If the bolt face is not perpendicular to the bore of the barrel, the bullet will seat off in the lands.

The vibration of the explosion pushing the bullet travels as a sine wave in the barrel. It has peaks and valleys. The bullet should exit the muzzle at a peak or valley because for that instant the barrel is motionless. If the bullet exits during the switching of the two, the barrel is moving. Most people just deal with it. If it is a real problem, the barrel can be trimmed. Browning came up with a device that adjusts the barrel length to find the sweet spot.

Last topic for internal ballistics is dirt. Dirt, grime, and grease can cause the bullet to seat differently after every shot. It is important to clean the action area, chamber, throat and bolt face religiously.

Human error makes the other discussed inconsistencies insignificant. Human error consists of misjudging distance, misjudging wind and mirage, flinching, wrong natural point of aim, and not knowing the limitations of their equipment and themselves.

A shooter has his rifle in shooting order and is able to shoot out to 1000 yards. Can he hit that white tail deer at 425 yards? If he knows that it is at 425 yards, sure he can; but how can he tell that it's at 425 yards. One way is a laser range finder. It could put him within a yard, as long as it is not raining or snowing. Many people purchase scopes with reticles that determine distances. For instance, the reticle in my scope is a mil dot reticle. The simple formula: yards equals 27.78 x object size in inches divided by mils gives me the yardage. A good example is the cover of the book. The cover of the book is a mil dot reticle with 0.2 mil dots. The height of the wall is 8' or 96". It measures 4 mils plus 0.5 mil from the crosshairs to the first mil dot plus 0.1 mils for the top mil dot equals 4.6 mils. 27.78 times 96" divided by 4.6 mils equals 580 yards. A calculator can be a lot to handle, so a card is made to quickly read values. Examples are located on my shooting card. Note the formula doesn't match the table. The mils are calibrated near 12x in Leupold riflescopes. The formula' constantly changes as the power of magnification changes. At 20x, the constant is 55.56. Premier Reticles can replace the reticle so that the formula's constant remains 27.78 at all powers.

Next, a shooter needs to account for wind. He has charts to tell him how much to adjust, but first he has to know the wind speed and direction to adjust. Buying a cheap wind gauge is the best way for him to learn how to estimate wind speed. He needs to make mental notes of the movement of the trees, grass, how the wind feels on his face, and what type of noise it makes while comparing it to the wind gauge. Another common practice is to drop some grass from shoulder height and note how far it floats away from him while comparing the results to the wind gauge. With a little bit of practice and a refresher every now and then, he is able to accurately account for the wind.

Body movements (flinching) and improper natural aim point are the most probable reasons for poorly placed shot of a novice. A shooter is ready to take a long shot. His rifle is on a bipod, and he is in the prone position. Between the time he squeezes the trigger and the bullet leaves the barrel, there is a lot of movement. The rifle is going to move, so let it move. It should only move in one direction—straight back. The school is simple, have a good shooting position with the rifle in line with the shooter's body and relax. The shooter should have a clear sight picture through the scope (one without shadows around the edges). He should then close his shooting eye and slowly open it. Where the reticle is aiming when his eye opens is where the bullet is going to hit. This is called the natural point of aim. A shooter's natural point of aim is adjusted by adjusting body position—not by using muscles to hold the rifle in place. The best toy a shooter can have in the prone position is a palm bag. A palm bag is a sock loaded with sand, rice, or plastic beads that fits in the palm of the shooter's non-trigger hand. The rifle is supported by the bi-pod in the front. The shooter places the palm bag under the stock near the butt plate with his non-trigger hand wrapped around it. By squeezing the bag, the shooter is able to make minor adjustment to the elevation of impact. The rest is practice. Every time he places the rifle to his shoulder and puts his cheek on it, it has to be done the same way.

Earlier, it was stated that the shooter wants the rifle to move straight back. The shooter can determine if the rifle is going to move straight back by pulling the rifle back a ¼" using the pistol grip. If it stays on target, he should make a good hit. If the point of aim changes when he pulls back, he needs to find out what is causing the point of aim to change and correct it.

Once the shooter is ready to shoot, he has to regulate his breathing. He wants to exhale and shoot before he inhales. His point of aim will be moving when he is breathing. After he exhales, he has about 5 seconds to adjust the palm bag and shoot before he becomes uncomfortable. If the shooter becomes uncomfortable, he should start with regulating his breathing again.

Everyone knows that a shooter is supposed to squeeze the trigger until it breaks. Many shooters make the mistake of wrapping their index finger around the trigger. The shooter should touch the trigger with his index finger between the tip and first joint.

For a good shooter, all the above becomes basic. Over 90% of the time when a good shooter blows a shot, it is because of poor follow through. As the rifle rockets back, a shooter should remain motionless and keep his eye focused on the target.

The most important accomplishment a shooter can make at the shooting range is to establishing his limitations in various positions and distances. He should be able to shoot a 6" (some say 8") target to hit the kill zone of a deer. He should only shoot at an animal at distances and positions that he can hit the kill zone. Once he establishes his limitations, he should continue to make improvements on his limitations until he sets new limitations.

For review remember the basics: natural point of aim, clean sight picture, consistent spotweld (cheek placement on the stock and shoulder placement), slight pull back, breathe, relax, aim, squeeze, and follow through.

A shooter has to be confident in himself and his equipment. He obtains this confidence through practice, practice, and more practice. Practice—but how?

The first item a shooter should have is a data book for each rifle. Every shot he takes should be recorded. He should record the date, temperature, humidity, altitude, wind, mirage, bullet and charge.

A shooter's first focus should be getting confidence in his rifle. He should use a bench and sandbags to group test the rifle. If the group is larger than two inches at a hundred yards, the shooter should look for something loose on the rifle—scope rings, action bolts, not fully setting the bolt handle, etc. If a shooter is shooting a group larger than 2" and can't find anything loose, he should seek help from a more experienced shooter at the range. The experienced shooters are easy to find. A shooter just has to look at the targets down range.

Rifles have limitations. Very few rifles can put a five shot group through a single bullet hole. Most factory rifles can only hold 1 MOA (1" group at 100 yards); however, many factory rifles with factory ammunition are only capable of 1.5 MOA accuracy. Target rifles can hold much tighter groups; however, it is like

334   The Cajun Sniper

adding horsepower to an automobile. The cost goes up exponentially with the reduction of the group size. A good target rifle and scope starts at $2,500.

If shooter is a reloader, he should find a load that works and stick with it. There are too many people that spend all of their time looking for the perfect load. Another error that reloaders make is they have different loads for different distances. One sniper match will cure him of that mistake. At a sniper match, he may have to shoot one shot at 100 yards and the next shot at 670 yards. A shooter needs to find a load that works well at all ranges.

Once the shooter is confident that his rifle is performing well, he should get off the bench and stay off of it. Using the bench and sandbags should be only used to test the rifle's ability—not the shooter's ability. He should get a piece of carpet or a shooting mat to lay down on. Many fabric rifle cases now open to make for a shooting mat.

A good practice routine is a cold bore shot, two rounds of make-it take-it, two five shot speed drills, five shots from every position, and distance shooting. A shooter should start inside of 300 yards because he can see the bullet holes with a good spotting scope without leaving the firing line.

The cold bore shot should be the first shot out the rifle—no practice shots. There should be a separate section in the shooter's data book for cold bore shots. In real life, the cold bore shot is the only one that counts. The rifle comes out of the case and the shooter should be able to drill a 1 MOA target out to three hundred yards on his first shot.

Make-it take-it is an event in sniper competition. The shooter shoots a single shot at five progressively smaller targets. The first target is 1.25 MOA and reduces in 0.25 MOA increments. Shooting a small group is good; but a shooter should be able to hit the object that he is shooting at. The shooter shouldn't get discouraged if he misses the 0.25 MOA dot. I rarely hit it, and I only know one person that consistently does. The shooter should see how close he can get to it.

The speed drill is shooting five separate 1 MOA targets in thirty seconds. The shooter should remember that it is better to take his time and only hit two of the targets and run out of time than to miss all five of them.

Positional shooting is next. The shooter should take five shots from the standing, kneeling, sitting and unsupported prone.

From positional shooting, the shooter can move out to distance shooting on freshly painted steel. He should read the mirage, call the shot, take it, and record it. In the data book, it is important that the shooter records the point of aim and the point of impact. He may develop a pattern that can be corrected. The shooter will see a piece of paint the size of a silver dollar missing where he hits the steel.

He should adjust if needed and take a second shot. Two shots at each distance from four hundred out should be all the shooter requires.

One of the biggest mistakes that shooters make is that they only go to the range on calm and bright sunny days. Initially, calm and bright sunny days are acceptable days to practice. Once the rifle patterns are set, the shooter should practice in whatever weather God throws at him—rain, dry, hot, cold, windy, total mirage and no mirage. The shooter needs to remember that the purpose of practice is to give himself confidence. The more different weather conditions he shoots in, the more weather conditions he will feel confident in shooting in.

Last topic on shooting, every shooter has a bad day every now and then. If a shooter finds that he is having a bad day, he should pack it up; head home; and enjoy the rest of the day. A good example is a law enforcement sniper match I shot. It was cold and raining. I could not hold a 1" group at a hundred yards. In the twenty-one events, all except three events were shooting sub-minute targets inside of a hundred yards. Needless to say, it was a bad day for my partner and me. The next weekend, I stripped everything off of my rifle, sandbagged it and got a ¼" group at 100 yards. I added the strap with no change. I put on the bi-pod, and the group opened to 2 MOA. I bought another bi-pod and the group dropped down to 3/8 MOA.

Trajectory is as important to long range shooters as it is to archers. A long-range shooter needs the flattest trajectory that will maintain a ½ MOA group size. Suppose a shooter is engaging a 20" tall by 11" wide human silhouette target somewhere between 900 and 925 yards with a 10 mph cross wind. He is shooting a .308 with a 168 grain match bullet with a muzzle velocity of 2400 ft/s. The shooter wants to aim for center of mass because guessing short will result in a low hit and guessing long will result in a high hit. He has to keep his error to 20" on elevation and 5.5" on windage. At 900 yards, his drop is 38 MOA; and his windage is 9.5 MOA. At 925 yards, his drop is 40 MOA; and his windage is 10 MOA. The difference in elevation is 28", and the difference in windage is 7". Chances are that he will miss the target. If the shooter moves up to a 175 grain bullet with a muzzle velocity of 2600 ft/s, his elevation error is 23"; and windage is 4". His chances have improved. If the shooter moves up to a 300 Win Magnum that shoots a 200 grain bullet with a muzzle velocity of 2950 ft/s, his error is reduced to 15" of elevation and 0" windage (windage is 0 because the scope adjustments are only in ¼ MOA increments). His chances of hitting the target are high.

The rifle's grouping error needs to be added to the trajectory error to get the outside limits. ½ MOA equates to 4.5" at 900 yards. If a shooter knows that the target is at least 900 yards but less than 925 yards, he should split the difference on his elevation adjustment—24 MOA using the 300 win mag. example. If the target is at 900 yards, he will hit 7 ½" high; and 7 ½" low at 925 yards. If the rifle is only capable of ½ MOA, the outer extreme is 4 ½". 4 ½" plus 7 ½" equates to 12", which is 2" outside of the target. The answer is to reduce the group size to ¼ MOA. A ¼" MOA group using a belted case is difficult to achieve. A custom chamber has to be made to remove the internal ballistic errors. This thought process set the design basis for the 300 TALLEY, which shoots a 200 grain bullet with a muzzle velocity of 2950 ft/s and holds a ¼ MOA group. This rifle gives me a definite advantage in distance shooting over law enforcement, military, and special ops that shoot a .308.

Breaking in a rifle is a necessary, long, and boring task. To properly break in a rifle, 200 rounds must go through it. There are several different recommended break-in procedures, and shooters should consult their rifle manufacturer's recommended procedures. A common procedure is to clean after every shot for the first 20 shots, clean after every 3rd shot from 21 through 60 shots, clean after every 5th from 61 through 100, and clean after every 10th from 101 to 200. The shooter should clean with powder solvent and copper solvent. Most match barrels are not guaranteed unless the shooter follows the manufacturer's break in procedure. The best day to break in a rifle is a rainy day because the shooter's emphasis should be on cleaning and not shooting. There is a period of the barrel stretching, bolt seating, etc. This period is called seasoning the rifle. An accuracy benchmark should not be taken before 120 shots are through the rifle.

Cleaning a rifle is the second most important part of shooting. The shooter should invest in a maintenance center; it's worth the money. He should start by using a small brush with a clean patch or a cleaning rod with a rag and clean the chamber. He should be careful not to damage the throat. He should then insert a bore guide, which is a device that keeps the glass bed eating powder solvent in the barrel. With the barrel sloped downward so that the solvent drains out the muzzle, he should use a brush and powder solvent—20 strokes. He should only push the brush from the chamber to the muzzle. He should remove the brush at the end of the barrel to keep from pulling it back through. He then should do 20 strokes of copper solvent. Then, he should keep pushing powder solvent patches through the barrel until they come out clean. A shooter should remember to wipe the cleaning rod to keep from putting dirt back into the barrel. Once all the debris is out of the barrel, the shooter should run dry patches until he no longer collects powder solvent. He then should lightly lubricate a patch with oil and pass it through the barrel. The shooter should then take a brush and some lubricant and clean the action and bolt. He should wipe down the outside and clean his optics. Before he goes to shoot, he should push two patches with rubbing alcohol on them to remove the oil.

The 300 Talley is a bolt action with a 29" Kreiger fluted standard target barrel. The stock is a McMillian A-2 Tactical. The trigger is a Jewell that is set at 2 pounds. The bolt and action are lapped. The real specialty is the custom chamber. It's made for 300 Winchester magnum with a Sierra 200 grain matchking bullet. The chamber's clearance is reduced to 2/1000". The throat is cut long so that the start of the boat tail lines up with the back of the neck of the casing. The 29" barrel gives extra velocity to have an edge at shooting distances. The bolt handle extension allows quick cycling of the bolt during rapid fire and allows cycling the bolt without moving out of the spot weld. The scope is a Leupold 6 x 20 Tactical with a 30mm tube. This gun is capable of a 5 shot ¼" group at 100 yards, and it has shot a 4 shot 3 ½" group with the fifth (probably cold bore) flyer at 1000 yards. The only drawback with this rifle is that it weighs 14 lbs.

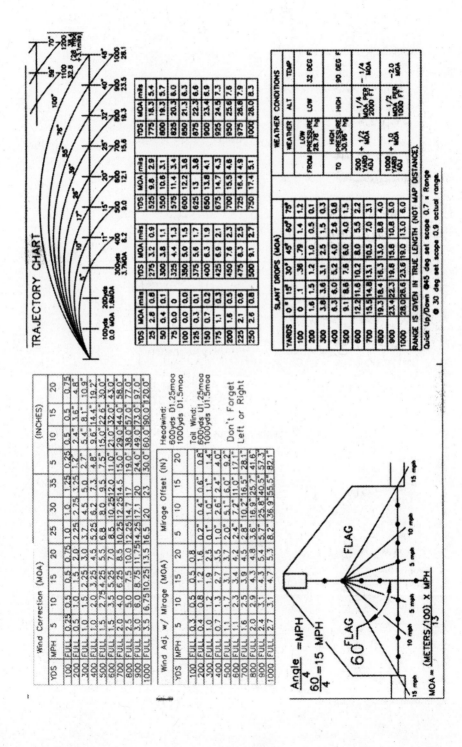

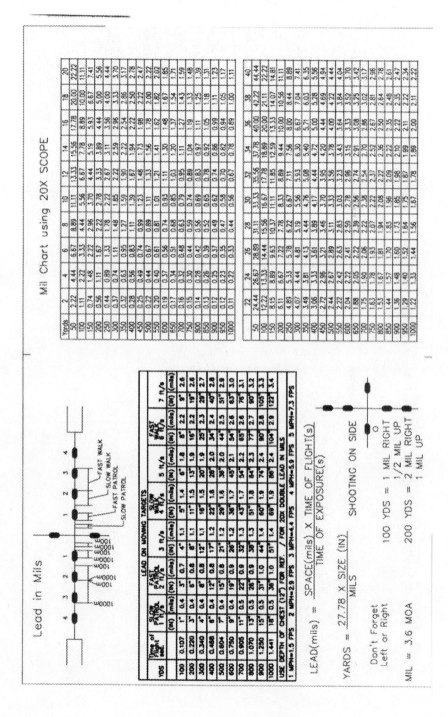

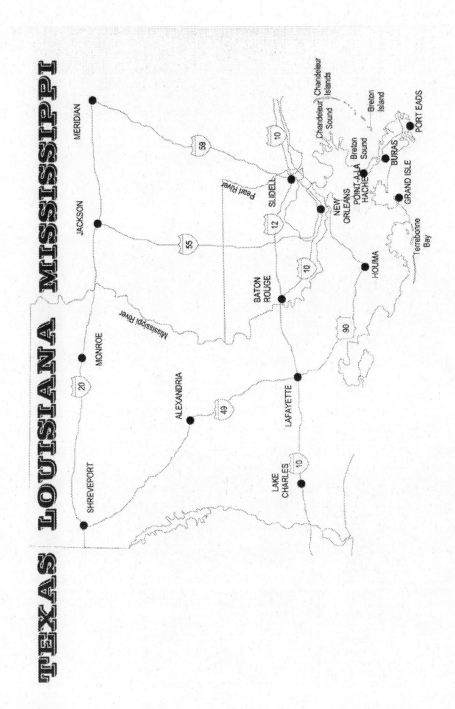

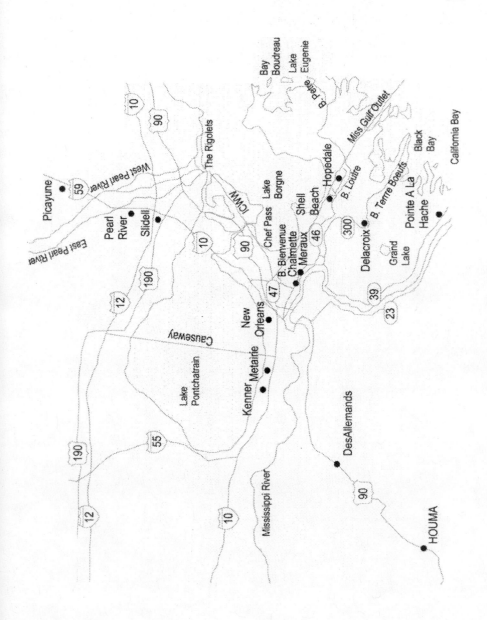

About the Author

Wayne Talley is married sixteen years to a wonderful wife. He is the father of three. Born in New Orleans, the nearby swamp was his childhood playground. He lived in southeast Louisiana nearly his entire life. He now resides in Houston.

0-595-31446-5